Belonging

A heart-wrenching story about love, loss and family secrets

Emma Dhesi

Rowanbrae Press

Copyright ©2020 by Emma Dhesi

www.emmadhesi.com

All rights reserved.

This book is a work of fiction. The characters, incidents, and dialogue are drawn from the author's imagination and are not to be construed as real. Any resemblance to actual events or persons, living or dead, is fictionalised or coincidental.

No part of this book may be reproduced in any form by any electronic or mechanical means, including information storage and retrieval systems, without written permission from the author, except for the use of brief quotations in a book review.

For any inquiries regarding this book, please email emma@emmadhesi.com

Cover Design by GetCovers

Editing by Rebecca Jones

Dedicated to SRF, with love

Contents

1. Chapter 1 — 1
2. Chapter 2 — 10
3. Chapter 3 — 18
4. Chapter 4 — 25
5. Chapter 5 — 31
6. Chapter 6 — 37
7. Chapter 7 — 43
8. Chapter 8 — 47
9. Chapter 9 — 54
10. Chapter 10 — 60
11. Chapter 11 — 69
12. Chapter 12 — 78
13. Chapter 13 — 87
14. Chapter 14 — 95
15. Chapter 15 — 103
16. Chapter 16 — 109
17. Chapter 17 — 118
18. Chapter 18 — 125
19. Chapter 19 — 131

20.	Chapter 20	139
21.	Chapter 21	146
22.	Chapter 22	152
23.	Chapter 23	159
24.	Chapter 24	167
25.	Chapter 25	173
26.	Chapter 26	181
27.	Chapter 27	188
28.	Chapter 28	195
29.	Chapter 29	203
30.	Chapter 30	211
31.	Chapter 31	218
32.	Chapter 32	226
33.	Chapter 33	234
34.	Chapter 34	242
35.	Chapter 35	250
36.	Chapter 36	258
37.	Chapter 37	265
38.	Chapter 38	272
39.	Chapter 39	279
40.	Chapter 40	285
41.	Chapter 41	291
42.	Chapter 42	299
43.	Chapter 43	306
Acknowledgments		311
About Author		312

Also By 314

Chapter 1

'They're coming,' Kathi called down the stairs to her son. 'Quick, you don't want to miss them.' She rushed back to the window. It was 5am, and the sun was up. Despite the early hour, Kathi, together with her fifteen-year-old, bleary-eyed son Jake, stood at the open upstairs dormer window, waving and cheering on the Byreburn Town Band as they drummed their way down the street.

Neighbours too were out in force, on their doorsteps or at their windows, each waving flags. Watching the band pass by at the same time every Common Riding filled Kathi with pride and reassurance. This day had been marked every year since the time of Robert The Bruce and its constancy persuaded her that all was right with the world.

She glanced over to watch her son leaning against the window. He was enjoying the scene, she knew, but his adolescent caginess wouldn't let him show it. To stop himself from getting carried away, he folded his arms in front of him. It was his smile that gave him away.

Kathi remembered when he'd been so small that she'd had to lift him up to look out of the window. Now he was taller than her, and one day soon he'd be taller than his father. A wave of love made her reach a hand over and ruffle his hair, even though she knew he'd hate it. 'Get off,' he complained, pushing her away. Scowling, he felt to check his hair was still in place.

'It's going to be a long day,' said Kathi. Once the Town Band had left them behind, the sound of their flutes and whistles fading into the background. 'I'll cook a fry up.' Jake went downstairs ahead of her and she had to resist ruffling his firmly gelled hair a second time.

'Are you going up to the High Street early?' Kathi asked when they sat down to eat. Even at such an early hour, Kathi was groomed and ready for the day. Her shoulder length sunshine blond hair sat easily, framing her face and making her sky-blue eyes pop. She prided herself on her slim figure and was careful about what she ate. She watched Jake tuck into his breakfast of fried eggs, bacon, black pudding and baked beans while she had her usual poached egg on toast. 'Yes,' Jake said, gobbling down a piece of bacon. It was going to be a fun day wandering up and down the High Street, seeing friends, and trying to blag alcohol from the older kids. Perhaps he'd see Lindsay.

'Will you come and watch the horses gallop with me and your dad?'

'I told the others I'd go with them.'

'I want you to come and watch with us. It's probably the last time we'll do it as a family.'

'You said that last year.'

'Please?' Kathi tried one last time.

'Alright, but I'm not doing it next year.' Gulping down a last mouthful of tea, Jake headed out the door. 'See you.'

Kathi went upstairs to get ready. Her husband Graham was still sleeping and when she tried to rouse him, he pulled her onto the bed for a cuddle. He'd been out drinking the night before and the smell of pub lingered. Maintaining his youthful physique was not as important to Graham as it was to Kathi. He was quite content to eat what he wanted. He had relaxed into middle age and his trousers might have been a little snug around the waist, but he felt it all balanced out with the physical work of the busy plumbing business he ran. Still sleepy, he rubbed his brown eyes, so like Jake's, and ruffled his dark hair, trying to shake away his hangover.

'Get off,' she laughed, 'you stink.'

'You love it,' he said, pulling her closer. 'Has Jake left already?'

'He's just gone.'

'You mean we have the house to ourselves?' He gave her bum a squeeze to stop her from escaping. After eighteen years of marriage, he still made her laugh, and she succumbed to his embrace. 'We could make this a new Common Riding tradition,' he joked afterwards.

'I think we already did,' Kathi said, giving him a quick kiss. She put on a necklace and earrings before checking herself in the full-length mirror. She wore slim fitting jeans, and a tailored shirt. Downstairs, she added a pair of Hunter wellies and a fitted Barbour jacket. When Graham finally showered and dressed, they headed up to the Common Riding festivities. They heard the horses before they saw them, a loud echo of hooves clip-clopping down the High Street to congregate in the Market Square.

Some of the animals relished the opportunity to show off. They were tall and gleaming in the bright summer sunshine. They held their heads proudly and lifted their legs high. Others bobbed their heads and twitched their tails, nervous of the chattering crowd.

'Can you see Jake?' Kathi looked around, trying to spot him. 'I told him to come and meet us for the horses.'

'Don't worry, he'll turn up when wants something, I'm sure.'

At last the riders kicked their horses into action, quickly gathering speed to gallop up the Kirk Wynd, a narrow hillside road leading past the church and up to the surrounding hills. The crowd burst into cheers, outdone only by the clattering of hooves against the ground. It required skilful handling to coax some before they found their stride.

At the rear were grinning children, only five or six years old, gleaming in their new riding hats. They were plonked on Shetland ponies by parents who ran alongside. Appreciative oohs and aahs carried them on as they were initiated into the traditions of the Common Riding.

Proud of her little town, Kathi looked around at the hanging baskets, fat with flowers and suspended from the streetlamps. Flags and bunting were draped from every possible spot, and the buzz from locals and tourists alike was palpable. The pomp and ceremony, the tartan and heather, bagpipes and drums all helped rekindle the last days of Byreburn's wild and lawless history. Just for a moment, the town felt young again.

Once the horses were out of sight, the crowds milled. Chatter and laughter filled the air, lifelong friends took photographs to mark the passing of another year. Kathi and Graham mingled with friends and family, grabbing coffee to keep themselves going after such an early start to the day. It was only 10am, but some headed to one of the town's many pubs to start the day with a pint.

'No wonder Jake didn't want to join us,' said Graham, indicating over Kathi's shoulder. Turning around, she saw him sitting on a low wall with friends. Beside him was a girl Kathi recognised and knew was in his year at school. There was something about Jake's body language that told her he was doing his best to flirt with the girl, to make her laugh and watch her smile. His big brown eyes followed the girls every more. His wide mouth was made even wider by the grin on his face. He unconsciously touched his dark wavy hair, making sure the gel was doing its job. Kathi looked at Graham with an expression that said, bless them.

'How old were you when you started getting interested in girls?' Kathi asked him.

'Only when I met you,' teased Graham, for which he received a playful punch on the arm. His phone pinged. 'Mum's heading home to get lunch on, shall we go with her?'

'Sure, I'll just tell Jake where we're going and follow you down.' When Jake saw her approach, his face fell and quickly turned red with embarrassment at being seen in the same proximity as the girl he was trying to impress. 'We're going to your gran's house for lunch, are you coming?'

'Yeah,' said Jake, 'I'll be there in a minute.'

'Hello Mrs Beattie,' said the girl next to Jake. 'I'm Lindsay.'

'Hello, Lindsay. Are you having a good day so far?'

'Yeah, it's fun,' she giggled.

'Don't be long,' Kathi said to Jake, leaving them.

It wasn't until lunch was over and they were walking back up to the High Street for the afternoon's festivities that Kathi looped arms with her son and said, 'Lindsay seems nice. Are you two friends?'

'Sort of,' said Jake, quickly colouring.

Kathi watched him go over to meet some boys from his year. They greeted each other with a cursory nod of the head, but Kathi noticed that the easy friendship they used to show each other was lacking. She couldn't put her finger on what it was, but Jake didn't look as relaxed as he used to be around them. It wasn't long before they moved on to watch the highland dancers at The Green, who were competing for the Common Riding Cup.

Jake was maturing, Kathi noticed. His body and face were changing, and he even moved differently these days. There were flashes of the adult he was growing into. He'd shot up what felt like a whole foot in the past few months and would undoubtedly be taller than his father. His shoulders had broadened, as had his jawline, but his torso and limbs had yet to fill out and strengthen. The result was he looked a like an overgrown fawn. He even had huge, deep brown Bambi eyes, and Kathi felt sure he would melt a few hearts in the not too distant future.

As Jake walked down the street, another three kids joined his group and Lindsay was one of them. Kathi observed how quickly the traces of maturity she'd noticed in Jake only a moment before had fallen away in the presence of the girl he fancied. He giggled childishly before play fighting with one of the other boys. Kathi's heart was torn between sentimentality that he was going through his first crush and sadness he was growing up so fast. She'd often looked forward to when Jake wasn't so dependent on her, but now that it was here, Kathi wanted time to slow down again. She silently made a wish Lindsay wouldn't break his heart.

Kathi's phone rang, and she answered without looking.

'Hi, it's me.' It was Cherry.

'Hi, how did you get on yesterday?' Kathi asked.

'She seems nice enough and wants to take the flat.' Not only was Cherry her best friend, but she also managed Kathi's portfolio of rental properties.

'What do you know about her?'

'Her name's Joanne Wylie, and she's got a job in the mill. She says she came here on holiday from Glasgow, fell in love with the place and moved down.'

'Do you think she'll stay or is it a whim?'

'I think she'll stay. She's been lodging with a friend for a couple of months, so she's not fresh off the boat, so to speak.'

'She's a Wylie. Has she got a family connection?'

'Oh, Kathi, you know I don't know about all that stuff. I'm sure you'll find out in good time.' Cherry laughed, unable to get used to the fact that everybody here was related to everybody else, one way or another. Even she had been until her divorce.

Like Joanne, Cherry was from Glasgow and had only moved to Byreburn when she married local boy Wayne. She, too, had fallen in love with the town, staying after her divorce. 'Her references all check out fine and she seems nice enough.'

'If you get a good feeling about her and everything checks out, I'm happy.'

'Excellent. I'll get all the paperwork sorted tomorrow.'

It was half-past nine that night when Jake walked through the door, more than a little unsteady on his feet. 'Jake,' Graham called through from the living room. 'Come in here, please.' Graham was on the sofa, pretending to read the paper. Kathi was in the armchair, laptop on her knees, working on her blog. The living room was sparse, like much of the house. It would have looked cold too, if it wasn't for the warm colours Kathi liked. Interspersed amongst the cool cream colours were vibrant teals and velvet reds. Yellow brightened the hallway and aquamarine the kitchen. Happy to leave the home décor to his wife, Graham didn't mind what the house looked like as long as he had his plasma TV.

Kathi favoured the clean lines and uncluttered feel of the fashionable Scandinavian designs. The sofa and chairs weren't ones you would sink into on a Sunday afternoon, but they were ideal for an hour or two of TV in the evening. The coffee table displayed a carefully curated selection of hard-backed books on whatever was interesting to her at the time. At the moment, it was house design.

The photographs on the walls were what made the room homely. Photographs of Jake at different ages were mixed in with family holidays to Spain and even South America. Kathi loved looking at the pictures of Jake. She was so proud of the young man he was becoming. A few years to go yet, she reminded herself as Jake came into the room like the condemned man he was.

'What time do you call this?' Graham asked.

'Sorry,' mumbled Jake, 'I lost track of time.'

'It's not good enough, Jake,' said Kathi.

'It's only half-past nine,' he snapped. 'Everyone else is still out. I'm the only one who has to come home early.'

'Have you been drinking?' Kathi asked.

'A bit.'

'A bit? You can barely walk.' Jake rolled his eyes.

'If we're going to let you stay out late,' said Graham, 'we've got to be able to trust you. You were told no alcohol, and to be home at nine o'clock.' Graham and Kathi looked at their son expectantly.

'Sorry,' he said.

'Alright, don't do it again. Drink some water and go to bed.'

'Is that it?' Kathi demanded when Jake was out of earshot.

'He's sorry. What else am I supposed to do?'

'Don't you think he needs punishing?'

'Oh, come on, it's Common Riding night. He'll have been with his friends and forgot the time. It's easily done.'

'You're a big softie,' Kathi tutted.

'Hey,' Graham said conspiratorially, 'do you think he fancies that Lindsay girl?'

'Yes, I do. You should have seen him with her this afternoon, being all goofy and trying to impress her.' Kathi smiled indulgently.

'Do you think we should have adopted a little girl as well?' Graham asked, surprising his wife with the sudden change of topic.

'Sometimes I do, but I like things the way they are,' said Kathi, glancing up at Graham, who was lost in his own thoughts. She looked back down at her laptop and saw a new message had arrived in her in-box. She smiled to herself. Thank you so much for the hashtag tip you gave us in your blog post last week.' Someone had written. It's been really helpful and I've already reached more people.

That was the sort of message Kathi loved to get from her readers. Helping others in the same position as her made all the effort worthwhile. Kathi considered herself a small-town girl who wrote a small-town blog about her small-town property business, and the ups and downs of being the mother of an adopted child. She wrote the blog under the pseudonym of HumanRacer (named after the first album of her first crush, Nik Kershaw) because she wanted anonymity.

The blog, Human Racing, was a way for Kathi to vent her frustrations, share her experiences and laugh at the things life threw at her. She worked hard on her property investing business and, like anything else, it came with its own headaches and heartaches. Motherhood too had its challenges, and the blog was a safe place to share her experiences around the subject of adoption. Human Racing was two years old now, and she posted twice a week, regular as clockwork.

Part of her weekly ritual was to brew a strong coffee, take it to her desk, put some music on and write whatever was on her mind that day. She never planned out her posts but spoke from the heart, and that was what seemed to resonate with her followers. Over time, her readership had grown, and she loved opening up the blog to see who had commented, in-boxed or started following her. It was reassuring to know she wasn't alone in her personal and business challenges.

By now it was late, and Kathi was tired. She'd been up since before 5am and it showed. She yawned loudly. 'Go to bed,' Graham said.

'The kitchen is a mess.'

'I'll do it.'

Kathi packed away her laptop and took their empty mugs through to the kitchen. She couldn't help herself from loading the dishwasher. 'Hey,' said Graham gently, 'I said I'd do it.' He put his arms around Kathi and squeezed her tightly. 'Another successful Common Riding,' he announced as if he himself had organised it.

They chatted about the day as they cleared the debris from the countertops and put the dishwasher on. It was an effort to get up the stairs, and Graham pulled her up by the hand. They heard Jake's music playing and rolled their eyes at each other. 'How can he listen to that stuff?' Kathi whispered.

Chapter 2

Jake had had absolutely no interest in watching the horses at this year's Common Riding. That was for kids and losers like his parents. He'd only said he'd join his mum to get her off his back. He hadn't wanted to watch anything except Lindsay. He didn't know why it had taken him so long to notice her, but now he had, she was all he thought about. All that thinking about one person got him down at times. It took up a lot of energy for very little return, but he was powerless to stop it.

Lindsay was there when he woke, she infiltrated his thoughts all day at school, and was most definitely there when he went to bed at night. He'd picture her laughing with her friends in class, or how her hair moved when she walked down the school corridor. Her hair was like dark chocolate and her eyes sparkled like the emeralds he'd seen in the local jewellers. He'd relived so many times the moment she'd first said hello to him on the stairs. He was going up to Geography, she was going down to French.

He'd blushed so heavily that his friends and hers had teased him mercilessly. His ears always went bright pink when he was embarrassed, it was one reason he was growing his hair. But it had been worth it, because now they always said hello to each other. They didn't say anything else, just hello, but it was enough.

But today, on the magical day that was the Common Riding, his world was shifting. The boys he hung around with had become attached to her group of friends and now they were sitting together on a low wall surrounding the post office, set back a little from the High Street. He'd managed to manoeuvre himself next to her, and they were laughing about a movie they'd seen. He did an impression of the comedy sidekick, and his heart rose like a kite in the wind to hear her laugh at his jokes.

'You're funny,' she told him, absently flicking her hair out of her eyes. That movement mesmerised him and for a few seconds he could do nothing but grin.

'Why thank you ma'am,' he said in an American accent, deflecting the fact he'd been staring at her.

'Jake,' someone said. 'Your mum is coming.' Immediately his face dropped and so did his head. What did she want?

'Hi Jake,' she said with that smile of hers fixed onto her face. She used that smile a lot these days, but he knew it wasn't real. It was a smile she put on for show, when she was pretending to be happy families. She looked ridiculous, too, dressed up like some country squire in her wellies and waxed jacket. All that was missing was a flat cap.

'We are going to your gran's house for lunch, are you coming?'

'Yeah, I'll be there in a minute.'

'Hello Mrs Beattie,' said Lindsay, surprising him. 'I'm Lindsay.'

'Hello Lindsay, are you having a good day so far?'

'Yeah, it's fun.' Lindsay giggled. Jake knew that was the effect of the wine she'd been sipping over the course of the morning and hoped his mum didn't notice she was a bit giddy.

'I wish she'd leave me alone,' he said when Kathi was out of earshot. 'She's always watching me.'

'She seems nice,' Lindsay said.

'Your parents don't harass you every minute of the day.'

'That is because my parents are in the pub. They've no idea where I am.' He looked away, embarrassed at having put his foot in it. Everyone knew Lindsay's parents were a wreck. Both of them were more or less alcoholics. 'Your mum seems alright,' she went on, 'and I bet you'll get a good meal at your gran's house.' They both laughed at that.

Jake pictured the full roast lunch his gran would be cooking up, as she did every Common Riding. He could smell the chicken as it came out of the oven. He pictured his dad carving it, the gravy boat filled to the gunnels, and his gran's roast potatoes. 'The trick is to use goose fat,' she said every time. Despite the lure of roast potatoes, he hesitated in getting up. He didn't want to break the magic that was sitting on a brick wall with the girl of his dreams. He knew that once he stood up, he'd never be able to recreate this moment of intimacy. He was scared she'd transfer her attentions to one of the other boys, and that would be that. He was about to tell her he wasn't hungry and that he was going to stay, but she jumped up in excitement about something, he didn't know what, and the bubble popped.

He called out a cheerio as he walked away, but the contents of a plastic bag someone was carrying distracted the others. He knew it was beer, but even if he wanted to, he couldn't stay and share it with them because his mum would immediately smell it on him and go nuts.

He grumbled to himself all the way to his gran's house. None of his friends were bothered he was leaving. All they were concerned about was the illegal booze. If his mum hadn't stuck her beak into his business, he could have stayed and joined in.

Gran's house smelled amazing and as soon as he walked through the door, the fragrance of roast chicken hit his nostrils and his stomach rumbled loudly in response. There was the usual hustle and bustle as the table was set and the food brought out. Kathi called Graham and his granddad through, and everyone sat down with the ease that comes with being part of a close family. Everyone, that is, except Jake. He was distracted by thoughts of Lindsay and what she might be doing at that exact moment.

'You're quiet,' said Graham.

Jake merely grunted in response, and so the conversation moved on. He didn't want to talk to them but was irked they didn't probe further into why he was so quiet. If they had, he'd have told them it was because they were spoiling his day by dragging him away from his friends, and he wished they'd all leave him alone.

The banter around the table was the same as it ever was. It amazed him how much they had to talk about. They saw each other nearly every day, yet never ran out of things to say. After lunch Gran roped him into loading the dishwasher while she and Kathi cleaned up around him. 'How's school?' she asked.

'Fine, just the same.'

'I saw you yesterday, hanging about the park.' Tiny shocks of alarm sprinted up his spine and from the corner of his eye he saw Kathi's head spin in his direction. 'We went up there at lunchtime,' he lied.

'My friend saw you a couple of days ago too.'

Jake looked over at his gran but said nothing. She gave him a look as if to say; I know what you're up to.

No more was said on the subject and before long they headed out the door. After only a few steps Jake said, 'I need to use the toilet, I'll catch you up.' He headed back to the always unlocked house and nipped upstairs to the bathroom. On the way back down, he swiped a can of lager from the fridge and hid it in an inside jacket pocket. He caught up with the others but tried to keep a physical distance from them in case someone noticed the can. His heart was in his mouth when Kathi looped her arm through his.

When they reached the High Street, he craned his head this way and that, looking for his friends, and with relief he saw they hadn't moved far from the wall. He joined them but was disappointed not to see Lindsay. He wanted to know where she was but didn't dare ask anyone in case it was obvious he fancied her.

Like a small flock of birds, they moved in unison towards the park to watch the Highland dancers. All the boys were a bit hyper and Jake soon got swept up in their energy. Someone jumped on his back and, startled, he nearly stumbled, finding his balance just in time. Whoever it was jumped off his back again, and what a delight it was to see Lindsay's laughing face. Not only had she joined the group, but she'd singled him out as special. She'd touched him, made contact, chosen him. They fell in tandem with each other at the back of the group.

'Look what I picked up.' He opened his jacket to show her the stolen can of lager tucked into his pocket.

'Nice one,' she said.

'Do you want to share it?'

'Definitely.' The ducked away from the group down a side street before heading over a small swing bridge and into the neighbouring Dukes Wood. In a place like Byreburn someone would know they were underage and call them out on their drinking, or even worse, tell their parents. Kathi and Graham would lay on the guilt trips, Lindsay's dad would probably give her a slap and so they looked for somewhere quiet to sit and drink.

They found a spot on the edge of the woods where the foliage afforded them some camouflage while letting them spy on the outside world. Jake sat as near to Lindsay as he dared, buzzing with excitement at being alone with her. He popped open the can of lager and an explosion of foam burst out, dripping over his hand. This added to the illicitness of their actions and they smiled at one another. Jake took a small sip before passing it to Lindsay. He watched her take a large gulp. She lifted the can to her lips and angled her head back, closing her eyes as she drank so that her lashes rested on her face.

They sat in silence, intermittently smiling at one another and taking sips of beer. This was the first time they'd been alone together. Lindsay pulled out her phone and put some music on. The two of them started bobbing their heads in rhythm to the beat. It was a strong beat, angry even. 'What is it?' he asked Lindsay.

'Eminem,' she said, handing him the phone. Lose yourself. That was definitely what he wanted to do most of the time. He wanted to lose himself in something bigger than himself, rather than live with how lost he felt every day.

'My eldest brother really likes him,' Lindsay went on. 'He's a bit old school.'

'It's good. I like it.'

'What happened between you and Hayden?' Lindsay asked.

'What do you mean?'

'Did you fall out?'

'Sort of.'

'You're better off without him. He's hanging around with Ryan these days. Ryan is only going to drag him down.' Jake wanted to ask more but held back. He reminded himself that Hayden had betrayed his trust, turned on him for no reason.

'Whatever,' he said.

The beer had loosened Lindsay's tongue, and she chattered on. Jake was content to sit back and listen to her. He was nervous about saying too much in case he said the wrong thing and she realised what a loser he really was.

Lindsay was sitting a little in front of him and he followed her long hair as it moved and swayed when she talked. She was wearing a cropped top, and he watched her spine bend and curve, each vertebrae working together in a fluid line.

She talked about the celebrities she followed and the reality shows she watched, none of which Jake was interested in. His mum watched one or two of the same shows and that was reason enough for him not to. Jake watched as Lindsay pulled a packet of cigarettes out of her bag. She took one, then offered the packet to Jake. As she did she said, 'your mum rents flats, doesn't she?'

'Yes,' said Jake, declining the cigarette. 'Her friend Cherry Anderson does it for her.'

'How do you get one?'

'What do you mean?'

'If I wanted to rent a flat from her, what would I need to do?'

'I've no idea,' Jake admitted. 'Why do you want to know?'

'I just wondered.' She thought for a moment. 'How much do they cost?'

'I haven't a clue, I don't pay any attention to her business.' Keen to move the conversation away from his mum, Jake asked, 'Do you want to go to The Green one day after school?'

She looked at him. 'Okay.' Lindsay shrugged her shoulders and took a drag on a cigarette. Jake couldn't work out what she was thinking.

'Can I have one?' He pointed at her cigarette.

'Sure,' she said, pulling them back out of her bag and offering the packet to him. Jake nervously eeked one out of the gold packaging and put it to his lips. The smell of tobacco was powerful this close up, and the filter absorbed the moisture from his lips. He didn't know what it would taste like and was nervous. Lindsay pushed down on the lighter and the small flame appeared as if by magic. He put the end of the cigarette into the fire, but nothing happened.

'You need to inhale,' she explained. As soon as he did the end glowed orange and his mouth filled with smoke. The spluttering came next, and they both laughed at his ineptitude. She playfully nudged his arm with hers.

The cigarette tasted disgusting, and it hurt his throat, but he enjoyed the light head it gave him. It made him woozy and feel a little out of control. He closed his eyes and listened to the noises around him. He heard Lindsay shuffle about and inhale her cigarette. He heard the cawing of the rooks as they went about their business in the treetops. In the near distance, he could make out the sound of horses' hooves as some of them made their way home. In the far distance he heard the dancers' accordion music blasting through a tannoy. The odd bit of laughter and conversation floated in their direction.

'Are you going to stay on at school?' Lindsay's question broke the reverie.

'My mum would kill me if I didn't. Why? Are you leaving?' He held his breath while he waited for her answer.

'I'm thinking about it. I don't want to be here any longer than I have to. At sixteen I can leave school, leave home, get a job. At sixteen I can start my life.'

Jake wondered when his life would start and whether or not he hated Kathi enough to want to leave. He was only 15 and the thought of leaving home now was terrifying. It was scary enough to keep him here in Byreburn. But if he did leave, where would he go? He stubbed out his cigarette and lay back on the ground, his hands behind his head.

Lindsay stood up. Her t-shirt rose and Jake was rewarded with a glimpse of her smooth, flat stomach. Her belly button winked at him before Lindsay noticed and pulled it down self-consciously. She held out a hand. Jake took it and levered himself up.

'Smile,' Lindsay said. She moved closer to him, held up her phone and took a selfie. 'I'm going to my brother's party tonight, do you want to come?' She flicked her fringe out of her eyes.

Jackpot. This was going to be the best Common Riding ever. Here he was, sharing a drink and a ciggie with the most beautiful girl he had ever met, and now she was asking him to a party. Her green eyes glinted at him conspiratorially. Jake worked hard at not blushing under her gaze. She flicked her hair again.

'Sure,' he said nonchalantly, 'sounds fun.'

'Give me your phone number in case we get split up.'

They'd swapped numbers before lurching back into town.

Chapter 3

With the excitement of Common Riding over, Byreburn got on with the day-to-day business of being a tight-knit community. The town's mills reopened their doors, and the looms were cranked back into action. The school rang its morning bell, and the shops opened for trade.

Kathi's business, too, carried on and she headed to the estate agent to collect the keys of a three-bed terraced house she'd newly purchased. She had arranged to meet her builder, Brian Weatherstone, at the house. He was usually late for their appointments and at first it had frustrated Kathi beyond belief but she had eventually grown used to it and she knew it meant she had an extra few minutes before she had to head out to meet him.

'Morning Brian, everything alright?' she asked while checking her watch. She wondered if she was late but no, unusually, Brian was exactly on time.

'Aye, fine.' Again this was unlike Brian. His usual demeanour was of doom and gloom. He always reminded Kathi of Eeyore from Winnie the Pooh. A nice enough donkey, just not very cheerful.

Kathi tried the various keys given to her by the estate agent until the right one fit and they went inside. The previous owner had lived there for over sixty years and from the choice of décor and the state of the electrical wiring, even a layperson like Kathi knew it needed a lot of work. When the owner passed away the only buyer willing to take on such a big refurbishment was her and so she purchased it from the executors for a good price.

It was Brian's first view of the house, but for Kathi it was a time to remind herself of its layout. She pulled out a copy of the surveyor's report and the notes she'd made on that initial viewing, jotting down fresh ones as she wandered the rooms.

The electrical consumer board was above the front door. They looked at it with horror. 'Say no more,' said Kathi, 'a full rewire it is.' The avocado suite in the bathroom made them giggle. 'How was this ever fashionable?' Kathi wondered out loud.

'Rip it out?' asked Brian.

'Definitely.'

The small square kitchen told its own story of family meals lovingly made on what would have been the latest in cookers. The units were no doubt fashionable in the 1980s, but now they looked tired and dated. The counter tops were worn away with years of food preparation and pots of tea being brewed. It was time to move those memories aside in readiness for new ones to be made by a young family.

In time they headed upstairs. All three bedrooms had retained their fireplaces, which lifted Kathi's heart. Too often they were ripped out to make a smooth wall against which a piece of furniture could be placed. Fireplaces were now considered a period feature which would be both aesthetically pleasing and could add value to the property.

'Oh look,' said Brian, tilting his head back. 'There's still some original cornicing here. It's not fancy, but it does add a little bit of grandeur.' He smiled at Kathi, who smiled back, happily bewildered by the cheerful Brian before her. Perhaps he was finally over the heartache of his ex-girlfriend leaving him? Whatever it was, she was delighted with the result.

When they had firmed up what needed to be done inside, they went out to the back garden. Because the property had been empty for so long it was completely overgrown. Rose bushes had gone wild and were competing for space with the pretty but invasive bindweed. The once neat lawn was now a meadow of tall grass and it was pleasing to see bees, butterflies and insects buzzing about the place, making merry.

'It's going to be lovely when it's finished,' said Brian, looking back at the house. This was one step too far.

'Everything okay, Brian?' Kathi asked. He looked at her sheepishly.

'Can you keep a secret?' he asked, clearly desperate to tell her. 'I've started seeing someone.'

'That's brilliant news,' Kathi said, genuinely delighted for him.

'Do you want to know who it is?'

'Who is it?'

'Cherry.' Kathi hoped her face didn't register shock but Cherry really was the last person she would have guessed. Brian didn't seem at all her type. In fact, Kathi was sure she could remember Cherry being rude, not that long ago, about the mass of hair on Brian's head and face. Brian had unruly curly hair and a thick beard which he let run wild.

'I'm happy for you. Two of my favourite people together,' A sudden dread zipped through Kathi's mind that if things didn't work out between them, her property team might fall apart and that would be a disaster because a reliable letting agent, and a good joiner who lived locally, were hard to find.

'When did you get together?'

'Almost a month ago now. To be honest, Cherry was never really my type. She wears a lot of makeup and can be, you know, a bit forceful.'

Kathi couldn't hide an understanding smile. Cherry often had to chase Brian up for jobs he was slow to finish or simply shout at him to get his invoices submitted or she'd never pay him at all. 'How you manage to make it through the day in one piece I'll never know,' she'd said to him many times.

'I bumped into her in the pub one night and we got chatting and we got on. Outside of work, she was really nice to me. Anyway, one thing led to another and here we are. I'd say we're a couple now. Except,' Brian turned serious. 'She won't go out with me for dinner, not even to Dumfries where nobody knows us. I don't understand why, but she always wants to stay in.'

'Maybe she wants to keep you all to herself,' suggested Kathi, which cheered him momentarily.

'Naw, I don't think it's that.'

'Maybe she just wants to take things slowly, it's early days after all.'

'Yeah, maybe,' he said thoughtfully, before snapping back to the here and now. 'Give me a set of keys and then I can get cracking. I've got a skip coming tomorrow, and I've roped in a couple of lads to help. It'll be a nice easy job.'

Later, at home, Kathi decided to write a blog post because the day had been positive and she wanted to share it. There were a couple of comments on her previous post and a new in-box message. There were a few new comments and a couple of emails, one from an account called DayOfReckoning. Very dramatic, Kathi thought to herself. She opened it and blanched at what she read.

You're a thief and a cuckoo who steals what doesn't belong to you, and one day you're going to die because of it. Bitch.

Kathi tutted, amazed at how bored some people were that this was how they amused themselves. Hadn't they anything better to do with their time. She pressed delete and began her blog.

She heard Jake open the back door. He was home from school. She went through and offered to make him a snack. 'Nah, I'm alright,' he said. Kathi knew that was code for, I've been to the sweet shop on the way home.

She knew that shop well because as a girl she'd visited it on her way home from school. It hadn't changed since she was a child, and although she rarely bought anything for herself these days, she loved going in. The atmosphere and smell bombarded her with memories and good feelings.

'How was school?' she asked, more out of habit than in expectation of a response.

'It was alright. A couple of guys got kicked out of class for fighting,' Jake laughed as he recalled the memory of it, while continuing to text. 'I think their parents will be called in.'

'Was anyone hurt?'

'I don't care, I hate them both. They're arseholes.'

'Watch your language.' Kathi observed her son. His face was deadly serious and she could see he really did hate these boys, that something must have happened between them. 'Have they had a go at you?'

'No.' Jake poured a glass of water, picked up his bag and went to his room. She saw he'd left his phone on the kitchen table and thought about looking at it, just to see what was going on in his life. He told her so little these days that she often had to resist the urge to snoop. She put the kettle on to distract herself before deciding to have a quick look, just in case something presented itself.

'What are you doing?' Jake demanded, appearing at the kitchen door like a reprimanding parent, and indeed Kathi did feel like she'd been caught with her hand in the cookie jar.

'I was going to check you haven't changed the passcode.' A condition of Jake having his own phone was that Kathi and Graham knew the passcode and could periodically check he wasn't up to anything he shouldn't be.

'Well, I haven't,' he said, clearly furious Kathi was actually invoking this condition. He grabbed the phone from her, gave her a filthy look and skulked away upstairs.

Kathi began preparing dinner and before long Graham came in from work. They exchanged news before Graham went upstairs to have a shower. Kathi couldn't resist going in to see Jake on the pretext Graham was home. She knocked gently on his door before entering and closing it behind her.

'Dad's back,' she told him.

'I'll be down when dinner's ready.' He was lying on his bed and to Kathi's joy was reading a book, his phone abandoned at the end of the bed. A flush of pride made Kathi smile down at him.

'What?' he growled.

'Nothing, it's nice to see you reading a book, that's all.'

'I do know how to read, you know.'

'I know, I just mean it's nice to see you doing something other than play on your phone.' This didn't warrant a reply, only an eye roll. Uninvited she sat down on his bed, picking a pair of socks up from the floor as she did so. Jake's room was a horror story of dirty clothes and used dishes. She didn't dare imagine what lay under the bed. He had a few posters on the walls of footballers she'd barely heard of, as well as a scantily clad Dua Lipa. Kathi only knew this because her name was on the poster.

'So, how are things? Was it a bit of a fright seeing the boys fighting today?' Again Jake didn't reply, pretending instead to read. 'There was a bully in my year at school. He was always picking on the boys who weren't as physically strong as him. No one liked him and avoided him as much as possible.' Jake silently stared at his book, but Kathi knew he was listening. 'Turns out his dad wasn't very nice to either him, or his mum. Eventually the dad left and I remember he took it really badly. What I'm trying to say, I guess, is that...' Kathi searched for the right words, '...often bullies are bullied at home and they're very unhappy. Picking on other people makes them feel better for a short time.'

'So what, we should feel sorry for him and do nothing?'

'No, of course not, just know that whatever he says to hurt you, it's not personal, it's not about you. It's him trying to feel better about himself.' As she said the words she knew they were futile. No amount of philosophising would lessen the impact of hurtful comments or shield against a punch or a kick or a slap issued in the playground.

'Are you finished?'

'Jake, have I done something, or not done something, that's made you so angry?' Jake turned away from her. She said gently, 'Remember, I'm your mum and I love you, no matter what.'

Jake wouldn't look at her so didn't see the effort Kathi put into not crying. She was determined not to break down in front of him but show she was strong and reliable, an unmovable wall of security and safety. She quickly ran through in her mind the tools she'd learnt at the training courses she'd attended on how to be a good mother. With as much calm as she could muster, she repeated, 'I am your mother and I love you no matter what.'

'No. You're not.' This time Jake looked her in the eye.

Chapter 4

Jake's words shocked Kathi. She thought she was prepared for the day he would say it, but in reality it was just like every other aspect of parenting; no amount of preparation was enough.

The anger he clutched at was part of his self-discovery. She knew this, but his words winded her. She gathered herself up off the bed and with as much control as she could muster, left the room. As soon as his door was shut she took a silent and laboured breath.

In her own bedroom she lay down in the dark. The shock slowly ebbed away and left in its place anger. She pursed her lips. Ungrateful brat, she thought, I've given him everything, how dare he treat me like this. After the anger was hurt. She burst into tears.

Graham came into the room, having showered off his working day. 'What's up?' he asked, switching on the bedroom light. 'Have you had a bad day?' Kathi nodded. 'You stay here,' he said, getting dressed. 'I'll finish dinner. Have a rest, you've been working hard lately.' He gave her a kiss, his skin slightly damp from the shower, and went downstairs.

Leaning against the headboard, her knees tucked up close, Kathi wondered if now was the time they needed professional help for Jake, to help him through whatever it was he was going through. She thought back to the little boy they'd met at Adoption Day. He wasn't yet two years old, cute with toddler chubbiness. He had big brown eyes and a mop of black curly hair. He was full of smiles and confidence as he played with the other boys and girls. He relished exploring the toys that had been set out to keep all the children entertained.

They had been so nervous that day, meeting their possible son. They needn't have been. When she and Graham had gone over to play with him, Jake been so open and happy to engage it felt like a natural fit. They had been told not to expect to fall in love straight away, that chemistry needs time to grow. But Jake's winning smile drew them in, and they knew he was the child for them. It was another five long weeks before they found out whether or not Jake had been matched with them.

It had taken Kathi and Graham a long time to get to the point of adoption. They had tried IVF three times with no success. Broke, emotionally exhausted and, in Kathi's case, physically burned out, they finally accepted they were not going to have a biological child. For this they grieved. For over a year they grieved. Then, little by little, they acknowledged they still wanted to be parents, and that adoption was the path for them.

The thrill of Jake's arrival soon turned to distress and exhaustion. The smiling little boy who welcomed them at Adoption Day turned into an angry, frightened and sad little boy. From Jake's point of view, even with the most careful of planning, he had been removed from a secure and loving foster family. He'd been ripped away from a mother-figure he loved and plonked into a foreign land. This new family spoke differently, they smelled and sounded different. Their home was unfamiliar, and he was expected to sleep in a strange bed. Hardest of all, Jake didn't understand why he'd been sent away to live with strangers. It was the second time he'd been abandoned. He clung, day and night, to the toy giraffe he'd brought with him. It was a lifeline, a link to his former life.

At first Jake rejected Kathi and Graham. He cried and railed against them and refused any attempts to be comforted by them. It took some time, but little by little he recognised they weren't going to hurt him. The tight knot in his stomach began to loosen, and he found his appetite again. The hard shell of protection he carried with him softened and his heart started opening. For two years Jake grieved for his foster parents and only after that was he fully able to attach himself to his new mum and dad. By year three the Beatties were a contented and secure family unit and so it remained until 18 months ago when Jake began to burrow back in on himself, withdrawing his usual chatter and good humour. His temper quickened, and he isolated himself in his bedroom.

It's normal, people said, he's a teenager, they all do that. Kathi clenched her fists but didn't say anything. She knew it was more than developing hormones. She saw him staring at her, watching her. His looks weren't hostile, they were curious. Sometimes he looked as though he wanted to ask her a question before changing his mind. She felt him trying to work out who she was to him, or what he was to her. She never prompted him. He'll ask when he's ready, she thought.

At times she felt he was seeing her for the first time. This is positive, she assured herself. It means he's maturing and seeing me as more than just his mum. She closed her ears to the possibility that he didn't like what he saw.

'Dinner's ready.' Graham popped his head around the door.

'I'll be down in a minute,' Kathi said, smiling at him.

'Are you feeling better?' Kathi nodded. 'Good, come and eat before it gets cold.'

The atmosphere at dinner was sullen. Neither Kathi nor Jake said very much, and Graham's attempts to lift the mood were met with monosyllables. 'For Christ's sake,' he said eventually. 'What's wrong with you two?'

'Ask her,' said Jake.

'Who's her, the cat's mother?' Graham snapped.

'Well, she's not mine.'

'Go to your room.'

Jake pushed back his chair so forcefully it tipped over. Kathi and Graham listened in silence to his footsteps thumping up the stairs and his bedroom door slamming shut.

'This can't go on,' said Kathi. 'He's only 15. I can't live like this.'

'What do you want to do?'

'I think we need professional help.' Graham's face fell. When they'd talked about this in the past, Graham had made it clear he didn't want outsiders poking their noses into his life ever again. The adoption interviews had been so intrusive, to the point where he'd felt the social workers wanted him to behave badly so they could call the whole thing off.

He'd felt the process had been a power trip for them. They'd picked fault with him and Kathi for being human, with histories and the mistakes that come with youth, rather than an ordinary couple who simply wanted to be parents. It was one of the reasons he and Kathi chose not to adopt again. They couldn't face the interrogation a second time.

'I don't think things are that bad,' he said. 'Families argue, it's normal.'

'This isn't a normal argument.'

'Kids tell parents these things all the time. They blame parents for everything. I did it myself. I remember shouting at Mum and telling her I wished I'd never been born. We don't need professional help.'

'Your background was different to Jake's. You didn't have the instability he had. Deep inside you knew your parents loved you no matter what. You knew they were your parents, and that was enough to give you the security you needed to say those things. Jake doesn't have that and I don't know how to give it to him.'

'I think you're overreacting. We don't need professional help.'

'Maybe you don't, but I do, and Jake definitely does.' Graham stared down at his dinner before deciding he wasn't hungry anymore. He put his plate in the sink and went through to the living room. 'Why are you so against this?' Kathi asked, following him.

'Because it's unnecessary.'

'For who?'

'For any of us. It'll be another pompous social worker rubbing our noses in what a bad job we're doing. It'll prove to them they were right in thinking we were no good and putting us through hell during those interviews. Do you remember that? How they looked down their noses at us? I'm not going through that again.'

'Graham, this isn't about us.'

'Of course it is, we're his parents, he's our responsibility.'

Kathi sat down on the sofa. She hadn't seen Graham's outburst coming and needed to think about how to respond. 'I didn't realise you felt so strongly about the social workers.' Graham didn't reply and wouldn't look at her, but he did sit down in the armchair. 'Do you think we're failing as parents?' Kathi asked.

'If you think we need to get professional help, then yes, I do. We should be able to handle this ourselves. This is our family and our business. It's nothing to do with anybody else.'

'That's your pride talking, not what's best for Jake.'

'Do you think he wants everyone to know his business? You know this town, within minutes it'll spread like wildfire that the Beatties are in trouble and that it's all because they adopted a child.' Aware that Jake was upstairs, Graham lowered his voice. 'They'll say if we hadn't adopted we wouldn't be in this trouble now.'

'Rubbish.'

'It's not. Which other kids do you know that are getting 'professional help'? I'll tell you, only those whose parents don't care about them, who can't look after them. We are not one of those families.'

'Jesus Graham, that's simply not true. This isn't the 1950s, you know. Lots of people get help when they need it. And no, I don't know of any other kids who are getting help because it's private and none of my business. If someone wanted me to know they'd tell me. And we wouldn't tell anyone about our situation because it's none of their business. There's no need for anyone else to know. We don't even need to tell your parents because, let's face it, that's what you're worried about, isn't it? They've never fully approved of us adopting, and this would only confirm they're right.'

'I don't want you to do this. I don't want any social workers involved in my life ever again.'

'Then I won't go to the social workers. I'll find someone else.'

'Who?'

'I don't know yet, I'll need to find someone else who can help.'

'I'm not happy about this.'

'I know, but it's not you I'm worried about just now, it's Jake.'

'If you go ahead with this,' said Graham, shooting out of his seat and heading to the back door, 'it's on you. I want no part of it.'

Chapter 5

Cherry hummed a tune that morning as she switched the kettle on, put two spoons of coffee granules into her favourite mug and got the milk out of the fridge. She pottered about the kitchen straightening this, aligning that, giving the spotless table a quick wipe down. When the kettle boiled she poured the water into the mug and, as she made her way along the hallway to her home office, burst into a rendition of The Beatles' It Must Be Love.

Her office was actually a box room with a window, but she had used her natural energy and efficiency to design and fit her desk, chair and filing cabinet, as well as a chair for her visitors, into the tiny space and still make it feel uncluttered. 'I should work for Ikea,' she liked to joke. She couldn't stop herself from humming and singing as she went through her morning routine, nor could she rid herself of the dreamy feeling that had been following her for the past few weeks. Brian's face flashed into vision and she remembered how his lips felt. A girlish giggle escaped her own lips. 'Pull yourself together, Cherry,' she chastised herself, mortified by her adolescent behaviour.

A notification came up on her computer screen letting her know she was due to do a flat inspection. She gave the tenant a call to remind them she'd pop round in a couple of days. While she was checking through her emails, she heard the front door to her flat open.

'Only me,' called a voice.

'I'm in the office,' Cherry sped to the door of the office and grinned as Brian made his way down the hallway. 'Morning,' she said coyly.

'Good morning gorgeous.' They embraced passionately.

'You know,' said Cherry as she put her fingers through is long hair, 'I love your hair, the curls you've got.'

'Why thank you,' he smiled. 'I like your hair too.' They kissed again.

'But do you know what would make it even easier for me to put my fingers through it? If it was just a teeny, tiny bit shorter.'

'My hair is my strength,' he said, hoping to persuade Cherry of its prowess. 'You know, like Goliath.'

'Samson.'

'Who?'

'Samson. It was Samson who got his strength from his hair.'

Brian kissed her again in a bid to change the subject. His ex-girlfriend had always been on at him to cut his hair but he loved his tresses. He thought they made him look like one of the Rock Gods he so admired.

'Kettle's just boiled,' said Cherry, satisfied she'd laid the seed of a haircut to germinate. When he came back from the kitchen Cherry gave him a packet of chewing gum. Cherry knew how hard Brian was working to break his smoking habit. Every time he felt like lighting up he was to take a piece of gum instead and think about kissing Cherry because, she told him, she didn't want to make out with an ashtray. So far Cherry's lure was enough and he hadn't smoked anything in over three weeks. 'I'm proud of you,' she said when he picked up the gum. 'I know it isn't easy.'

They talked through the jobs due that day, some were small maintenance ones, others more complicated. Now that Brian had quit his marijuana habit he'd started sleeping better, his head was clearer and, bit by bit, he'd gained more energy. Only a few weeks ago Brian hopped from job to job as the whim took him, never really finishing any of them and then fending off a barrage of insults from Cherry, who was constantly placating irate tenants. It was only his natural skill as a joiner and his cheap rates that kept him employed.

'I've spoken to Kathi about the refurbishment on her new place,' Cherry said. 'I've told her you can do it, but I need you to do all the maintenance jobs for my clients first.'

'I need to start that refurb soon,' Brian told her. 'You know she doesn't like to hang about after a sale has gone through.' Brian looked nervous all of a sudden, shifting in his seat.

'What's wrong?' Cherry asked.

'Och, nothing.'

'Don't och nothing me, what's wrong?'

'I was in Murray's shop and Kathi's son, Jake, was there with a couple of pals.'

'And?'

'I saw him shoplift some sweets. It was nothing major and we've all done it at least once, but I don't know whether I should say something to Kathi or not.'

'You should, definitely you should. She's his mum, she has a right to know. I'd want to know if it was my child.'

'I suppose so, but I don't want her to lay into him or anything. It might be a one off and like I said, we've all done it at one time or another.' Cherry raised an eyebrow indicating he could speak for himself. Brian stood to leave. 'Have you ever wanted any?' he asked.

'What?'

'Kids?'

'At my age? Don't be daft.'

'What about marriage?'

'Once was enough for me, thank you very much. Hey, I hope you're not getting any ideas Brian Weatherstone?'

'Don't you be daft,' he said. Cherry got up and walked him to the door. After a prolonged and passionate goodbye she stretched like a cat in front of the hearth and headed back to her office. She stopped in front of the hallway mirror to check Brian hadn't ruffled her thick, short blonde hair too much in their embrace. She moved her hands over her face, smoothing out the wrinkles. She removed a tiny clump of mascara from underneath one of her blue eyes and smiled at herself.

She felt unusually at peace with the world. Her life generally went from one small drama to the next, and that was the way she liked it. It kept her on her toes and stopped life from getting dull. She had to admit, though, it was nice to have a bit of respite from the soap opera and enjoy how good life was at the moment.

Grateful to have escaped her marriage to Wayne she'd jumped feet first into her new lettings business and although it was hard work and seven days a week, she enjoyed being in charge of her own time and how successful, or otherwise, her business was. She was proud of how well she'd done.

After her divorce from Wayne, a number of people turned against her, but equally she'd made good friends of her own, friends that proved to be loyal during her difficult divorce. While Cherry acknowledged that the downside of small town living is that nothing is private and everybody knows your business, the upside is that, once you've been initiated into the gang, membership is lifelong. Something about Byreburn had wormed its way into Cherry's heart and while the easy option after the divorce would have been to leave, she liked being part of this gang and felt affection for the town.

Cherry loved the fact Byreburn took pride in its traditions, its festivals, its sons and daughters who travelled the world and took their culture with them. She loved the outrage inhabitants felt at any unwelcome change within the town, and the efforts made to retain Byreburn's high standards for itself.

Through making good friends and providing an excellent service for the town, Cherry had earned her place in its heart and that made her happy. She felt she belonged. She looked out of the office's small window and watched the River Esk flow pleasingly through the town. She smiled, content with her lot in life.

Today was Kathi's day to upload her weekly blog post. She'd been thinking all week about a book she'd read and wanted to review. She had written some notes and just needed to put them all together.

She brewed her coffee, put some music on and logged into her site. There were a couple of messages, one from DayOfReckoning, the same sender as the other day.

I see you're ripping off another family not giving them what they deserve, the person wrote. You're a fat, greedy cow filling your fat, greedy pockets with things that don't belong to you. You'll pay for it bitch.

Shivers slithered down Kathi's spine. Was is it coincidence that she'd picked up the keys to a new property recently? Could DayOfReckoning be related to the woman who had lived at the property? There was something creepy about the message, not simply because it was aggressive but because it was personal. I can't let this derail me, she thought, today is blog day, I have to keep my readers happy. Stubbornly Kathi wrote the blog post she'd been planning and pressed publish. When Graham got home that night she asked what he made of the message.

'Who's it from?' he asked.

'I've no idea, someone calling themselves DayOfReckoning. I don't recognise the name.'

'What do they mean you're ripping people off?'

'Your guess is as good as mine.'

'Don't worry about it,' said Graham, 'I bet it's not even a human, I bet it's one of those bots you hear about. It goes around the internet writing random stuff to random people.'

'Yes,' Kathi conceded. 'Maybe you're right.' She wasn't convinced though, there was something about the message that felt personal or familiar. She couldn't put her finger on what it was exactly, but the message didn't feel at all random.

'I don't know,' he said. 'I just can't take it seriously. I can't believe anyone we know would do that. I'm convinced it's someone looking for cheap kicks. Have you replied?'

'No,' said Kathi. 'What would I say? Sorry you think I'm an evil bitch but hope you're enjoying my blog?'

'What do you want to do?'

'I don't know, I really don't. Do you think I should tell the police?'

'That seems a bit over the top. Maybe you could mention it to Jamie when you next see him?' Jamie Armstrong was one of the local bobbies, and a good friend of Graham's.

'There's no harm in broaching it with him, I suppose.'

Chapter 6

Jake and Lindsay started heading up to The Green most afternoons after school. Jake hadn't really been sure she wanted to so nearly melted through the floor when she came up to him after the bell had rung and asked him if he wanted to go with her. He'd tried not to look smug as they'd left the school grounds and headed up the street, over the Kings Bridge and to The Green by the river.

'Do you want to go to Maths?' Lindsay asked today as the bell was ringing to denote a change in class.

'Not really.' Instead, they ran out of the school grounds and up to The Green. The day was sunny and dry so they plonked themselves on the grass. 'What's your mum like?' Lindsay asked. The question took him by surprise.

'My mum?'

'Yeah, what's she like?'

'She's alright, I suppose.'

'She's really pretty. And she's her own boss?'

'I guess so.'

'That's cool. She's her own boss and answers to nobody. I want that.' Jake thought about whether or not that was true and he supposed it was. She worked a lot, he knew that. She was never off the phone from Cherry and that dope head Brian. Now that he thought about it, yes, she was the boss.

'Do you want to own your own company?' he asked her.

'I don't care what I do as long as I get out of here.' She stretched out her arm and moved it from left to right, showcasing the entire town of Byreburn.

'I couldn't agree more,' he said, hooking his arms around his knees. 'I want to get out of this place as soon as possible.'

'What's your dad like?'

'He's nice. More easy-going than Mum.' Lindsay took her cigarettes out and lit one.

'What about your parents? Why are they like?' He took one of her cigarettes while he waited for her to answer.

'Dad can be really funny. Sometimes he makes us all laugh. I like him then.'

'And your mum?'

'She's quiet, never says much. Even when she's drunk, she doesn't say a lot.'

'What about your brothers?'

'One is alright, but one is like Dad. You're adopted, aren't you? Hayden told me.' Jake's body stiffened a little at the question but Lyndsay asked in such a matter-of-fact way that he knew instinctively she wasn't judging him and didn't take offense.

'Yes,' he said. 'You asked Hayden about me?' Hayden had been his best friend but they'd fallen out recently.

'Have you ever met your other mother?' said Lindsay, opting not to answer his question.

'My birth mum? No, I haven't.'

'Do you want to?'

'All the time. I think about her all the time.'

'Where does she live?'

'In Glasgow, I think.'

'You don't know?'

'That's where she lived when I was born. I don't know if she's still there.'

'That's exciting.'

'You think?' Exciting was not a word Jake would have chosen to describe his situation.

'Definitely. You've got a whole other family out there. I wish I did. If I did, I'd go and look for them because they couldn't be any worse than the one I've got. In fact, I wish mine had put me up for adoption.'

'No, you don't. You don't know what it's like not to be wanted.'

'Don't I?' Jake turned to look at her. 'My parents don't want me,' she said. 'Christ, they don't want each other. I wish they had given me up for adoption because then I would be with a family who really wanted me. Like your mum and dad.'

'Your parents might be useless but at least they're yours, you belong to them. You know where you fit in this town. I don't.'

'You fit. Everyone knows your mum and that you're her son. You are a Beattie.'

'Then why don't I feel it?' They finished their cigarettes and lay down on the warm grass.

'What are you thinking about?' Lindsay asked at length.

'How I can find my birth mum.'

'Easy,' she said, 'internet. You can find everyone on the Internet.'

'Yeah, maybe.' Lindsay might be right about that but he had no clue where to start. A brief image of their imagined reunion flashed through his mind. The image was vague, two blurred figures talking and moving, but the feeling was powerful. It was a feeling of connection and belonging. With Marie there was no animosity or burning desire to escape. With Marie, Jake felt calm and at peace. How lovely to always be happy and content.

Perhaps he should look for her? His brow furrowed as he thought about how he might find his birth mum. As far as he knew, not even Kathi and Graham had her contact details. It was impossible.

Cherry's phone pinged, reminding her that she had a flat inspection in an hour. She decided to have a shower before heading out. Turning the radio on for company, she washed her hair, lathered her body and shaved her underarms. To check she'd razored all the stubble, Cherry ran a finger from the top of her armpit to the bottom. It was right at the bottom she felt a lump. It was small and solid, as if a small bouncy ball had been placed just under the skin. She felt it again and wondered if it was a large and badly placed pimple. A second inspection confirmed it wasn't.

Cherry stepped out of the shower and with her towel wiped the steam off the bathroom mirror, but it steamed up again just as quickly so, irritated, she left the warmth of the bathroom and went into the chill of the hallway. An ocean of goose-pimples erupted and her wet hair dripped over her naked skin.

She stood as close as she could to the wardrobe mirror in her bedroom, stretching her arm up and pulling the skin taut, trying to see what she was sure she felt. 'Bloody hell,' she cursed, grabbing her glasses from the bedside table and putting them on for a closer inspection. Still she couldn't see anything, so she ran her hand once again over her armpit. There was no denying the lump.

Cherry stepped back from the mirror to look at both her breasts, searching for a clue, anything she might have missed. She couldn't understand how a lump had formed without her noticing, after all she'd been so careful and observant. Breast cancer was not a stranger to her family. Her grandmother and aunt had both succumbed to it, and a cousin had been lucky enough to catch it early and survive. Have I caught it early? She asked herself.

The shock left her slightly breathless and lightheaded and she sat on the bed, oblivious to her shivering. Memories of her ill and bed bound grandmother were interspersed with those of her aunt in hospital prior to moving home and being nursed around the clock. She remembered too the smell of both women in their final days. When Cherry's grandmother was dying, she had thought the smell was the general smell of death. To her child self, the smell was peculiar and the sum of its parts. When her aunt was ill, the adult Cherry recognised those parts; urine, stale breath, disinfectant and used air. She did not want that. That was not to be her destiny.

Her first instinct was to drive to the nearest emergency room, announce she had breast cancer and demand it be removed immediately. Instead, she picked up her phone and called the local doctor's surgery.

'We can fit you in on the twenty-third,' the receptionist said.

'That's nearly two weeks away,' said Cherry.

'It's a very busy time.' The receptionist sighed audibly.

'I need an appointment sooner than that. I found a lump and I need it taken out.'

'Let me look at the computer,' the receptionist conceded. 'I can fit you in with Dr Brown next Tuesday.'

'I'll take it, but if there's a cancellation, will you call me? This is urgent. I don't want to die.'

'Absolutely, I'll call you.'

Cherry struggled to get on track after the call. Her hair had started to dry so wouldn't behave when she tried to style it. She'd been naked for so long she struggled to get warm. Her coffee had gone cold, and she didn't have time to make a fresh cup before the flat inspection. For the rest of the day Cherry felt wrong-footed and couldn't seem to pull herself back into focus. Without realising it, her hand would move to her underarm, searching out that marble-sized lump. In quiet moments she envisaged herself lying in a hospital bed surrounded by friends and loved ones, so many in fact they could only be there for one reason; to say goodbye.

After the flat inspection, she headed back to the office. She sat at her desk, picturing her funeral. It would be here in Byreburn because this was her home now, this was where she had built her new life. She'd ask everyone to wear bright colours because she didn't want people to be sad. She wanted them to celebrate how fabulous her life had been.

Forget that, she thought, I want everyone in black. She wanted them to mourn her life because she'd been taken too soon. There was still so much she had yet to achieve. She wasn't ready to call it quits.

Panic bubbled, she felt dizzy, as if she were about to step out into thin air. She slumped down to the floor, crouched over. She wasn't ready to leave this earth yet. There was so much she wanted to do and achieve with her life. She was too young. In time she slowly stood up and felt a little better. She could see out the window to the River Esk and it calmed her. She saw a couple of school kids down at the riverside and checked her watch. It had only just gone two o'clock in the afternoon. There was a boy and a girl. Cherry squinted to try to make out who they were. At the same time as seeing cigarette smoke ascend skyward she recognised one of the boys. 'Jake,' she gasped, 'you wee bugger.'

Chapter 7

It was Saturday night and Lindsay had invited Jake to another one of her brother's parties. He'd been to a couple of them by now and although he was getting to know people, he still felt out of place. He could see people looking at him as if he shouldn't be there. He was sure the only reason he was allowed in was because he was with Lindsay. Before going to the party, they had gone to the supermarket to buy some alcohol. They'd be able to get a few cans of something depending on who was working the till.

Tonight it wasn't anyone they knew and Jake would have given up at that point, but Lindsay was not to be defeated. They hung around close to the drinks aisle and when a slightly shabby woman appeared, Lindsay asked her if she'd buy them some booze. She looked at Lindsay and at first Jake thought she was going to say no. But when she looked over to Jake, something made her change your mind, and she agreed.

'Score,' Jake said to himself. He and Lindsay gave her some money and waited outside for the woman to bring the beer out to them.

'Thanks so much,' Lindsay said. 'The guy on the till is a real stiff.'

'No problem,' the woman said. 'I remember being your age.' She winked at Jake. 'Don't tell anyone though, eh?'

'We won't,' Jake said, grinning from ear to ear. It felt so rebellious to be obtaining illicit booze. He could barely contain the added exhilaration that shot through him, brought on by the simple fact he was doing this with Lindsay. He looked over at her and she looked as pleased as him. Jake knew he'd gone up in her estimation. This was a win on all fronts.

'You off to a party?' the woman asked.

'Yeah,' said Lindsay. 'My brother is throwing a house party. Do you want to come?' The woman thought about it for a moment.

'Are you both going?' she asked.

'Yes.'

'Will your brother mind?'

'No, the more the merrier.' Jake wasn't sure her brother would see it that way. 'Come on,' Lindsay said, linking arms with Jake. They began to move away, but Lindsay turned around to the woman. 'You coming?' She began following them. 'What's your name?' Lindsay asked.

'Joanne.'

'I'm Lindsay. This is Jake.'

'Hi,' said Jake.

'Hello, Jake.' They walked on. 'Are you two together?'

Jake held his breath, wondering what Lindsay would say and praying she'd say something like not yet, or, I want us to be. Instead, she laughed and said, 'We're just friends.'

They heard the music blaring as soon as they turned onto the street. The sound of the bass was intoxicating. It spoke of good fun, laughter, excess and being with Lindsay. I bet Hayden never gets invited to parties like this, Jake thought. The thought pleased him. Lindsay seemed to know everybody there. She waved or said hello to people Jake had never even seen before. Sometimes he was amazed at how much older than him she seemed. He felt like such a kid next to her.

They went through to the kitchen and put their drinks in the fridge to cool, taking some that were already chilled. The three of them stayed in the kitchen, leaning against the cupboards, watching people coming and going. After a few minutes, they started chatting. 'Where are you from?' Lindsay asked Joanne. 'I've not seen you around.'

'I'm new to Byreburn. I moved here a couple of months ago from Glasgow.'

'What brought you here?'

'I got a job at the mill.' Joanne smiled at Jake. She used a hand to brush her overgrown fringe out of her eyes and tuck it behind an ear. Jake couldn't help but notice how greasy her hair looked. There was something unkempt about her. Her clothes were too big for her, even though she was big herself. She looked like she just threw on whatever was closest to hand. Not like him. He chose his clothes carefully and gelled his hair to within an inch of its life, each strand placed with precision. He tried to watch Joanne without her noticing but whenever he cast a glance in her direction, she was watching him.

'What about you, Jake?' She asked. 'Are you Byreburn born and bred?'

'Yeah,' he answered noncommittally. How could he ever answer that question? If he said no, that would open up more questions than he wanted to answer.

'Oh yeah?' she said, raising her eyebrows. 'What about your mum and dad?'

'Them too,' said Lindsay, offering her cigarettes around. Jake took one, but Joanne declined.

'Nasty habit,' she said to Jake. 'But don't worry, I won't tell.' She nudged his arm and gave him another wink, grinning the whole time. For some reason, this made him laugh.

'Cheers,' he said to Joanne, lifting his can of lager. 'Cheers,' she replied, lifting hers. The kitchen filled up and pushed them out into the living room. Joanne squeezed herself into a small space on the sofa, forcing the other occupants out. She patted the space next to her and indicated Jake should sit next to her. He looked to Lindsay for backup, but she had moved off and was talking to some guy who left school last year.

Deflated, he sat next to Joanne, scowling at the boy talking to Lindsay. 'Don't worry about it,' Joanne said, looking in the same direction. 'She's not interested in him.' Jake blushed. He felt his ear tips heat up and redden. 'She likes you, I can tell.' Jake turned to look at her, surprised.

'How can you tell?' he asked her.

'By the way she looks at you.' Joanne nodded her head in Lindsay's direction. 'She's not hooked her arm around his, has she? Not like she did with you. Give it time. These things always take a bit of time.'

'Do you think so?' he asked. Jake looked at Joanne, trying to work out if she was mocking him or not, but her face was dead straight. She meant every word she said. He tried not to, he tried to be cool, but Jake's face lit up and his lips parted into a wide smile. Joanne turned to look at him. 'I know so,' she said.

Chapter 8

The renovation had begun in Kathi's new property and, with Brian, she was waiting for the two lads to come and finish ripping out the old kitchen and bathroom. Once that was done, the electrician and plumber could start their role in modernising the house. Kathi loitered while Brian tinkered about the kitchen. She checked her watch. 'They're late,' she said.

'They'll get here, don't worry,' said Brian. He cleared his throat. 'I saw Jake the other week.'

'Oh yeah?'

'Yeah, he was in Murray's shop with a couple of pals.'

'Was it after school?'

'I think so.'

'Was he buying sweets? I've told him I don't want him doing that.' Kathi made a mental note to have a word with him that night.

'The thing is, he didn't exactly buy any sweets.' Kathi looked properly at Brian and saw how nervous he was.

'What do you mean?' she asked. 'Either he bought sweets or he didn't.'

'He didn't buy any sweets,' Brian repeated.

'Wait, you mean, he stole them?' Brian looked guilty, as if he'd been the one caught steeling. 'Oh my God, I can't believe it. Are you sure, Brian? Are you sure it was him?'

'Yes, it was definitely him.'

Embarrassed, they both fell silent. Kathi's immediate thought was, what had she done for Jake to start stealing? Her brain re-ran her parenting life at high speed, searching for a moment when she'd given him the impression that this was okay. The two lads came in and broke the silence.

'You're late,' Kathi barked at them, making a point of looking at her watch. 'Don't forget you're paid by the hour and I know both your mums.' They looked at the ground, shifting from foot to foot, their shoulders slouched. Their sudden appearance gave Kathi the excuse she needed to let her anger bubble to the top. 'Make sure they pull their weight,' she said before storming to the car. Kathi pulled out her phone and called Graham. 'He's shoplifting,' she blurted out as soon as he picked up. 'Brian caught him shoplifting.'

'Who's shoplifting?'

'Jake, who else would it be?'

'Are you sure? Is Brian sure? Has he had a little too much to smoke?'

'No, he's stopped all that now. Brian watched Jake steal sweets from Murray's shop. What are we going to do?'

'Calm down, Kathi, it's not the end of the world. We'll have a chat with him, tell him not to do it again, and leave it at that. All kids go through this phase. Don't make too big a deal of it.'

'How can you be so calm?'

'We've all stolen from Murray's, it's like a rite of passage. Even I did it when I was about his age. It's not a big deal.'

Frustrated by Graham's apparent lack of concern, Kathi got back out of the car and marched the two minutes to her mother-in-law's house. At this time of day Iris would be doing her housework. She liked routine and was incredibly house proud, the combination of which meant Kathi knew she'd be home. She knocked on the door and went in. 'Hello Iris, it's only me,' she called.

'I'm in the bathroom, come on up.' Sure enough there was Iris on her hands and knees scrubbing the floor with a hard brush. 'This is a surprise,' she said, getting up and sitting on the closed toilet, a little out of breath.

'Why don't you use a mop?' Kathi asked impatiently.

'What's up with you?'

Kathi sighed loudly. 'Jake has been seen shoplifting and when I told Graham he was completely unconcerned.'

'Och pet, they all do it. Was it from Murray's?' Kathi nodded. 'Graham was caught doing exactly the same thing. All the kids do it at some time or other. I think Murray factors it into his pricing because his biscuits cost a lot more than the Co-Op.'

'I'm worried that this is just the start of things, though. What if it begins with stealing a few sweets and then escalates to housebreaking?' Iris looked at her and laughed.

'Kathi come on now, you're over-reacting. It's just a few sweets. Have a quiet chat with him and leave it at that. Don't embarrass the boy.'

'I don't want to embarrass him, but I do need to knock it on the head, or at the very least address the issue. We've read about this, about adopted kids who start lying and stealing as a way of dealing with abandonment.'

'And of course we don't know what his real parents were like,' Iris said before she could stop herself.

'What do you mean 'real parents?''

'Sorry, I meant his other parents, his, what's the word...'

'Birth. His birth parents. What have they got to do with this?'

'I only mean we don't know what sort of people they were, do we? We don't know anything about his father, for example.'

'I can't believe I'm hearing this.' Stunned, Kathi felt like time had rewound 15 years and all the explanations as to why she and Graham wanted to adopt had fallen on deaf ears.

'Some things are genetic, Kathi, and that's a fact.'

'Yes, hair colour and eye colour, not criminality.'

'Oh, now don't cry,' said Iris, her tone impatient. 'All I'm saying is, there are things we don't know about and they might have an impact on his future behaviour.'

'Being abandoned is what will have an impact, not whether his birth parents were drug addicts or alcoholics.' Iris raised her eyebrows but said nothing. 'What was that look for?'

'There was no look, Kathi, I just think you're over-reacting to Jake taking a few sweets. He's a good boy inside, this will just be a phase.'

'Unless of course his parents were evil animal killers,' said Kathi with as much sarcasm as she could muster, 'and it's made his way into him.'

'Don't be ridiculous, you're exaggerating, but it can't be denied we inherit from our parents and we don't know what he got from his.'

'I'm his parent. I came to you for support but instead you've called me fanatical and more or less said my child is a criminal. Thank you very much.' Feeling ridiculous but unable to stop herself, Kathi stormed out of the house and back to her car. What she wanted to do was go home and sulk, but she needed to buy paint so reluctantly headed to the hardware store.

She wandered the aisles feeling lost and unsure about how to talk to Jake about his shoplifting. It may well just be a phase, but what if it wasn't? What if he ended up in the dock one day and it was all her fault because she didn't take action now?

By the time she'd lugged the paint to new property, dropped it off with Brian and arrived home it was after lunchtime. Hungry, she made a sandwich and a pot of tea before flopping in front of the telly. Graham came in the front door.

'Hi, I've been trying to call you,' he said.

'My phone is on silent.'

'Are you alright?'

'What do you mean?'

'Mum phoned and told me what happened.'

'Oh, did she now?' Kathi felt her blood begin to rise again. 'Did she tell you what she said?'

'She told me you were very upset, and she was worried about you.'

'Pah,' Kathi snorted.

'She told me things were said and taken the wrong way.'

'I'll bet she did. She more or less said Jake was bound to turn out bad because his birth parents, or should I say his real parents, were.' Kathi's anger dissipated as she said it out loud. 'I thought they had accepted the whole idea of adoption now that we'd explained everything to them. I thought they understood which issues would and would not affect Jake.'

'We have explained and they are accepting but there are always going to be bits about Jake's life we'll never know and that's okay. We just have to help him come to terms with it.'

They sat in silence for a few moments. Kathi's tears spilled, so Graham sat down and put his arms around his wife.

'Your mum was really hurtful,' she said at length.

'Try not to take it personally. They're a different generation and haven't done the reading. They haven't done the courses or talked to the experts like you have. Remember what the adoption people told us? Part of being an adoptive parent is being an educator.'

'I know,' Kathi nodded, 'but it's so hard.' Graham held his wife tightly. 'Alright,' she said. 'Let's do this your way. We'll have a chat with Jake and say no more about it.' After dinner that night, Kathi and Graham sat Jake down at the kitchen table.

'I didn't do it,' said Jake.

'You were seen,' said Graham.

'By who?'

'Brian.'

'That loser? You can't trust him. Everyone knows he's not right in the head, he takes too many drugs.'

'Jake,' Kathi reprimanded, 'Brian is a friend of mine and your elder. You will show him some respect.' Christ, thought Kathi, I sound like my grandmother.

'Why? He's making up stories about me, calling me a thief. I don't call that respectful.'

'He's concerned about you and he did the right thing by telling me.'

'Your mum's right,' said Graham. 'We're simply concerned. You're a smart kid, you know stealing is wrong. I want you to promise us you won't do it again.'

Jake took his time before saying, 'I'm sorry. I don't know why I did it. Someone dared me and I couldn't back out. I'm sorry, I won't do it again.'

'Come here, son,' said Graham, getting up. He put his arms around Jake and hugged him tightly. Kathi also wanted a hug. She was proud of how mature Jake was being about this. She put her arms around them both but Jake pulled away.

'I've got homework to do,' he said and went to his room.

Graham looked at Kathi and smiled. Kathi smiled back, but she was hurt by Jake refusal to hug her and it left her feeling uneasy for the rest of the evening.

A seed had been planted in her mind, one she didn't want to germinate. Looking for reassurance, and once they'd gone to bed, Kathi lowered her voice and said to Graham, 'I've been wondering, do you think it could be Jake?'

'Could what be Jake?' he asked.

'The troll. Do you think it could be him? He's so angry with me at the moment. Maybe he's found out the blog is mine and is punishing me.'

'Stop it Kathi, you're being ridiculous.' Graham was annoyed. 'Trolling is everywhere. You knew you might have people say nasty stuff when you began this bloody project. You're putting our lives online so it was only a question of time before someone figured out it's you. Now they have and they're making the most of it. Don't try to blame Jake. He's having a tough enough time as it is, he doesn't need you thinking he's a stalker.'

Kathi put her hands up in front of her, palms towards Graham, indicating she capitulated.

Chapter 9

Jake was very pleased with how he'd handled his parents. He'd quickly clocked how united they were on the subject of his shoplifting and figured he'd best play the long game and apologise. If he continued to deny it he'd get in more trouble, and he didn't want to be grounded. The relief on his parent's faces when he apologised was laughable. They were so gullible.

He jumped onto his bed, bottom first, and checked his social media. It was the usual banter, and he soon grew bored so moved on to messaging Lindsay. They were spending a lot of time together and the messaging was near constant. She seemed to understand him in a way nobody else did, nor did she judge him the way he knew the others did. She gets me, he smiled to himself.

When he'd first told her about the shoplifting, she'd laughed and teased him a bit but didn't lecture him on what a bad person he was, or give him a guilt trip.

I can't believe Brian grassed me up, he thought. He knew Brian had caught him in the act that last time, but given how much weed the man smoked, Jake thought he'd be the last person to tell tales.

It first happened when Jake and a couple of classmates had gone to Murray's to get some sweets at lunchtime. The shop was busy, a little chaotic, because Murray always struggled to keep the school kids under control.

The shop had two short aisles of goods, the shelf units reaching just higher than his waist. He stood in the middle aisle, facing Murray at the till. He was deciding which chocolate bar he wanted when the thought popped into his head like a cartoon speech bubble. He wondered how it would feel to steal something, to pick up a chocolate bar and walk out of the shop. His heart thumped vehemently just at the thought.

Impulse took over and Jake picked up a couple of bars, put them in his trouser pockets and tacked onto three boys leaving the shop. Before he knew it he was out in the open air. He picked up his pace, leaving the other boys behind, and jogged back to the school grounds. Only once did he look behind him, and it gave him a kick to see he'd made it to freedom. There was no Murray running after him and shaking a fist, or Jamie in his police car, sirens blaring. Bold with adrenaline, he'd pulled out one of the bars and eaten it in three bites.

Lying on his bed at home, he smiled at the memory. He dug out a chocolate bar from his schoolbag and opened it. Today's booty. Stealing from Murray had been so easy and made him feel so powerful that he'd done the same thing for a couple of weeks now. Not every day, of course. He didn't want to make it to look too obvious.

When Brian caught him in the act Jake couldn't help himself, he grinned and even gave Brian a cheeky wink before walking out the store. His smile faded at Brian's betrayal, however. He considered making an anonymous call to the police about Brian's drug habit, but dismissed the idea. For some reason, he felt sure he'd end up the one in trouble.

Jake's phone pinged. It was an unknown number. He opened the message.

Hi Jake, it was good seeing you the other day. Let me know if you need someone to talk to. Joanne.

It took him a moment to recognise the name, then it hit him. She was the woman who had gone to the party with him and

Lindsay. He'd bumped into her again a few days later when he was at The Green. He'd had another run in with Kathi, about what he couldn't exactly remember. Probably something to do with his smoking or the language he used. He'd stormed out of the house and run all the way to The Green. By the time he got there, he was knackered. He wasn't able to run as far since he'd started smoking. Even his football coach had commented. 'You need to lay off the fags,' he'd told Jake.

Out of puff, Jake had taken a seat on one of the benches that lined the river flowing alongside The Green. He'd pulled out a cigarette and cursed when he realised he didn't have a lighter or matches. 'Hi, Jake,' a voice had said behind him, making him jump.

'You gave me a fright,' he said, putting his hand over his chest. He looked at her, trying to place her.

'You don't remember me?'

'I do, I just can't remember your name.'

'Joanne.'

'That's right! We met at the party.'

'I bought you alcohol.'

'I remember. Thanks for doing that. Did you have a good time?'

'It was alright. How are things with Lindsay? Are you together yet?' Remembering their conversation, Jake blushed.

'Not yet,' he admitted.

'You need a light?' she asked, indicating the packet in his hands.

'Yes, please.' She lit it for him. 'I thought you didn't smoke.'

'I don't. I saw you run into the park. You looked upset. Everything aright?'

Jake looked at her, still unsure as to whether or not Joanne was teasing him, but again she looked sincere. It was a genuine question. She even looked concerned. 'Yeah, fine.' He wasn't entirely certain he wanted to open up to this strange woman.

'Are you sure?' she pressed. 'I remember being your age. I found it really hard. My mum didn't understand me at all. She was really difficult to live with.' Jake inwardly sneered. She didn't have a clue about what was going on in his life. 'I was adopted,' Joanne went on. That made Jake sit up straight. 'My adopted mum just didn't understand me.'

'You were adopted?' Jake wanted to be sure he'd heard correctly. He didn't know anyone else who was like him.

'Yes, when I was a baby.' This was so close to Jake's own situation that his pulse quickened. If she'd been in the same situation, would she tell him what he needed to know?

'Me too,' he said.

'Ah, then we understand one another.'

'What happened? With your mum, I mean?'

'My adopted mum?' Jake nodded. 'We never got on and in the end I had to cut her out of my life. For my own sanity, do you know what I mean?' Jake nodded.

'Yes,' he said. 'I do.'

'Can I tell you a secret?' Joanne asked.

'Of course. If you want to.'

'That's why I'm here, in Byreburn.'

'To escape your mum?'

'To find my birth mum.'

'Really? She's here?' Joanne nodded this time. 'Do you know who she is?'

'I do.'

'How did you find out?' This might be the answer he was looking for. If this woman can tell me how to find my birth mother, I can leave Byreburn with somewhere to go.

'I got my adoption papers. My birth mother's name is on there.'

'Can I do that?'

'How old are you?'

'15.'

'Then no. You have to be 16 or over.' Jakes heart deflated with disappointment. He thought he'd found an escape route. 'Only one year to wait, though.'

'I don't think I can wait that long.'

'Are things that bad?' Joanne asked. Jake nodded. 'What's your adopted mum like?'

'She's awful. She's always on at me. Nothing is ever right, or enough. She's always butting into my business and wants to talk feelings all the time.' Jake felt he'd gone too far. A little voice in the back of his brain whispered that he was being disloyal to his parents. 'Sorry,' he said. 'You don't want to know all that.'

'You don't need to apologise to me. I know what you're going through.'

'What will you do when you find your mum?' Jake asked.

'I don't know exactly.' Joanne's face saddened. 'But it's got to be better than with my adopted mum,' she said quietly. 'Wouldn't you agree?'

'I guess so.' Jake had thought only abstractly about his birth mother. Meeting her was never something that felt possible before. Now, he was sitting next to someone who had been through what he was going through at this very moment in time. Here was someone who was actually finding her birth mother. This re-framed everything in his mind. A wonder of possibilities opened up before him as he sat there on that riverside bench.

'What will you do when you find your real mum?' Joanne had asked.

'My real mum,' Jake had repeated. He'd smiled at Joanne. 'Whatever she wants,' he'd said.

Jake looked at his phone and began to message her back.

Hi, good to hear from you. Things are just the same

Come by the flat any time. I remember what it's like

Jake was unsure how seriously to take her offer, so left things open.

Thanks.

The next day, Kathi was still ill at ease with Jakes' response to her the previous night. Something was going on inside Jake and she wanted to help him get to the bottom of it. She knew Graham would think her crazy, maybe even angry, but she didn't care. It was Jake's mental health at stake, and that was worth them disagreeing. She wouldn't go back to the social workers, but would find someone qualified and experienced in helping adoption families. Through her blog she had some good ideas of where to start, but a lot of people were based in Glasgow or Edinburgh. She needed someone closer to home.

Searching through some forums, she found a new practice that had opened up in Dumfries, a much easier place to get to than the cities. The therapist was called Brenda Wilson, and already the forum had a few good comments about her. Beggars can't be choosers, she thought, and sent an email asking for an appointment.

Chapter 10

Sitting on a chair in the waiting room of the counsellor's office, Jake's right leg couldn't keep still. He tapped his heel up and down like a jack-hammer trying to dig its way through the floor. He didn't want to be there because he didn't think he had any issues that needed to be 'worked through' as Kathi kept saying.

On the car journey over he'd refused to speak to her, and had decided he would refuse to speak to the counsellor as well, whoever she was. It would all turn out to be a waste of time and he wouldn't have to go again. He'd glared over at Kathi to silently show her how angry he was.

A small woman with short wavy hair eventually appeared in reception and called Jake's name. Kathi stood up. 'Yes, that's us.' She indicted Jake, who refused to acknowledge the woman.

'Come on through,' she said. To emphasise his point, Jake stomped loudly down the corridor to the woman's office, Kathi close on his heels. The woman closed the door behind them and indicated they take a seat.

'Good to meet you both today,' she said. To Jake she said, 'I don't know how much your mum has told you about the session but let me explain a little about how it works. Sorry, I should have asked, have either of you seen a counsellor before?'

'No,' said Kathi. 'We've not.'

'Okay, well my name is Brenda and people come to see me about all sorts of things and at different ages because, you know, as we go through life we come across situations or feelings that are difficult and we need help to understand them. At all ages.' She paused for a few moments and smiled at Jake. She had a round, open face and he found it harder to glare at her than he did at Kathi. 'Now,' Brenda went on, 'there's no set way that this works, and we can talk about anything you want, but I thought we might start with a game.' Jake rolled his eyes, he wasn't a child. 'Don't worry,' Brenda laughed, 'it's nothing too daft, but it is a nice way to break the ice.'

Jake glanced at his mum and enjoyed the look of horror on her face. He knew she'd hate the idea of playing or doing anything that involved getting down on all fours pretending to be an animal. Brenda pulled out a blanket and a plastic ball, the sort that are used in children's ball pits.

'We each take a side of the blanket,' she instructed, 'and then put the ball in the middle. The aim is to roll the ball around the edges of the blanket without letting it fall to the ground.' Kathi got up and took a section of the blanket, but Jake remained seated with his arms folded. There was no way he was doing that.

'Jake,' said Kathi in a tone that said get up, but he ignored her.

'I know it can seem a bit daft,' said Brenda, 'but it's just a bit of fun to help us relax.' Still Jake sat with his arms folded. He wasn't going to make this easy for Kathi. 'Not to worry, maybe we can try it later,' said Brenda before she and Kathi sat down again.

'Kathi, when you got in touch to make the appointment you told us things are a bit tough at the moment. Tell me a little bit more about what's going on.'

'Well,' she said, 'I've noticed that Jake's behaviour towards me had changed over the last eighteen months or so. He's become very moody and verbally aggressive.' Jake sat motionless, staring at the floor. 'We had an argument last week,' Kathi continued, 'and Jake told me he doesn't see me as his mother. It was clear from the way he said it that it was more than just an angry outburst, but that something else is going on. When my husband talked to him about it later, Jake admitted that some of the kids at school have been teasing him about being adopted. We thought it might be helpful for him to have someone neutral to talk it through with.' Brenda nodded and turned to Jake.

'Dad didn't think that,' he said. 'Dad doesn't think this is a good idea and neither do I.' Jake dared Kathi to deny that this was all her doing and that she was putting them both through this for no good reason. 'It's a waste of everybody's time,' he said.

'That sounds really horrible, Jake,' said Brenda. 'It must be very upsetting to hear people say things like that about you and your family.' She paused and watched him for a moment. 'Is there anything you'd like to add to what your mum said?' Jake shook his head and Kathi looked at Brenda apologetically. Jake knew she felt his sullenness reflected badly on her, but he didn't care. Brenda smiled at Jake before saying, 'Right, here's what we'll do. Kathi, I'll ask you to sit in the waiting room while Jake and I chat for forty minutes or so, at the end of which we'll ask you to come back in and we can all have a few words before finishing. Does that sound okay?' Kathi nodded and looked at Jake, hoping for some sort of response.

Brenda stood up and opened the door, indicating it was time for Kathi to make her exit. Jake bet she felt strange leaving him in the company of someone else and more than a little frightened of what he might say about her. He watched her go out to the waiting room.

As soon as Kathi left the room and Brenda had closed the door, Jake relaxed. He lifted his head to look at Brenda properly for the first time. Her Southern Irish lilt was soothing and now that he took the time, he could see she had a kind face and although he wasn't able to articulate it at the time, he felt sure she wouldn't judge him for his behaviour and fleetingly wondered if she too was adopted.

'The importance we put on adoption can come and go in waves,' said Brenda, sitting down. 'For ages you can be getting on with your life, not thinking about it at all, and then all of a sudden something happens and bam, it hits you, and being adopted is all you can think about. Is that what's happening for you now? You've gone ages without even thinking about it but suddenly people at school are saying things and it's on your mind all the time?' Jake thought about what she said and decided that was exactly what had happened but he wasn't about to admit that to her.

'Is that what's happening for you, Jake?' Brenda prompted him.

'Look,' he said. 'I'm only here because of her.' He indicated Kathi outside. 'I don't want to talk to you.'

'You didn't want to come here today?'

'No.'

'So why did you?'

'Because Mum arranged it.'

'You are a big person, you could easily have refused. Why didn't you?'

'What do you mean?' Jake didn't like the way the conversation was going. He felt Brenda was about to ambush him into admitting something or tricking him into telling her something private.

'I mean that you are too big for your mum to physically pick up and put in the car.'

'So?'

'Well, it suggests there is some part of you that wants to be here. It suggests you have worries you'd like answers to or at the very least to understand a bit better.'

'Such as?' Despite himself, Jake was curious to hear what she would say.

'How you feel about being adopted. How to manage other people's response to you being adopted.' Jake stared at his shoes and noticed how scuffed they were. He needed a new pair. 'Jake? Do you want to tell me how you're feeling right now?'

'There's nothing to tell. I don't want to be here full stop.' Did he? If he'd been asked that when in the car, he would gladly have turned around and driven straight home again. But now that he was here, talking to Brenda, he hesitated. 'What is it that scares you about being here?'

'I'm not scared.'

'You know that what we talk about here is confidential. I hope you know that this is a safe space. Whatever you're thinking about or worrying about, we can talk over here. I can help you put some of your thoughts in order, lessen the confusion.'

'How can you do that?'

'By listening to you. By being on your side. I am here for you, not your parents or anyone else. I am here to help you.'

Everything in his body screamed not to do it, not to open up and make himself vulnerable. He'd done that with Hayden and look where it got him? Ditched. 'What if you don't like what I say?'

'It is not my place to like or dislike anything you talk to me about. I am here to help you like what you say; to help you like you.'

Don't trust, his body shouted. Less loudly this time. Against his better judgment Jake said, 'Alright.'

'How do you feel about being adopted?' Brenda asked.

'I don't know. Confused.'

'That's natural. There's a lot to process.' Brenda paused before asking, 'Does your adoption get talked about at home?'

'Sometimes,' Jake said at length.

'What sort of things are said?'

He thought for a moment. 'Mum might ask if I've got any questions about it, you know, about my birth mum or foster parents or whatever.'

'Do you ever have any questions?'

'Yeah, but the timing never seems right. By the time she asks the moment has passed or I can't remember what it was I wanted to know. And sometimes I can tell she doesn't really want to talk about it. She just feels she ought to.'

'What do you mean?'

'Well, sometimes I'll think about it all, you know, and there's something I want to know but I don't want to ask because I don't want to...'

'Don't want to what?'

'I don't want to upset her.' Jake coloured at admitting this. It acknowledged he did really care about Kathi, despite his behaviour towards her.

'That's very thoughtful of you, Jake,' said Brenda. 'There're things you want to know about your life but your concern for your mum's feelings stops you.' He blushed again. 'But you know, I think that must be quite tough on you because you're left with a mix of questions and emotions and no way of answering them. They're left spinning around in your head with no way out.'

They sat in silence for a moment, thinking over what Brenda had said. 'If you were to ask your mum a question when you wanted to, not when she asked you, do you think she would be upset?' Jake imperceptibly shook his head. 'Have you asked her if talking about it upsets her?' He looked at the floor and didn't answer. 'Jake, I don't know you or your mum, we've only just met, but the fact that your mum has come here today with you tells me she loves you very much and wants you to figure out what's going on in your head. Ultimately, she wants you to be happy and my gut tells me that if asking questions helps you, she'll do her best to answer them.'

'But what if she does get upset?' he asked, unsure whether or not to trust Brenda's instinct.

'If she does get upset, that's okay. If you get upset that's okay too. It's an emotional thing to be talking about. Do you have a Life Story Book?'

'Yes.'

'Do you ever look at that?'

'Sometimes.' Jake thought about the album his foster parents had put together and handed to Kathi and Graham when he was officially adopted. It had photographs of him at various ages, photos of his foster parents and their house. Mementos of days out and birthday parties had also been placed in the album, all to give a Jake a sense of his place in the world. Sometimes he hated that book, at other times it was the only connection he had between now and then. His two different lives. They sat in silence for a few moments until Brenda said, 'I don't know your story, Jake, but it is your story. You have the right to know and understand it as best you can.'

Jake couldn't help himself and tears escaped, falling quietly one after the other down his cheeks. Brenda had spoken what he'd been feeling for a long time, and the relief that someone understood what he needed was overwhelming. While Brenda handed him a tissue, she asked what the kids at school were saying about him.

'That I must have adoption disease, or they call me orphan boy. They say my real mum didn't want me because I'm so ugly.'

'Those are unkind things to say.'

'Maybe it's true.'

'Do you think that's the reason your birth mother couldn't look after you?' Jake shrugged his shoulders. 'I don't,' she said. 'I think there will have been some really serious reasons your birth mother felt she couldn't look after you. Not what the kids at school are saying.'

'I know she was young,' he said, 'and that she didn't have a job.'

'I imagine looking after a new baby when you're very young and have no money would be very hard.' Jake nodded. 'I'm wondering if what the kids at school said has upset you so much because there's a bit of you that thinks it was your fault your birth mother couldn't keep you.'

He put the tissue to his eyes and held it there.

'If you think it was your fault, then you might feel very guilty and very unlovable. Perhaps you feel that if even your birth mother couldn't love you, then who could?'

Through his tears, Jake looked at Brenda with surprise. Again she'd said something that, without realising it, had been troubling him for a long time. 'Even if she was young and had no money,' he said, 'she must have had a mum and dad, or friends who could have helped her. If she really wanted to keep me, she could have done. She could have found a way. But she didn't. She didn't think I was worth it.'

'The situation may have been out of her control, or she didn't feel she had a choice. That's something you may never know.'

'People have babies all the time, even when they're young or have no money. They find a way because they think their baby is worth it.'

'What about Kathi and Graham?' she asked gently. 'Do they think you're worth it?'

'I guess so.'

'I think so too. That tells me you are lovable and that it wasn't your fault your birth mother couldn't look after you.' Jake nodded and said, 'I suppose so.' His body shivered in response to his tears subsiding and it was clear he'd had enough for now.

'Why don't we leave it there for this week,' she said. 'We've covered a lot of stuff. We can have a think about it over the coming few days and chat more next time.' Jake wiped his face, immediately conscious of his red cheeks and puffy eyes. He didn't want Kathi to know he'd been crying. Brenda stood up and went to the door. She looked at him and gave a nod of encouragement before opening it.

Kathi came in and sat down, looking at both of them expectantly. Jake knew she wanted him to tell her what they'd talked about. Brenda stepped in. 'What Jake and I discuss is confidential, and it's up to him what he wants to share.' She looked at him. 'Is there anything you want to tell your mum today?'

'No,' he said, not yet ready to share. Jake knew Kathi would be devastated to be left out in the cold like that, but she'd have to wait.

Chapter 11

Kathi felt very low over the next few days. Recent events had stirred the pond and doubts about her abilities as a mother had resurfaced. In not being able to conceive, she had pulled Graham down the adoption route against the advice of his family, and perhaps even his own wishes. Kathi worried that Jake's recent behaviour and her reaction to it proved how incompetent she was. It fed into Kathi's insecurities of not being strong or capable enough to nurture a child who had been emotionally traumatised. She wondered why it was that Graham never had these doubts, and why he'd been so calm about the shoplifting when it freaked her out so intensely. She saw it as further proof she wasn't a good enough mother.

Trying to make sense of it all, Kathi lay in bed longer and longer each morning, unwilling to start the day. Only when she heard the front door shut and felt the silence of an empty house, did she drag herself out of bed.

In her little office, cup of coffee in hand, Kathi switched on her computer and logged into Human Racing. There was one message from DayOfReckoning.

Who do you think you are taking what doesn't belong to you? Your husband thinks you're a fat whore and you're an ugly bitch.

The words on the screen made her feel queasy. She flushed at the thought of some man sitting at home on his computer thinking those vile thoughts, and maybe even laughing as he hit the send button. She closed the email and tried to ignore it, but every time she remembered it was there, a hot flush of embarrassment went through her. This was the third message from DayOfReckoning, and she was certain it wasn't a bot. The message was different each time, and it was personal. She made a mental note to talk to Graham about it that night.

She tried to focus on writing the new blog post, laying bare her concerns about Jake. She needed some support from her friendly followers.

She was desperately worried about Jake and felt she was the only one who was. The questions Jake was undoubtedly asking himself, combined with the teasing she knew he was getting at school, had changed his personality for the worse. It was at times like this she felt the most alone. She knew of no other parents in her situation who she could call and share her worries.

Friends with non-adopted children would reassure her that this was simply adolescence making itself felt, but Kathi knew it was more than that. She knew it but couldn't articulate it in a way that made sense to others. She couldn't find the words to describe the loathing on Jake's face when he looked at her or the rage in his voice when he spoke to her. This was not him simply pushing boundaries, it was him trying to push her away, to prove he was right all along with his belief he was unlovable.

'I can't deny,' she wrote, 'that there are times I do find him unlovable and I want him to disappear. When he tells me, with such contempt, that I'm not his mother, I feel utterly worthless. I want him and the way he makes me feel to go away. Later, when I've calmed down, I hate myself for feeling this way because I know it's his own fears that make him do it.'

With a heavy heart, she published the post and forced herself into the shower. As much as she wanted to hide in bed all day she needed to check on the refurbishment and make sure repairs elsewhere were going ahead as planned. She also had a house viewing. She wasn't in the mood for any of it. Cherry had sent her a text message asking her to call. This early in the morning meant it wasn't a social call, and Kathi put that task to the bottom of her list. She didn't have the head space to deal with much more.

Over at the refurbishment, things were progressing fine. There were only a couple of things Brian needed her input on, and she was relieved to see that the labourers were doing a good job. With that in hand, Kathi heading to the property viewing. Only after that did she pluck up the courage to go and see Cherry.

'You look dreadful,' said Cherry when she walked through the door. 'Are you alright?'

'I didn't sleep well, that's all.'

'Go make yourself a coffee, it'll help wake you up.'

'Joanne Wylie's been in touch,' said Cherry once they'd sat down. 'She says the kitchen sink has been leaking and one of the curtain rails coming off the wall. I messaged you because I wanted to get the okay from you first, but I went ahead and asked Brian to go round and check it. Is that alright?'

'Absolutely, thank you.'

'Nothing to worry about, Kathi,' said Cherry. 'It's just snagging, it always happens.'

'Thank you, Cherry, I don't know what to do without you.'

'Fall apart,' Cherry laughed.

'Cheer me up, tell me you and Brian are madly in love and are going to live happily ever after.'

'Did he tell you about that?' Cherry turned bright pink at the mention of his name.

'Yes, he did, and I don't mind telling you I was a bit surprised.'

'You were surprised?' she guffawed. 'How do you think I felt? That's why I didn't tell you myself.' She got up from her desk and went to the office door, peeking out to make sure

Brian hadn't quietly come in. 'My God Kathi, he's the last person I ever saw myself with. He dresses badly, he's got that awful hairy beard, and you've seen how he can drive me up the wall.' Kathi nodded. 'But we bumped into each other at the pub and got chatting. Outside of work he was dead funny and easy to talk to. After a few drinks I thought, what the hell.' Cherry giggled as she sat back at her desk and took a swig of coffee. 'Anyway, we had a good time and so started getting together a few evenings a week. It was all very casual to begin with but, don't laugh, I think I really like him.' Kathi saw from Cherry's expression that she was smitten.

'I think he feels the same way,' said Kathi. 'He's been positively cheerful the last few weeks. He's even been on time for our meetings together. He's like a new man.'

'Oh, you've got me to thank for that. He's stopped smoking and is even off the booze.' Cherry grinned.

'Well, however you're cajoling him into it, it's working.'

'I bumped into Graham the other day,' said Cherry. 'He told me you're getting nasty messages on your blog. Is that what's getting you down?'

'That's part of it.'

'What's in the messages?'

'That I'm ripping people off by buying their houses, that I'm money grabbing and evil. One of the messages even described me as a cuckoo. I got another one today telling me Graham thinks I'm fat and ugly. Who would do this?' Kathi couldn't help herself and burst into tears.

'Is that all?' Cherry said, coming round to Kathi's side of the desk. 'You should hear the things people have said to my face, never mind over the Internet. Don't worry about it, Graham is probably right that it's daft kids.'

'I don't think it is. There's something about them, maybe it's the timing, but whoever it is seems to know what I'm doing and when I'm doing it. Usually after I've blogged about it. It makes me think I must know them, or they know me.'

'But the blog is anonymous, not even I know the name of it.'

'Maybe they figured it out? Maybe it's someone whose house I bought and now they regret it? Oh, I don't know, I'm getting suspicious of everyone.'

'Well, there are some sick people out there, that's for sure. I agree with Graham though, it'll be kids or a robot or something. Can't you just block them?'

'Maybe you're right,' Kathi conceded, drying her eyes. If both Graham and Cherry thought the same thing, perhaps she was overreacting, seeing more to it than there was. 'Yes, I am sure you're right. I'll block them and that'll be that.'

'Right madam, what else is going on? How are things with Jake?'

'Terrible.'

'What's he up to now?'

'Brian caught him shoplifting and I was mortified. Graham and Iris think I made a big deal of it. They don't seem to be as concerned that this might be the start of something.'

'The start of what?'

'I've read about how this kind of thing can escalate for adopted kids. It's a way of filling a void and making them feel better. Before they know it they're house breaking and there's no way back. What if this is where it begins?

'What if it isn't? What if he's just like all the other rogue teenagers in this town looking for a bit of excitement?'

'Do you think I'm being ridiculous too?'

'No, not at all, I think your worries are genuine. I just don't have an answer for you.'

'Me neither,' Kathi said with a defeated smile.

'I'm afraid I've more bad news for you. I saw your Jake smoking cigarettes.'

'What?'

'A couple of days ago. He was down by the river with a few other kids and they were smoking away. How old is he?'

'Fifteen.'

'Well, tell him to give it up.'

'Are you sure it was him?' Kathi was working hard to stay calm on the outside because inside her blood was bubbling and bursting, each pop making her a little more angry and a little more helpless.

'Absolutely, I'd recognise him anywhere. He was with that girl we saw him with at the Common Riding.'

'Lindsay, Lindsay Irving?'

'I think that's her.'

'I knew it,' Kathi spat. 'I knew she was a bad influence. I went to school with her dad and he's no good. Why is she hanging around with Jake?'

'He's a hottie.'

'He's fifteen.'

'He's still a hottie, especially to someone his own age. Look at the other boys in his year; gangly, spotty and totally gormless. Not Jake, he's a hottie.'

'Stop saying that, he's a child.'

'Not for long a darling,' she teased. Cherry couldn't help but laugh at her friend's shocked expression. 'Anyway, it is not the girls you should be worried about, it's the ciggies. You need to get that knocked on the head.'

'Easier said than done.' Kathi burst into fresh tears. 'Oh, Cherry, what am I going to do? He hates me so much and won't let me even touch him. I can't find a way to get through to him.'

'Why do you think he hates you so much?'

'In all honesty, I think it's because I didn't give birth to him. I tell myself it's a phase and he'll grow out of it, but the longer it goes on, the less convinced I am.'

'After all you've done for him, that's harsh.'

'Don't think badly of him, please. He can't help it, he's confused.'

'That's as may be, but you're an amazing mum and he needs to know that.'

'Thank you.' They sat silently for a moment before Kathi said, 'I don't know what to do.'

'Come here,' Cherry gave her friend a hug. 'Sometimes life's rubbish, isn't it?'

'You're telling me,' Kathi agreed.

'Listen,' said Cherry, her tone suddenly serious. 'I've got something to tell you, but I don't want you to panic, and it's probably nothing anyway.' She took a deep breath. 'I found a small lump on my breast.'

'Oh,' Kathi gasped, but a stern look from Cherry made her reset her face to neutral.

'I've got an appointment with Dr Brown next week, so we'll see what comes of that. I don't want you to panic, because I am and I need you to be calm for me.'

'Sure, of course, whatever you want.' Kathi nodded. She marvelled at her friend. 'You should have stopped me wittering on about such trivial things.'

'Don't be daft.'

'Let me come to the doctor with you.'

'No, it's okay, I'll be alright. I just had to tell someone before I exploded.'

'Absolutely not. I'm coming with you, you're not doing this by yourself.'

'Are you sure?'

'Completely. You're not doing this alone.'

'Thank you, Kathi, I'll feel a lot better with you there.' She took a sip of coffee, but it was cold and she grimaced. 'Don't tell anyone, will you? Especially Brian. I don't want to put pressure on him.'

'If that's what you want.'

'It is. Right, I'm kicking you out, I've got lots to do today. It never rains, but it pours.'

Shocked at Cherry's news, Kathi made her way home in a daze. Cherry's illness put so much in perspective. Kathi and her family were going through a difficult time, yes, but none of it was unsurmountable. Jake would eventually come through this bad patch, and as for the trolling, this was of small concern next to the health of her best friend.

To cheer herself up, and maybe put a smile on Jake's face, Kathi popped into the Silver Spoon to pick up a cake for pudding. She browsed what was on offer, made her purchase and headed to the door.

'Hi Kathi,' said a voice. It was a woman Kathi didn't know. Despite being seated, it was clear she was a large, full bosomed, woman. She had short dark hair that sat limply around her skull, and large brown eyes. She was sat at the table by herself and laid out in front of her was a full afternoon tea.

'Hello,' Kathi said.

'You don't know me?'

'Sorry, no.'

'I'm Joanne Wylie, I'm renting your flat on the High Street.'

'Oh,' said Kathi, smiling, 'I see. Nice to meet you.' Kathi couldn't keep her eyes from the table. There was so much food, but only one person. She looked for a second place-setting, but there wasn't one.

'I'm hungry,' Joanne said, reading her face. 'I didn't have any breakfast.' Embarrassed at being caught out, Kathi made apologetic noises as if to say she hadn't been thinking that at all. 'It's alright, you're not the first person to look like that. But they don't know I didn't eat this morning and am making up for it.'

'How are you settling into Byreburn?' Kathi asked, keen to move off the topic of Joanne's obviously vast appetite.

'Great, just great,' she said between mouthfuls of sandwich. 'I'm getting to know the way the town works.'

'Oh right, and you're making friends easily enough?'

'Absolutely, people are very chatty here.'
'That's for sure,' Kathi smiled with recognition.
'It's amazing what people will tell you.'
'I'd best be off,' said Kathi. 'Nice to meet you.'

As soon as she got home Kathi took Cherry's advice and went online to block whoever this DayOfReckoning was, but when she logged on she found another message waiting for her. This time it was in direct response to Kathi's post of that morning.

A shiver of fear went down her back, and the hairs on her arms stood to attention. It was clear enough now that this was no robot. This was someone following Kathi's posts and responding as and when they appeared. The knowledge that someone had it in for her and stalking her every move was chilling. Kathi's next question was who in Byreburn hated her enough to do this?

She did a Google search on the handle name, DayOfReckoning, but nothing obvious presented itself and the only profile she found was of some girl who lived in New Mexico. She went to Facebook and looked at her list of friends. There were a number of people she'd met once or twice at conferences or who were friends of friends. She decided to cull her friend's list to only those people she actually knew. She inspected her privacy settings and changed them so only friends could see her posts. Back at her blog, she blocked DayOfReckoning. Those simple actions made her feel much better and as if she had taken back control of her online life.

Chapter 12

Joanne stood staring at the large, hand painted, wooden board that said Dunlop's Stables. The track to the actual stables stretched out in front of her, so far that she couldn't see the buildings from where she was standing. She turned her head left and right. There was nothing but rural B-road either side of her; no traffic, not even a bus stop. She was stuck.

Ever since she'd attended the Common Riding, Joanne had been mesmerised by the giant beasts she watched gallop up the Kirk Wynd. When they first cantered and skipped down the High Street towards Market Square she had been terrified. The biggest animals she had come face-to-face with until that point where the German Shepherds she used to see being walked around her Glasgow housing estate. Their owners would let them defecate in the little green space that was called a playground, but they never picked up after the dogs, not like she saw the dog owners in Byreburn do.

At first she laughed at the silly people who cleaned up after their dogs but she had to concede it was nice not to check your feet all the time and even she noticed it meant the kids could play without fear of landing in dog shit when they fell over. Joanne remembered the occasion that had happened to her. She'd tripped and fallen, hands first, into a cold pile of dog faeces. She'd held up her hands in horror and wailed loudly. If her hands had been chopped off, she wouldn't have felt any worse.

The other kids had quickly sensed her vulnerability, started laughing and calling her smelly and the 'dog shit girl'. Crying loudly, she ran home, hands in the air. This was when her dad was still alive, and he had guided her to the bathroom and helped her to clean up. The humiliation and the taunts lasted for only a few days, but Joanne remembered it vividly. When she thought back to that day she could still smell it on her hands.

When the Common Riding horses went past her, she'd backed away in fear. 'They'll no harm you,' said a man standing next to her. Easy for him to say. Scared as she was, she couldn't look away. A horse stopped right in front of her, lifted its tail, and a fountain of amber liquid shot out onto the road. It hit the ground with such force that it bounced back up again, forcing Joanne to move back in alarm.

She looked at the rider. He was oblivious, calmly chatting to another rider until his steed had finished and walked on. Joanne looked at her neighbours for their reaction, but nobody gave it a second glance.

What's wrong with these people? She wondered to herself. To her, this whole day was weird. Why would anyone choose to get up at 5 AM and march up and down empty streets, she did not know. When she listened to the speeches, she had no idea what they were saying. It was some weird Border's Scots. It might as well have been Greek.

As the shock of it all began to ease, Joanne found she was more able to take everything in. She noticed the flower posies all the children carried. She noticed everyone was wearing coloured ribbons. The horse riders weren't wearing tracksuit bottoms and a jumper, but clean jodhpurs, shining black boots, smart fitted jackets and lush, velvety riding hats.

The horses themselves had been cleaned. Even she could see that they had been groomed to within an inch of their lives. Their manes had been styled into designs Joanne would have been proud to wear.

The next time one of the giants stopped next to her, she held her breath but didn't back away. It took all her courage, but she didn't move. She looked up at its face and was surprised to see long eyelashes. Its long sleek face ended with a muzzle that looked so silky and inviting she almost reached a hand out to touch it. But when she saw the horse's enormous, grass stained teeth, she had second thoughts.

Her eyes drifted down the horse's neck to its body. Its coat was a glistening, rich chestnut. The only time she'd seen hair that colour was on an advert and she knew that wasn't real. When the horse walked on, she watched its leg muscles move with strength and certainty in a way she would never move.

From that moment on, Joanne was transfixed. She watched them all with fascination and awe. She watched the riders with admiration. They sat astride their horses with confidence and were in absolute control of those magnificent beasts.

Joanne wanted to feel that. She wanted to feel in control of something so potentially wild, and when she watched them gallop up the Kirk Wynd with speed and ease, she wanted to feel the earth move beneath her. She wanted to experience the thrill of travelling fast, her bare face to the elements. Her heart beat faster just at the thought.

She watched the smaller ponies canter past, but they didn't have the same appeal. No, she wanted the real McCoy. She wanted power and authority.

And so here she was at Dunlop's Stables, about to have her first lesson. It had seemed such a great idea when she booked, and she'd been counting down the days.

'How are you going to get there?' someone at work asked.

'What do you mean?'

'The stables are three miles out of town and you don't have a car.'

She hadn't thought about that. 'I'll get a taxi,' she said. There were a few sharp intakes of breath. 'What?' she asked.

'It will cost a fortune. Taxis aren't cheap.'

Someone else said, 'you could get the bus?'. Joanne's eyes lit up. That was a much better idea. It took a bit of digging around, but she found a bus timetable. The trouble was, there was no stop near the stables. When she got on the bus, she asked the driver which was the nearest stop and he told her not to worry about it, he'd stop at the road end for her.

She gratefully got on board and so exhilarated was she by her adventure, she almost skipped off the bus when the driver told her she'd arrived. She watched the bus drive away and now here she was, in the middle of nowhere, she was brimming with second thoughts.

Who are you kidding? Said a voice inside her head. You are not designed for this. This is for country people, not a city girl like you. Now that she was here, any enthusiasm or confidence that she could be like one of those Common Riding riders evaporated into the atmosphere as quickly as hot breath on a frosty day.

Fear reared its ugly head and if a car had happened to pass by at that moment, she would have thrown herself in front of it and begged to be taken away from this place. But there was no car in sight, and she couldn't even hear the rumble of one in the distance.

She stood in front of the Dunlop's Stables sign for a long time until eventually she felt ridiculous. She either walked down the track to the stables or she walked back to town. The next bus wasn't due for hours yet.

Reluctantly, and with a furrowed brow, she made her way down the half-mile track to the stables. By the time she arrived, she was out of breath and cross with herself for putting herself in this position. She slowed down a little as she neared at the stables. She could hear voices, but nobody was in sight. She walked into the middle of the yard, trying to avoid the horse dung that was dotted about the place.

She had planned on wearing her trainers, but someone recommended she wear wellies instead. She didn't have any, so bought some new floral ones from the hardware store. This was their maiden outing, and she didn't want to get them dirty. She stood in the yard for what felt a long time. This world, the world of yards and wellies and pitchforks, and of the outdoors generally, was alien to her. She didn't belong.

'Hello there,' said a man coming out from one of the stables. 'You must be Joanne?'

'Yes,' she answered more gruffly than she meant to. 'I've been waiting.'

'Sorry,' he said. 'I didn't hear the car pull in.'

'I got the bus.'

'I see,' he said. 'That'll explain it.' He smiled at Joanne and she felt her shoulders fall a little. 'I'm Donald,' he said. He gave her the once over and took in her clean boots. Joanne's shoulders rose again. 'Have you ridden before?'

'No,' she said.

'What made you want to give it a try?'

'I went to the Common Riding. I saw the horses there and wanted to ride one like that.'

'No problem,' he said cheerfully. 'Come on and we'll get you started.'

Donald led Joanne into the stables and she was hit immediately by the warm, sweet smell of hay. Just stepping over the threshold lifted her spirits. She heard the horses in their stalls as they shifted from foot to foot, pulled hay out of their feeders and nickered to one another.

They walked the length of the building until they reached the last stall. Housed inside was a grey pony, chomping happily on its hay. Joanne's heart sank. 'I don't want that one,' she said. 'I want one of those.' She pointed to the statuesque Cobs and Draft Horses they'd walked past.

The man chuckled, which made Joanne feel even more self-conscious and ridiculous. He must have noticed he'd hurt her feelings because he stopped laughing and explained that, 'these horses are for experienced riders.' He led her back towards them, stopping in front of one of the stalls and calling a horse over. The horse manoeuvred towards them but as soon as it realised there were no treats for an offer, moved away again.

'There are beautiful, aren't they?' Donald said. Joanne stepped closer to the gate and reached a hand out.

'Yes,' she said. The horse turned its head to give her sniff but was unimpressed and turned away again. For a reason she couldn't explain, Joanne felt hurt by this rejection.

'Don't worry,' said Donald. 'He's only interested in what food you have.'

'Why can't I ride him?' Joanne asked.

'He's young, and he's strong. He's also a little temperamental.' The man leaned against the stable door, his arm hooked over the top. 'He'll know in a heartbeat that you've never ridden before and will have a lot of fun.' He paused before pointing back to the grey pony. 'Betsy, on the other hand, is sweet natured and a lot older.' Donald pointed over to the grey pony. 'She will look after you and help settle you in.'

What is he talking about, Joanne thought. I will be in charge, not Betsy. They walked back over to the pony. 'Betsy,' Joanne said. What sort of name is that for a horse? She wanted a Duke or a Hunter, not a Betsy.

A couple of people came into the stables at the other end and they waved to Donald but continued chatting. Joanne watched them. They looked lithe and strong. Not like her. She pulled her jumper down a little way.

'Come on,' said Donald. 'Let's get Betsy out and meet her properly. She's not had a walk today and will want to stretch her legs.'

Joanne watched as Donald went into the stall and put a halter over her head. He led her out into the yard, Joanne watching from a distance. Now that Betsy was out of the stall, she looked bigger than Joanne originally thought. 'Come on,' said Donald, 'let's tack her up.'

Donald introduced Betsy to Joanne, after which he thoughtfully took his time to name all the tack and show Joanne how to put on.

They put the saddle and stirrups on. He showed her how to insert the bit into Betsy's mouth and then made her do it. At first Joanne was squeamish, but when Betsy didn't object and the bridle was securely in place, Joanne couldn't help but feel pleased. She smiled at the man, excited at having learned a new skill.

Once Betsy was tacked and Donald had fitted Joanne with a riding hat, he told her how to mount the horse. It looked so easy when she saw other people do it, but now she was standing next to Betsy the stirrup felt a long way off the ground and she was hesitant to lift her leg up that high. For one thing, she didn't think she could. For another, even if she did manage to get her foot into the stirrup, she knew she'd never be able to heft herself up into the saddle. She stepped back from Betsy. 'Do you have any steps?'

Donald hesitated but didn't say no. He silently went back into the stable and brought out a set of steps that were obviously designed for children. Joanne didn't care. She climbed the steps and put her left foot into the left stirrup before swinging her right foot over her back. She wobbled a bit but managed fine and was exhilarated at actually sitting on a horse. Donald moved the steps and Joanne felt suddenly towering off the ground. It gave her a little adrenaline rush.

Donald showed her how to hold the reins, then led her around the yard. Joanne's hips moved backwards and forwards in time with Betsy's strides. After a few circuits Donald was handed a horse that someone else had tacked for him.

'Shall we head out?' he asked.

'Yes, please.' Joanne grinned from ear to ear.

Donald took her out over the fields and through the nearby woods. Joanne had never before spent this much time in the wilderness. She felt exposed and vulnerable. There were no buildings to protect her from the elements, nobody to hear her if she screamed for help. Her fears faded though as Donald chatted on. He seemed happy to talk whether she listened or not.

The horses, too, seemed happy to chat between themselves. They snorted and brayed and from time to time Donald's horse would pull, as if keen to gallop on ahead. Betsy on the other hand was happy to plod along and enjoy the view, for which Joanne was thankful. It was that first ride out that taught Joanne she was not in control. Donald was right, Betsy was the one in charge. Surprisingly, it felt reassuring to know she was being looked after. She patted Betsy on the neck to say thank you.

It was when they were on their way back to the stables that Donald asked her, 'do you want to try a trot?' Joanne nodded. 'Give her a gentle kick and she'll know what to do.' Joanne did as she was told and sure enough Betsy picked up the pace.

Joanne couldn't find her rhythm, bouncing about the saddle and feeling out of control, convinced she was going to fall off. She didn't know what to do to slow Betsy down again. They clip clopped into the yard, the sound of hooves on cobbles reverberating off the stable walls. Joanne was a little out of breath from trying not to fall off and was keen to get back on solid ground.

She didn't wait for Donald to tell her what to do or get the steps for her. She unhooked her right foot and swung her leg back over. She misjudged how high up she was and plummeted to the ground. The force of the fall made her lose her balance. She stumbled and fell, her bulk crashing to the ground, her left foot trapped in the stirrup. Joanne closed her eyes as pain shot through her bum and up her back.

Donald jumped down off his horse and ran round to assist her. With effort he helped her up and unhooked her left foot. 'Are you alright?' he asked, worry etched on his face.

'Of course I'm not bloody all right.' Two other people came running over to help, which only made Joanne more embarrassed. The more fuss they made, the more foolish she felt. Eventually she snapped, 'I'm fine, leave me alone.' The couple drifted away, muttering between themselves.

'How are you going to get home?' Donald asked.

'The bus, how else would I get back.'

'Do you want a lift to the bus stop?'

'No.' Joanne handed him back the riding hat and stormed out of the yard. She cried as she walked the half mile to the road end. Who did she think she was to even try to ride a horse? She didn't belong here. She was angry with herself for forgetting that and getting carried away, and she was angry with Donald for witnessing her humiliation. The bus couldn't come soon enough.

Chapter 13

'How are you?' Brenda asked.

In the consulting room, he gave Brenda a quick look before averting his eyes to the floor. The truth was Jake didn't know how he was and he didn't know what she wanted him to tell her. Brenda was sat across from Jake in her small, Dumfries office. Kathi hadn't told her any of what was happening at school. She wanted Jake to tell Brenda himself. He'd been furious when she told him she'd made another appointment. He'd found it humiliating to be picked up halfway through the school day, because somehow or other news had broken that he was seeing a shrink. He knew people were talking about it amongst themselves and funny looks were being sent in his direction. Jibes had progressed from reminding him his mum didn't want him to what a psycho he was.

His plan had been to duck out of school before Kathi turned up. That way he'd be able to avoid the walk of shame across the school grounds to her car and going to the session at all. But when the opportunity for him to leave arose, he hadn't taken it. Instead, he'd let it slip by and when he had seen Kathi pull up outside the school gates, he'd joined her with no fuss.

As soon as he got in the car, he plugged in his earphones. He refused to look at her and instead stared out the passenger window. They travelled the thirty minutes in silence, but he was all too aware of her secretly wiping tears from her eyes.

His conscience told him he should say something, but he didn't know what.

'When your mum called yesterday,' Brenda continued, 'she said she was worried about you. Do you know why she's worried?'

'I've been shoplifting.'

'What did you steal?' Brenda's tone was curious rather than judgmental.

'Just some sweets from the corner shop.'

'Do you know why you stole them?'

'For a laugh,' he said, shrugging his shoulders. 'Because I could. It wasn't a big deal, it was just some sweets.'

'Does your mum disapprove of you stealing?' He nodded his head. 'What else does your mum disapprove of.'

'I dunno.' He thought for a minute. 'She doesn't like it when I answer back.'

'What else?'

'She doesn't like my friends.'

'Anything else?'

'She doesn't like it when I remind her she's not my mother.'

Brenda let that hang in the air for a moment, after which she said, 'Your birth mother wasn't able to look after you, for whatever reason, and she put you up for adoption. I imagine that one of the difficulties for you is that you had no say in it.'

'Were you adopted?' Jake asked, giving her a quick look.

'No, but I've worked with lots of young people who were. What they've told me is that having no say in their lives is one of the hardest things to come to terms with. Do you think you could be feeling that way too?'

'Maybe. I didn't ask to be born, I didn't ask for any of this. If my mother couldn't look after me why did she have me?' Jake looked at Brenda now, urging her to give him an answer. 'Why didn't she abort me?'

'That is something you may never have the answer to. Would it have been better if she had?'

'Maybe. At least then I wouldn't feel like this.'
'Like what?'
'Like I'm useless, like I'm a waste of space, a burden to Mum and Dad.'
'Are you a burden?'
'Of course I am.' He was cross with her for asking such daft questions. 'I'm not their child. I'm giving them all this grief and the only reason they haven't kicked me out before now is that they're legally tied to me.'
'What have you done that's so bad?'
'Nothing,' Jake mumbled.
'It can't be nothing. It must be something you think is bad enough to make your parents not love you anymore.'
'They don't love me.'
'Don't they?'
'No. How can they?'
'Why can't they?'
'Because I'm difficult, I make their life difficult.'
'In what way?'
'I get in the way. Dad has his own plumbing business and works all hours. Mum spends all her time in empty houses with Brian, or writing this blog she thinks I don't know about. Running their businesses is what they really love.'
'Everybody has to work.'
'Not twenty-four seven. And anyway, I know they regret adopting me because they didn't adopt any more children, did they?'
'Have they said that to you?'
'Of course not.'
'Why of course not?'
'Because they're not horrible people.'
'Could it because they love you and don't think you get in the way? Could it be that you are enough and complete the family they want?' He shook his head, his eyes fixed firmly on the weave of the carpet. 'It's not because they love you?'

Again he shook his head. 'Why could it not be because they love you?' Brenda goaded him gently. 'Jake, why could it not be because they love you?'

'Because who could love me?' He blurted, angry at Brenda for making him say it out loud. 'Not even my own mother loved me. She gave me away.' Brenda slid a box of tissues across the coffee table that sat between them. They sat in silence for a minute, while Jake let out some of the hurt he'd been storing away all these years. His body juddered with each sob but in time it lessened and Brenda asked, 'How does it feel to consider yourself unlovable?'

'I feel angry, angry and ashamed. Ashamed of being unwanted, ashamed of my anger and ashamed that, I dunno, Kathi and Graham are duty-bound to me.'

'Duty-bound?'

'Yeah. They've got to look after me whether they like it or not.'

Brenda leaned forward in her seat. 'I've heard a lot of adoptees tell me they're unlovable or that they're undeserving of love. What I've learnt, though, is that in time you will feel differently. You'll begin a process of healing, you'll develop a sense of self and find where you belong in the world. You are unique. You are a person who can love and in turn be loved. Being adopted will become just another part of your life, it won't define you. You are at the start of this process and this is the toughest part.'

She sat back again and let Jake digest some of what she'd said. 'As you get older,' she continued, 'and get to know yourself better, you'll begin to see what's great about you, and what your strengths are. You'll begin to understand that your mum and dad will never abandon you, no matter how much you try to push them away. The day will come when you realise they love you for who you are and because of who you are.'

Jake's tears rolled down his face at the idea someone might love him for who he was.

'You've worked hard today, Jake. Let's finish up there. You've talked about some very difficult emotions and I know it hasn't been easy. Take a few calming breaths and then we'll call your mum in.'

Even though this was their second session with Brenda, Kathi was still shocked to see Jake's red and blotchy face, his puffy eyes.

'Come in, Kathi,' said Brenda. 'Take a seat. Jake has had quite a tough session, would you agree?' Brenda addressed her question to Jake, and he nodded. 'He's worked really hard and I'm very proud of him. Jake, is there anything you want to tell your mum?'

What he wanted to do was curl up on her knee and tell her everything he was feeling. He wanted to be cuddled and feel safe in her arms, like he did when he was a small boy. He wanted life to go back to the way it had been. Instead he said, 'No, nothing.'

'Well, listen,' said Brenda in her soft accent, gently encouraging. 'I think it would be beneficial if we meet again next week to try to understand a little bit more about what's going on. What do you say?'

'Yes please,' said Kathi, taking the opportunity offered. Jake silently agreed. Something had shifted within him. He didn't know what, but he felt it in his stomach. It was tangible.

Jake and Kathi drove the whole way to Byreburn in silence, each bound up in their own thoughts. Only when they turned onto their street did Jake say, 'Tell me about Marie.'

They had had this conversation many times over the years, but Jake never tired of hearing it because each time he absorbed a new detail, or Kathi remembered something previously forgotten. When Jake was little, these conversations had covered the basic facts of her name, what colour of hair she had and how old she was. As Jake got older, he became interested in her likes and dislikes and wanted to know about any hobbies or pastimes Marie had.

Once, on a day trip to Glasgow, Jake had been hyper because he thought they would see Marie there. He'd been confused when Kathi and Graham told him that even though this was where Marie lived, they wouldn't see her. It took him a long time to figure out why this was, and when he did, he felt stupid at his own foolishness.

They pulled up outside the house, and Kathi switched off the engine. 'Her name is Marie. She was seventeen years old when she got pregnant. She lived in Glasgow and that's where you were born, in the Royal Infirmary. She has brown eyes and dark hair likes yours.'

'I know all that.'

'What is it you want me to tell you?'

'Something new, something I didn't know before.'

'I'm not sure I have anything new to tell you, Jake, I'm sorry.' Kathi reached out and stroked his cheek and for a few moments he accepted her affection, but all too soon his frustration floated to the top. He grabbed his schoolbag and got out the car, slamming the door.

Before he stormed out of the car Kathi turned to look at Jake and stroked his face gently. His profile was still that of a child. He'd let his hair grow longer, and it made him look much younger than his fifteen years.

She knew what Jake wanted to know about Marie, but those facts were messy and complicated. He was too young to make sense of Marie's life at that time. She didn't want to shatter the image of perfection Jake had of his birth mother, not yet. He wasn't mature enough to take in Marie's abusive childhood, her addiction to heroin, and the means by which she paid for it.

Kathi racked her memory, digging around for some small detail from the notes she'd been given about Jake when they adopted him. Out of the fog emerged the remembrance that Marie had enjoyed Maths at school, just like he did. It was a small detail but one Jake could grasp at and which might make him feel a step closer to her. She thought about going in to tell him, but hesitated. The moment had passed.

Kathi felt as lost and bereft now as she did before the visit to Brenda. She wanted to mend Jake's heart but didn't know how. She felt stranded in the dark about how to help him get through this. How did a parent reassure their child that they were loved and valued and wanted? She pulled out her phone and called her grandmother, Marjorie.

'Only me,' she said.

'You sound a bit down, what's up?'

'I don't know what to do about Jake.'

'What do you mean?'

'He's so angry all the time and is taking it out on me. I know why he's doing it, but it's so hard.'

'Oh Kathi, love, I'm so sorry.'

'I don't know how to make him understand just how much we love him.'

'I don't imagine there is anything you can say. I imagine this is something he needs to figure out by himself.'

'How can I speed that up?' Kathi asked in the hope Marjorie had an answer.

'Oh, love, you can't. It's one of those awful things we have to learn by ourselves.' Marjorie paused before going on. 'When your parents died, you were so angry. It took you a long time to come terms with it.' Kathi had been twenty-three years old when her parents were killed in a car accident. It didn't matter that she was an adult or that it had been an accident, she was furious with the world for doing this to her. 'You lashed out at those closest to you. You said things to me that you didn't mean, and that you would never have said under any other circumstances. But you needed to work it all out somehow. That's what Jake is going through now. He's working out how to manage the loss he has experienced.'

Kathi cringed when she remembered the hurtful things she'd said to her grandmother at that time. 'You're right,' she said. 'I know you are, but God it hurts.' To stifle the sound of her sobs, she placed her scarf over her mouth.

'You'll get through this, I promise.'

They hung up, and Kathi took a moment. 'Pull yourself together,' she reprimanded herself, slapping her cheeks in a bid to do so. After taking a deep breath, she hauled herself out of the car. The routine of domesticity didn't end even when you wanted it to.

Chapter 14

On Saturday mornings Jake usually went to football practice, but it had been cancelled that day, so Kathi suggested they take a hike up to the Thomas Telford Memorial. She looked surprised when Jake agreed to go, and he enjoyed unfooting her slightly. The memorial was perched high on one of Byreburn's three surrounding hills, both protecting it from the outside world and providing safe passage for the River Esk that flowed through the town.

Jake used to feel that the cold, clear water pouring down from the hills with its loud rumble was a comforting soundtrack to their life in Byreburn. Nowadays it felt like a prison moat, keeping him there.

Before they left Kathi had packed some biscuits and a thermos of hot chocolate into a holdall. She put it on her back and they headed out. As they walked through the town Kathi said hello to just about everybody they passed. She seemed to know everyone. This used to make Jake feel special, now it made him resentful. She had been born and raised here, with no dark secrets in her past. Everyone knew her and she knew them.

The route to the monument took them up the High Street before turning left up the steep Kirk Wynd, following in the steps of the Common Riding horses. As soon as they left the bustle of the main town and hit the quiet walking path, the silence between them amplified. Jake could tell Kathi wanted to say something, but she held her tongue and he wasn't about to make things any easier for her. He was enjoying her discomfort. Because he was taller than her now, he could more than match her stride for stride, and they kept a good pace. It wasn't often Jake thought about his birth father, but at times like this, when he was doing something physical, he wondered if he looked anything like him, or shared his physique or height.

It was September now, and the air had turned cool. The sun still shone brightly, but the atmosphere didn't warm up like it did in the summer months. The moorland heather was in full bloom, swathes of purple stretched out in front of them and its light fragrance floated, like invisible ocean waves, in the air. As the path got steeper, the sky got bigger, and Kathi had to stop a couple of times to catch her breath. Jake stopped with her, making a point of hiding his own breathlessness by looking out over the valley.

As he did so, he couldn't help but notice the beauty of this part of southern Scotland. It didn't have the craggy, rugged beauty of the north of the nation, instead its hills rolled, they were green and fertile. Graham always commented that they might not have the majesty of the Highlands, but they were friendlier and more welcoming.

Jake looked over at Kathi, who was smiling down on Byreburn with its long High Street and solid stone bridge that crossed the River Esk. He knew she was thinking of the generations of her family that had crossed it before her. She said it every time she came here.

Jake started up the hill again, Kathi could follow when she wanted. He was already seated among the heather next to the monument by the time she arrived. He'd found a large hollow in which they could shelter from the wind as they drank their hot chocolate and ate their biscuits. Kathi slumped down beside him, completely exhausted. It gave him a little bit of pleasure to see her struggling, showing her age and frailty.

She took the holdall off her back and Jake opened it, pulling out the picnic. He opened the biscuits first and ate them fast, suddenly hungry. He felt like he could eat for Scotland recently. When Kathi could breathe again, she poured them both a cup of hot chocolate and its sweetness tasted delicious after the exertion of the climb. They watched the wind whip the clouds overhead, speeding their way to who knew where.

The events of the last few days and the gallons of fresh air he'd inhaled that morning inspired openness in Jake and he asked, 'Do you and Dad love me?'

'Of course,' Kathi said quickly.

'Do you think you love me as much as you would have done your own child?' Kathi was about to answer, but she stopped herself, which made Jake nervous. It made him think she was trying to work out how best to tell him that no, she didn't, that she would have loved her own child, any child, more than she loved him.

'Yes, I believe I do,' she said eventually. She turned to look at Jake, but he kept his eyes firmly fixed on the valley spread out below them. She put her arm around him and asked, 'Do you think I do?'

'I don't know,' he shrugged. 'I guess we'll never know unless you have a baby.'

At length, Kathi said, 'I've never been pregnant. I've never given birth and felt a newborn in my arms, so I don't know what it feels like. What I do know is that the love I feel for you is the strongest love I've ever felt. I know you are the most precious person in my life and I want nothing more than for you to be happy and secure.' Kathi paused. 'Do you think you love me as much as you would your birth mother?' He was surprised by the question and turned to look at her.

'I don't know,' he said. They sipped their chocolate, and he ate another biscuit. 'I don't –' Jake stopped, uncertain how to go on.

'You don't...'

'I don't think you do love me as much as you would your own child. I don't think it's possible.'

'Why is it not possible?' Kathi's voice trembled.

'Because I'm not yours, not really. I don't belong.' From the corner of Jake's eye, he saw her surreptitiously wipe a tear away. He felt so powerful having this control over her, being able to make her happy or sad depending on his whim. At the same time, he knew he was being cruel, and that she didn't deserve to be treated this way.

'Jake, you do belong. You are my child. You are my son and I love you more than I love anybody else in my life. I know you belong to me. I hope one day you'll understand that, in here.' She placed a hand over his heart. Embarrassed, he changed the subject.

They finished the hot chocolate and headed back down the hill. By the time they got home, they'd put some distance between themselves and their conversation at the monument. It gave Jake time for reflection, and to his surprise he felt a little comforted by Kathi's words. He believed her when she said she knew he belonged to her.

In his room, after dinner, Jake heard the doorbell ring. Curiosity made him lean over the banister to see who it was. His stomach sank when he saw PC Jamie Armstrong in the frame of the door. In uniform.

'Hi Graham,' he said. 'Is Jake home?' Jake moved back up against the wall, out of sight. He knew why Jamie was here.

'Jake,' called Graham, 'come down here a minute.'

Graham, Jamie, and Kathi were waiting for him in the living room. He decided to try the same tactic as before, to say sorry and that he'll never do it again.

'Jake,' said Jamie, looking embarrassed at having to explain to his best friend that his son was a thief. 'We've had a report that you've been shoplifting in Colin Murray's shop.'

'It was just once,' said Graham. 'He has apologised and promised he won't do it again.' Jake's stomach dropped. Not only had he continued stealing, but now he'd been caught lying.

'I'm afraid it wasn't just once,' said Jamie. Kathi and Graham looked at Jake.

'Mum, Dad, it was just the once, I promise.'

'Jake, we know it was more than once because you were caught on camera each time.' Jake gritted his teeth.

'Jamie, I'm so sorry,' said Graham, his face puce with embarrassment. 'We'll talk to him again and put an end to it. Won't we, son?'

'Yes,' Jake said very quietly.

'Is there any chance we can put this down to a childish prank that went wrong? He won't do it again, I promise you.'

'I'm sorry Graham, I canny let it slide,' said Jamie. 'Murray says it's happened too many times and wants an end to it.'

'He's only a kid.'

'I know, so this time,' he turned to Jake, 'you're going to be let off with a warning. You must also apologise to Mr Murray and pay for the items you stole. If you do that, no charges will be pressed.'

Jake nodded his head in silence.

'Right, well, he'll expect your apology tomorrow, and he'll give you a bill for the stolen goods.'

Jake nodded again, his teeth still gritted, then went to his room.

'Jamie, I'm so sorry,' he heard Kathi say. 'I'll go with him to Murray's and make sure he apologises. I'll also pay the bill.'

'Don't worry, Kathi,' Jamie said, lowering his voice. 'It happens all the time.'

Jake closed his bedroom door. He didn't want to hear any more.

The next day, Kathi marched Jake over to Murray's shop. There were a couple of people there, chatting to each other and to Murray. Kathi and Jake waited until everybody was gone before she pushed him towards the counter. 'Jake's got something to say,' she said 'Haven't you?'

'I'm sorry,' he mumbled.

'I didn't hear you,' said Mr Murray at the same time as winking at Kathi, which really annoyed Jake. He was standing right there.

'I'm sorry,' he said louder.

'Sorry for what?'

'For stealing from the shop.'

'Good, thank you. I know it seems like a fun thing to do at the time, but remember Jake, I'm one man who owns one small shop. This is how I earn a living to look after my family. When you steal you hurt a lot of people, including your mum.' She grunted in agreement. 'When you do things like this, she feels let down and upset that her son would behave so badly. Think about that before you do something else you might regret.'

He reached over to the till and took out a receipt. 'This is the value of what was stolen.' It was just under twenty pounds.

'My God, Jake, just how much did you take?' Kathi said.

'It was just a few sweets,' he said. She paid the bill, and they left.

'I can't believe how much the bill was. I was expecting it to be a couple of quid, but twenty pounds.'

'Alright, I'm sorry.'

'I hope you are. I hope you won't do it again. Twenty pounds.' Kathi shook her head in disbelief.

'Stop going on about it, I've said I'm sorry.'

'I'm so embarrassed.'

'You are embarrassed? Nobody is more embarrassing than you. I hate you,' he shouted. He left her, stunned and silent, and stormed up to the high street. He needed to move, do something physical to release the rage that was burning inside him. He cut up through some backstreets before turning onto the High Street. Headed down, he took the corner too quickly and went straight into Joanne.

'Whoa there,' she said. 'Where's the fire?'

'It's her,' Jake burst out.

'Kathi?'

'Who else?' He kicked the wall.

'What happened?' Joanne led him back onto the side street. It was more private.

'I got caught stealing some sweets, and she's made a huge fuss about it.'

'Och,' Joanne dismissed his crime. 'I have been caught shoplifting loads of times and there's nothing wrong with me.'

'Exactly, everybody does it. I wish she'd get off my case. I know she thinks it's because, you know, I'm... I'm bad.'

'Ha, she can talk.'

'What do you mean?'

'Well, it is not as if her family is any better. She's told you about the other baby, I suppose?'

'What baby?' Jake's mind was flooded with images of a blonde-haired, blue-eyed baby that Kathi really wanted.

'The baby her mum and dad had, before she was born.' Joanne lowered her voice. 'Out of wedlock.'

'Wait, you're telling me her parents had another child?' Joanne nodded. 'Where is it?' Joanne shrugged her shoulders. 'How do you know about it?'

'It's common knowledge. I'm surprised you didn't know.'

'She's never mentioned it. Does she know?'

'I would have thought so.'

'I wonder why they didn't keep it?'

'Out of wedlock,' Joanne repeated. 'Couldn't do that in those days, especially somewhere like Byreburn.' Joanne lowered her voice again. 'Gossip.'

Again the image of the blonde-haired, blue-eyed baby popped into his mind. 'Was it a boy or a girl?' he asked.

'Does it matter?'

'I suppose not.' But somehow it did. Was it another boy like him? Abandoned at birth, cast out into the world without a second thought? Did Kathi's parents ever try to find the baby? Was his real mum looking for him?

'Next time Kathi gives you grief for the choices you make, remind her that her family is no better. Everyone has secrets, Jake. Never forget that.' She watched him for a little while. Eventually she said, 'You should look for your birth mum. It's your right to know what happened. Maybe she's looking for you too.'

'I wouldn't know where to start.'

'Have a look in your mum's office, see what you can find there. Tell me what you discover and maybe I can help.'

Chapter 15

Joanne Wylie and her friend Sharon were sprawled over the two sofas that engulfed almost all of Joanne's living room. Rain had moved in over Byreburn and it pelted the windows. The sky was a low and heavy, and as dark as only a Borders sky can be. Neither of them were working that afternoon, so decided to make a duvet day of it. They'd been watching re-runs of Friends and had now moved onto Dirty Dancing with a large box of Milk Tray. High on strawberry creams and diet coke, they were singing along to the soundtrack, giving it some welly from their respective sofas.

Joanne's tablet was balanced on the arm of her sofa and she heard a gentle 'ping' as a message popped into her account. Still singing, but not quite too loudly, Joanne clicked into the message.

'Who's your message from?' Sharon asked.

'It's just my mum, she's got a new smart phone and I canny get rid of her.'

Buoyed by the music and the fact that Baby was about to get her man, Joanne let out a large whoop, heaved herself off the sofa and began a celebratory jiggle around the bare room, her large hips swaying to an internal calypso. Encouraged by her friend, Sharon too got up and made attempts to imitate the Dirty Dancers.

The flat had recently been renovated by Kathi, the carpets had a fluffy look to them, the countertops were unscuffed and the walls were blemish free. Despite the newness of the decor, Joanne's meagre belongings made the place feel shabbier than it was. The sofas were well worn, cheap charity buys. All she could afford at the time. She used a crate she's picked up from her work at the mill as a coffee table and there were no pictures of any description on the walls. Only the television was new.

'Let's open some wine,' said Joanne, boogieing her way into the kitchenette. 'Prosecco,' she announced. There was a bottle of Co-Op's own brand chilling nicely in the fridge door. She pulled it out, popped the cork and poured some into two decorative champagne flutes she's splashed out on at the Silver Spoon Cafe and Gift Shop. It was four o'clock on a rainy Tuesday afternoon and as Joanne and Sharon clinked cheers, they grinned at each other in delight at how decadent they were.

The afternoon stretched into evening and once they'd finished the Prosecco, along with a family sized bag of Kettle Salt and Vinegar crisps to soak it up, they opened a bottle of Chardonnay and danced along with Sandy and Danny in Grease. They ate a couple of oven pizzas which allowed them to open a final bottle of wine and settle down to cry at The Notebook. As the end credits rolled Sharon looked at the time.

'Shit,' she said, 'I'd better go. I'm absolutely hammered and I start work at eight tomorrow morning.' With slow, woozy movements she gathered her stuff and went home. Joanne was left alone on the sofa, dozing, building herself up to make the move to her bedroom.

Her tablet pinged again, another message from her mum, complaining about Joanne's Nana, who was an interfering old bag. Mind you, Maureen, her mum, was no better. She'd lied to Joanne for years, and it was only by chance she'd found out. If she hadn't had the good sense to look around her mum's bedroom, she would never have found that series of letters.

At first they hadn't made any sense, so she'd stuffed them back in their drawer. A few years later she found the letters again, but this time she was intrigued enough to find out more. A bit more rummaging and she made the connection. Maureen wasn't her birth mum, she'd been adopted.

The tablet pinged again. The afterglow of the wine had faded, and Joanne was left feeling alone and depressed. She pictured Maureen's face and was immediately irritated.

Joanne had been well looked after by her adoptive parents, Maureen and Michael. She had never lacked for anything, including affection, but Maureen and Michael had, unintentionally, instilled in her the understanding that she was lucky to have parents who looked after her so well and would send her into the world with prospects. Joanne never understood why she felt that way until she discovered she'd been adopted.

Maureen didn't like to talk about Joanne's birth mother; who she was or why she'd been put up for adoption in the first place. Joanne had never understood that the very mention of her 'real mother' hurt Maureen at her core and Maureen was never able to explain to Joanne how not being able to have a baby made her feel inadequate as a woman and as a wife.

When Joanne reached the age Jake was now, she had no one and nowhere to turn to. The insecurities she already felt were amplified when Michael died from stomach cancer. Joanne never recovered from his loss. It echoed too closely the loss of her birth mother.

Joanne's behaviour became erratic and volatile. She stayed out late, drank, smoked and went with boys, all in a bid to fit in and to forget she was a misfit. Maureen didn't know how to respond to this angry, ungrateful child and bit by bit began to back away. This of course made Joanne feel even more rejected and so the spiral continued.

Her behaviour isolated her from the other kids at school. They made fun of her, described her as bad. 'You have bad blood in you,' said one girl. 'My mammy told me.'

When she realised this was how people felt about her, Joanne began to believe it. It must be true, she thought to herself. Why else would she have been given up at birth? She must be intrinsically bad, and her real mother had felt it right away.

Joanne put up a barrier between her and the rest of the world, and that barrier stopped any new hurt from entering her sphere. She had sectioned off the old hurts and locked them away in her stomach. To feed those hurts and keep them drowsy, she fed them – alcohol, drugs, food – so that they wouldn't want to rise up in rebellion. The fat around her waist grew thicker and thicker, making her stomach too comfortable a place to leave. No new hurt could penetrate because it would be packed away in her stomach.

As an adult, that defensiveness evolved into attack – the best form of defence. She sabotaged relationships and opportunities even before they began. Female friendships came and went, and any man who seemed interested in her was ignored or lashed out at. Jobs were short-lived because she found one reason or other to be late, to call in sick or fight with colleagues.

At 16 years old she requested her adoption papers and find out the name of her parents, but she didn't know what to do with that information. This only heightened her frustration because she knew she was only one step away from her birth mother, but she was unable to get up and walk.

That frustration turned into a fixation which turned into hatred for her birth mother for rejecting her. She began to plan a way of finding her birth mother, but it wasn't until 20 years later that Joanne hit the jackpot. Of all things, it was a simple Google search that told Joanne her parents lived in Byreburn.

When she first visited Byreburn, she'd been nervous travelling so far from home. She'd never been out of Glasgow before and the adventure had been liberating. It had been thrilling heading out into the unknown.

She'd booked herself into the cheapest B&B she could find and stayed two nights. The town was so small she felt everyone must know she was a stranger. She spent her time walking around the town and getting to the know the streets. By evening she was feeling a bit lonesome. It was Saturday night, and she was bored sitting in her room by herself. She wanted a drink.

There were only a couple of local pubs to choose from so she picked one, ordered a drink and sat by herself at a corner table. The pub began to fill up, the alcohol loosened tongues and lowered inhibitions, and in time Joanne began to chat with the people around her. Just passing through, she'd said when people asked her why she was there. One of the pubs had a late-night disco, and she danced until 1 a.m..

The next morning, her hangover aside, she felt great. She felt like she'd come home. She applied for a job at Milton Mill in the packing department, and Cherry helped her find the small one bed flat off the High Street. With no husband or family to tie her down, it was an easy decision to escape Glasgow and start again.

Joanne was loving her new life in Byreburn. The freedom of being somewhere new gave her strength and a sense of possibility she'd never experienced before. She was able to shake off her family name and the history that went with it.

'I don't understand why you're going there,' her mum had said. 'What is there that you can't find here?'

Of course they both knew what was there, but neither wanted to say the words out loud.

Byreburn would never set the world alight, but the people here were industrious and busy. They gossiped and interfered in each other's lives, just like Joanne's Glasgow estate, but here the comments were about people letting the side down and standards slipping. They were not about people getting above themselves by looking for a job or seeking a better way of living.

Byreburn and the mill were giving Joanne a second chance. The work wasn't exciting, but it was regular and the people she worked with were nice. But more than that, she was paid at the end of each week and the pride she felt when she looked at her bank balance each Friday was greater than she ever would have believed.

She felt like Kate Winslet standing on the prow of the Titanic and shouting 'king of the world' as loudly as she could.

Chapter 16

'Brian, get in here,' Cherry called through from her office. She'd been there for some time, trying to work out what to say to him. To her frustration, and against her better judgment, she was falling in love with Brian Weatherstone, faults and all. This made life very difficult, for it was clouding her judgment and she wasn't able to rip into him as she'd once done.

She was accepting less than the best work from him because she knew how hard he was trying to stay sober. That said, there were too many complaints from tenants about either shoddy work or him not turning up at all. If things carried on like this, she'd not only lose her reputation but her business, and that was not acceptable. Something needed to be done.

Brian shuffled into her office looking like a puppy who knew he'd eaten his master's slipper. He hovered in front of her desk until Cherry told him to sit down. 'Right, what's been going on?' she demanded. Before he could respond she said, 'I have had tenant after tenant phoning me to complain about your work. That is not good.' When Cherry was angry, her Glaswegian accent asserted itself and was enough to frighten most people. Brian stood no chance. 'But to top it all off, Kathi tells me you're way behind on her refurbishment. That is terrible.' She paused for effect. 'Don't forget Brian, most of both our work comes from her, and she's my friend. It's in both our interests to make sure she and her tenants get the best from us.' She gave him a hard glare. 'Do you understand?'

'Of course I understand, I'm not a child. She's my friend too.'

'Then tell me what's going on.'

'I will if you give me a chance.' Cherry sat back in her seat, placed her hands in her lap and raised an eyebrow to indicate he may proceed. Under her steely gaze, Brian faltered. He was always taken off guard by her transformation from gentle princess at home to wicked queen in the workplace.

'You're asking me to do too much,' he said eventually. 'I'm jumping from place to place, running about all over town and always in a rush.'

'What do you mean all over town? The town is two square miles max.'

'Jobs take time and I need my breaks. There's only so many hours in a day.'

'Nonsense Brian, you're giving me excuses.' She leaned forward, elbows on the desk, cross he was making such feeble excuses for not doing what he knew he should. 'Don't try to kid a kidder.'

'I am not making excuses, you don't know what my days are like. You sit here in your nice comfy office barking orders and expect me to jump at your command.'

'Bollocks,' she snapped back. 'I expect you to do your job, the work you're paid for.'

'I do my work.'

'Aye, but not very well.' They eyeballed each other across the desk, both feeling badly done to. It was only in the stillness that Cherry noticed Brian's hands were shaking. She looked at them and then again at his face and noticed how pale it was. She decided a new approach was needed.

'Brian, babe,' her voice softened and took on an appeasing tone. 'Something is not right with you and I want to help. Talk to me.' To Cherry's amazement Brian began to cry. She was so amazed she didn't know how to respond. Seeing a grown man cry was not something she often, if ever, came across. In fact, Cherry had probably only ever seen a man cry on the telly. 'I didn't mean to make you cry,' she said, feeling awkward, 'I'm sorry.'

'It's not you, well, not just you.'

'What is it then?'

'It's everything.'

'Are you drinking again?'

'No, but I want to. Every day is a nightmare and the longer time goes by the harder it gets.'

'You've never said.'

'I didn't want you to see how much I'm struggling with it all.'

'Don't be daft, that's what I'm here for.' Cherry's eyes drifted back to Brian's shaking hands and she only now began to realise he was finding this sober malarkey harder than he let on. 'But you're not drinking?' She asked again.

'No, but I might as well be. I can't sleep at night, I can't concentrate on anything and I keep forgetting things. It's only when you phone and shout at me that I remember I'm supposed to be somewhere else.' They both smiled. That had certainly been the pattern of the past week or so.

'Do you need to get some help?' Cherry asked. 'You know, professional help.'

'No way.' Brian was horrified by the idea. It would be all round the town within minutes. 'People think badly enough of me as it is, I can do without that stigma.'

'There must be someone who can help. Ask the doctor.'

'No, I will do it by myself. I can do it, I'm just tired.' They sat quietly for a few moments before Cherry asked Brian what he wanted to do about the situation. 'Just carry on, I suppose, until it passes.'

'I can wait, Brian, but my business can't and neither can yours.'

'What do you suggest?'

Cherry took a few minutes to think about it before saying, 'Here's what we'll do: At the end of each day I'll draw up a schedule for you for the next day. That way you know exactly where you need to be and when, without worrying about it. If a job takes longer than planned you call me and I'll let the client know. If it finishes quicker than planned, you get an extra break. How's that?'

Brian looked uncomfortable. 'Think of it this way,' she said. 'I will be your secretary. If anyone calls you about a job, get them to call me to arrange a time. Just like a PA would do.' That did sound better, Brian conceded.

'Okay,' he said without conviction.

'It's temporary, Brian, just until you're feeling better. It is the only way I can see of moving forward and not losing business. And I want to be of help. Believe it or not, I care about you.'

'Do you?'

'Of course I do.'

'Alright,' he said, 'let's try it and see how it goes.'

'Brilliant.' She pulled out a piece of paper and together they planned out his day. 'I probably haven't said it enough,' Cherry told him as they walked to the door, 'but I am really proud of you for kicking the drink and everything. I don't think I appreciate how hard it is for you, but you're doing brilliantly.'

Cherry had arranged to meet Kathi at the Silver Spoon Café and Gift Shop for lunch. She arrived first and had a browse around the gifts. When Kathi arrived she was paying for large wooden letters that were painted red and sprinkled with glitter, spelling the word 'love'.

'Oh yes?' Kathi inquired, peering over Cherry's shoulder. 'For anyone in particular?'

'It's for me,' Cherry protested, blushing brightly. 'I need a bit of that from your tenants.'

'Oh yes?' Kathi said again.

'I'll tell you over lunch.' They found a table, and each ordered the soup 'I spoke to Brian,' said Cherry. 'I think I've got to the bottom of what's going on with him, so there shouldn't be any more issues. Only thing is, your refurbishment might have to wait a few days until he has caught up on his jobs for the tenants. I need to get those finished and keep my clients happy, but after that he'll be straight over to get cracking.'

'Is everything alright with Brian?' Kathi asked.

'So, so, but the important thing is,' Cherry lowered her voice, 'he's still off the booze.'

'Good for him,' said Kathi. 'He's tried it before, but I don't think he has managed this long. You're a good influence on him.' Cherry didn't respond. 'What's wrong?'

'I really like Brian, more than I would normally admit.' Cherry took a quick look around checking nobody was listening. 'And like you, I am so proud of him making this change in his life. But I worry.'

'That he'll fall off the wagon?'

'More than that. I'm worried he's doing it for me, not for himself. What if things don't work out between us and he hits the drink again because it was only ever for me and not for him?'

'Either way, isn't it a good thing he's stopped?'

'That's what I thought at first, but now I'm not so sure. You know him better than me. Does he have a habit of falling apart when things get tough?'

'He's had his struggles,' said Kathi. 'Not so much because things fall apart but because they never get any better, despite his best efforts. Life's been pretty hard on Brian, and I think he expects it to stay that way. Occasionally he gets his hopes up and when things don't work out as he thought, he gets angry with himself for being so optimistic. He blanks it out the only way he knows.'

'What if the same thing happens with me and him? I don't know if I can handle that responsibility.'

Kathi's stomach involuntarily dropped. This was exactly what she'd worried about when Cherry and Brian first got together; that it wouldn't work out and their great team would fall apart. 'You know what,' she said, 'you're over-thinking it. You're worrying about something that might never happen. Just take one day at a time.'

'How is Jake?' Cherry asked, keen to change the subject. 'Is he being any nicer to you?' Kathi shook her head.

'Things are going from bad to worse.' This time it was Kathi's turn to lower her voice. 'Jamie Armstrong came by the house the other day. Jake's been caught shoplifting in Murray's. You can imagine how mortified me and Graham were. I took him over to the shop, he apologised and we paid for what he'd taken, but I'm scared this isn't the end of things, just the beginning. I'm scared he's either going to carry on the way things are, or that they'll get worse.'

'Did you have a word with him about the smoking?' Kathi nodded. 'You might need to have another chat with him. I saw him again down by the river.' Kathi put her hands over her face and shook her head despondently. 'What does Graham think about it all?'

'I know he sees things differently to me, but that's because he doesn't feel shut out.'

'What do you mean?'

'Jake doesn't seem angry with Graham, the way he does with me. It's as if I'm the one to blame for him being adopted; not Graham and definitely not his saintly birth mother, Marie.' Kathi took a breath. 'Sorry, I shouldn't say that. I know things were hard for her, but I can't help it sometimes. I feel like I'm the baddie in this scenario and that everything I do is thrown back in my face.'

'Oh Kathi, that must be horrible. He doesn't know how good he's got it with you.'

'That night, after the first shoplifting incident, Jake apologised and said he wouldn't do it again. Graham gave him a hug, and I wanted to as well, but when I went over Jake pushed me away and made an excuse to leave the room. Graham didn't pick up on it, but I knew it was a snub. I just knew he was pushing me out of the equation.'

'What did you do?'

'Nothing, what could I do?'

'I know it's hard,' Cherry tried to reassure her friend, 'but try not to worry. He'll come good in the end.'

'I hope you're right.'

As soon as he got home that day Kathi jumped on Jake. 'Cherry says she saw you smoking again. Is that true?'

'No, of course it's not.'

'Don't lie to me, Jake. She saw you.'

'I'm not lying.'

'Just like you didn't lie about the shoplifting? Tell me the truth..'

'Alright, I have one now and again.'

'Why, Jake? You know how bad it is for you. It's because of that Lindsay Irving girl, isn't it? I knew she was a bad influence on you.'

'You don't know what you're talking about.' Jake shouted at her as he stormed up the stairs to his room. Kathi followed him up.

'Yes I do. I know her family, don't forget. I know them better than you do.'

'It's not as if your family are any better.' Jake slammed his bedroom door in her face.

'What do you mean by that?' She banged her fists on it.

'Oh nothing,' he shouted from behind the door.

'No,' Kathi turned the handle and went in. 'What do you mean?'

'Your parents. They were no angels.'

'My parents? What have they got to do with this?'

'They did stuff they shouldn't have done.'

'You're talking in riddles, what do you mean?'

'They had another baby. Before you.'

'No, they did not. Why on earth would you say that?'

'They did.' There was something in Jake's tone that made her stop short and listen.

'Who told you that?'

'Everyone knows except you, it seems.' There was no way he was going to tell her who told him. 'So don't pretend I'm the baddest guy in town. Plenty of people have done far worse than me.'

'Where is this child, then?'

'How should I know?' Jake stood up and moved towards her. 'Now get out of my room.' He pushed her back with more force than he intended. She stumbled back out of the room and he slammed the door once more.

Before dinner that night Graham came to his room. 'You've really upset Mum this time. What happened between you two at the shop?'

'I told her that her parents had another child, before they had her.' Now that Jake had calmed down, he felt bad for having blurted this out. 'She was annoying me,' he explained to Graham. 'She made me feel like I'd murdered someone when all I'd really done was steal a couple of sweets. It wasn't that serious.'

'It's serious to your mum. Stealing is stealing, no matter what it is. But how did you hear about there being another child?

'Is it true?'

'What do you think?'

'I don't know and I don't really care. I just said it to piss her off.'

'Language.'

'Sorry. Well, is it? True?'

'No, son, it's not. Whoever told you that is winding you up.' Jake indicated he didn't think they were, that his source was reliable.

'If it's not true,' he asked Graham, 'why is Mum so upset?'

'How would you feel if you knew people were spreading gossip about you, saying your dead parents had another child hidden away somewhere?'

'Do you have any other children?'

Graham laughed, 'I can barely keep up with you, I wouldn't have the energy for another.'

That didn't answer the question. 'Do you?' Jake repeated.

'No, son, I don't.' Graham didn't laugh this time.

Chapter 17

The next morning, before getting into the daily routine, Kathi went for a walk to clear her head. Cherry's news about Jake's smoking, and his behaviour in general, had knocked the stuffing out of her and she didn't know how to poke it back in.

She walked down the High Street, over the King's Bridge and down Thomas Telford Road. The route took her past Jake's school, and she made sure not to look over in case he saw her and thought she was snooping. She went past the sports field and into the adjoining woods. It was a popular walking spot, but at this time of day it would be quiet. There were a few dog walkers to say hello to, but nobody to disrupt her train of thought. Next to the pathway was a steep decline to the river, which was low-lying today because there hadn't been a lot of rain to make its way down from the valley hills.

Large, glossy rooks chattered overhead. They were gathering materials for their nests, sometimes dropping an overambitious branch. On the other side of the river was a heron, still and aloof, its beak held high as if in disapproval of the noisy rabble in the treetops.

Kathi went through in her mind all the little comments and insults Jake had thrown her way recently; you're not my mum, you're so selfish, I hate you, I wish you'd never adopted me, you don't even try to understand what I'm going through. She found this last accusation particularly hurtful because she felt all she'd done for the past eighteen months was try to see things from his point of view.

She thought about his shoplifting and how little remorse he'd shown despite being caught and made to apologise. She remembered how earnestly he'd told her he hadn't been skipping school and wondered whether or not this was another lie. Kathi reflected on how tough the teenage years can be. They're a time when all kids start to question who they are and how they fit into the world. She recalled how hard she'd found it and tried to remember how her parents had handled her teenage angst.

She'd read enough to know that this could be a very difficult period for many adopted children. They either knew nothing about their birth family and were left hanging, or what they did know wasn't particularly life affirming. Alternatively, their birth families came with memories of neglect, abuse and trauma.

She and Graham had drip fed Jake information about Marie over the years until now, at the age of 15, he knew almost as much as she did. What they hadn't yet shown him was his full adoption file. They didn't feel he was old enough to see it there in black and white, written in abrupt, professional and medical shorthand.

Jake's birth story was not one of trauma and abuse but it was one of abandonment. The woman who had carried him in her womb for nine months, who had given him life, and may even have held him in her arms, had decided she wasn't able to keep him.

Whilst Jake's rational brain might have understood that Marie wasn't able to look after him properly or that if she had kept him, he may still have ended up in care, his body and his heart knew deep down that Marie didn't choose him. There would forever be a question hidden within him that asked, what did I do wrong?

It made Kathi's heart ache to know she'd never be able to remove that question or eradicate his feelings of never being quite good enough. She wished Jake could spend a day outside of his body, to watch himself and observe. From a distance he'd be able to see what a wonderful child he was and just how much he was loved.

She wished he could see what a handsome and imaginative boy he was, filled with curiosity about how the world works. She wished he could admire his own resilience the way she did. She wanted him to be amazed, like she was, at how he jumped right back from any setback life threw at him. She wanted so much for him to give himself the credit he deserved for simply having been through what he'd been through. If he could see all that, he'd see there was nothing wrong with him and none of this was his fault.

But he couldn't. What, Kathi asked herself, could she do to help him through this? What could she do to stop him getting comfortable on that downward slide he seemed determined to ride? She wanted to give him a secure sense of his own identity, but knew that was something he was going to have to figure out in his own time.

Identity. What did that actually mean and did it change over time? Since Jake had dropped his bombshell about a possible other child, her own identity had shifted every so slightly. A small crack had appeared in the solid wall of security her ancestry had given her. Her life in Byreburn wasn't quite what she thought it was.

Kathi crossed over the river via a small wooden bridge and looped back into town. Border weather could so often be drab, but today it was bright and clear and for that she was thankful. The rain would have sunk her spirits even further. As it was, she felt as low as a snake's belly.

She found herself at Granny Marjorie's house and knocked before opening the front door. 'It's only me,' she called out. Marjorie made her way down the stairs, her housecoat on. It never failed to amuse Kathi that she still wore a housecoat at home. It transported her back in time to the 1950s and a vision of a young Marjorie, not this spry elderly woman, taking it one step at a time.

'Is everything alright, Kathi?' Marjorie asked when she got to the bottom of the stairs. She put a hand up to her granddaughter's face. 'You're very peaky.' Now that she was here, Kathi didn't really know what it was she wanted to say. Marjorie took her hand and led her into the tiny kitchen at the back of the house. It was dated and immaculately maintained. They sat down at the small leaf table.

'Tell me about my mum and dad.'

'What do you want to know?'

'How old were they when they met?'

'They weren't much older than Jake is now, when they first got together. I think they were 18 or 19.'

'Was it love at first sight?'

'I wouldn't say that,' Marjorie chuckled. 'They'd known each other since they were bairns. But once they started courting, there was no going back.' Marjorie smiled at Kathi. 'A bit like you and Graham.'

'How long were they together before they got married?'

'Quite a long time. Three or four years, I think.'

'And how long after they were married did they have me?'

'Very soon.' Marjorie looked at her granddaughter quizzically. 'I thought you knew this?'

'I did. I'm feeling nostalgic today, I guess. Did Mum have any boyfriends before Dad?'

'A few, yes, she was a very bonny girl.'

'Were any of those serious?'

'Not particularly. Is there something you're worried about?'

Kathi desperately wanted to tell Marjorie what Jake had said, but scared to upset her grandmother. What if it was all nonsense, said only to upset her? She didn't want to pass that onto Marjorie. It was difficult enough talking about her parents without bringing slander and gossip into the mix.

'Are there any photos of Mum and Dad when they first got together?'

'Yes, I'm sure there are. Why don't you go into the living room and have a look through the photo albums? I'll make us a pot of tea and some biscuits.'

The living room was cold. It wasn't used often, and Marjorie wouldn't put the heating on until November. Kathi shivered involuntarily when she went in, but soon forgot about the cold as she began to pour through the old photograph albums. To do so was to step back in time. Sitting on the floor, flipping the pages of the albums was comforting, like putting a soft and well-worn blanket over herself.

The clothes people were wearing, their hairstyles, the house decor and cars, were all from a bygone era. One that now felt so innocent compared with today's world of fast connections and global travel. Marjorie came in with the tray. 'Found anything?' she asked.

'There's some lovely ones of Mum as a girl. She looks so sweet.' Kathi showed her gran.

'I remember that dress,' Marjorie said, 'I made it for a cousin's birthday party. Your mum loved it and wore it every chance she got.'

Together they made their way through one album, then another. In time, Kathi's mum, Carol, grew up. Her hair changed style and colour, her makeup became increasingly colourful until it was full of the vibrancy of the 1980s.

'Oh my goodness,' said Marjorie, shaking her head. 'Would you take a look at that dress?' Carol was dressed in skin tight satin leggings and a baggy pirate-style top. Her hair was long and crimped. 'She thought she was Kate Bush.'

'She was beautiful,' said Kathi.

'Yes, she was.' Marjorie touched her daughter's face in the photo and quickly pulled her hand away. She stood up on the premise of looking out the window, but Kathi noticed her pull out a tissue from her housecoat pocket.

'I'm sorry, Gran,' Kathi said. 'I don't mean to upset you.'

'You haven't sweetheart, you haven't.'

Only two pages later, Kathi stopped in her tracks. There was a photo of both her parents, holding hands, at a family function. Both looked... Kathi couldn't quite find the word. The best she could come up with was preoccupied, as if they had just had an argument or were just about to. Carol's face was very pale, and she had no makeup on, no crimped hair. The polar opposite of the previous photos. Kathi was on the floor, surrounded by photograph albums. Marjorie sat on the sofa and looked over her shoulder.

'Mum doesn't look very well here,' Kathi said, pointing at the photograph.

'Does she not?'

'No. She looks very pale, and she's got no make-up on.'

'Oh yes, you're right.' Marjorie's tone was light, but it sounded forced.

'What year was it?' Kathi asked. They looked at the front of the album. 1971. Marjorie's fingers tapped lightly on her knee. 'Do you know,' she said, 'I think that was the year your mum had a really bad bug. She was laid out for weeks. Oh yes, I remember now.'

'You've never mentioned it before.' Kathi quizzed.

'No? Well, it was such a long time ago and I've forgotten most of your mum's ailments.'

'But this photo reminded you?'

'Yes, it has. Now, do you want some more tea?'

'Yes, please. I'll come through to the kitchen in a moment.' Kathi watched Marjorie busy herself with the cups on the tray. She couldn't get out of the room quick enough.

Kathi looked back at the photo of her mother. There was definitely something going on behind the eyes. Kathi flipped forward a few pages. The next photograph of her Carol was over a year later. This struck Kathi as odd. There were plenty of photographs, just none of Carol.

Kathi looked closer at the first photograph after of her mother after that long absence. Was she imagining it, or did Carol look like she'd put on weight? Her face looked round, her breasts and stomach looked fuller. But it was hard to be certain because Carol was no longer dressed in figure hugging leggings. Instead, she was wearing jeans and baggy T-shirts, all of which hid her body.

The lurching feeling that had been swaying in Kathi's stomach tilted fully when she put it all together. She knew she didn't have the full story, but it seemed all too clear that Jake's tale about another baby was very possible. 1971. It was before her birth and before her parents were married. Was it possible Kathi had a sibling out there?

Chapter 18

Cherry sat with Kathi in the surgery waiting room, but she found it difficult to sit still. She shifted her body one way and then another. She stood up, paced back and forth and sat down again.

'Oh God, Kathi,' she said, 'I'm so nervous.'

'I know,' said Kathi, giving her hand a squeeze.

The surgery was busy. There were mothers entertaining babies who were waiting for their jabs. There were the elderly with their sticks and zimmer frames, who slowly and noisily sat themselves down and heaved themselves up. She recognised a good number of the faces but an unspoken rule ensured there was just enough eye contact to say hello but not enough so that uncomfortable questions could be asked.

Only those who seemed to make a vocation of attending the surgery liked to discuss, in clear voices, why they were there and the history of their illness. Cherry recognised it in her own parents, which made her smile. The smile faded all too quickly as she realised that this would soon be her life as well.

Too nervous to make small talk with anyone, she was thankful to have Kathi there to deflect any unwanted chat. While Kathi chatted Cherry distracted herself with social media. So engrossed was she in a video of a little boy who could see properly for the first time after being given glasses, that she didn't notice Joanne Wylie and Sharon come in and sit opposite her. It was only when Cherry's name was called that she looked up and saw them.

'Hi Cherry,' said Joanne. 'What are you doing here? Hope everything is alright?'

Joanne's tone was light enough, but there was something about the way she looked over Cherry's shoulder she didn't like. When she turned around, it was clear Joanne was looking at Kathi. She smiled, ignored Joanne's question and followed Dr Brown through to her consulting room.

'I found a lump,' she blurted as soon as she sat down. 'I know what it means because my gran, my aunt and my cousin all had breast cancer. My gran and aunt died. My cousin was lucky because she caught it early. So you see, I know it's cancer and I need you to remove it before it gets any bigger.'

When Cherry had run out of breath, she stopped to watch Dr Brown consult her notes and waited intently for the doctor's response.

'Okay Cherry,' she said, 'let me take down a few details and then I'll have a look at the lump itself.'

After the examination, Dr Brown said, 'I can't say for definite what the lump is, but the fact that it's solid, rather than soft and pliable, gives me enough concern that I'm going to refer you for a biopsy.'

'Do you think it's cancer? It is, isn't it?'

'I don't know for definite but given your family history, your age and the texture of the lump, it's best to be cautious.'

'I knew it.'

'I will request an emergency appointment, but even then it can be three or four weeks until you're seen.'

'That's ages.'

'I agree it's longer than ideal, but we'll get you seen as soon as possible.' Dr Brown put the details into her computer and produced a referral letter. 'Give this to reception and they'll have it sent on today.'

Cherry took the letter and glanced over it. 'I'm shaking,' she told the doctor, and held out a hand.

'I know it's hard,' said Dr Brown, 'but try not to dwell on it. Carry on as normal. Remember, it could be benign.' Dr Brown tried to be cheerful as Cherry left the consulting room but Cherry knew there was a good chance her lump was carcinogenic.

In the waiting area, Joanne was sitting next to Kathi, and they were chatting. 'Everything alright, Cherry?' Joanne asked. 'You're white as a sheet.'

'Oh, I'm fine, Joanne, just routine stuff. Why are you here today?' Cherry didn't know why she asked, and immediately regretted it.

'Oh, it is not for me.' Joanne leaned in close. 'It's Sharon. Morning-after pill.' Her eyes widened in disapproval, implying she would never get herself into such a situation.

'Sorry to hear that. Listen, we've got to go, come on Kathi.'

'Look after yourself, Cherry,' Joanne said, winking.

'What was she winking at me for?' demanded Cherry as soon as they were out of earshot. 'You don't think she, you know, fancies me, do you?'

'Well, you are a hottie,' Kathi teased her.

'Oh, don't, it's not even funny. Have you seen her?'

'Never mind that, what did the doctor say?'

'Oh God, I totally forgot, I've got to hand this into the reception. Wait here a minute.' Cherry dived back into the surgery to hand over the form.

'Can you ask them to let me know about any cancellations?' she asked the receptionist. 'I need an appointment as soon as possible.'

'Uh-huh,' the receptionist replied, looking the form over, before dropping it into a filing tray.

'Don't forget to send that,' Cherry said. 'It's important.'

'We will, don't worry.'

'I'm a bag of nerves,' Cherry announced to Kathi when she came back outside. 'I can't think straight.'

'Come on and I'll take you for a drink.' They began walking towards the High Street. 'What did Dr Brown say?' Kathi asked.

'She wouldn't commit one way or the other, but she said it felt abnormal and so has requested an appointment for a biopsy.'

'When will that come through?'

'Not for weeks yet. I don't know how I'll be able to wait that long and not go crazy.'

'It'll be fine, Cherry, I promise.'

'That's a big promise to make.' Cherry rummaged around in her bag and pulled out some chewing gum. 'Maybe this will help,' she said, sticking a piece in her mouth. 'Thanks for coming with me today, it was a real help.'

When they reached the pub Kathi ordered them each a glass of wine and they sat at a table near the window. Cherry took a large gulp of wine. 'I needed that,' she said. 'What was Joanne saying to you?'

'She's very... she's quite...'

'Straight to the point?'

'Yes.'

'I know what you mean, but I like that about her.'

'She was asking about my business and how it was going. She seemed very interested and said she's going to buy a flat one day.'

'Not on the wage she's on, she won't. What? Don't look at me like that, it's true and you know it.'

'Has there been any plumbing work done at her flat since she moved in?'

'I don't think so. Why?'

'There was something she said about Graham that seemed a bit odd.'

'What?'

'She asked if it was hard knowing my husband out on plumbing jobs all the time. It was a weird question, and the way she said it made me think she knew something I didn't.'

'What on earth could she know about Graham?'

'That's the thing, I don't know. All this stuff with the troll and the other baby has got my mind playing tricks, I suppose. What if Graham has a secret love child hidden away somewhere?'

'Back up a minute,' said Cherry. 'What other baby?' Kathi brought her up to speed.

'Kathi, that is crazy talk and you know it. If your parents had had another baby, you'd know about it. End of conversation.'

'You're right, I know you are. It just thrown me a bit, that's all.'

Joanne sat back in her chair in the doctor's surgery. Her legs didn't quite reach the floor, and she swung them, just a little, back and forth, back and forth. She was pleased to have chatted with Kathi.

It was strange to sit so close to Jake's mother, and Joanne had taken in every detail of her face. She reluctantly admitted that Kathi was pretty, in a blond sort of way, and she was envious of her straight white teeth. But other than that, it was pleasing to see she was as ordinary as anyone else.

She wasn't going to speak to Kathi at first, but once her friend had been called through to the doctor and the two of them were left sitting side by side, she couldn't resist starting up a conversation.

'Hi Kathi.'

'Hi Joanne.'

'I hope Cherry's alright,' Joanne had said to her, but Kathi was engrossed in a magazine and didn't answer. That irked. 'I said, I hope Cherry's alright.'

'Yes.' Kathi smiled and went back to her magazine.

'Is it easy to buy a flat?' She could see Kathi didn't want to talk to her, but Joanne ducked her head down to make Kathi look at her.

'Sorry, what did you say?' Joanne enjoyed seeing the forced smile on Kathi's face.

'I said, is it easy to buy a flat?'

'If you've got the deposit ready, yes, it's easy.'

'How do you get a deposit?'

'You save up.'

'I work at the mill, I'd have to do a lot of saving.'

'You'll do it, I'm sure,' Kathi said, giving up on her magazine.

'Maybe.'

'You're not from here?'

'No, I'm from Glasgow. You ever been?'

'Yes, often. We go up for day trips, or to the theatre.'

'Who's we?' Joanne asked, getting up to stretch her legs.

'My husband, my son, and I.'

'Oh, right. I don't have a husband.' She stopped in front of Kathi and stared down at her.

'I see.'

'I lived with my mum before I came here. It must be hard.'

'What must be?' Kathi asked.

'Knowing your husband is out working all the time. On emergency call outs.' She used air quotes to emphasise those call outs.

'What do you mean?' Joanne noticed the startled look on Kathi's face.

'I'm all done,' announced Cherry, emerging from the consulting room. 'Come on, let's go.'

'It was nice to see you again,' Joanne said, watching Kathi head out the door.

Chapter 19

Jake and Lindsay were sitting in a secluded spot along the river's edge. It was October now, summer was well and truly over. Leaves were dropping from the trees and the long sunny days were now chilly and misty. They'd skipped school to go somewhere they could escape the confines of the classroom, and the ever observant eyes of the town gossips. It had rained recently, and the grass was damp. The cold slowly made its way through their uniforms like frost creeping over the forest floor. They didn't care. They felt free and reckless gazing up at the sky, blowing cigarette smoke into the air, smoke that matched the grey clouds almost perfectly.

'Has she said anything about the baby?' Lindsay asked.

'No, nothing. I think she's angry and has stopped talking to me.' They each took a drag and, much to Jake's envy, Lindsay blew perfect smoke rings up to the heavens. To him it was such a neat trick and gave Lindsay an air of sophistication he wanted to emulate.

He remembered Common Riding when they had first started getting to know each other. It seemed a lifetime ago when in fact it had only been a couple of months. He'd fancied her like mad at that time. Her long brown hair had been like a magnet to him. He loved the way she'd intermittently flick it over her shoulder and the way she had of twitching her head to the side to move her fringe out of her eyes.

Jake would watch her at school, talking to her friends, and it embarrassed him now to think of how much he'd showed off in front of her, trying to make her notice him. At that time he'd badly wanted to kiss her, but the closest he'd ever come to kissing was with that girl at the Christmas dance. She'd moved in to lock lips, but he'd backed off. He still didn't know what he was scared of, but he was.

Lying on the grass now, watching Lindsay blow smoke rings, he was amazed to think about what good friends they'd become. He no longer showed off when she was around because almost immediately all his obsessing over her had vanished. It felt great to have the pressure of impressing someone lifted from his shoulders. He still thought she was beautiful and amazing, but she was also his best friend.

'Who cares anyway?' Lindsay said matter-of-factly. 'I mean, think about it, it was years ago so everyone's forgotten. And let's be honest, the baby is probably with a really nice family and living an amazing life. Like you.' She took another drag. 'And whose family isn't fucked up?'

Jake turned his head to look at her, moved by a sad note in her voice. He knew better than to ask anything, though. Lindsay would tell him what she wanted to share and there was no use pushing her. From where they were lying, he could see the dark purple bloom on her cheekbone.

'We should get out of this town as soon as we can,' Lindsay said.

'Yeah.'

'Where should we go?'

'London.'

'London?' She scoffed. 'Not far enough. It's just the same as here, only more of it. No, we need to set our sights higher and bigger.'

'Like where?'

'New York? Los Angeles?'

'Maybe.'

After a pause Lindsay announced, 'Australia.' She said it with such certainty that Jake knew instinctively she'd get there, that's where she would achieve her dreams. 'Sandy beaches, clear blue waters, barbecues.'

'Sharks, snakes, deadly spiders.'

'Wanna come?' Lindsay asked, ignoring his sarcasm.

'Sure.' But he wasn't. He wasn't sure about anything except he wasn't happy here. Would he be any happier elsewhere? He didn't think so because he didn't even know what it was he was unhappy about. Even in Australia he'd still be Jake, he'd still not know where he came from or who his real mother was. Going to the other side of the world would only take him further away from finding the truth.

'You still hanging about with that Joanne?'

'Sort of. It's mostly just text messages.'

'I don't know what you see in her. She's old.'

'She's nice.' Jake found it hard to articulate to Lindsay what he liked about Joanne. There was something sympathetic about her. She didn't judge him or tell him his mum was amazing like every other adult. Maybe it was because she didn't quite fit in and was an outsider, just like him. Too often these days he felt like a cuckoo in the wrong nest and Joanne seemed to understand that. She was also the only person who agreed he should look for Marie by himself.

Kathi and the adoption people were always trying to keep her a secret, but he wanted to meet her, to look in her eyes and ask all the questions that had been building up over the years. What was her favourite colour? What car did she drive? What job did she have? Did she have any more children? Did she love him? So afraid of what the answer might be he hadn't acknowledged, even to himself, that what he really wanted to ask was did she want him back?

He hoped she regretted giving him up and wanted to be reunited, but he was terrified the answer would be no. He was scared she'd tell him she'd never wanted him and was glad when he was born because then she could finally be rid of him. Once he was out of the way she'd be free to have more children, cute babies that didn't cry and that she could shower with kisses and cuddles and never let go of.

If she were to say that to him he knew he'd never recover. The blow would be too much. It would be like turning into a ghost, he'd wander the streets and never be seen. People would walk straight through him and shiver.

At times he felt guilty for wanting Marie so much. When the hormones raging through his system exhausted themselves and slept, guilt raised a finger and tut-tut tutted. How could he be so disloyal to Kathi and Graham who loved him so much? They had given him a home when nobody else had. They were patient and forgiving of the vitriol he spat at them. How could he repay their kindness by wanting to be anywhere else but with them?

'You don't sound sure,' Lindsay said.

'About what?'

'Coming to Australia.'

'I am, I want to come.'

'Let's take a boat there, an all-inclusive luxury liner. We'll sleep as long as we want to in our cabin, we'll eat as much as we can at the eat-as-much-as-you-can buffet. We can go to the evening shows and drink champagne and eat fancy finger foods.' Jake smiled, enjoying the image Lindsay conjured. 'We'll dock at Sydney and be so fat they'll have to roll us down the gangplank.' This made them laugh, and they rolled from side to side on the grassy riverbank, in imitation of the steep plank.

All of a sudden Lindsay let out a roar that started right down in the pit of her stomach. As soon as she ran out of air she took a breath and started again. Jake saw tears run from the corner of Lindsay's eyes down to her temple and pool into the folds of her ear. He roared too. At first it was to keep her company, but with each breath it became more heartfelt and little by little he expelled days of frustration and confusion. Afterward they were both exhausted, panting with the exertion of using their tar infected lungs to full capacity.

In the distance the school bell rang, marking the end of the academic day. Jake got up first, then pulled Lindsay to her feet. Their bums were damp from the grass but their bodies were warm from the rolling and the roaring. Lindsay dished out a couple of extra strong mints and they sucked on the sweets as they made their way back to school.

'Don't forget,' said Lindsay when they got to his road. 'Australia.' She punched him playfully on the arm and moved on towards home.

As soon as he got through the front door his phone pinged. It was Joanne.

Any news about RM?

It took him a moment to realise RM stood for Real Mum.

Not yet

What's stopping you?

He didn't have an answer, so didn't reply. Not long afterward another message came through.

??

I don't know where to look.

Kathi will have an adoption file. Find it.

Jake looked at his watch. It wasn't yet four o'clock, his parents wouldn't be home for another hour yet. Feeling clandestine, he made his way to Kathi and Graham's study. He stood on the threshold, looking around the small study. On Kathi's side the room was filled beyond capacity with folders and files, books on shelves and on the floor, newspaper cuttings, decorating magazines and even Graham's trade catalogues. He never needed to go into this room other than to occasionally use Kathi's computer. Even that he hadn't done in ages, not since he'd been given his own laptop. He didn't know where anything was kept and couldn't see an obvious place to start.

He took a deep breath and walked stridently to Kathi's desk, one ear cocked in case she came home unexpectedly. He pulled open the desk drawers and had a rummage, but mostly they were filled with old pens and rubber bands, business cards and mailshots, or receipts from DIY stores like B&Q and Homebase.

He moved over to her bookshelf, upon which were folders labelled with the properties Kathi owned, and the paperwork relating to each. There were bank statements neatly filed, a key cupboard with more keys than seemed necessary. There were lots of folders labelled tax, but nothing labelled Jake or Adoption. He looked amongst the magazines piled on the floor. Nothing. He moved over to Graham's side of the room. His desk was sparse, only his laptop, one tray of filing and one pen pot. No drawers to look through. He had five lever-arch files, some for invoices, some for tax. Again, nothing that hinted at Jake's adoption. By now the tension had built to tipping point and it was with relief he exited the room, certain he hadn't left any signs of his intrusion, but he never failed to be disappointed at how little escaped Kathi's notice.

In the safety of his bedroom he messaged Joanne

Nothing in her office.

Look in the bedroom.

She'll be home any minute

I just saw her go in the Co-op

He stood outside his parents' bedroom, not knowing what to do next. Sure, he wanted to find his adoption papers, but he didn't want to get caught snooping. He'd been in enough trouble recently. Still, he knew Kathi and Graham had been selective in what they'd told him about Marie and why he had been put up for adoption. There was stuff they weren't telling him, and he had a right to know. It was about him, after all. He was just about to enter the room when he heard Graham come in the house.

'Jake, you home?' he called.

'Upstairs.' Relieved to be off the hook for now, Jake snuck into his own room and messaged Joanne to tell her his dad was home.

Graham knocked and stuck his head round the bedroom door. 'Good day?' he asked.

'All right,' Jake said, making a pretext of unpacking his schoolbag and sorting his homework. Graham was looking at him in a funny way.

'What?' he demanded.

'Nothing.' He looked like he wanted to say more but said only, 'I'm going to have a shower.'

Jake slumped on his bed, all too aware that his parents were watching his every move and trying to second-guess him. He felt like they were waiting for him to make a mistake, to get something else wrong and give them the excuse they needed to kick him out. It went through his mind a lot these days, that he should save them the trouble of finding a reason to get rid of him and go of his own accord.

In the plan his imagination had devised, he'd to head to school but instead of turning left he'd turn right towards the High Street and the bus stop. From there he would take the bus to Glasgow because that was where Marie lived. That was where he would find his real mum. All he had to do was find her address, and he'd make his way to her. He dreamed about it time and again.

At night he dreamed about taking a bus that dropped him off in front of the garden gate of Marie's semi-detached home. The lawn would be neatly mowed and flowers would sit primly in their weeded flower beds. There would be a car parked in the driveway and the front door would be white, with a multi-coloured glass panel through which he would see Marie's blurred outline as she came to open it. The door would open and there she'd be, dressed in simple jeans and a t-shirt. For some reason he could never see her face. It remained as blurred as it had been behind the glass. He'd blink, but she'd remain unclear. He'd rub his eyes, but still her face would be washed out, and he'd be unable to tell if she was pleased to see him on not.

The dream would always turn into a horror show because a miasma of disappointment would rise up from the lawn and engulf him, pulling him away from her. He'd stretch his arms out to her for help, pleading with her not to let him slip out of her life again, but she'd remain where she was. He would sense her confusion and embarrassment and in the end she would close the door again. Just before the miasma covered his face, Jake would wake up. He wouldn't sit bolt upright, gasping for air as if escaping a nightmare, like he'd seen in movies. Instead, his eyes would pop open, calmly and quietly, is if merely surprised. After a while, he'd fall back into a dreamless sleep.

Jake felt something on his arm and, startled, sat up.

'You fell asleep.' It was Kathi, smiling at him. She enveloped him in her arms and, feeling disorientated, he let her. It felt nice. 'Dinner is on the table. Come down when you're ready.' She stood up to leave, but before she did, she reached out a hand and tenderly moved some strands of hair from his eyes.

'I'm sorry,' he said, surprising them both.

'For what?'

'For everything.'

'We'll get through this.'

'Will we?'

'Yes.'

'How can you be sure?'

'Because you are a smart, resilient boy and with time you'll figure out what's going on in there, and there.' Kathi placed one hand on his head and one over his heart.

'Thanks Mum,' he said, smiling. Kathi left his room, closing the door quietly behind her.

Chapter 20

It had been a few weeks since Kathi had last received a message from her troll, and she'd begun to think that whoever it was had grown bored and moved on. She also thought that if it had been Jake, things had so improved between them that perhaps he didn't have the need to take his anger out on her anymore.

Feeling positive about the upward trend in their relationship, Kathi was inspired to write a new blog post about the small moments upon which a mother or father can look back upon and think, I handled that well; today I was a good parent.

'As parents you plough through the day, cajoling your kids into putting their clothes on to keep warm, giving them unhealthy snacks to make them eat healthy meals, loading and unloading the endless dirty washing basket and refereeing the never ending arguments about how much iPad time is enough. In amongst all that are the moments that send endorphins shooting around your bodies and give you the best type of natural high. Like when your child laughs at your joke, or in a quiet moment comes in for a hug, or maybe even asks for advice. Those are the moments that make life's mundane chores worthwhile.

I had one of those yesterday. For the first time in a long time my son and I had a frank and heartfelt conversation, at the end of which he smiled at me. Not with sarcasm or because he wanted something but because, for those few moments, he lowered his guard and let me love him. His beautiful smile was like a firecracker going off in my heart and I felt so proud that for the first time in a long time, I managed to say the right thing. And that, my friends, is no mean feat!'

Just then a new message arrived, and without a second thought Kathi opened it. She was confronted with a photograph of herself, scowling, looking as though she'd stepped into an abyss. Kathi's stomach dropped. Like ripping off a plaster, it removed any pretext she had of anonymity. Whoever this troll was, they were not a bored kid, and they had not moved on. They knew who she was, and they were here in Byreburn. This meant that despite her efforts to the contrary, she had not only opened up her private life to the faceless Internet but to a walking, talking, emailing person who did not like her.

Prank or no prank, Kathi felt vulnerable and scared. She felt caught out by both the troll and by Graham, who had advised her not to write the blog in the first place. He didn't want their lives put out there for everyone to see. The longer she looked at the photo, the more she panicked. Fear forced her up and out of her study and into the kitchen where she could hide from her computer.

If she couldn't see the message, then she could tell herself it wasn't there, that it was merely a cruel trick of the light, or that perhaps her laptop was developing a sense of humour. But the lure of the mystery beckoned her, and after a few minutes she marched back into the office, her expression set in grim determination.

She looked at the photograph and tried to work out when it had been taken. She was outside the refurbishment property and wearing her green coat, so it must have been a cool but not cold day. The last time she'd worn that coat was the day she found out about Jake's shoplifting. Judging by the scowl on her face, Brian must already have told her about the stealing and she was on her way to the car or to see Iris.

Kathi next attempted to work out where the photograph had been taken from. Betty's Beauty Parlour was in the background, which meant it must have been taken from the park end of the road. There was a small World War One memorial park. Beyond that was the Duke's Wood. In the wood were lots of walkways and hidey-holes in which a snooping troll might hide.

Curious, Kathi drove to the property and walked towards the memorial park. She turned around to face her property, outside of which she was pleased to see Brian's van. Cherry's new schedule for him was working.

On her phone she looked again at the photograph. Yes, this was definitely the place from where it had been taken. The fact the photo had been taken early one midweek morning suggested the person was local. Byreburn was not on the way to anywhere. You had to make a decision to come through the town.

Kathi's next question was who would be interested enough in her to go to the effort of sending vicious emails and follow her around town so early in the morning? She felt sure she knew the person, but for the life of her couldn't think who it might be.

'Are you alright, Kathi?' It was Marjorie. She followed Kathi's line of vision. 'What are you looking at?'

'Oh, nothing in particular.'

'Don't hang about street corners too long,' she joked. 'You know how people like to talk around here.' Ever busy, Marjorie moved on with a full bag of groceries that needed to be put in the fridge, chuckling at her own joke.

Kathi slowly turned three hundred and sixty degrees, trying to think of anybody who lived nearby who might hate her enough or was bored enough to come down to the park and take a photograph of her. There were a lot of popular walks through the Duke's Wood, some leading up to the surrounding hills, others looping back into other parts of the town.

The road on which she stood and where the memorial park was situated, led up to the High Street. It was only a few minutes' walk and so the person could easily have come from that direction. Alternatively, it could be somebody who lived on the street itself, or was angry that she'd bought the property in the first place. Eventually her eyes rested again on Marjorie, only now disappearing out of sight.

Like an arrow from the back of her consciousness, a thought broke through. It didn't stop on Go; it didn't collect £200; it went straight to Mayfair and suggested, Could it be the missing child?

Kathi thought back to her conversation with Marjorie, who mentioned that Carol had been very ill in 1971.

She called Graham. 'I know we've talked about this, but are you sure you haven't heard any rumours about my mum and dad having another child?'

'Are you still worrying about this? Babe, Jake only said that to wind you up.'

'I'm not worrying about it, I just wondered.' There was no way Kathi was going to share her theory with Graham, he already thought she was obsessing over it, and perhaps she was, but there was something about this hunch that resonated, and deep in the pit of her stomach she felt she was on to something.

'Not that I've ever heard of,' said Graham. 'Look, I've got to go, I'll speak to you later.'

Kathi and Graham's terraced house didn't have an attic, but it did have limited storage space in the eaves and many moons ago, when her parents had died, she'd hidden away a suitcase of old letters and documents and memorabilia. Nostalgia rather than anything practical had made her hang on to the ephemera. She dragged it out of its hiding place and brought it, complete with dust and cobwebs, to the kitchen table. She placed it down delicately and gingerly opened the lid.

Inside was a haphazard jumble of items. They looked as if they'd been thrown in randomly, and perhaps they had been. One by one, she removed each item and gave it the once over, looking for anything with Carol's name on it or that mentioned a baby. She found certificates relating to the births, deaths and marriages of her ancestors, going all the way back to the 1800s. There was even a last will and testament dated 1804. He must've had a bit of money if a will was necessary, she thought. In amongst the official documents were studio portraits of long ago relatives in their tight corsets and high collars. Their clothes and stern expressions made them seem as close to her life now as aliens from Jupiter. There were more recent snapshots of families gathered at Christmas and of children singing around a birthday cake. Many of the faces she recognised, but a lot of them she didn't, and Kathi supposed they must be her mother's Glasgow family.

When she happened upon the snapshot of a woman and child who looked so different from the rest she was forced to stop and look more closely. Judging by the hairstyle and clothes, this photo had been taken in the 1970s. Instinct told Kathi this photo didn't belong with the others. This woman did not belong in Byreburn.

The woman was kneeling on the floor, her arms reaching out to a girl in the foreground, as if beckoning the child to sit on her knee. There was something about the woman's body language that told Kathi she was the girl's mother, but they didn't look alike.

The girl looked six or seven years old, but instead of smiling at the camera like her mother, she was scowling at whoever was taking the picture. Kathi couldn't decide if something had just happened, or was about to happen. She stared hard into the child's eyes, as if she might divine something prophetic from the expression. But nothing came, and so she looked at the room itself. It was a living room and sparsely decorated by today's standards. The carpet, the walls and even the furniture looked to be various shades of brown or beige, and Kathi couldn't discern any clues as to where this was or who these people were. She flipped the photo over and on the back was written 1979 Lola, but it wasn't clear if Lola was the woman or the child. Kathi wondered whose the handwriting was, and who thought these people important enough to keep a photo of them.

Kathi started packing away all the things she'd pulled out of the case, giving them a second glance as she did so. A piece of sky blue paper caught her eye. All that was written was a partial address, Cressland Place. She put the paper on the table next to the photo. For some reason, Kathi knew the two were connected. She put everything back in the case and closed it. With the photograph and strip of paper, she headed to her computer.

Into Google she typed the street name. It brought up a number of Cressland Places, in different towns across the UK and beyond. For no other reason than desperation, she added the name Lola to the search. There, at the top of the results page, was the thumbnail of a census report. Next to it was some text picked out from the census that mentioned both Cressland Place and the name Lola. Kathi clicked on the result. Up popped a page telling Kathi she could only access this page if she paid for it.

'Bugger,' she muttered. She searched around the Internet a bit longer, trying to find the information for free but unable to she bowed to her curiosity and opened an account with Ancestry. They seemed to have what she needed. She went through the motions of opening the account, but it was only when she put her credit card details into the system that Aladdin's Cave fully revealed its treasures. In there she found access to a plethora of births, deaths and marriages, ships' records, wills and obituaries, photographs of gravestones, phone directories and employment records, not to mention a kaleidoscope of newspaper archives. Opening a new page, she typed Cressland Place Lola, and clicked on the link. This time she was taken straight through to the image of the census return. Kathi greedily looked through the return, gathering what information she could. Lola was seventeen years old, she lived at number 12 Cressland St, her mother was Euphemia and her father Harold. The names jarred with Kathi. They didn't seem quite right, after all, who the hell was called Euphemia these days? Or Harold, for that matter. The elation Kathi had felt only a moment ago began to deflate and when she looked at the census date. 1921. This was not the Lola she was looking for. Cross with herself for thinking she could solve the mystery so quickly, Kathi stumped to the kitchen and poured a glass of wine. It was four o'clock, Jake would be home soon, she'd better start thinking about dinner. She replenished her glass and mulled over the mysterious Lola. It wasn't until she'd finished the second glass of wine that it dawned on Kathi it was nearly five o'clock and neither Jake nor Graham were home. She checked her phone. No messages. As if on cue, Graham opened the door.

'Is Jake with you?' she asked.

Chapter 21

'No,' said Graham. 'Isn't he home yet?' Seeing the concern on his wife's face, Graham said, 'Don't worry, he'll have gone to Hayden's house to play Fortnight or something.' Kathi picked up her phone and rang Jake's number. It went straight to voicemail, so she left a message. She next called Hayden's mum.

'Hi, it's Kathi, Jake's mum... Yes, fine thanks. Listen, I don't suppose Jake's at your house, is he?' Kathi looked up at Graham and shook her head. She rang Marjorie and Iris in case he'd popped in to see them, but they hadn't seen him.

'I'm worried,' Kathi told Graham. 'I can't help but think something has happened.'

'I'm sure there's a reason why he's late and anyway it's only just after five o'clock.'

'Something has happened, I know it has.'

'Alright, give it an hour and if he's still not back, I'll have a drive around,' Graham said. 'See if I can find him.'

An hour later, Jake still hadn't turned up. She tried Jake's number again, but still it went through to voicemail.

'I'll come with you,' Kathi said to Graham as he headed out the door.

'You stay here, call me if he comes back.'

'Graham,' Kathi grabbed his hand when he reached for the car keys, 'do you think he's run away?'

'No, I don't. I think he's mucking about with his pals somewhere and lost track of time. But he's gonna get such a bollocking for worrying us that he won't to do it again.'

'Don't get angry with him,' called Kathi, but he had already closed the door. The last thing she wanted to do was eat, but for the sake of something to occupy herself, Kathi began, half heartedly, preparing dinner. For her nerves, she poured another glass of wine. 'Jake will be hungry when he gets home,' she said out loud. 'That boy eats so much these days. He's late, he'll be extra hungry.'

'Who will be?' Kathi jumped and spun round at the sound of Iris's voice.

'Jesus, you gave me a heart attack.'

'Who are you talking to?'

'Myself.'

'First sign of madness, that.'

'What are you doing here?'

'Graham called me.'

'Here, give me that.' Kathi was chopping carrots, wielding the knife around so erratically, chopping them into smaller and smaller pieces until they were of no use for anything. Iris nudged her aside and took over. 'Fill the pan,' she instructed. 'Put it on the hob to boil.' Kathi did as she was told. 'Is it mince you're cooking?' Kathi nodded. 'Get it from the fridge, then.' As she did so, the front door opened again. Both women turned expectantly.

'Only me,' said Marjorie. 'Not turned up yet?'

'Not yet,' said Iris with a tone that said "he will".

Marjorie took quick stock of the situation and began peeling the potatoes for boiling. She and Iris moved easily around each other, gathering what was needed. A lifetime's experience of preparing family meals showed itself in their hands as they added a sprinkle of salt or dollop of butter, a stir of the pan. Kathi meanwhile paced between the front windows and the back, her ears attuned to the sound of approaching cars.

Eventually she called Graham, who told her there was no sign of him.

'I'll walk down to the King's Bridge, see if he's gone that way.'

'No need, Dad is on it. Stay there in case he comes home.' With nothing else to do, Kathi sat in the kitchen nursing her wine. Before she realised she was even thinking it, Kathi asked, 'Who is Lola?' Both women looked at her, faces blank. 'I found a photograph of a woman and a child. On the back it said Lola 1979.'

Iris looked at Marjorie. 'I can't remember anyone called Lola, can you?'

'Maybe she was a friend of your mothers.' Something in Marjorie's body language told Kathi she was hiding something, but she didn't ask anymore.

'Maybe.' Kathi knew she wasn't. She was certain Lola was connected to their family, but thought it best not to say anything in front of Marjorie. 'I am being trolled,' she said after a while.

'Trolled?' Marjorie asked. 'What's she talking about?'

'I have no idea,' said Iris.

'It's when somebody sends nasty images or messages on the Internet.'

'What did your troll do?' Marjorie said.

'Sent some nasty emails, you know, things like you're a horrible person, you're ruining people's lives, buying all the houses I do. Oh, and I'm a terrible mum.'

'That's not very nice, is it?' Iris said.

'No,' said Marjorie. 'What can you do about it?'

'Nothing, I don't know who it is.'

'Why are they focusing on you? How do they know you?'

Kathi blushed. She hadn't told them about the blog. 'I write a diary about my life and put it on the Internet.'

'So other people can read it?' The two older women looked at each other in disbelief.

'But now they've sent a photo of me, by the memorial park.'

'So they must be local then?' Iris said.

'But that's just it, there's nothing on my website that says where I live, only that it's the Borders.'

'They must've found out.'

'Yes, but how?'

Iris shrugged her shoulders.

'Is that why you were hanging about the park when I saw you the other day?' Marjorie asked. Kathi nodded.

'I was trying to figure out where they were standing when they took the photograph, see if I could work out which direction they came from.'

'And did you?'

'No, they could have come from anywhere.'

They were silent for a while as Marjorie put the potatoes on to boil and Iris flavoured the mince. Kathi picked up her phone in case Graham had rung and she hadn't heard or Jake had messaged to say he was on his way home. Nothing. She went to the front door, opened it and stepped out onto the pavement. The cool air was refreshing after the heat of the kitchen, but too soon she was cold and went back in.

'So who do you think your troll is?' Iris asked.

'They are not my troll.'

'Why would you put your diary on the Internet?' asked Marjorie.

'It's not exactly a diary, it's my thoughts on parenthood, running a business, that sort of thing. It is not my actual diary.'

'Well, that's a relief because publishing your diary before you're dead would be a daft thing to do. What's it called again, trolling?'

'Yes.'

'I've heard about that,' said Iris. 'You know that nice woman who does the history programs?'

'Lucy Worsley?' said Marjorie.

'No, the other one, Mary something.'

'Mary Berry?'

'No, she's the cooking one.'

'Mary Beard.' Kathi put them out of their misery.

'Mary Beard, that's it, well she's been trolled. I read about it in the newspaper. People said some horrible things to her. I don't know why, all she wants to do is tell us a bit of a history.'

'She's a very clever woman,' said Marjorie. They all grunted in agreement. Marjorie's face suddenly dropped, and she turned a horrible white colour.

'What, what is it?' Kathi demanded.

'I don't like to say.'

'Spit it out, Marjorie,' said Iris.

'You don't think the troll…' Neither Kathi nor Iris had thought of this but now Marjorie had said it out loud they fell silent, thinking about whether or not it possible. Kathi decided it was.

'Oh my God.' Her voice was high, almost shrill, unable to control the panic flying around inside her. 'Please God, please God, please God,' she muttered over and over while dialling Graham's number. 'Do you think it's the troll that's done it?' She asked him as soon as he picked up.

'Done What?'

'Taken Jake.' Graham didn't answer. 'Do you think it could be?'

'No, no, it's too far-fetched.'

'But you do hear about things like that happening.'

'Not in Byreburn. People here don't get kidnapped.'

'Remember that guy who disappeared?'

'He wandered off drunk, that's different.'

'Is it?'

'Yes it is, stop scaring me.'

'It's nearly nine o'clock, we should be scared.'

'I'll call Dad, see if he's got news.'

Kathi looked at the other two. Even Iris couldn't hide her worries now. Marjorie grabbed her granddaughter's hand in desperation.

Chapter 22

'She's booked another appointment for me to see the shrink.' Jake was slouched on Joanne's sofa. He'd bumped into her after school, they'd got chatting and she'd invited him home for a cup of tea. After the tea, Joanne said she was having a glass of wine and offered him a beer. He was delighted and said yes.

This was one of the reasons he liked her so much; she didn't treat him like a child. She made him feel like an adult or at the very least nearly an adult, rather than a 15-year-old teenager. The beer wasn't very tasty, a bit bitter, watery and fizzy. But just cupping the can in his hand made him feel grown up, and he practiced holding it in different ways, finding the right place for it to feel comfortable and casual.

It wasn't as easy as it looked because the can was big in his hands and so cold it made his fingers chilly and he was forced to put it on the table. He hoped Joanne didn't notice his ineptitude, although he was fairly sure that even if she did notice, she wouldn't care.

He watched Joanne pour her wine and take a long gulp. Watching her, and young as he was, he recognised that Joanne was not one of life's winners. That was another reason he liked her. He wasn't one either. Lyndsay wouldn't admit it, but neither was she. He wasn't able to put it into words, but Jake felt he and Joanne were misfits together. Neither of them were from Byreburn, neither of them belonged here, but for different reasons they found themselves in this town and had to find their own niche.

'Why did you move here?' Jake asked. 'If I could choose where to live, it definitely wouldn't be here. It's a shit town where nothing happens.'

'Oh, I wouldn't be so sure of that.'

'What you mean? Nothing exciting ever happens.'

'Byreburn might be small and unexciting, but there are worse places. At least you're loved here, you've got prospects.'

'Where did you used to live?'

'I grew up with my mum and gran in a council flat on an estate in Glasgow. There were no jobs and too many drugs. There was lots going on there, but none of it good. My nana wasn't like your grannies. She didn't care about me like they do about you.' Joanne took another swig of her wine. 'She was horrible to me and my mum, always telling us how useless we were. She made Mum's life miserable with her drinking, her dirty language and quick hands.'

'Why was she like that?' Jake asked.

'Mum says it was because Granddad left her with no money and a baby to look after. But, you know, that happens to lots of women and they don't turn out bitter old witches. Mum left as soon as she could and married my dad. She said he made her feel special for the first time in her life. I know they were happy together in the beginning. Mum said so.' She sighed heavily and for the first time Jake felt a bit sorry for Joanne.

'You might not think you've got much,' she said to him, 'but it's better than it could be. Where do you think your real mum lives?' As she asked, she leaned over and offered him a cigarette.

'Have you started smoking?'

'No. Someone left them here. Take one, I won't tell.' Jake took one, and she lit for him. 'Well?' She prompted. 'Where do you think she is?'

'I know she's in Glasgow. Mum – I mean Kathi – told me. I think she'll be married. She's probably got other kids by now.' He took a drag.

'What do you think her house is like?' Shy at first, then warming to the picture, he told Joanne about the semi-detached house and picket fence he often dreamed about.

'It sounds nice,' she said. 'If I had another mum, that is what I'd want too. And when I turned up at the door she'd open it, know who I was and welcome me in with a big cuddle.' She didn't tell Jake that in this daydream she'd be slim with white teeth and long shiny hair. In her fantasy, she was the sort of daughter a mother couldn't help be proud of.

'In my dream,' Jake said, 'I look just like my mum. We have the same hair colour and eye colour, and we like the same things. If she hadn't had to give me up, we would have done everything together and been best friends.' He took another drag, Joanne refilled her glass.

'Did you ever find your adoption papers?'

'No, I can't find them anywhere.'

'You've not looked hard enough. Kathi must have the information somewhere, she can't keep it secret from you forever.'

'I know, but I've looked everywhere. I can't find it.'

'Maybe she's got a safe deposit in a bank somewhere and keeps all her secret stuff there.'

'I don't think so,' Jake laughed. 'She might be well off but she's not a big time crook with a load of gold stashed away in the bank on the High Street.' The beer was making him lightheaded.

'Where is it then?'

'I don't know. Why are you so interested, anyway?'

'Because you're my friend and you have the right to know who your real mum is. You deserve to know. She's probably been looking for you all these years and doesn't know where to look. Did you ever think about that?'

'Do you really think so?' Jake had never considered that Marie might be looking for him. His eyes shone at the very idea.

'I know so. I've seen it on the telly, that program about long-lost families being reunited. Mums never forget about their kids, they always want to find them. Your mum will be the same.'

Jake had seen that program and realised Joanne was right. His mum really was trying to find him. He felt it in his soul. He felt her calling his name through the airwaves like a homing beacon, bringing him back to where he belonged. 'Have you got a basement in your house? What about an attic?'

He sat bolt upright. 'Yes, we've got space in the roof, Mum calls it the eaves. There's loads of stuff up there. I bet that is where she keeps it.'

'Bingo!' said Joanne, and they clinked drinks. She got him another beer from the fridge.

'No,' he said. 'I should go really.'

'Why?'

'They'll be wondering where I am.'

'I bet they've not even noticed. You said it yourself, Graham is always working, and all Kathi thinks about is her property empire and how to rip people off.' Persuaded, he took the can. 'Do you know what I heard?' Joanne said, opening a fresh bottle of wine. 'I heard she pays a backhander to the estate agents, if they help secure the deal.'

'She wouldn't do that.'

'She so would, she's no fool is Kathi. All the investors do it, how else can they buy so many properties at low prices?'

'Is that what she does, buy them for low prices?'

'Absolutely. That's what she did with this place and the one she's doing up now. That's people's inheritance, and she's robbing them of it. That's what I don't like about the whole business.'

'Why do you rent from Mum if she's so bad?' Joanne looked at him, making him feel like a simpleton.

'I didn't have a choice, did I? Your mum and Cherry have the whole town sewn up. And I've got to live somewhere, haven't I? I can't go back to Glasgow.'

'No, I guess not.'

'Tomorrow, when she's out, go up to the eaves and I bet you'll find what you're looking for.' She heaved herself up from the sofa, swaying slightly from the afternoon drinking. 'I am starving, I'll bang on a pizza. Margarita or Hawaiian?'

'Hawaiian. I love hot pineapple.' This made them both laugh. Jake moved over to beside the telly and looked through Joanne's DVD collection. 'Let's watch a movie,' he said. 'A comedy.'

Joanne chose Anchor Man. 'It's an oldie but a goodie,' she said. She put the film on and they settled down to watch. It felt nice there in Joanne's little flat. He could relax on the sofa, not hide in his bedroom by himself. He felt at home. The sounds of Joanne moving about the kitchenette and making dinner were comforting. He had no fear of being nagged by Kathi to do his homework, turn his phone off or put away his Switch. This is what life should be like, he told himself. If he was with his real mum, it would feel like this all the time.

'I'd better go home,' Jake said once the movie and the pizza were finished. 'I've got that appointment with the shrink tomorrow and Kathi is going to love the fact I've been out late. I bet she makes a big deal about it, blows it all out of proportion like she always does.'

'Don't go, then.'

'It gets me out of school,' he said, only half joking. The truth was, he wanted to go to the session. Despite his reluctance and the tears of last time, he did feel a lot better afterward and for a time felt closer to Kathi. Plus, he couldn't deny it was comforting to have someone listen to him without judging and who had no agenda of their own. He didn't fully understand what it was about this tiny Irishwoman that made him feel safe. Even when she was challenging him he didn't feel criticised. All she wanted was for him to think about how he was feeling and by doing that understand himself better. What he did find difficult was that his opinions and feelings changed from day to day, hour to hour even. It was impossible to make sense of them when they wouldn't stand still long enough for him to take a good look.

What had surprised Jake the most about the sessions was that they were confidential. He had fully expected everything he said to be reported back to Kathi, and so really it would have made no difference who he was talking to. The fact that Kathi was not privy to the conversation and would only be told what he was happy to share was a revelation. It left him free to be honest with Brenda. Not entirely honest, though. There were still things he felt about his parents he didn't like admitting to himself, never mind someone else, confidential or otherwise.

'I've always thought it was a waste of time,' Joanne interrupted his thoughts.

'What was?'

'Therapy, counselling, whatever you want to call it. Sitting around talking about yourself, having a moan to someone you've paid. It's not going to make your problems go away.'

'No, I suppose not.'

'Are you listening?'

'Yes, I am.'

'Doesn't seem like it. Why don't you tell her you don't want to go?'

Jake thought about how he could explain it to Joanne without sounding like an idiot, but he knew she wouldn't understand. If he told her that Brenda gave him a safe space and he really needed that time just now, she'd laugh in his face. He also had a niggling feeling that if he did manage to tell her, she would be jealous. 'It gets me out of school,' he repeated.

'See you,' she called to him as step-by-step he made his way down from her flat to street level.

'Jake,' she called down to him. He slowly turned round to look back up at her. 'Remember not to tell Kathi you were here. She won't like it.' Joanne closed the door and went to her bedroom window from where she watched him meander his way down the High Street.

Just before Jake got to his turnoff, Joanne saw Graham's van screech to a halt. He got out and started shouting at Jake, but quickly realised he was drunk. It was clear Graham's anger dropped away, and instead he helped Jake into the van.

Chapter 23

Graham opened the back door into the kitchen and his expression told Kathi all was not well. As soon as she saw Jake she rushed to him, desperate to reassure herself, he was unharmed.

'Jake,' she said. 'Thank God, are you alright? We've been worried sick.'

She held his face in her hands and only then noticed his eyes were bloodshot and his pupils dilated. She sniffed. 'Have you been drinking?'

'He's had a couple of beers, that's all.' Graham spoke for his son.

Jake noticed the room was filled with grannies and only then did it begin to dawn on him that he was in real trouble. He felt his only choice was to brazen it out. Granny Marjorie had always been the softest on him, so he made a beeline for her.

'Granny,' he beamed and swayed his way over to her. 'Lovely granny, what are you doing here?' He leaned over her at the kitchen table and hugged her a little too forcefully. Marjorie patted his arm, a little embarrassed.

'They're all here because they were worried about you,' said Kathi. To Graham she said, 'Where was he?'

'I found him on the High Street, on his way home.'

'Where were you?' Kathi turned again to her son.

'Nowhere,' he slurred, still grinning.

'Don't give me that,' she snapped. 'You don't come home after school, you don't tell us where you are and to top it all you stagger home drunk.'

'Says you?'

'What do you mean?'

'You're not exactly sober yourself, are you?' He picked up the empty bottle of wine on the table. 'It only takes one glass and you're pissed. You are what they call a cheap date.' He said this with such relish that Kathi wanted to lash out at him, but she wrapped her arms around herself instead.

'Where have you been?'

'I am not telling you.' Jake's expression flipped from a smile to revulsion before returning to the smile again as he focused on Iris. He sat down next to her. 'Granny Iris, there was no need to worry, I was with a friend.'

'Which friend was that?' Iris asked.

'Oh, nobody you know.'

'Tell us where you've been,' demanded Kathi, her face thunderous.

'Calm down, Kathi,' said Graham. 'Let Jake go to bed. We can talk about this in the morning.'

'Yeah, Mum,' mocked Jake. 'Let's talk about in the morning. There's a good little woman.'

'I don't think you realise what big trouble you are in young man,' said Kathi, marching over to him. Jake's face contorted into a sneer and he imitated her in a high-pitched whining voice. The humiliation of being talked to like that in front of everybody, the fear of being out of control of the situation, and the effect of her own alcohol consumption, removed Kathi's rationale and she slapped Jake hard across the face. 'How dare you,' she shrieked. 'You ungrateful brat.'

Everyone in the room flinched at the sound of Kathi's hand connecting with Jake's cheek. 'Kathi, control yourself,' said Iris.

'No, I won't control myself,' Kathi shot back. 'He's been getting away with too much for too long. Shoplifting, smoking, now drinking. What will be next? Burglary? GBH?'

'Mum, you are overreacting as always.' Jake rubbed his face. She'd knocked the bravado out of him, but not his disdain.

'That's easy for you to say,' said Kathi. 'You are not the one at home worrying about your child, wondering if he's been abducted.'

'Abducted? What are you talking about?' Jake looked at her as if she was mad. He looked at the others for an explanation for his mother's madness, but they looked away, embarrassed. 'What?' Jake demanded. 'What's going on?'

'Nothing is going on,' said Marjorie. 'We were simply worried about you. We know you're a good lad and wouldn't disappear without telling anyone, and so when you didn't come home from school we were worried. Your dad and granddad have been out looking for you.'

'I'm sorry,' he said to his grannies. 'I didn't mean to worry anyone. I caught up with a friend after school and lost track of time.'

'Which friend?' Kathi asked. 'Who's been plying you with alcohol?'

'A friend.' Jake turned on her. 'Why don't you leave me alone, woman. You are always on at me about something. Can't you take the hint? I don't want to talk to you. I don't want you in my life. You're not even my mum.'

'You see?' said Kathi, appealing to the others. 'Do you see how he treats me, the things he says to me?' She turned back to Jake. 'I am your mother, whether you like it or not. We're stuck with each other and I don't care how angry you get, I am still your mother. You can like it or lump it.'

'Stop pretending,' challenged Jake. 'Stop pretending to be happy families.'

'There's nothing happy about this family right now.'

'Then why don't you kick me out? That's what you want to do, isn't it? You hate me, I know you do. You wish you'd never adopted me and so do I because I hate you too. I hate you all.'

Jake stormed out of the kitchen and ran up the stairs two at a time before slamming his bedroom door. Kathi looked at Graham, terrified by what had just happened. She put her hands over her mouth, not trusting herself. Marjorie stood up and went to her granddaughter. She put her arms around Kathi and let her sink into her body, defeated.

Iris began to move the dishes from the sink to the dishwasher. 'You shouldn't of slapped him,' she said.

'She knows that,' said Graham. 'Just leave it, Mum.'

'He's only a boy,' she said. 'He doesn't know what he is saying. It was the drink talking, not him.'

'If this is your attempt at making me feel better, it is not working.' Kathi couldn't keep sarcasm out of voice.

'You shouldn't have slapped him,' repeated Iris, looking this time Kathi. 'He's just a child, a hurt child. I put up with a lot of bad behaviour from Graham but I never slapped him.'

'Yes, Iris, you've let me know many times that you are a saintly mother who never made any mistakes. You've made it clear that you think I have failed. Not only could I not get pregnant, but now I can't even look after the child I have been given.'

'That's enough, Kathi,' said Graham.

'No, it's not. I've only just started.'

Graham, his jaw set, headed into the living room. 'That's right,' she called after him. 'Walk away like you always do. Leave it to me to pick up the pieces, to fix the situation.'

'I'll go up and check on Jake,' said Iris.

'Kathi,' coaxed Marjorie. 'Stop.' She took Kathi's hand and led her upstairs. Kathi lay down on her bed, weeping all the while. Marjorie sat next to her, rubbing her back and trying to soothe her.

'I miss them,' said Kathi.

'I know you do, darling.'

'I miss having Mum to talk to. She always knew what to say. I need her. I might be a grown woman, but I still need my mum. It's not fair.'

'I know, I know,' soothed Marjorie. 'I miss them too. You know, when your parents died, it was you who kept me going. My husband was taken from me too soon, then I my daughter and son-in-law. You were all I had left.' She leaned over and kissed her granddaughter's wet cheek. 'I'm so proud of you and everything you've done.'

'I don't know what to do about Jake or how to make things better. What do you think Mum would tell me to do?'

'She'd tell you you're doing a great job with Jake. She'd remind you that the teenage years are difficult and you've just got to ride them out as best you can.'

'It doesn't seem enough.'

'Sometimes enough is all we can do.' Marjorie was silent for a little while and stroked Kathi's hair. 'I think she'd tell you to keep trying to talk to Jake, even when he rejects you. He'll come round, eventually.'

'Do you think so?'

'I know so. He's a good kid and has two parents who love him and want to protect him. That's as much as anyone can expect.'

'I don't know if I can go on. It's all too much.'

'What's too much?'

'All of it; being a mum, being a wife, running a business and being a good friend. I don't think I can do it.'

'Yes, you can.'

'How do you know?' Fresh tears sprung up.

'Because you have to. What other choice do you have? What choice do any of us have except to have a good cry and then get on with things?'

'Stiff upper lip?'

'Exactly.' Marjorie smiled at Kathi and gave her another kiss. 'Get some sleep, things will feel different tomorrow.'

Within a minute Kathi was sound asleep, as if she'd been waiting for permission. Marjorie sat for a long time with her, not wanting to burst this rare moment of tranquillity. By the time she dragged herself away and returned downstairs, Graham was alone at the kitchen table, a beer in his hand. 'What a night, eh?' Graham tried to joke. Marjorie sat down next to him and put her hand over his.

'Jake is home safe and sound,' she said. 'That is the main thing.'

'How is she?' Graham indicated Kathi upstairs.

'She's asleep.'

'She's opened a can of worms.'

'Maybe she's right, maybe there are things that needed to be aired.' Graham took a swig of his beer. They heard Iris coming down the stairs. Both had forgotten she was with Jake.

'Is Jake alright?' Graham asked.

'He will be. He's upset, that's all. Where's Kathi?'

'Asleep,' said Marjorie.

'It is not often I am angry with that girl, but tonight I am. What was she thinking?' Iris directed her question at Marjorie.

'She was scared and desperate.'

'She shouldn't have slapped him.'

'No, she shouldn't, but she did.'

'What did Jake tell you?' Graham asked.

'He's very confused.' Iris sighed a deep and heartfelt sigh. 'I don't think he knows what he's angry about or why he behaves the way he does.'

'Why is he so angry with Kathi?'

'Because he can be, I think. He knows you both love him, but it's as if he needs to test that love, to make sure.'

'Did he say who he was with tonight?'

'No.' Iris shrugged her shoulders. 'Does it really matter? He is his own person. If he didn't want to get drunk, he wouldn't have done. I have seen enough people in this town self-medicate to know that's exactly what he did tonight.'

'He better not do it again. I don't think I can take another night like tonight.'

Kathi stirred when Graham got into bed. Her face was pale and her eyes had dark circles under them. She was still fully dressed and Graham got back out of bed to help her into her pyjamas.

'I'm sorry,' Kathi murmured.

'What about?'

'It all, but mostly for slapping Jake. Do you think he'll ever speak to me again?' Kathi's body was floppy with fatigue, making it difficult for Graham to change her.

'Everything will seem better in the morning.'

'Will it?'

'Yes.'

Kathi moved Graham's face to look at her. 'Are you angry with me?' He ignored her question. 'You are, aren't you?' Kathi's face crumbled and Graham couldn't help but soften.

'I'm not angry,' he lied, 'but you said some hurtful things tonight. Mum was really upset.'

'I'm sorry I upset her but it's true, she's never approved of us adopting.'

'Kathi,' Graham's tone was abrupt. 'Let's not talk about this now. You are drunk and I am tired.' He got back into bed and switched the lamp off. He left Kathi crying for a few moments before relenting and pulling her into him. He kissed the top of her head.

'I can't do this anymore,' Kathi said softly.

'Do what?'

'Any of it. I know I have to, but I don't want to.'

'That's the drink talking. I have never known you to give up on anything.'

'I'm a dreadful mother.'

'No, you're not. Anyone would find this difficult.'
'But they wouldn't slap their son.'
'Maybe not.'

Kathi fell asleep again within minutes but Graham lay awake a while longer wondering why his family was falling apart and for the first time he considered the possibility that Kathi was right and perhaps they did need some help after all.

Chapter 24

Jake woke early the next morning. He was sweating, his mouth was dry and furry, and when he rolled over his head exploded inside. He had to hold his breath and stop his body from making any movement until the pain subsided.

He sat up and eased his feet off the bed. It took him a moment to gather his thoughts and stitch together the events of the previous night. He remembered being at Joanne's house and then the cold night air hitting him. Instead of sobering him up, it seemed to make him even more drunk. He remembered misjudging the kerb and stumbling.

The next thing he remembered was his dad standing next to him on the pavement. He couldn't remember what Graham said, but he was angry. They got into the van and Jake remembered how warm and cosy it felt and he briefly dozed off.

Jake cringed at the memory of his grandmothers sat around the kitchen, witnessing him drunk. He'd had alcohol before, but nothing like last night. Previously, he and a few friends had only ever passed around a can or two of beer to share. The next morning he'd been a bit tired, but that was all.

Today he felt like death warmed up, and the back of his throat was itchy and dry from the cigarettes Joanne had given him. Without a shadow of a doubt, his parents will have smelled the smoke. He lifted his right hand and sniffed. The tobacco smell lingered on his fingers and they were even a little discoloured. He disgusted even himself.

In the bathroom, he stuck his mouth under the cold tap and lapped up as much water as he could before splashing his face. He looked in the mirror. His eyes were bloodshot and ringed with dark circles. His left cheek was red. He put his hand to his face and felt the warm sting of Kathi's slap.

To mask the embarrassment of his own behaviour, Jake blamed Kathi. There was no way he'd let her off the hook for this. In fact, he'd make her suffer by reminding her that she'd beaten him.

Jake dug around the bathroom cabinets and found some paracetamol. He swallowed two before getting in the shower and dressing for school.

Downstairs, the mood was sombre. His parents were eating breakfast at the table, but it was clear they were deep in their own thoughts.

'Morning,' said Graham. 'How are you feeling?'

'All right.'

'Do you need any painkillers?'

'I found some in the bathroom.' Jake sat down and poured himself a bowl of cereal.

'Jake?' said Kathi. He kept his head down and refused to look at her. 'About last night. I'm really sorry. I shouldn't have slapped you and I'm very sorry I did.' Still Jake didn't speak. 'I'd been so worried about you and I felt so hurt by what you said that I lost control and I am so very sorry.'

'Jake, your mum is talking to you.'

'Tell her,' he said, suddenly pumped up by his own power, 'that I hate her. Tell her I'm glad she's not my mum because my real mum would never have hit me.'

Carried away by his own righteousness, he abruptly stood up, cast Kathi filthy look and left the house. On the way to school he picked up a can of Coke and a packet of crisps and by the time he'd finished them he felt nearly back to normal.

'You look awful,' declared Lindsay when she saw him.

'I got wasted last night,' he told her.

'You went out and didn't invite me?' She teased. 'Some friend you are.'

'I was with Joanne.'

'Oh.' Lindsay touched his face. 'Is she the one who slapped you?'

'No, that was Kathi.'

'You must really have pissed her off.' Jake jolted at Lindsay's assumption it was his fault.

'Why do you think that?' he asked.

'Think what?'

'That it was my fault?'

'Wasn't it?' Jake looked away. 'All I'm saying is, that's not her style. She must have been really angry.'

'She was drunk.' Lindsay's face registered surprise, but she didn't say anything. 'I should report her,' Jake said.

'Will you report my dad at the same time? Please?'

'Do you want me to?' Jake looked at his friend, unsure if she was joking or not. He would gladly drop Tommy Irvin in it if Lindsay gave the nod.

'Nah,' she said. 'I can't be bothered with the hassle.'

The bell rang, and they gravitated towards class, negotiating the stream of other kids. 'I didn't think she had it in her, to be honest,' Jake said as they walked up the stairwell. 'She's usually such a sap, always wanting to talk about our feelings and stuff. Actually, it was a bit of a relief.'

'Aren't you seeing your shrink today?'

'She's not a shrink.'

'What is she?' Just in time they reached Jake's classroom and he waved goodbye without answering her question.

As soon as he sat down Jake switched off from what was going on around him and sunk into his own thoughts, confused by the events of last night. He didn't recognise it was Kathi's feelings of shock that had driven her to react so violently towards him. Lindsay was right; slapping him was totally out of character for her. Nor did Jake recognise that he was hurt by the slap. Not a physical hurt, but an emotional one. He was hurt that the person he trusted and depended on so intently could be that angry with him. That hurt manifested itself as anger. *She shouldn't have hit me, no matter how upset she was.*

Mixed up with that anger was guilt. Guilt he had worried her so much, that he had belittled her to such an extent she felt trapped and lashed out. He knew this because he recognised it. It was how he felt nearly all the time. Regardless, his anger and pride would not allow him to forgive her and when she picked him up later, to go to Brenda's office, he was sullen and wouldn't look her in the eye.

Kathi tried to make conversation in the car, but he rebuffed her each time. It was easier not to engage because if he did, it might open a wound he didn't want to examine. It was easier not to speak at all than risk being vulnerable. Anyway, wasn't that what Brenda was for?

'Please talk to me, Jake,' Kathi asked for the final time. 'We'll never get past this otherwise.'

'There's nothing to talk about.'

'Yes, there is. We had a huge fight last night. We can't ignore that.'

'We didn't have a fight. You hit me.'

'I am so sorry for doing it, I wish I could take it back, really I do.'

'You can't.'

'No, I know I can't. However, I can apologise and talk about why it happened.' Jake tutted, making it clear he thought this was a waste of time. 'I slapped you because I was hurt and angry. We had all been so worried about you, had even begun to think you'd been kidnapped. When you walked through the door, I cannot tell you how relieved I was you were safe.'

Kathi glanced over at him, but Jake was examining his fingernails intensely. 'When I realised you were drunk, my relief turned to anger that you'd been drinking, God knows where, while I had been sitting at home expecting the police to call any minute and tell me you were dead.'

Jake heard Kathi's voice break before she took a deep breath and composed herself.

'Why did you think I'd been kidnapped?' he asked, despite himself. He saw Kathi's cheeks colour and knew there was something she was keeping from him. 'Well?' he demanded.

'I have been getting trolled online.'

'What does that have to do with me?'

'Whoever it is lives in Byreburn. They emailed a photograph of me outside the new property.'

'I still don't understand how that involves me.'

'Perhaps it doesn't, but whoever the troll is, is aggressive and threatening. When you disappeared I worried that perhaps the troll had done something to you.'

Jake thought about this for a moment, but dismissed the idea as ridiculous. 'Who on earth would want to take me? For Christ's sake mum, this is Byreburn, not Los Angeles. Things like that don't happen here.'

Kathi smiled at him. 'That's what your dad said.'

Jake turned the radio on and channel hopped for a bit, but nothing felt right so he switched it off again. He looked out the passenger window. 'Why is someone trolling you?' Kathi didn't answer, so he turned to look at her. Again her cheeks were bright red. This time she switched the radio on. Jake let things lie for a moment, but curiosity compelled him to ask again. 'Why are you being trolled?'

'I don't know. Trolls are crazy, bored people. Why do they troll anyone?'

'It's someone in Byreburn?'

'I think so. Or they live nearby.'

'Who have you pissed off?'

'Nobody I know of. I can't think who it is. I have racked my brains but have no idea.'

'You must have some idea.'

'Well, I did wonder... the person who told you about there being...'

'... another baby?'

'Yes, about that. Did they mention anything about where the baby is?'

'The baby is here?'

'No,' Kathi jumped in, 'at least I don't think so. Have you heard anything?'

'Why don't you ask Gran?'

'I don't like to, I don't want to upset her.'

'But you think the baby is the troll?'

'I know it sounds ridiculous –'

'– it does.'

'It's the only thing I can think of.'

They pulled up outside Brenda's building, and Kathi switched the engine off. 'I'm glad we had this chat,' she said. 'I'm glad I could tell you why I was so upset. I overreacted, but now you know why. Can you forgive me?'

Kathi smiled at Jake and he was on the verge of smiling back, but he sensed that as soon as they stepped out of the car and broke this bubble of security and safety, life would return to its difficult and confusing self.

For a few minutes he'd lowered the protective shell he usually hung around his shoulders, but when the car door opened so did the bubble. He quickly lifted the shell back onto his shoulders.

'No, I can't.'

Chapter 25

Brenda called Jake and Kathi through to her office. 'Good to see you again,' she said, and made some small talk to ease them in. As soon as they were seated she could tell something was wrong. Kathi's lips were pursed and her eyes were bloodshot. Brenda took a moment to decide how best to start the session. 'How have things been since I saw you last, Kathi?'

'Not great, if I'm honest.' Kathi lowered her eyes, glancing now and again in Jake's direction. 'We had a bit of an incident last night.'

'Oh yes?'

'Jake didn't come home from school yesterday. By six o'clock we naturally got worried. We phoned around friends and family to find out if anybody had seen him. They hadn't. My husband and father-in-law went looking for him. He turned up halfway along the High Street and it was clear he'd been drinking and smoking.'

'What time was this?'

'After ten o'clock. Graham and I were both furious. He won't tell us where he was, which makes me assume the worst.' Kathi looked across at Jake, but he was motionless, his expression giving nothing away. 'If I'm honest,' she said to Brenda, 'I don't know what to say or how to handle the situation.' She turned back to Jake. 'You're only 15.' There was a desperation in her voice which he found pathetic. It was as if she thought that by reminding him of his age he'd suddenly become an obedient pre-schooler.

'Before last night,' Brenda asked, 'how were things between you?'

'I thought they were going well,' said Kathi. 'I don't know what went wrong. Maybe you can talk some sense into him.'

'What I will do,' Brenda reassured,' is have a chat with Jake now and perhaps help him understand what's going on.'

'You're very quiet today,' Brenda said to him when they were alone.

'I've got a sore head.'

'Is this your first hangover?'

'Yeah. I've had a few drinks in the past, but not as much as last night.'

'What did you drink last night?'

'Only lager.'

'If you're smoking as well, that can make the hangover worse.' Jake didn't respond. 'Do you want to tell me what happened last night?'

'Not really.'

'It might be helpful in understanding what's going on in your head.' Brenda stayed quiet for a while, giving him the chance to speak, but he didn't so she went on. 'It probably doesn't feel this way to you, but for someone of your age to drink heavily there is usually a reason. It might simply be you wanted to know what it was like, or that it happened unintentionally. Inexperience means you don't yet know your body's limits. But my instinct tells me that you wanted to get drunk.' Still, he said nothing.

The eagerness he'd felt last night about the session, in the warm buzz of his second beer, had evaporated as quickly as the buzz and now all he wanted was to be at home in his bed, with his head under the pillow, and to stay there until everyone had calmed down. It was one thing to have the breathing room Brenda gave him; it was another to use it.

'What would you think if I said you'd done it to punish your parents?'

'For what?'

'For being your parents?'

'That doesn't make sense.'

'What I'm wondering is, with all the different emotions you are going through at the moment, could anger be one of them? What can happen is that an adopted person is angry with their birth mother for not keeping them. But she's not here to be told about that anger, and so the next best person is the adopted mother. Do you think that could be happening here?' Jake dropped his shoulders a little, he was beginning to feel more at ease. Brenda's soft voice and light brogue was soothing, she seemed able to spellbind him into opening up and even though he was self-aware enough to realise it, he didn't feel the compulsion to fight against it, as he would have done if anyone else had asked him these same questions.

'Maybe,' he said at length. 'I have been thinking about her a lot recently.'

'What's been going through your mind?'

'Mostly wondering what she looks like now, where she's living and if she's had any more children. Children she's kept.'

'Anything else? Anything you fantasise about happening?' Jake's teenage hormones seeped out and he couldn't help giggling at the word fantasise. 'Let me rephrase. Is there a scenario you think about that involves your birth mother? For example, adopted people often imagine meeting their birth mother and wonder what that would be like.'

'Yeah, I guess I've wondered that too. I have imagined going to her home and what we might talk about.'

'What do you talk about when you meet?'

'We talk about when she got pregnant, why she didn't want to keep me.'

'What does she say?'

'I don't know.' Now that he was asked to say it out loud, his mind went blank.

'Ask her now.'

'What?' For a brief moment Jake panicked, thinking Brenda was going to magic Marie from out of nowhere. He watched her, mouth agog, as she got up and moved a chair to face him.

'Imagine Marie is in this seat. What would you ask her? Remember, this is the first time you've seen each other since you were a baby. If she was here, what would you say to her?'

'I don't know,' he said, swallowing down growing hysteria.

'Really? The woman you've wanted to meet all your life, your birth mother, sitting right here, and you don't know what you want to ask her?'

'No... yes.'

'I think you've got some idea. There's no right or wrong. You simply want to tell her what's in your heart.' Jake stared at the empty seat in front of him, feeling ridiculous. He took a breath, trying desperately to think of something to say.

'I suppose I want to ask why,' he said to Brenda. 'I want to ask what was wrong with me that she didn't want to keep me.'

'Tell her, say that to Marie.' Brenda indicated to the empty chair.

'I want to know why you didn't love me, why you got rid of me. Did I cry too much?' Suddenly it all poured out. 'Was I ugly? Maybe you took one look at me and just didn't like me. Whatever the reason, I hate you for it, it's all your fault. You brought me into the world so you should have looked after me. This is your fault, not mine, so why is it me that feels shit? Why do I feel horrible and that nobody can love me? Because it makes sense, doesn't it? If you can't love me then who can?'

'Very good Jake, now take Marie's seat. What would she say to you?'

You're mad, he thought. How could I know what she's thinking, if I knew that I wouldn't be here. Reluctantly he moved into the opposite seat, trying hard not to roll his eyes.

'I left you because I couldn't look after you,' he said, surprising himself. 'I was so young, not much older than you are now. My mum and dad had kicked me out and I couldn't do it by myself. When you were born I couldn't look at you. I heard you crying, and it was too painful. I knew I couldn't keep you, so I didn't want to look at you and fall in love with you and then have to let you go. I cried and cried so much. I was scared and hurt and angry. I was so confused. I would have been no good for you. You're better off without me.'

At the end of his outburst, Jake wept openly. He couldn't help it, and he didn't care. Brenda let him have a minute before helping him breathe and calm down. 'It's my hangover,' he said by way of explaining his tears. It may have been true, but when he thought back on it, he knew it was because the things he had imagined Marie saying hurt so much. His worst fears had been said out loud.

'Is there anything else you want to ask her?' Jake's brain felt numb and depleted. He rummaged around in his mind for something but came up blank. Just before saying so to Brenda, he said, 'Do you want me back?'

Brenda indicated Marie's chair, and he moved over.

'No,' he said.

Kathi and Jake were silent on the way home. Jake's face was drawn and his eyes were red rimmed. Kathi knew something had occurred in the therapy room, something monumental for her son, but she felt boxed in and helpless because she had no right to be told what they talked about. It was Jake's decision about what he shared with her, and given what had happened between them over the past twenty-four hours, she was not in his circle of confidence.

As she drove, she wracked her brain as to who she could approach to find out. Who would Jake confide in? Her first thought was Hayden, but she hadn't heard much about him recently. Perhaps they'd fallen out? The person he seemed to spend most of his time with was Lindsay Irving, and this made Kathi uncomfortable. She didn't know Lindsay very well, but she knew her family by reputation and had gone to school with Lindsay's father, Tommy.

It was well known Tommy was a drunk who beat his wife. For a reason Kathi would never understand, Annie refused to leave him. She had always been a quiet woman, even at school she had barely said boo to a goose. Tommy's destiny at school was to be a drunk and a bully, and he had fulfilled it. The rest of the Irving family weren't much better, and Kathi did not want her son falling for one of them. She didn't want him throwing away his future on a pretty face, for there was no denying Lindsay was a pretty girl who used her long, chocolate coloured hair to good effect. It made Kathi feel queasy to think she might have to pander to Tommy Irving's daughter to get what she needed, but if it meant she understood what was happening with Jake, then so be it.

'Was it Lindsay Irving you were with last night?' she asked him, trying hard to sound casual and non-judgmental. Jake didn't respond.

'I wouldn't be angry if it was. She's a nice girl. I just want to know who it was, otherwise I am left to imagine the worst.'

'What on earth could the worst be in Byreburn? It is not exactly known for its seedy nightclubs, gambling dens or red-light district.'

'How do you know about places like that?'

'Jesus Mum, get a life. I'm 15, not eight. Can we just stop talking about this? Leave it alone. You're always sticking your nose in. There are some things that don't concern you.'

'Everything in your life concerns me. As you said, you're 15 years old, not 20. I am responsible for you, it is my job to get you to adulthood in one piece and if you're creeping about the streets at night, I can't do that.'

A pheasant ran out onto the road, forcing Kathi to swerve, nearly hitting an oncoming car. The other car beeped loudly and, already flustered, Kathi pulled the car over and got out. She was scared of this new, secretive and argumentative side to her son. It left her feeling out of control. He was too big now to be manhandled into the car, too old to be bribed with sweets or threatened with a stony count to ten. Kathi was utterly out of her depth and didn't know how to get back to shore. It took her quite a while to compose herself, by which time Jake had begun beeping the horn. She got back in and took them home.

As soon as they pulled up outside the house Jake stormed from the car and into his bedroom. Kathi remained where she was, trying to understand what had just happened. She wanted to phone Graham and ask him for the answers, but she knew he didn't have them. Instead, she gathered up her things and went inside.

She slugged her way up the stairs and cocooned herself under the duvet. She wished she could be stronger, could wash off Jake's words and attitude and not take it personally, but today she couldn't. The past 18 months had nearly broken her and she couldn't forgive herself for the events of last night. She'd handled the situation badly and said so many wrong things. In the afterglow of the argument, snippets of the parenting books she'd read popped into her head, reminding her of what she should have said, compounding her feeling of failure.

Later, Jake peeked through the door of Kathi's bedroom and saw she was sleeping. Events that morning had really shaken him, but if he wanted to know what Marie would actually say to him, he had take matters into his own hands. He closed Kathi's bedroom door and cautiously made his way to the small door on the landing that opened onto the eaves of the house. For the moment his hangover had subsided, the adrenaline of snooping had forced his brain to focus on the task at hand. It wasn't a large space, but Kathi had filled it.

That said, it was with a surprising ease that Jake found a large lever arch file simply named Adoption.

'Bingo,' he said.

Chapter 26

Cherry was having a good day. She'd agreed to let a flat to a nice couple moving to the area, and she'd just conducted a very easy flat inspection. When tenants looked after their flats, it made her life a lot easier.

To celebrate, she popped into the Silver Spoon Café for a coffee. School was out, and the kids were swarming on the Spar convenience store, the chip shop and the ice cream parlour to stock up on sweet and starchy foods. They were ravenous after a full day of stretching their brains. The Silver Spoon was off the hit list for most pupils. Only a few girls came in for a juice and a cake.

She ordered her coffee and took a table by the window. 'They're like gannets,' she muttered to herself.

The hardware store was situated diagonally opposite the Silver Spoon and Cherry's eye wandered over to the goods displayed in the window, stopping at a dustpan and brush covered in bright flowers. The view was interrupted by Brian's van, which pulled up in front of the store. Brian jumped out and into the shop. Cherry took a sip of her coffee and when she next looked up she saw, walking in front of the hardware store, Jake Beattie and Joanne Wylie.

Cherry was more than a little surprised. They were deep in conversation; it didn't look like they were exchanging polite niceties. Why would a boy of 15 be hanging about with a woman in her late forties? She was pretty sure there was nothing silly going on, Joanne didn't seem the type and Cherry was generally a pretty good judge of character.

When she'd carried out the checks on Joanne to rent the flat there had been no red flags. Joanne was a bit rough around the edges, it was true, but Cherry had been impressed by her apparent ambition to get herself out of her Glasgow estate and begin again somewhere new. She said she wanted to start a new life. Cherry certainly understood that feeling. It had been one of Wayne's attractions. Byreburn was a small town where everybody knew and cared for each other. Despite quarrels and disputes, the community was strong. A far cry from her own upbringing in a rough city. Wayne had turned out to be a bit of an idiot, but Byreburn continued to appeal and she could understand why Joanne felt that way too.

But how did they know each other? It seemed unlikely they hung about in the same circles, and Joanne wasn't a particularly alluring woman. She was middle-aged, overweight and not particularly attractive, so Cherry didn't think this was a schoolboy crush. And whilst Joanne seemed decent enough, Cherry had never considered her charismatic or as the sort of person who drew people to them.

She was about to take out her phone and send a text to Kathi, letting her know what she'd seen, but Brian came out of the hardware store, waved and came over to sit with her. They chatted about this and that, and when the conversation lulled, Cherry looked at him and nearly told him that she might have cancer. But she couldn't think of the words to use, and she was scared of either chasing him away or making him feel obliged to stay with her. No, she wasn't ready to tell him just yet.

When he was leaving Brian took Cherry's face between his hands, kissed her tenderly. Cherry blushed, much to his obvious delight. Once he'd gone Cherry went to the counter to pay. She heard the girls at the other table giggling over the kiss, and the waitress smiled ruefully. 'Who's the cat that got the cream?' she said.

'Me? Don't be daft.'

'Not you. Brian. I've never seen him look so happy. He's a different man.' Cherry blushed again. Annoyed with herself at being so embarrassed, she left quickly, relieved to be outside and away from the giggling. Just up the street she saw Lindsay Irving coming out of the chemist.

'Hi Lindsay,' she called, catching up with the girl. 'Listen, can you help me with something?'

'Maybe.'

'I saw Jake Beattie with Joanne Wylie earlier today. Are they friends?'

'They might be.' Lindsay was defensive but Cherry saw enough in her expression to know Lindsay didn't approve of Jake's choice of friend.

'How long have they known each other?' Lindsay was silent. 'Come on, I can see you don't like her, but Jake obviously does. Do you know why?'

'He says she understands him, that they're are both outsiders. That's all I'm saying about it.'

'So they're good pals, then?'

'You could say that.'

'Thanks Lindsay, that's all I needed to know.' Cherry pulled out her phone to call Kathi. There might be nothing in it, Cherry told herself, but Kathi ought to know. Kathi's phone rang, but she didn't pick up.

'Oi, Cherry,' called one of the tradesmen Cherry used to do the bigger jobs Brian couldn't manage. 'You got a minute?'

'Sure,' she called back and hung up the phone.

After what felt like an eternity, the day of Cherry's hospital appointment arrived. She'd put plans in place for while she was away and had asked Brian to keep an eye on things.

'I'll have my phone with me,' she told him, 'so if it's urgent, leave a message and I'll get back to you.'

'No problem,' Brian reassured her.

'Are you sure it's okay for me to leave you in charge like this? It is not your responsibility, I know.'

'It is absolutely fine. I just wish you'd tell me what's going on, that's all.'

'I told you, I am knackered. I need a few days off and I'd like to see my parents. I haven't seen them in ages and they're getting too old to make the trip down here.' Brian looked sceptical.

'Is it us?' he asked. 'Do you need a break from us?'

'No, Brian, I promise.' She kissed him tenderly. 'I really like 'us'. I think it's going well, don't you?'

'Yes, I do.' He pulled her close and wrapped his arms around her. 'I will miss you,' he said.

'I will miss you, too.' She looked at Brian and was flooded with affection for this man who made her laugh and made her feel fabulous, and who also had the capacity to frustrate her more than anyone else. She didn't dare contemplate she might be in love with him, not now. 'It is only a couple of days, I'll be back before you know it.'

Cherry drove the two hours to the hospital. Brian waved her off, and she chastised herself for nearly crying. 'Don't be ridiculous, woman,' she said to herself. 'You're not leaving forever.' The journey seemed to drag. Whilst she was keen to get it over and done with, she didn't actually want to arrive because that would bring her closer to her fate. Normally a positive person, Cherry was all too aware of her family history, which had taught her things don't always go your way.

The Screening Centre was in Glasgow's city centre so she decided to park at the Buchanan Shopping Gallery car park. Afterwards she'd go shopping and treat herself to something new. She'd either be cheering herself up or celebrating a near miss.

The walk from the car park to the Screening Centre was only ten minutes, but it was a miserable ten minutes. Clouds hung low in the sky. They were fat with water despite it having rained all morning. It seemed that as soon as one cloud had emptied itself, another took its place. The wind, too, was out in force, channelling up the streets. It was all Cherry could do to keep her umbrella functioning.

The centre was on the third floor of an office block and, because her head was down and pushing through the rain, Cherry almost missed the entrance. Once she saw it, she leapt inside out of the wind and into the comparative warmth of the foyer. In the lift she shook the drips off her umbrella, breathed deeply and repeatedly adjusted her weight from one foot to the other.

The lift door opened onto the reception desk and waiting area. Armed with her referral letter, Cherry approached the desk.

'Hi,' she said, handing over the letter. 'I have an eleven thirty appointment with Dr Gill.' The receptionist looked at the letter before saying, 'Take a seat.'

The centre was busy. There seemed to be a lot of doctors and nurses coming in and out of consulting rooms, beckoning women to follow them. After what felt like an age, Cherry was called through. Dr Gill was a no-nonsense type of woman. Her tone was authoritative, and Cherry felt reassured that the woman knew what she was doing.

'Right, Cherry,' she began. 'Today we are going to take the biopsy of the lump you found. Before I do that, however, I want to examine you once more, and do an x-ray. This is just as a precaution, you understand, so that I know exactly what I am looking at. Okay?'

Before Cherry could answer she was shown through to the x-ray room where a gentle nurse guided her through the process. It was a cold and somewhat painful procedure, but the nurse was sympathetic and efficient and before too long Cherry was given a gown to wear before being led back to Dr Gill's room. Dr Gill asked her to sit on the examination table where, much like Dr Brown had done, Cherry was lifted and prodded, moved and palpated. 'I am sorry, my hands are so cold,' said Dr Gill. 'I got cold coming into work this morning and can't seem to warm up.'

Cherry attempted to make small talk but was too distracted. Just as Dr Gill finished a nurse came in with the x-ray films. 'Thank you,' she said to the nurse. 'Let's have a look at the film, shall we, Cherry?' She opened the envelope and had a look. 'Cherry. It is such a pretty name.'

Dr Gill placed the film up on the light board and examined it more closely. Cherry looked at it too, trying to see what the doctor saw. 'Do you see this area of white?' Dr Gill asked. 'That is where we'll take the biopsy.' Cherry looked at the images. She could see the area of white, but it didn't mean anything to her.

'Is that the tumour?' She asked.

'That is what we'll find out,' smiled Dr Gill. 'Until we have those results, let's not worry.'

Cherry sat back down on the examination table. Her mind was blank while around her the nurse prepped her for a local anaesthetic and Dr Gill prepared her instruments. Cherry felt as though she had been removed from the scene and was simply an observer. This was only one in a handful of occasions that Cherry felt powerless, a passive player in her life.

She couldn't help think that this was how it must have begun for her grandmother, her aunt, and her cousin. They, too, must have sat in a consulting room like this, static with fear, while someone gave them the news their lives were about to be turned upside down and may even die. The setting seemed too ordinary for such an extraordinary event.

Meekly, Cherry followed the nurse's instructions to lie down, lift her arms, and hold still. Cherry withdrew into herself while the doctor gave her the anaesthetic before inserting a needle and withdrawing the test tissue. Cherry closed her eyes and listened to her heart thumping violently deep within.

Quickly and quietly Dr Gill and the nurse tidied up, asked Cherry to dress, and sent the sample for analysis.

'You'll be pleased to know it's all done,' said Dr Gill. 'You shouldn't feel too much pain, but once the anaesthetic has worn off you might feel a dull ache. Just take some painkillers, it won't last longer than a day.'

'When will you get the results?'

'In a few weeks. Once I have received them, the nurse will arrange a follow-up appointment.'

When she left the consulting room Cherry felt faint and had to sit in reception for a few minutes. In an attempt to put a barrier between herself and the rest of the world, Cherry pretended to check her emails. When she had composed herself she lifted her chin and headed back out into the elements.

Chapter 27

The day Jake had found his adoption folder, he'd quickly opened it and stared at the first page. He'd stared at it for a long time without actually taking it in. His mind had been a blur of seemingly endless questions about what might be contained within that lever arch of folded, crumpled, hole punched pieces of paper.

The faceless image of Marie at her front door, which had haunted so many of his night times recently, emerged out of the folder like a phantom, and he quickly shoved it under his bed. He was scared. He was scared because this folder had all the information he'd been looking for, written down in black and white. What if he didn't like what he read?

His dreams became erratic and were filled with pieces of paper. He dreamed that he came home from school and the folder was lying open on his bed. Each piece of paper that had been carefully hole punched and tidied away was flying up into the air and were swirling round and round his room. He tried to pluck them from the air and put them back where they belonged. He was scared Kathi would come in and see that he'd stolen the file. As if displaying how angry the folder was with his deception, the swirling paper gathered pace and seemed to dodge around the room, avoiding him.

The more frantic his attempts at snatching them, the faster they billowed until eventually his bedroom window blew out of its cavity and landed on the pavement below. Every single sheaf of paper followed the window outside and disappeared over the town and out of sight. He was left staring after them, desperately trying to think of a way he could put everything back before his mum came home. In his dream there was a knock at his bedroom door. The knock woke him up, breathless and hot with guilt and panic.

After enough nights of this he realised he had to either read it or put the folder back in the eaves. But Pandora's box had been found, and he couldn't rest until he'd revealed its contents. He bunked off school one afternoon when he knew Kathi would be out. Barricading himself in his room in case she surprised him, Jake gathered his courage, took a deep breath and lifted the cover.

He soon saw that the papers were filed by date, the newest on the top, so he flicked right to the back. Where better to start than at the beginning? When he got to the back, the first thing he hit upon was a photograph of a girl. She looked just like him, only a couple of years older. At first he was confused. Was this a sister he didn't know about? If it was, why was there a photograph of her here? It couldn't be a new picture because it would've been at the front of the folder and anyway, there was something about the photograph that looked old, it wasn't digital. Underneath was a label that read Marie Robertson.

The shock of seeing his birth mum so unexpectedly sent a hot flush of adrenaline around his body. He had to stand up and go to the window for a few moments before the draw of Marie lured him back. He spent a long time staring at her face, trying to take in every blemish on her skin, every strand of her hair. He tried hard to read the expression in her eyes. He wanted to know what she was thinking when this photograph was taken. The longer he looked, the more he noticed. He noticed how lank her hair was, that she had dark circles around her eyes and just how pale her skin was. He saw too that even though her lips were set in thin defiance, her eyes gave away how scared she was. Despite her tough and cold expression, she was still a child. This photograph could have been of Lindsay.

Seeing her face put so much into perspective from him. Yes, he was still angry with her for giving birth to him in the first place, but he could now begin to put himself in her shoes. If he got someone pregnant how would he feel? Would he want to be a father at 17? No, he wouldn't.

Jake turned the page and saw a photo of himself as a newborn baby. This was a picture he had seen before. A copy of it was in his Life Story Book that used to get wheeled out every now and again whenever Kathi thought he was asking too many questions. He enjoyed looking at it, but even from an early age he knew it showed only half the story, the positive story. He knew there was another hidden chapter of his story that was darker and negative, but which was almost more important.

His Life Story Book shone a white light on how wonderful his foster family had been. It marked with pride all his milestones and achievements. But it left so much unanswered. It was this commonplace, lever arch file marked Adoption, that would fill in the gaps.

Jake took his time that afternoon, trying to understand what each bit of paper meant and how to fit it into the jigsaw of his life. There was medical form after medical form and it took him a while to work out that he had been born with a heroin addiction and that he had spent the first month of his life in intensive care, detoxing. He was born a junkie.

He felt sorry for his infant self. He had seen babies around town and they were swaddled and carried and cooed over. They were held and cuddled and kissed. He'd always watched with fascination at how these tiny humans were treated as precious cargo by the adults around them. It was clear from the paperwork that this had not been his experience.

His infant days had been spent in a plastic box, surrounded by machines and clip charts and beeps. He hadn't been nourished by a warm and soft breast, but by a nurse with a bottle. He hadn't been cuddled and kissed, he'd been handled and measured and monitored. He didn't have a memory of this, but somewhere in his body he knew that was the way it had been.

There were a lot of letters back and forth between Kathi and Graham, and the authorities. Most of it was dry correspondence, but a lot of it was reports about them. They had to undergo a series of interviews before being accepted onto the adoption register, but for the first time he was aware of just how in-depth they were. He read about the deaths of Kathi's parents and how that had affected her. He read about how she and Graham had met, about Graham's childhood and just how uneventful it had been. The biggest conflicts in his youth seem to have been with his parents when he opted not to go to university but learn a trade instead. He had no desire to leave Byreburn. Graham had been a golden, blue-eyed boy, who had succeeded at everything in life. How could Jake live up to that? He couldn't. He'd already failed multiple times.

There was information too about why they wanted to adopt. All Kathi had ever told him was that she wasn't able to have children. He didn't realise they had twice tried to have children via IVF and had twice failed. He wondered if he was their third disappointment.

He next came to a document headed 'Later In Life Letter'. It was addressed to him, and when he looked at who the sender was, he saw it was the social worker who had been in charge of his case.

Jake's bedroom door rattled, giving him a fright. 'What is it?' he barked.

'Dinner is ready.' It was Kathi.

'I'm busy. I'll be down in a minute.'

'Oh right, erm, sorry Jake, come down when you're ready.' She was embarrassed. He knew what she thought he was doing and although he too was embarrassed, he preferred she think that than know the truth.

The mood had been broken, and he was actually glad to step back from his history for a moment. He felt instinctively that the letter was going to tell him the circumstances under which he had come into being and self-preservation told him he first needed to come up for air.

He tried to act normal at dinner, but his parents could sense he was distracted. 'Everything all right?' Graham asked.

'Yeah, fine.' Jake only half listened as they burbled on about their respective days. Inside, he was nervous and scared about what he was going to read. He even questioned whether or not he wanted to know. The fact that he was born with a heroin addiction cast a shadow, and it seemed unlikely he was conceived out of love.

'Jake. Jake?' Graham's voice brought him back to the present. 'What's wrong with you?'

'Sorry, nothing. I've got a headache, that's all.'

'Do you want some painkillers?' Kathi asked.

'No thanks. I'm tired, that's all. I'm going to have an early night.' He felt their stunned silence as they watched him put his plate in the sink and head upstairs. In his room he put the chair back under the door handle, sat on his bed and picked up the letter.

Dear Jake,

This letter is designed to give you a full picture of your early years. It is normal to have a lot of questions about your birth parents and the circumstances that led to your adoption. A lot of these will have been answered by Kathi and Graham, I am sure. Right from the beginning it was clear they were a couple who were devoted to you and who would do their best to give you open and honest answers to your questions, and do what they could to help you through the inevitable periods of curiosity and confusion surrounding your formative years.

Your birth mother, Marie Robertson, was born in Glasgow in 1986. She had a difficult childhood and was abused both physically and sexually by her father. As a way to escape, Marie ran away from home aged 15. Not long after this she began to take drugs, which quickly escalated to heroin. In order to pay for her habit, Marie took to prostitution.

When Marie became pregnant she received no medical care and so when she went into labour she took herself to Stobhill Hospital. Very quickly it became evident that you too were addicted to heroin and would need round-the-clock care. Marie was in no position to look after you properly and at that point it was decided, for your health and security, you should be taken into care.

To Marie's credit, she understood she would not be able to give you the care you needed and signed your custody over to myself and the social work department on 16 April 2003.

Your first five weeks were spent in intensive care at Stobhill Hospital, allowing you to be safely weaned off your heroin addiction.

Once the doctors were happy with your physical health, you were moved to a very experienced and loving foster family, Heather and Dean MacIvor. Whilst you were being looked after by the McIvors, it was my role to find a suitable forever family for you. As is the nature of this type of process, and because we wanted to ensure we found you the right family, it took us nearly 18 months to find you the best home we could.

As soon as Kathi and Graham met with you in 2005, they said they felt a connection and so we progressed with the application. At first they visited you at the McIvor's house, and under supervision. Once you had become used to them, Kathi and Graham's visits progressed to trips out of the home, at first for an hour, then progressively longer.

After six weeks of increasingly regular and longer visits, you then had an overnight visit. That went well, so the next time it was two nights. I am pleased to say that this went as well as could be expected and so you joined your new home.

As with any upheaval of this scale, it took time for you to adjust to your new environment, and to trust that Kathi and Graham were there to look after you. Because you were so young when all this happened you probably don't remember any of it and so I hope this letter will fill in some of the practical steps that were taken to find you a safe and loving home. I hope it also gives you some answers about your birth mother and the circumstances of her life that meant she wasn't able to look after you either physically or emotionally.

My memory of you is as an inquisitive and lively child who loved to run and be active. Even at that early age it was clear to see you were developing a lovely sense of humour. I know that your foster parents loved you dearly and were so happy for you when you found your new forever family. I am sure they have told you themselves, but they wanted nothing but the best for your future.

It has been a pleasure knowing you, best wishes.

Chapter 28

The next night, after dinner, Jake slouched upstairs. He shut the door and plugged himself into his iPhone, putting a barrier between him and the outside world. He'd sensed Kathi looking in on him at one stage, but had pretended not to notice and she closed the door. It had been a shit day at school. He hadn't been able to focus on any of his lessons that day, but more than that, he didn't want to.

'Are we keeping you?' One teacher after the other had asked. What he wanted to say was yes, you are. There were so many more important things he could be doing that day than sitting in a classroom ignoring information he'd never use past exam day. He also wanted to tell them how unimaginative they were, each of them asking the same boring question, 'Are we keeping you?' Sarcasm that has been rattled out by teachers for the past two hundred years. And you tell us we need to try harder, he wanted to yell. Instead, he grumbled 'no sir,' or 'no miss.'

Sitting in class, he had felt his phone vibrating as message after message hit his notification centre. He was desperate to read them and see what was being said because he knew everyone was gossiping about him. He also wanted to throw his phone in the river because he didn't want to face the taunts about him being adopted and unwanted, the jibes about being different from everyone else, for being an outsider.

Because that's what he was; an outsider. He's listened too many times to Kathi reassure him that he was their son and that he belonged in Byreburn, but he knew differently. He knew in his core that these were nothing other than placatory words, a way of making him feel better. They weren't actually true.

He was convinced, too, that when they were alone together, Kathi and Graham discussed how much they regretted their decision to adopt all those years ago. If they'd been able to see where the future led they would never have gone through with it.

But they couldn't see the future and so here they all were, bound up in a package of regret and resignation. They weren't bad people; Kathi and Graham would wait until he was 18 before they told him to leave. They'd wait until he was old enough to make it on his own. The trouble was, he wasn't sure he wanted to make it. If he was going to struggle like this, every day, for the rest of his life, he wasn't sure it was worth it.

At lunch break, he'd read through the messages. They were the same as every other day - freak, weirdo, nobody wants you, I don't want to catch what you've got, your mum didn't want you, go back to where you came from.

He couldn't prove who had sent them, and even if he could it wouldn't do any good. That wouldn't stop the bullying. He knew Hayden was behind some of the messages and his betrayal hurt the most. Jake couldn't understand why he was so keen to ditch their friendship and impress the class bullies, who would drop Hayden as soon as they got bored.

'Why did you send it?' he'd asked the first time it happened.

'Send what?' Hayden had kept his voice light, feigning innocence, but they'd known each other since they were three years old. Jake knew all of his expressions. He'd stared as his friend, willing him to admit it and apologise. He wanted Hayden to explain it away as a moment of madness that he immediately regretted and which he of course hadn't meant. But Hayden stayed silent.

'Whatever,' Jake said at last. They hadn't spoken since.

Today after lunch he and Lindsay had snuck down to the river for a quiet cigarette, each of them putting some distance between themselves and the mundanity of school life. 'Just ignore them,' she said.

'Aye, says you,' Jake replied. 'Nobody would ever send you these messages.' Lindsay had three older brothers ready to batter anyone who attacked their sister, except of course their father. Both their phones pinged. Someone had sent a meme about him to the whole class.

'He's an idiot,' said Lindsay. 'Ignore him.' She was, as always, straight to the point. It was one of the things he liked about her.

'I wish he'd fuck off and die,' Jake said, angry and irritated. He couldn't shake off the taunts. They went round and round his head and led him to imagine another world in which he would beat up everyone who bullied him. He'd leave one for dead, a couple of others bruised and limping. That would teach them not to mess with him, that he was to be feared and respected. That was the power Jake needed to put an end to the shitty life he had now, and begin a new, easy life. A life in which he was confident and funny and popular.

That night, when everyone else was asleep in bed, he messaged Lindsay.

You still up?

Yes

They bantered back and forth, their messages interspersed with comments on, or shares of, messages about the people they loathed. With each message, Jake's frustration built. At one point it erupted like hot lava and he threw his phone across the room. He shoved his head under his pillow and let out a silent scream. When his blood cooled, he rescued his phone from the floor, scared he'd broken it.

Lying on his bed, he attempted to block out the voices running through his head and to expel the imaginary arguments and fights he'd have with the boys at school, but they wouldn't budge. They remained there, fixed. They spun round and round his brain like a zooped up carousel and when they couldn't go any faster his mind jumped to thoughts of Marie and the life they should have had together, and maybe still could have.

So began a new round of torment. The pressure in his brain swelled and swelled like a bicycle pump, pushing horrible thoughts into his brain, and that had no means of escape. He needed a way to release the pressure.

Do you wanna go for a drive? He messaged Lindsay.

???

I'll be there in 10

It was 11.38 PM. His parents would be asleep by now and it would be safe to go downstairs without fear of Kathi sneaking up on him and wanting to talk about their feelings. He'd come to dread those chats because he knew she wanted more from him than he could give. Anyway, she'd have taken her sleeping pills by now and would be dead to the world. Driving her to medication, for he knew deep down he was to blame, was another thing for him to feel guilty about. It's her own fault for adopting me, he told himself.

Kathi always put her car keys in the dish beside the back door. Jake quietly picked them up and reached out for the handle. Just before turning it, he had a thought and went into the living room. He took a bottle of vodka down from the drinks cupboard.

Out on the street he looked for Kathi's car. Luckily she hadn't been able to park right outside the house and he had to walk a few hundred metres down the street, which meant his parents were less likely to hear the car being started. If they did hear a car, they wouldn't suspect it was theirs. Now that he was there, sitting in the driver's seat, he began to regret his decision. But he'd told Lindsay he'd come and get her, and he didn't want to lose face with her.

On only three occasions had Graham allowed him behind the steering wheel to move the car and change from first to second gear. He wondered now whether that was enough practice for him to take the car by himself.

He looked around the street, his heart thumping quickly with the audacity of what he was about to do. The road was clear, there was no traffic or people. There weren't even any house lights visible. He started the engine and in the dead quiet of the night it sounded to him like a Formula One race car. The revs were deafening. A deep breath, a foot on the clutch, he moved into first gear.

'Can you feel the biting point?' Graham had asked him. 'Move your feet slowly and smoothly and when you feel the engine bite, the car will move.' He did as Graham had instructed but didn't manage to keep things smooth when he lifted his foot off the clutch. The car sprung forward and bumped the one in front.

'Fuck.'

No alarm went off, so he put the car into reverse. The camera on the back of the car leapt into action and, with more success, he moved the car slowly back, giving himself enough space to manoeuvre onto the road.

Once safely out and moving forward, he changed into second gear. The dashboard told him to move it up to third gear, which he did. For a few moments he relaxed, but then he came to the end of the road and had to turn left towards Lindsay's street. He managed to move back down into second gear but didn't manage to stop. Instead, he swung round the bend and hoping for the best. Luck was with him and there was no other traffic. Under instruction from the car, he moved again into third gear and drove steadily up the hill to the estate Lindsay lived on. He changed into second gear so he could slow down and swing into the estate and Lindsay's street. He crawled along until he saw her waiting for him on the street, a few doors up from her own house. He stopped the car, and it stalled.

'Oh my God,' said Lindsay, getting into the passenger seat. 'What are you doing?' The look on her face told Jake she was impressed, and that was good enough for him. 'Oh man,' she said, 'vodka.' She opened the bottle, took a swig, and grimaced.

'Where do you want to go?' he asked.

'Let's go down to The Green.' she said. 'Nobody will be there.' She took another swig. 'Can you turn the car around?'

'No!' Jake laughed at himself and the situation they were in, enjoying his own daring.

'You'll have to go round the block.'

Slowly, and with a lot of laughing, he took the car around the block and back down the hill towards the King's Bridge and then turned left towards The Green, which was a small playground and parking area by the river.

They got out of the car, taking the vodka with them, and sat themselves on the swings. It was chilly, and they zipped up their jackets. Cigarettes lit, they took turns to drink the vodka, letting it warm their bodies from the inside out. It wasn't long before the alcohol loosened their tongues.

'Dad's on a bender tonight,' Lindsay told him. 'If you think your mum is an idiot, you should meet my dad. He's the biggest loser there is.' She took a drink. 'I'll tell you what, Graham might not be your real dad, but he's a hell of a lot better than mine.'

'Why doesn't your mum kick him out?'

'That, my friend, is the million dollar question. Because she is as big an idiot as him. The woman has no self-respect.'

'What about your brothers?' he asked. 'Can't they get rid of him?'

'I think they're scared of him, too. Well, maybe not Thomas anymore, but the other two are. Thomas and Dad had a big fight one night and Thomas moved out. Dad's never picked a fight with him since.'

'Australia,' Jake reminded Lindsay. 'We've just got to bide our time. Hey, we should get jobs, start saving.'

'I am totally up for that. What shall we do?'

'I could be a taxi driver, my driving skills are brilliant.'

'Yeah, and I can be a chef because I know how to heat beans in the microwave.' They laughed at how funny they found themselves.

'Mum said her first job was washing dishes, even I could do that.'

'I don't like doing that at home, never mind for someone else.'

'Aye, but the difference is we'd get paid.'

'We're too young.'

'Mum was only 14 when she had her first job.'

'Can't do that now.'

'Health and Safety,' they said in unison, with mock gravitas.

'I wish someone would do a health and safety check at my house. I don't think my parents would pass the test.'

'Maybe we can sell stuff on eBay, I hear about people doing it all the time.'

'What would you sell?'

'I don't know. We could sell your dad?' The vodka had kicked in and they found this hilarious. They rolled around laughing and came up with lots of idiotic things they could sell to make a profit and bring them closer to their escape.

'We should go home,' Lindsay said later. 'I'm tired and cold.'

'Let's get in the car and put the heater on.' They piled in and he blasted the heater, as well as switching on the seat warmers.

'Oh, this is luxury,' sighed Lindsay, reclining her seat. 'My bum is toasty warm.'

'I don't want to go home,' Jake said, suddenly very certain.

'Where do you want to go?'

'Anywhere that is not here, wherever the road takes us.' If Marie could leave home at 15, so could he. He looked at the petrol gauge. 'The tank's full.'

He and Lindsay looked at each other for a long time before Jake finally put the car into first gear.

Chapter 29

The road was haloed by fluorescent blue, the ambush of ambulances and police cars made it feel narrow and cramped. The tall trees that formed a tunnel above the road felt oppressive rather than protective.

In Graham's rush to get out of the van it stalled, but neither he nor Kathi noticed as they ran to the police tape and made to go under it. A duty officer stopped them.

'That is my son,' Graham pointed to the car and yelled, desperation and fear removing all self-control. Jamie Armstrong saw them and came over.

'Kathi, Graham, calm down.' He put his hands on Graham's shoulders. 'Jake is fine. He's bruised, and a bit concussed, but it looks as though he's fine.'

Kathi's shoulders dropped with relief to know her son was alive. 'What happened?' she asked Jamie.

'I don't know exactly, but it looks like he lost control of the car and it went into the bank.'

Kathi looked over at the car. It was on its roof, angled in the middle of the road. Even in the dark she could see it was dented and grazed like a child's knee. 'One thing you should know,' continued Jamie, 'is that Lindsay Irving was in the car with him.' Kathi and Graham stared at him, speechless, waiting for him to finish the sentence.

'And?' Graham asked.

'Her injuries are more serious. She's unconscious and on her way to Dumfries to be checked out.'

'Oh God,' whispered Kathi. 'This is dreadful. Should I go with her in the ambulance? It feels like someone should.'

'Her parents are on their way. What would be really helpful is if you can go and get some clothes for Jake and follow in the van? He'll need something to go home in.'

'But –'

'Kathi, let them do what they need to do. You can follow in the van. You'll need it to get home later.'

'He's my son, I want to be with him.'

Jamie shifted his gaze from one to the other, choosing his next words carefully. 'Jake has said he'd rather be alone at the moment. He's very shaken and is in shock.' Jamie's tone was firm and Kathi found herself complying. Although secretly relieved to have someone else tell her what to do, she was all too aware of Jake's rejection, even at a time when he must have been feeling in need of a friendly face. 'Stop pushing me away,' she wanted to shout at him.

On the road to Dumfries, Graham and Kathi were mostly silent. The sun was rising and now that the initial shock had worn off they were intermittently exhausted and cold. Kathi turned on the heating.

'What were they doing?' Graham thumped his hand against the steering wheel. 'He's only ever had a couple of goes in the car, not enough to think he can actually drive it.'

'Well, he obviously did because that's exactly what happened,' Kathi snapped. 'I told you he was too young.'

'You always know what's best, don't you?' Graham shifted in his seat, gearing up for a fight. 'You are the one who said he needed to see a counsellor which, as far as I can see, has only made him worse. Drinking, shoplifting and now car theft, yeah the counselling has really helped, hasn't it?'

'Don't try to make this out to be my fault. I am not the one who put him behind the wheel of a killing machine.'

'Don't be so melodramatic. How could I have known he'd sneak out at night?'

'Anyway, you're the one who told me shoplifting wasn't a big deal, that everyone does it, that I'm overreacting. If you'd backed me up and taken a firm stand on things we might not be in this situation.'

'That's right, blame it on me, it's always my fault, just like everything else is my fault.' They were shouting loudly at each other by now, temporarily feeling better at having someone else to blame.

'That's right,' Kathi retorted. 'It is your fault. You are so busy trying to be Jake's friend that I'm the one left to do the parenting. You have no backbone.'

'Rubbish. If it wasn't for me, you wouldn't be able to swan around buying up half of Dumfrieshire.'

'If it wasn't for me, you wouldn't have a business at all.'

'Yeah, and my life would be a lot less stressful.'

'You tell yourself that if it makes you feel better.'

Graham put his hand down on the van horn and left it there, the uncomfortable noise an outlet for his aggression. Kathi focused her eyes on the passenger window and Graham kept his firmly on the road.

'Swanning around?' Kathi said after a while, unable to stop herself. 'Is that really how you see me?'

'No, not really.'

They both laughed a little, feeling better at having flushed out some of their anxiety. Quickly Kathi's laugh became sobs. 'Do you think he'll be okay?' she asked.

'I don't know.'

'Why didn't he want us in the ambulance? Why does he keep cutting himself off from us?' Graham didn't have an answer for her. 'Why was Lindsay there?' she continued. 'Oh God, I hope she's alright. You see this sort of thing on the news and pray it'll never be your child who is reported dead or in hospital with severe injuries, or having killed someone else on the road, or –'

'Enough Kathi, you can't think like that. We don't know what happened or even that it was Jake's fault. I can't remember what Jamie said now. Maybe he wasn't even driving, maybe it was Lindsay.'

Graham was hopeful, but wrong, of that Kathi was certain. The thought that her son was the cause of this accident made Kathi's stomach clench, like there was a python inside her, flexing its muscles and squeezing the strength out of her.

The image of the car, upside down in the middle of the road, reared up in front of her. The flashing blue of the emergency vehicles caused her to close her eyes; they were too glaring against the black sky. She searched her memory for a sign of Lindsay but couldn't see her. There had definitely been two ambulances, but Kathi couldn't recall seeing where the paramedics had been positioned. She could only see Jake's body on a stretcher and the medical staff around him.

'Did you see Lindsay?' she asked Graham.

'I don't remember seeing her.' Graham paused, replaying his own version of the scene. At last he shook his head. 'No, I didn't.'

At the hospital they were directed to critical care. They followed the orange stripe lining the floor and walls, half walking, half running. They wanted to be by Jake's bedside as soon as possible, but something about the institutional feel of the hospital prevented them from picking up too much speed. The first person they saw was Jamie Armstrong, who calmly took them to nearby seats and told them to sit down.

'I'll get the doctor,' he said. A few minutes later he returned with the duty consultant.

'You are Mr and Mrs Beattie?' he asked.

'Yes,' Kathi stood up, but the consultant sat down and she followed his lead.

'Jake has had a lucky escape,' he said. 'He has a mild concussion and has sprained his left wrist, but that's about it. We're going to keep him in for 24 hours' observation, then he'll be free to go, unless of course anything else arises. But I don't think it will.'

Kathi and Graham simultaneously exhaled, letting relief wash briefly over them.

'What about Lindsay?' Graham asked. 'Is she alright?'

'Her situation is more serious. She's currently unconscious and we're doing a few more tests. We're just waiting for her parents to arrive.'

'Oh God.' Kathi put her hands over her mouth and sunk further into her chair.

'Are they on their way?' Graham asked.

'An officer is bringing them over,' said Jamie. Jamie, and the doctor looked at each other before the consultant said, 'I will leave you with PC Armstrong for now and I'll see you when I come to do the next round of checks.' He smiled at them in an efficient and professional manner, the smile never quite reaching his eyes. Instead, they seemed to express both sympathy for them and anger at their failure to control their son.

Humiliated, Kathi's strength crumbled, and she burst into tears. Graham put his arm around her but he didn't like how uneasy Jamie looked nor how he cleared his throat, preparing himself to switch from friend to police officer.

'Graham, Kathi.'

They looked up at him and, sensing he wasn't going to sit down, stood up. Graham took a step away from his friend, knowing he wasn't going to like what he heard.

'A bottle of vodka was found in the car and a blood test has confirmed that Jake was above the legal alcohol limit which in Scotland, as you know, is less than one drink. Not to mention the fact he's under age to both drive and drink.'

'Okay,' said Graham slowly, buying himself some time to take in what Jamie was telling him. 'What does that mean?'

'Well, for an adult it would normally mean an automatic loss of license and a fine. It might even mean a prison sentence.'

'And for a child?' Inch by inch Graham's face paled.

'Because of his age and the fact he has no prior, it's likely he'll be fined and be disqualified from driving for a period of time.'

'But he doesn't have a license.'

'As you know, in Scotland you can get your license at 16 years old. He might not be allowed to do that. He might have to wait until he's older.'

'Will that be the end of it?'

'Not necessarily.'

'It will depend on Lindsay,' said Graham, the realisation creeping up on him slowly. Jamie nodded. Suddenly exhausted, Graham sat back down on the chair. He was winded by the knowledge he was powerless to help his son. Graham held his head in his hands as if to stop himself falling onto the floor. Sensing her husband's defeat, Kathi gathered herself together and nodded her understanding to Jamie.

'I am going to see my son now,' she told him.

Kathi stood in the doorway of Jake's room, watching him sleep. His arms, on top of the blanket, were pale and bruised in places. The blues and violets had spread like ink. A bandage was wrapped tightly around his wrist. His cheeks were flushed red with the heat of the hospital, but underneath that his pallor was pale.

There was a single, neat cut on his forehead that looked as though it had been drawn on by a make-up artist, so precisely was it placed below his hairline. He looked small and vulnerable there on the bed. Kathi had to work hard not to collapse into another flood of tears. Instead, she made herself busy by quietly unpacking the few belongings of his she'd brought with her, placing them in the tiny cabinet beside his bed.

She fussed over how neatly they were folded and placed upon the shelf before moving a chair closer to his bed and sitting down before rising again, adjusting the chair's position, and sitting down once more. Even then she made one further change.

She pulled out her phone and muted it. She looked at her emails but couldn't get comfortable. She shifted and twitched in her seat, crossing her legs first one way and then another until she felt Graham's hand on her shoulder. She put her hand over his and found some stillness. Graham took a chair and placed it on the opposite side of the bed.

Kathi looked again at her emails, but they soon dissolved into a blur as she thought back to being here after the car crash of her parents. She remembered the same feeling of otherworldliness. Hospitals feel like a world outside of the normal, where time and light and reality collapse in on themselves and become meaningless. Hours become days, doctors and nurses become surrogate parents and carers, your future is in their ability to take or preserve life. Vending machines become restaurants, laughter becomes unseemly.

The smells and sounds of that time were ones she hoped never to relive and yet here she was again, sitting by the bedside of someone so precious to her, who gave her life a meaning she never would otherwise have known. Here she was again begging some unknown power to help a loved one and cut her some slack, to do it for them if not for her. The powers that be hadn't listened last time. Both her parents died that day, and she wondered if it was worth asking for help this time. She didn't think it was.

'Graham, will you say a prayer?' He looked at her in some surprise.

'Jake's going to be all right.'

'Is he? Even if he makes it out of hospital in one piece, will he be alright?' Graham closed his eyes and put his hands together. Kathi watched his lips move as he issued a silent prayer. 'Maybe God will listen to you,' she said.

'Where do you think they were going?' Graham asked. Kathi didn't answer because she didn't want to acknowledge the possibility that he was trying to leave them. Jake's eyes blinked open, and he groaned slightly, at which Kathi and Graham leapt up. They put their hands on each of his in an attempt to reassure him. 'Jake darling, it's Mum and Dad. We're here and we love you.'

Chapter 30

The first thing to hit Jake when his eyes blinked open was thirst. His mouth was dry and when he licked his lips, they were cracked and shrunken. The next thing he was aware of was his mum's voice. Although he couldn't make out what she was saying, just the sound of her voice was reassuring. But he was confused. He didn't know where he was. He suspected he was in a bed, so thought he must be at home. But the room was far brighter than his bedroom, and the mattress felt different. Then he heard his dad's voice. 'Son,' Graham said. 'We're here. How do you feel?'

As Jake adjusted to the light and as the room came into focus, he realised where he was and wanted straightaway to fall back asleep. Graham's face was haggard, his eyes were black and filled with fear. Jake couldn't look at him and turned his head away. He saw Kathi. The initial relief he'd felt at hearing her voice disappeared with a snap, and he resented her very presence. He was embarrassed to be there in hospital, having got another thing wrong and all too alert to her judgment. He couldn't bear to see her disappointment. 'Go away,' he told her. 'I don't want you here.' He closed his eyes and turned his head back towards his dad.

'Jake,' Graham said. 'Your mum has been so worried about you, we both have.' Jake didn't say anything. 'Son, your mum loves you, don't be like this.' Graham's voice was gentle but Jake could hear the disappointment in his voice.

'Jake, please.' Kathi's voice was whiny and begging. It irritated him. 'Tell me what I have done wrong.'

'Go away,' Jake said again, still not looking at her. He could feel them both making eye contact with each other. 'Go away,' he said again, louder. He heard her walk to the door, open it and leave. Only then did Jake open his eyes and look at his dad. He reached out a hand. 'I am so sorry, Dad,' he said with tears in his eyes. 'I'm so sorry.'

'It's alright son, everything is going to be all right.' Still holding Jake's hand, he pulled his chair closer to the bed and sat down, both hands now on Jake's. 'Can you remember what happened?' He looked right into his son's eyes and Jake knew he was trying to read whether or not he would tell the truth.

He didn't know whether it was the drugs or because he was genuinely so scared about what had happened, that Jake told him. Normally he would have been too ashamed to admit how he felt about the bullying at school, or the fights with Kathi. He normally would have hidden the fact he couldn't stop thinking about Marie or that he was compelled to do something reckless and fun. He'd wanted to take the car and the vodka. He'd wanted to collect Lindsay and drive to The Green. He'd been happy sitting on the swings with her. The vodka and the cigarettes had made him feel great. For those few hours he'd felt free from restraint, free from being watched and free from the tedium of everyday life. He hadn't wanted it to end. Neither did Lindsay.

'Where is Lindsay?' he asked, suddenly terrified. 'Is she okay?'

'No, son, she's not.' Graham gripped his son's hand more tightly. 'She's unconscious at the moment and is in a bit of a bad way.'

'Is she going to be all right?' he asked, not sure if he wanted the answer.

'I don't know. The doctor couldn't tell us anything until he'd spoken to her parents. All I know is what I've told you.'

Jake felt the earth open up, and he sank gratefully down into it. He didn't want to hear anymore, and he didn't want to know that he had hurt her; that he may even have killed her. He couldn't look at his dad and didn't want Graham to look at him because the shame was too great.

Jake replayed the events of last night but remembered it only in flashes. He remembered struggling to get the car going and bumping the one in front. He remembered the headlights picking out Lindsay standing on the street waiting for him. He remembered the relief at making it to The Green in one piece. He remembered the vodka burning his mouth and throat and stomach before it released its warmth into his veins. He remembered that wonderful feeling of relaxing as his alcohol-infused blood moved around his body and into his muscles. It felt good to wash away the pain and dissatisfaction he felt with life and sink into a lovely bubble of just him and Lindsay. The rest of the world could disappear.

Jake knew she felt the same because they'd talked about their futures together. They'd talked about escaping to Glasgow or Manchester or London, and the luxury cruise liner to Sydney where they would begin new lives; lives they had created for themselves and which were full of adventure and laughter. In their new lives they would fit like square pegs in square holes. Now that dream might be over.

'Jake?' Graham's voice brought him back to the present, and he turned to look at him. 'Son, why are you so angry with your mum? She doesn't understand what she's done wrong.'

'Yes, she does. She knows.'

'Has something happened between the two of you that I don't know about?' Jake shook his head. 'Then what? She's your mother, she loves you and she at least deserves an explanation.'

'She's not my mother and I wish you would all stop pretending she is.'

Graham hung his head and looked so sad Jake almost regretted his words. Instead he said, 'I'm tired, I want to sleep.' At the same moment that Graham stood up, the door burst open so violently they both turned to look.

'You.' It was Lindsay's dad, Tommy. His face was scrunched in anger, his eyes were red and wild. He pointed at Jake. 'You murderer.' Jake froze. Murder? Did that mean Lindsay was dead? Kathi came in after him, shouting and trying to grab him. Graham moved around the bed to get in between Tommy and Jake. Annie, Lindsay's mum, stood in the doorway, helpless to stop her husband.

'Calm down, Tommy,' said Graham. 'This won't help anything.'

'Your son nearly killed my baby girl. She is lying in there fighting for her life.' The knowledge Lindsay wasn't dead gave Jake courage.

'Like you give a shit,' he sneered.

'What did you say?'

'You heard me.'

'Jake, stop it,' barked Kathi. Tommy turned to her.

'What kind of parent are you that you let your 15-year-old son out at night to drive around drunk, nearly killing innocent children?'

'Innocent?' Kathi hit back. 'There's nothing innocent about Lindsay. What was she doing sneaking out at night meeting boys?'

'Don't try to blame my baby girl.'

'Please, spare me the theatrics.'

'What can you expect though?' Tommy turned to look at Jake. 'He's not even yours, just some kid you picked up off the streets. Who knows where he came from.'

To Jake's amazement, Kathi slapped him across the face. Tommy lifted his fist as if to punch her, but at the last minute pushed her instead, but with enough force she stumbled back against the wall. Graham went to her, took her in his arms and was about to say something to Tommy, but Jake got in before him.

'What about you? Where did they dig you out from? The man who beats his wife black and blue, who abuses all of his children and whose daughter hates him with every fibre of her being.'

For a moment they were all silent, watching Tommy as he took in what Jake had said. It was as if nobody had ever called him out on his abuse before, and perhaps they hadn't.

At first all Jake saw was shock pass through Tommy's eyes, before his face whitened at the knowledge his dirty secret had been aired. His head and neck now turned puce with rage, and Jake almost laughed out loud with hysteria and panic as Tommy lunged for the bed. Jake was certain he would kill him if he got hold of him. He tried to scramble out the other side but even with the drugs and his adrenaline he was slow to move and Tommy grabbed his arm, pulled him back down on the bed and put his hands around Jake's throat. He wasn't aware of anything except the hatred in Tommy's eyes and the strong smell of whisky. He didn't notice Graham trying to pull Tommy off, Kathi and Annie screaming for help, or two police officers rush in and tackle him from behind. As soon as Tommy's hands left Jake's throat, his replaced them. This time as a protective shield while he coughed and gasped and tried to regain control of his breathing.

Tommy was hauled from the room, Graham and Kathi stood in front of the bed in a last bid to protect their son. Amongst all the commotion the doctor and a nurse came in to check Jake had no injuries and once satisfied there was no harm done they left, shutting the door behind them.

As soon as the door closed, Kathi broke down. She was frenzied and rambling. Graham was holding her and trying to calm her down, worried she'd do herself damage. Jake felt bizarrely at ease. He could see and hear Tommy through the glass panel in the door. His arms flailed, casting himself as the badly done-to, overwrought father, tormented by the boy who hurt his daughter. Who could blame him for getting angry? Jake heard him say.

In time, the commotion and excitement in the ward died down and everything went back to normal. For the rest of the day Jake could tell that the nurses were gossiping about what had happened, and who wouldn't? Jake was pleased because for a while at least it took people's attention away from his own stupidity. He told his parents they didn't need to stay, that he was fine and wanted to be alone, but he succeeded only in expelling them to the waiting area. They wouldn't leave the hospital.

Jake dozed off and on, the pain from the accident coming and going depending on his drug dosage. When the pain subsided he slept, thankful for the escape from his own guilt and shame at having got something else wrong. He felt he couldn't get anything right anymore, and yet it didn't seem so long ago that life had been easy.

He and Hayden had been best friends. They'd played football together, they'd played on his computer console, school was alright and he loved his parents. Now the reverse was true, and he didn't understand why. Worse, there was nothing he could do about it. The only saving grace in his life recently had been Joanne and Lindsay, one of whom he'd rendered unconscious. He wished Joanne was here because she'd know what to say to make this better. She'd be able to make him feel a little less worthless. For the first time he wondered where his phone was and assumed it must have been left in the car. He'd ask Jamie for it next time he saw him. Actually, it was a relief to be free of it for a while.

A nurse came in. 'Time to check you out,' she said. 'Make sure everything is working as it should be.' Jake smiled half-heartedly at her but didn't say anything. He was feeling low and couldn't think of anything to say. In addition, his throat hurt from when Tommy had tried to strangle him.

'You'll be looking forward to going home?' the nurse said.

'Yes,' he croaked.

'You came in with your friend?' He nodded. 'What's her name?'

'Lindsay, Lindsay Irving. Do you know how she is?'

'She came round about an hour ago.'

'She's not unconscious anymore?'

'That's right, and she's talking, which is a good sign.'

'She's going to be all right?'

'It is early days, but it looks like it.' Jake hid his face behind his hands. He didn't want the nurse to see his tears, but she sat down on the bed next to him.

'Would you like to see her?' she asked. 'She's asking for you.' Jake sat up, feeling like he'd been given a lifeline.

'Yes,' he said, wiping his eyes. 'But what about-'

'her parents have gone to the police station so won't be back for another while. Do you want to go and say hello?'

'Yes,' he smiled.

The nurse brought a wheelchair and wheeled him over to intensive care. 'Just a few minutes,' she said, giving Lindsay the once over to make sure she was up to it. After she'd gone Jake pushed himself closer to the bed and put his hand in hers.

'Lindsay,' he whispered. 'I'm sorry. I'm so sorry about it all.'

'It wasn't your fault,' she said. 'We were both to blame. And you don't need to whisper,' she teased. 'What have I missed?'

'Oh my God,' Jake laughed. 'It all totally kicked off. Wait till I tell you.'

Chapter 31

It had been a condition of Jake having his own mobile phone that Kathi and Graham know the passcode. When the nurse brought in the clear plastic bag with Jake's dishevelled belongings in it, his phone was sitting on top of his clothes and shoes. It had a crack down the front of the screen, but other than that it didn't look too damaged. 'Do you know where Jake is?' Kathi asked the nurse.

'His friend has regained consciousness. He's gone to see her.'

'Oh, thank God. Is she going to be alright?'

'All her test results are good, it looks like she's going to be fine.'

The shadow that Lindsay might not pull through had been hanging over her. Not only was she worried about the girl herself, but the severity of her injuries would have a huge impact on Jake and what he was charged with.

She'd managed to avoid Jamie Armstrong so far, but knew it was only a matter of time before he pulled them aside and told them what was going to happen to Jake.

Once the nurse had left the room Kathi hesitated for only a second before removing the phone from its bag and going into the waiting area. She knew she shouldn't but she couldn't help herself switching the phone on and waiting to be asked for the passcode. She punched in the number they had agreed upon and, if she was honest, was surprised that he'd kept his word and the agreed code.

All too quickly the phone began to ping as notifications came firing in from his apps. She looked through them trying to discern any clues as to what was going on in Jake's life to make him think stealing a car and driving drunk was a good idea, or fun, or daring, or whatever it was he was trying to achieve.

Her eyes widened, and her stomach dropped. Message after message arrived deriding her son for being adopted and unwanted, for not belonging and being a freak. Seeing these words aimed at someone she loved so much and who was now lying in a hospital bed enraged her. She tried to see who had written the messages, but she couldn't necessarily tell from the sender's handle name, and she couldn't understand why some of them disappeared into the ether, untraceable.

Thinking it was her own ineptitude, she switched to another app, one she was familiar with. This time there were messages of concern. News of Jake's crash had spread like spilt milk and people were curious. Kathi knew she and Graham would be quizzed a lot over the next few weeks, and she dreaded it.

As she scrolled through the messages one name jumped out of her. Joanne Wylie. Why would she be messaging Jake? She opened the message and looked at the thread. It went back for months, to not long after Common Riding, in fact, soon after Joanne had taken the High Street flat.

Perplexed as to how they had become friends in the first place and wondering if perhaps there was another Joanne Wylie, Kathi read through the correspondence. Her face flushed and her head spun as she read the comments Jake had made about her: How much he hated her, how nosy she was and how little she understood him. He complained that she didn't even try to see things from his point of view. Lies, thought Kathi, I have tried so hard.

Her horror intensified when she saw how Joanne had egged him on in his thoughts. She repeatedly referred to Kathi as not being his real mum. His real mum was somewhere else and she would understand him. Joanne reminded Jake that he was young and had a good chance of finding Marie and being able to build a life with her, the life he should have had.

A chill went down her spine when she saw that Joanne had coaxed him into looking for his adoption file. She shuddered at the thought of him reading those notes. He was too vulnerable and angry to be shown what had been written about Marie's state of mind at the time, or her lifestyle and how he was conceived. Kathi knew that if he read those notes now, it could do irreparable damage. So engrossed was Kathi that she didn't notice Graham until he sat down beside her.

'Is that is Jake's phone?' he asked. 'I'm amazed it's still working. Should you be looking through it?' he teased. 'You know what he's like about his phone.'

'I'm glad I did,' said Kathi. 'I don't care if it's the wrong thing to do. At the end of the day, he's my son and I haven't done enough to protect him. That ends as of today.' Kathi handed Graham the phone. 'Read that,' she said. 'Read it.' They sat in stony silence as Graham read through the dialogue.

'Who is this Joanne Wylie?' he asked.

'One of my tenants.'

'A tenant? Why is she texting our son? Is something going on between them?'

'No, it's nothing like that, but you're right. Why is she texting him? They can't possibly have anything in common. She's older than me.'

'We have to talk to him about this. The things she's saying are playing with his emotions.'

'No.' Kathi looked at him sharply. 'I don't want to say anything to him just yet. I don't know what it all means.'

'It means she's sticking her nose into something that doesn't concern her and causing a lot of trouble.'

'Exactly, but why?' Kathi switched the phone off and put it in her bag. 'Don't tell him I've got it. If he asks just say it must have been lost during the crash.'

'Kathi, I don't feel comfortable doing that.'

'Please, I need a bit of time to figure out how to handle this. He wants a new phone anyway, so he need never know.'

'On your own head be it.'

'Did you ask Jake why he's so angry with me?' Graham shifted in his seat and wouldn't look at her. 'Well, what is it?' she snapped. 'It can't be any worse that what I've just read.' She indicated to Jake's phone in her bag.

'Just more of the same, there's nothing really to tell.'

'Tell me what he said. I need to know.'

'He said you knew why he was angry. That you're not his mum and we should all stop pretending. I promise, that's all he said.'

'It's not fair. Why is it me that's getting the brunt of his anger? What have I done that's so bad?'

'Nothing, you've done nothing wrong.'

'It's not fair.'

'No, it's not.' Graham moved closer to his wife and put his arm around her. She shook him off and stood up.

'Don't patronise me,' she hissed at him.

'I'm not,' he said, offended.

'You don't know what it's like. I've done everything for that boy. I've nursed him when he's been sick, I've cooked all his meals, I've been to all his school concerts, his football matches.' She slapped her sternum. 'It's me that's carted him from activity to activity and comforted him when he's fallen out with Hayden. Me.'

Kathi paced up and down before stopping in front of Graham. 'And yet it's you who gets all the kind words and the hugs and is taken into his confidence. It's you he goes to when he needs comfort.' She stood over Graham and pointed her finger at him. 'It's not fair and I-'

Jamie Armstrong's luminous police vest caught her attention, and she stared at him with ill-concealed fear. Graham turned to look and stood up when he saw who it was.

'Graham, Kathi, will you take a seat?' Jamie's face was pale and at first he couldn't look either of the in eye.

'Just tell us,' said Graham with forced calm. 'Please.'

Only now did Jamie looked at them. 'Let's sit down.' Silently the three of them sat. 'It's not good news, I'm afraid. He's going to be charged with drink driving, driving without a license and endangering the life of a minor. It means there will be a fine to pay, he'll be banned from gaining his license and most likely go to court.'

'To court?' Graham asked. Jamie nodded.

'It might mean a six-month sentence.'

It had been two weeks since Cherry had undergone the biopsy, after which she'd stayed with her parents for a couple of nights.

The day after the biopsy had been the worst. She'd felt like the lump was punishing her for disturbing it, and Cherry had felt so sorry for herself that day she'd even asked her mum to make her favourite childhood dinner; mince and potatoes. While she lay on her parents' sofa, snuggled up under a duvet, she let herself be treated like a child.

That very first spoonful of mince transported her back to a time of innocence and carefree schooldays. She felt again the security she had done as a child, watching Saturday evening television while eating her dinner of mince 'n' tatties. Maybe there would even be tinned peaches for pudding.

She looked over at the blank television now and caught her reflection on the screen. Gone was that carefree childhood. What she saw now was a woman who might be dying. Coming face-to-face with her own mortality was terrifying, and she cried into her tatties.

'Don't cry, pet,' her mum coaxed. 'It'll be fine, don't you worry. You are young and strong. I've never known anything to get the better of you.' The older woman put her arm around her daughter and squeezed her tightly.

'I don't know what I'd do without you, Mum.'

That was two weeks ago and here she was again, this time to get the results. The same nurse as before ushered Cherry into Dr Gill's consulting room and where she was instructed to take a seat. Cherry obediently sat. She could barely breathe for nerves. She was sure that if she took a breath, her body would relax and she would vomit.

She didn't hear a lot of what Dr Gill said. It was all medical talk, but when eventually she stopped speaking and looked at Cherry, Cherry said, 'Sorry Dr Gill, I didn't catch any of that. Do I have cancer, or not?'

'You have Stage-1 breast cancer.' Cherry's face fell, her fears had been confirmed. 'Cherry, this is good news.'

'Good news?'

'Yes, thanks to your observation, you have found the cancer early. This means we can remove it straight away. You may need to undergo some radiation therapy but you should have a one hundred percent recovery.' Dr Gill sat back in her chair and waited for Cherry to take in the news.

'Are you sure?'

'Based on the biopsy there's no reason to think otherwise.'

'Thank you, Dr Gill, thank you. Look at me,' she held up her hands, 'I am still shaking.' They talked through the operation and what would happen if the radiation therapy was necessary.

'One thing I've noticed, Cherry, is that nobody has come to the centre with you.'

'I haven't told anyone except my best friend and my mum.'
'Why not?'
'I didn't want to worry anyone.'

'I see you live a few hours away,' said Dr Gill, looking at her notes. 'You are going to need help during your recovery. You don't need to tell everybody, but I suggest you tell one or two people you trust and who will be able to help you in the weeks after the operation.'

As she stepped out onto the street, Cherry felt like she'd been given a new lease of life. It was still raining, but the downpour didn't feel oppressive. Instead, it felt like it was washing away her old gripes and complaints, making way for new opportunities and adventures. She knew her mum was waiting for her to call, so she dialled her number straightaway.

'It is Stage-1, Mum.'

'What does that mean?'

'It means we caught it early and they can remove it. The doctor thinks I should have a one hundred percent recovery. One hundred percent.'

'Oh darlin', that's brilliant news, really brilliant.'

'I'll be home later, we can celebrate.'

'Absolutely. I'll let everyone know.'

After they hung up Cherry was tempted to check her email but stopped herself. No, this was a day to focus on the here and now, to take in the world around her and enjoy herself. She put her phone away and headed to the shops, just as she had planned to do the day of the biopsy itself.

That night she and her parents celebrated with champagne, and the next morning her brother Ross, and nephew Sam, came over with cake. It was later that day Kathi called.

'Did you get your results?' she asked.

'Yes, all good news. Stage 1. I need an op then will be back to normal.'

'That's brilliant news. I'm so happy for you.' Cherry could hear Kathi smiling on the other end of the phone.

'Me too! How are things there?' Kathi filled Cherry in on what had happened since she'd been in Glasgow.

'Oh my God, Kathi, that's awful.'

'Can I ask, when you did your checks on Joanne Wylie, were there any red flags?'

'None, but I'll have another look. Anything wrong?'

'I found a whole load of text messages from her Jake's phone.'

Cherry gasped. 'I totally forgot to tell you,' she said to Kathi. 'I saw the two of them chatting on the High Street one day.'

'When?'

'Maybe a couple of weeks ago now. I was going to tell you, but it totally slipped my mind. They weren't doing anything, but I remember wondering how they knew each other.'

Later, when they'd rung off, curiosity compelled Cherry to look again at Joanne's online application form. Still nothing jumped out at her. Joanne's guarantor was her mum, Maureen. I'll give her a quick call, she thought, see what's what.

Chapter 32

The next day Jake was told he could go home. Once he was dressed and had gathered his stuff together, a nurse brought a wheelchair in which to take him to the hospital entrance. Graham and Kathi hadn't yet arrived, so he had a bit of time to kill.

'Do you want to see your friend before you go?' the nurse asked. Lindsay had been moved out of critical care but was still being monitored. Her face and arms were bruised and the sight of them renewed Jake's guilt. He wondered if he'd ever stop being angry with himself for hurting his friend so badly.

'I wish you were coming home too,' said Jake.

'I don't. It's much nicer here than at home.' Lindsay smiled, but neither of them laughed because it was too close to the truth.

'Have your parents been back?'

'Mum has. She doesn't say much. I keep telling her to leave him, but she just tells me to drop the subject. I don't know why I bother.'

'Will you forgive me? Will you still come to Australia with me?'

'You dafty,' she said softly, 'of course I will.' She paused before asking, 'Has Jamie Armstrong been to see you?'

Jake lowered his eyes. He was terrified of the conversation that was yet to come. The conversation when he was told what he would be charged with and whether or not he'd go to prison. 'Not yet, but I know it's coming.'

'It'll be alright. I'm not going to press charges.'

'Your parents or the police might. I don't think we have a say in it.'

'But I'm to blame just as much as you. We were both in that car.' Jake appreciated Lindsay trying to make him feel better but he knew it was him behind the wheel and that he was ultimately responsible.

'Lindsay, I'm so sorry, I wish I could change what happened.'

'Stop it. I'm fine and I'm not angry. It's you we need to worry about now.' She gave him a play punch on the arm, but Jake grabbed her hand and squeezed it tightly. To stop himself from breaking down completely, he changed the subject.

'I've been thinking,' he said. 'I'm going to go and see my birth mum. I'm going to find out where she lives and as soon as I'm well enough I'm going to go.'

'How will you find out where she lives?'

'I don't know yet, but I will.'

'Are you sure you want to find her? It's a big step.'

'Never been surer. I can't stay here, not after all of this.' Jake indicated the hospital and Lindsay's injuries.

'Good luck.'

'When are they letting you out?'

'I'm trying to stay here as long as possible.' She lowered her voice. 'I've been making stuff up, telling them I have pain when I don't, that sort of thing. I'm not ready to go home yet. Will you come and visit?'

'Definitely. Don't stay here too long though, I'll miss you.'

'Okay, lovebirds,' said the nurse. 'Time to say goodbye. Jake, your parents are here.' She wheeled Jake to the lift. 'Tell me something,' she said when the doors closed. 'Why is that lovely young woman not your girlfriend?'

'We're just friends,' Jake explained, his face colouring. The nurse made a noise as if to say she didn't believe a word of it.

Graham and Kathi were waiting in the car at the hospital entrance. They both jumped out as soon as they saw him, Kathi taking his bag from the back of the wheelchair. Graham opened the backseat door and helped his son manoeuvre out of the wheelchair and into the car.

'I'm fine, Dad, honest.' Graham turned to the nurse and thanked her for all her help. 'No problem,' she said. She looked in to where Jake was sitting. 'You take care of yourself now.'

'I will, thank you.'

Graham and Kathi got back in the car, and they began the journey home. Jake could see his parents looking at each other. He knew there was something they wanted to tell him. 'What is it?' he asked Graham. Graham looked in their rear-view mirror.

'Jamie came to see us.'

'What did he say?' Jake's voice was small. Here it was, the moment he had been dreading.

'He says that you are going to be charged.'

'But Lindsay said she wasn't going to press charges.'

'It is not up to Lindsay, I'm afraid,' said Kathi. 'It is the Crown who have decided to pursue the case.'

'Dad, what does this mean?'

'It means you're going to be charged with drunk driving, driving without a license and endangering the life a minor.'

'What will happen if they find me guilty?'

'There will be a fine. You won't get your license for quite a while. And... It could mean a custodial sentence.' Graham looked in the rear-view mirror again, trying to gauge his son's reaction. Jake's face paled and he couldn't stop his tears. The events of the last couple of days and the uncertainty of Lindsay's prognosis had taken its toll. Any bravado he may have felt had long since disappeared. He now felt like the young teenage boy he really was.

'Jake, try not to worry,' said Kathi. 'We're going to do everything we can to make sure that doesn't happen. We're going to get the best lawyer we can.'

Jake ignored her. He looked out of the window and tried to put his thoughts in some kind of order, but he had no idea of where to start. Kathi reached a hand over to take one of his and for once he didn't snatch it away. He was so caught up in his own fear he didn't even notice.

'Jake, are you okay?' Graham asked.

'Yes,' he said on autopilot and without conviction.

The rest of the journey passed by in a blur. Jake could hear his parents' voices, he knew they were discussing their plan of action but for the time being it was all too much. He didn't want to listen. He didn't want to acknowledge the seriousness of his situation or that there was the possibility he could go to prison. If he thought about it too much, he wasn't sure he'd be able to recover.

The sympathy for Marie that Jake had initially felt when he read his adoption file was now replaced with an anger that stemmed from sadness. He flitted between being furious at how he had been conceived and the ease with which he had been thrown away, and angry at how careless Marie had been to get pregnant in the first place.

Before he returned the lever arch file to its space under the eaves he'd taken a photo of the picture of Marie. He looked at it every day in case he could find out a little more about her, that perhaps there was some kinetic thread between them that neither knew was there.

In hospital and during his recovery at home he had so much free time that his brain went wild with thoughts and daydreams of Marie. It got to the point where he was obsessed and couldn't think about anything other than where she was and what she was doing.

When he returned to school he enjoyed a brief bit of fame. Everyone wanted to hear about what happened and what Jamie Armstrong was going to charge him with. They all wanted to know how Lindsay was and if she was still speaking to him. But after those first few days of attention, life returned to normal. His bruises vanished, his cut healed, all evidence of his accident faded away.

But something inside of Jake had changed permanently. He no longer saw the point of his life in Byreburn. It all seemed so trivial in comparison to what was out there waiting for him. Namely, his birth mother and the life he should have had. His schoolwork suffered, for which his teachers told him off daily. It was the year before exams and his year group were constantly being drilled on how important it was for them to work hard this year in preparation for a future that depended on good results. Jake didn't care about exams. He cared about finding Marie.

The only person Jake could talk with about this was Joanne. He'd gone round to her flat one day after school and told her about finding the folder and how neatly everything had been filed. He showed her the photograph of Marie and had been delighted when she said how beautiful Marie was, how alike they were. He'd even told Joanne about Kathi not being able to have children.

'Does the file tell you where she is now?' Joanne asked.

'No, nothing after I was adopted. I hoped there might be a letter or a toy or something from her. You know, a keepsake.'

'Has the file got her date of birth?'

'Yes, why?' Joanne smiled at him conspiratorially. 'Let's see what we can find out,' she said, logging on to her tablet and the National Registers of Scotland. She typed in Marie's name, date and place of birth. The first document they found was her birth certificate. Joanne paid for the download and emailed it to Jake. They peered at the certificate on screen and all the information matched what they knew about her.

'Let's see if she got married,' said Joanne. They searched again and this time three entries came up that were possible matches to a Marie Karen Robertson. 'I am not going to buy them all,' said Joanne. 'But you can do a Google search and see what comes up. I bet she's on social media somewhere and you can compare photos.' Jake nodded and grinned like an idiot, he didn't know any of these things were possible. 'We'll do one more search,' she said. She searched the death records. Jake's face fell and Joanne said, 'Well, she was a junkie.'

Jake didn't take a breath while they waited for the results to come up but let out a sigh of relief when nobody matching her description showed up. Joanne sat back in her seat and looked at him. 'The rest is up to you, Jake.'

It took him three days to find her. He searched under each of the three names listed, a day for each. Typically, hers was the last and it wasn't through Marie herself he found her but through a friend of hers. She'd been tagged in a photo and as soon as he saw it he knew it was her. He searched a little deeper and found more photos. There was no question that this was his Marie. He was so excited but didn't know how to celebrate. He texted Joanne.

I found her online. It's definitely her. Unmistakable. I can't believe it.

Brilliant news. Where is she?

In Glasgow.

Got a number or an address?

Jake had a look at her profile but she'd kept most of it private so he couldn't see. His phone rang, it was Joanne.

'In the file, did it list her address, or her parents address?'

'I can't remember, I'll call you back.'

Jake snuck back along to the eaves and carefully removed the adoption file. In the safety of his bedroom he went straight to the back and found an address. He texted it to Joanne.

What are you going to do with it? he asked her.

She didn't reply for ages and he got really jittery. He wanted to know what she was up to. To calm his nerves he went back online, staring at each and every photograph of Marie and wondering who all those people with her were. There was one man who cropped up time and again and Jake thought he must be her husband. He felt sick when he realized the two little girls who kept showing up must be her daughters. One looked just like her husband and one looked just like her. And just like him.

Jake ran to the bathroom and retched into the toilet. Whilst he always knew it was more than likely she'd had more children, seeing their smiling faces, their arms wrapped around her, having what by rights should have been his, was too much. That single moment of realization ripped his euphoria in shreds and he was left feeling as bruised and worthless as before. If anything, he felt worse. His phone pinged, it was Joanne.

Marie's address and phone number

Jake immediately phoned Joanne. 'Where did you get this? Are you sure it's right?'

'I phoned her parents, told them I was an old classmate and I was organizing a reunion. Easy as that.'

'You spoke to her mum?'

'Yes.'

'That is my granny,' he said, awed that someone had spoken to a blood relative. 'What did she sound like?'

'Normal, I guess. Actually she sounded old.'

'Anything else?'

'Well, I think she'd been drinking. Look, never mind that, the point is you know where Marie is. You can go and see her.'

Jake was silent and felt sick all over again. It was one thing to search for her, it was another to find her. He was terrified. 'What if she doesn't want to be found? She's got a new family.'

'Of course she wants to be found. You are her child. Her first born. She was too young before, she's not anymore.'

'Do you think so?'

'Absolutely. This is what you said you wanted. You've got the information now, the rest is up to you.'

Chapter 33

It had been three weeks since the crash and things were strained at home, even the sessions with Brenda weren't helping. Jake had become so obsessed with Marie he felt like Gollum, coveting the photograph of her like she was his very own precious. He spent far too long looking at her house on Google maps. But he was nervous. He was scared of making his dream a reality. What if Marie didn't want to see him? What if they had the wrong person? He'd be right back at square one.

He couldn't avoid it forever, though. The lure of her was so strong that he gave up fighting it and devised his plan.

He had been to Glasgow before, but only on day trips with Kathi or Graham, one of them driving to wherever it was they were going. The last time they'd gone it was to the Science Museum. Hayden had gone with them and together the boys had tried out every challenge and puzzle the museum had on offer. Afterwards they headed into the city centre and had Vietnamese food for lunch. Kathi and Graham had raved about it, but Jake and Hayden later agreed it tasted just like Chinese.

Jake recalled how much fun that day had been. Nobody was bullying him, he and Hayden were still best friends. He had no thoughts of Marie and there was no Lindsay or Joanne in his life. On that day trip, he didn't need to worry about where they were going or how they'd get there. His parents had it all under control, they dictated the day.

It wasn't as much fun standing alone in Buchanan Street bus station trying to figure out how to get to Rutherglen. Google Maps told him to walk to Central Station, which he did. The station felt really big and busy compared to Dumfries. It took him a bit of time, but he figured out where to buy his ticket and which platform to wait on. He kept expecting someone to stop and ask him what he was doing there by himself, but that's the thing about cities; you can disappear and nobody will ask any questions.

The train was empty when Jake got on and he took a window seat in a bank of four, stretching out and enjoying his freedom. It was short-lived. Because the train didn't leave for another ten minutes and the carriage filled up and made him nervous, especially when a man sat down opposite him. Jake watched the man for a bit. It was hard not to. He twitched and jolted continuously, seemingly unable to sit still, forcing the others in the bank of seats to move away. He was dressed in dirty grey tracksuit bottoms and a hoodie, with a ripped black parka over the top. His hood was up, but Jake could still hear him muttering to himself. It wasn't aggressive talk, but he was clearly a psycho. Jake couldn't help but wonder from where he'd gotten his clean, white Nike trainers. They looked as if he'd only got them that day.

Jake had nearly decided to move seats when the man looked up and stared at him. He must have clocked Jake's fear because he looked at him as if to say don't dare move. Jake didn't. Instead, he looked out the window and did his best not to catch the man's eye in the window when they went through a tunnel.

Jake knew from Google that he only had four stops to go, but each time they pulled into a station he looked around for the sign. He needed reassurance he hadn't gone too far. At Rutherglen he got off the train and looked around for the exit. Jake was disappointed to see the psycho had also got off and tried desperately to look like he knew where he was going. The psycho might take him for a soft touch and try to mug him. Jake had heard his mum talk about things like that happening in Glasgow. Luckily the man walked straight past him, oblivious to the fact Jake was even there, which was fine by him.

Jake made his way up the stairs and through the barrier, and again his nerves kicked in. He was close, so close, to finding Marie and seeing her, speaking to her, reuniting with her. He banished any thought that she might not want to see him.

When he'd started out that morning he was nothing but excited and thrilled at the prospect of his journey to Glasgow and seeing Marie's face light up when she realised who he was. Joanne was right, mums always wanted to find their long-lost children. But now that Marie was within reach, he faltered. His nerves reared up and scared him for a moment, but he pushed them back down. He couldn't come all this way for nothing. He had to find out if they had a future together.

Jake consulted Google again and got the directions to her street. It was a nine-minute walk. He knew what her house looked like because of the hours he'd spent pouring over Google's satellite view. It looked just the way he'd imagined it. A garden out front with a fence, and a driveway down the side. It was the picture of a happy family home, a home that had a Jake shaped hole in it. He felt in his bones that Marie was waiting for him to find her.

He looked around the main street, taking in all the shops and cafés, memorising the route from the station to the house. This was going to be his new home, his new neighbourhood. It was so loud and rough compared to Byreburn's High Street. There was rubbish being blown about by the passing cars, horns beeping at delivery lorries who were blocking the road, people everywhere. It excited him, the prospect of his new city life. A life full of adventure, where there were new things to do every day, the opposite of Byreburn's rural quiet, where nothing of any interest ever happened.

He took a turn off the main street and then another, each street becoming quieter and more suburban than the last. The houses looked just like those he'd seen on Google, so he knew he was in the right place. Eventually he hit her street and his legs slowed. By the time he reached number 54, her house, they nearly buckled. He could see into the living room window and saw someone moving inside. His heart beat with force, like a hammer bell at the funfair being struck repeatedly, ever faster.

He ducked across the driveway to the neighbour's house and hid in front of their hedge until he caught his breath. That was her, he knew it, that was Marie. His mother. Mum. For a few seconds he was paralyzed. This was the moment he had dreamed about and played out in his mind's eye time after time after time. He wanted it to be perfect. He wanted to take in every moment and savour it. It would be the first time only once.

'Come on, Jake,' he geed himself on. 'This is it. If you don't do it now, you'll never know.' He took a deep breath and with purpose stood up, walked down the short path to the front door and rang the bell. The chimes inside played a tune that sounded tinny and old-fashioned. It wasn't a solid ding dong like Kathi had. This was something he'd heard on a soap opera once, and for some reason he was disappointed by it. 'If it's good enough for Marie,' he told himself, 'it's good enough for me.'

Nerves got the better of him and he rang the bell again, this time a different tune played. As soon as he pressed the button, he regretted it because the woman who answered the door was cross at his impatience and the last thing he wanted to do was anger his mother before he'd even met her. The frown on her face disappeared when she saw him.

'Yes?' she asked. Jake couldn't speak. This was her, and she was even more beautiful than he had imagined. Her curly hair was glossy, her big brown eyes sparkled and her wide smile was just like his. 'Can I help you?'

'Are you Marie Robertson?' he asked.

'I was, who are you?'

'It's me,' he blurted. 'Your son.'

For a second he saw confusion in her eyes before he saw it turned to horror and her face turn as pale as winter. She took a step back and put a hand on the wall to balance herself. She stared at him but didn't say anything. She looked so shocked Jake thought he should say something. 'My name is Jake. I'm 15 years old. I'm your son.'

She slowly reached her hand out and put it on his shoulder to guide him inside. He saw her look around the street before she closed the door. She didn't want him here. Jake clenched his teeth together, determined not to panic. She ushered him into her living room. There were two enormous sofas on either side of the room and a large TV which was switched on but muted.

She came into the room after him and they both stood there, staring at each other. He couldn't take his eyes off her. He realised he was staring at her too hard because she turned away. He responded in the same way. He watched the television, distracting himself from this hideous situation.

'How did you find me?' she asked.

'Internet.' Jake kept his eyes on the television.

'But how did you get my details?' Marie switched the TV off and faced him.

'I found my adoption papers. Your parents are at the same address. They told me where you live.'

'Why did they do that?' Jake watched her clench her hands so tightly they turned white.

'My friend said she was an old friend of yours and wanted to invite you to a school reunion.'

Marie closed her eyes, but he couldn't tell why. 'Are you here by yourself?' she asked. He nodded. 'How did you get here?'

'Bus and train. I got the bus from –'

'Don't tell me, I don't want to know.' She paced up and down the room, which made him nervous. He didn't want to upset her, so decided not to say anything else. Instead, he looked around the room. There were framed photographs everywhere, on the walls, on the mantelpiece and even on a couple of side tables. He saw a photograph of her in a white dress, standing next to a man, and went over to look at it. It was Marie's wedding day. She looked so happy. On the mantelpiece were school photographs of the two girls at varying ages. Her daughters. The photographs were the same as Kathi had of him at home, also framed and hung on the walls.

Both girls had long hair that had been brushed and styled into a plait with care and attention. He hated those girls. They had taken all the love that should have been his. If they didn't exist Marie would be happy to see him, she would want him to come and live with her.

'Hayley is the eldest and Beth is the youngest,' said Marie, coming to stand next to him. Jake looked at her and said, 'I'm the eldest.' This made her cry for some reason and it took a little while before she said, 'Why have you come?'

'To be with you. You must have wondered where I was.'

'I have -' she hesitated.

'Jake.'

'Jake. I have Jake, every day, and I hoped you were well and healthy and had a mum who looked after you better than I ever could have done.'

'I did get a mum, and she's nice, but she's not you. Now that you're older...and I'm older and you don't need to look after me...you know, because I'm not a baby anymore...I thought I could come and live with you...be a family, a proper family. I've always wanted sisters and I'm no trouble, honestly.'

'Jake,' Marie tried to interrupt him, but now he'd started he couldn't stop himself from talking.

'I can pack a suitcase and bring only what I need so you don't even have to come and pick me up. I don't mind sharing a bedroom, or even sleeping on the sofa if there isn't enough room. I'm easy to get on with so won't be any trouble.'

'Jake,' Marie tried again.

'I'll go to school and work really hard. I'm clever and will get good grades and you'll be proud of me and you won't regret letting me come to live here and letting me be your child.'

'Jake, please stop.' She took him by the shoulders and shook him to make him stop talking, but he couldn't.

'I won't be any trouble, I promise, I just want to be a family, I just want to be with you.'

Marie put her arms around him and squeezed him so tightly that he couldn't take a breath and had to stop talking. When she let go, she took his face in both her hands. She smiled the slightest smile. 'You're a beautiful boy,' she said. 'Won't your mum be worried about you?'

'You are my mum.'

'No, I'm not,' she stood apart from him. 'I gave birth to you, but I'm not your mum. I have a family. Hayley, Beth and Chris are my family. You have your own family.' Tears spilled down his face no matter how hard he clenched his jaw. 'You have to go home and forget all about me.'

'But why, what did I do wrong?'

'Nothing, you did nothing wrong.' Marie held him by the shoulders and looked intently at him. 'This isn't your fault.'

'I must have done something. Whatever it was, I'm sorry, I didn't mean it. Please don't send me away again.'

'I'm sorry Jake, I am so sorry but we are never going to be a family. When you're older, you'll understand you shouldn't have come. I can't give you what you want. I'm sorry.'

'Please,' he begged, 'please don't send me away again, I'll be good.'

'I know you will, I know you'll be good.' She took a ragged breath. 'I know you are a good boy, but you still need to go home.'

'This is my home.'

'No,' she was stern. She wiped away her tears. 'This is not your home. I am not your mum. You have to leave now.' She left the room, and he heard her open the front door.

Jake looked around the living room, searching for inspiration or some way of making her change her mind and letting him stay. But he couldn't come up with anything. In the hallway he looked at her, praying she would have a change of heart, but still she wouldn't look at him. Desperate, he walked up to her, stopped and gave her one more chance, but she still wouldn't look at him. Her eyes, red rimmed, wouldn't lower to his level. Shame made its presence known. He had made a fool of himself. He ran from the house, trying to hold it together until out of sight. He heard her shut the door behind him, but he didn't see her tears.

Chapter 34

Like a mad dog he ran and ran, always on the precipice of falling, his jaw still clenched. He ran past the express supermarket, the budget store and post office that he thought would be his local shops. But he would never come here again, he would never help Marie with her errands on a Saturday morning. He would never help Marie with anything.

At the station, he didn't know what to do. The focus and thought of Marie that had kept him going earlier in the day had evaporated. He stopped and looked around. All he saw were strangers. The station itself looked enormous and unfriendly, and he felt like everyone was watching him, knowing he didn't belong. He tried to make himself invisible by turning against a wall, his face touching the cold surface. He closed his eyes and tried not to panic, but he couldn't put his thoughts into any order and felt a million miles away from home. He was lost and abandoned, not sure which way to go next. He wanted simply to disappear, to be transported back to his bedroom where he could forget this ever happened.

'Are you all right, son?' A man's gruff voice made him turn with a start. The man was wearing a uniform, which Jake took to be that of a station guard. His humiliation moved up another gear. All he wanted was to be left alone, and now someone official was involved. Of course he could make something up, he could lie, but by now any strength or determination or courage he had had that morning was well and truly spent.

He knew he looked pathetic because the man didn't ask him anything else, he simply said, 'Come with me lad, we'll get you sorted out.'

He led Jake into the ticket office and sat him down on a chair. Jake sensed the man was going to take care of him because he allowed his mind to wander back to Marie's house. He relived looking at the house and seeing her through the window. He saw again the photographs around the living room and the smiling faces of Beth and Hayley. He hated them. They had taken his mum. She should have been his.

The ticket office door opened, breaking his dream state, and a huge policeman came in. He dwarfed the small, cramped office and looked down at Jake. The officer's body was bulked out by his vest and belt, the tools and gadgets of the job hanging from his person, all of which added to his size and intimidated Jake. If he had already felt young and lost, the appearance of this police officer only intensified it. Jamie Armstrong never looked this scary, he never made Jake feel like this young a child. This officer made him realise just how out of his depth he was, and he didn't know how to get to the shallows.

'Hello,' the officer said. Jake didn't reply. His chin was wobbling because he'd been clenching his jaw for so long, and it ached. The muscles were so tired he no longer had any control over them. 'What's your name?' he asked.

'Jake,' he managed to whisper. The officer crouched down beside him. 'Jake,' he said again.

'You lost, Jake?' He shook his head. 'Where do you live?'

'Byreburn.' The policeman looked up at the ticket officer and they discussed where Byreburn was. Neither of them knew.

'Byreburn?' the policeman asked. Jake nodded his head.

'Byreburn.' The ticket officer went to a computer terminal to look it up.

'You're a long way from home,' he said to Jake. To the police officer he said, 'It's in the Borders.' There was some discussion and it was decided Jake would be taken to the nearest police station from where Kathi and Graham could be contacted.

'I'm not a child,' Jake argued. The last thing he wanted was his parents knowing where he'd been. 'You don't need to do that.'

'In the eyes of the law,' said the officer, 'I'm afraid you are.' Jake's humiliation reached new heights. He was led back through the train station, down the road and into the police station. He considered making a run for it, but realised he had nowhere to run.

At the police station Jake was placed in front of a desk and another officer, a woman this time, asked him questions and filled out a form with what he told her. When she felt she'd asked enough questions, she phoned Kathi.

Jake sat rigidly on the chair, listening to the conversation. He could imagine his mum at the other end, either in the car or at work, and he wondered what would happen to him. Would she come and get him, or would he have to get back on the bus on his own? He hoped he'd be able to go back on his own.

The WPC looked up and asked, 'Do you have any money?' Jake nodded. 'How much do you have?' He pulled out his wallet.

'£20,' he told her. She chatted with Kathi and it became clear he was going to be taken back to Buchanan Street bus station and put on the next bus to Dumfries. Before hanging up, she handed the phone to Jake. Reluctantly, he put it to his ear.

'Jake? Jake, is that you?' Kathi's voice was calm and measured and Jake knew she was working hard not to overreact.

'Yes.'

'Are you all right?'

'Yes.'

'Where have you been?' He didn't answer. 'Jake, please, what's been going on?'

'Nothing.' He could feel the WPC watching him. He handed her the phone.

'Mrs Beattie? Don't worry about anything, I'll put Jake on the next bus and I make sure he lets you know what time it will arrive.' The woman officer was nice enough. She even offered him a can of coke from the vending machine, which he accepted gratefully. As soon as she asked him, a sudden thirst came over him. While he gulped down his drink, she filled out her report, talked to colleagues about other cases, and at the same time tried to persuade one of them to take Jake to the bus station. Nobody wanted to, and so she reluctantly got up to do the job herself.

With a lot of sighing, more than Jake thought necessary given all she had to do was drive a car, she gathered her things and led him through a maze of corridors and out to the car park at the back of the building. Jake hoped they'd go past some cells and see some real criminals he could tell Lindsay about, but they didn't.

It was a succession of offices, some open plan, others closed to the outside world, with Inspector or Chief Inspector written on the door. There were three offices marked as interview rooms and in one of them, through the glass panel in the door, Jake saw a man and a woman. She was seated, and he was standing. She glanced at Jake as he passed by, and in that moment he saw someone who had given up on the world. That was how he had felt in the train station, his head against the wall. He'd felt like his whole world, his future with Marie, had crumbled down in front of him like the pictures of Aleppo he'd seen on the telly. Rubble everywhere.

The WPC told Jake to get into the passenger seat of the police car. 'Can I trust you not to pull a gun on me?' she joked.

'Do you have a gun?' he asked.

'No, only special ops have guns, not your bobby on the beat.'

From the safety of the car Jake relaxed enough to take in the city and was again struck by just how different it was to Byreburn: the traffic, the people, the buildings, everything was bigger and busier and for some reason grubbier. What he noticed most of all was the graffiti. Some of it was just words he could barely make out, other stuff was amazing. There were huge murals of faces and cityscapes, animals and even a skeleton. He wished he could create something that monumental. They went over a huge flyover that rainbowed the River Clyde. On the other side, they hit traffic and came to a stop. 'You're a long way from home,' The WPC said. 'Did you run away?'

'Sort of.'

'What happened? Rutherglen train station is not the place most kids run away to.'

'I went to see someone.'

'Who was that?'

'My mum.'

She paused, obviously confused. 'I thought your mum was in Byreburn?'

'I mean my real mum.'

'Are you adopted?' Jake didn't respond, making it obvious he didn't want to talk about it, but she ignored the hint. 'Do you not like your adopted mum?' Again Jake didn't answer. 'I'm adopted,' she said. 'For years I hated my adoptive parents. I blamed them.'

'Blamed them for what?' Jake asked despite himself.

'Anything, you name it, but especially for the fact I was adopted in the first place. My birth mother wasn't there for me to shout at, so my adoptive one was the next best thing.'

The traffic lights turned green, and they made it as far as the front of the queue before they turned red again. 'I also blamed myself. I knew I must've done something wrong. Even as a newborn, something made my mother not want me or love me. Who else's fault could it be?' She glanced over at Jake, but he couldn't look at her and kept his eyes firmly on the road ahead.

'Did you ever find out?' he asked at length.

'Find out what?'

'What you did wrong?'

'Yes.' He turned to look at her now, unsure whether or not she was telling the truth.

'What was it?' he asked.

'Nothing.'

'What do you mean?'

'I had done nothing wrong. It wasn't my fault. How could it have been? I was only a baby. No, I had done nothing wrong.' The traffic light changed again, and they hit a run of green lights, making good time through the city centre. 'It took me a lot of time,' she continued, 'a lot of therapy and a lot of talking to realise it. But I got there.' She took advantage of her special status as an officer of the law and parked illegally right outside the bus station. She walked Jake into the ticket office and while they waited she said, 'I'm a good judge of character, you know. It's something I've learnt on the job.

'I can tell you're a good kid who comes from a good home. Your mum loves you, I could tell that from how worried she was about you.' She made him look at her. 'You'll get there, okay, you'll get there. It's hard, but you'll figure all this out, eventually. I promise, you'll find your place in the world.' Jake was taken aback by just how much she seemed to read him. She seemed to know things about him even he didn't know. Before he could say anything he was summoned to the ticket counter.

At the bus stand the bus was waiting but not yet ready for boarding. Luggage was being loaded while the driver had a last cigarette. The WPC spoke to the driver, who gave Jake the once over. He reluctantly opened the door to let him on.

She came on board with him and sat him at the front where the driver could keep an eye on him. 'Right,' she said, 'get your phone out and text your mum so she knows when to pick you up.' She watched him send the message. 'Good luck with it all.'

With a wave, she disembarked and disappeared into the crowd. The driver closed the door again and Jake was left alone. In the quiet of the coach, he sat back and let his adrenaline dissipate. Tired, he leaned his head against the window and as soon as the engine started he fell asleep.

Jake didn't know how much time had passed before he woke up, but the seat next to him was occupied by an old woman who was knitting. 'I've got to sit here,' she said as soon as she saw he was awake. 'Normally I sit there, where you are, but the driver said I couldn't move you. How far you going?' Jake instantly took a dislike to her and turned to look out of the window. He didn't know where he was and wondered how long he'd been asleep. 'You were asleep for an hour,' said the old woman. 'Where are you getting off? She asked again.

'Dumfries,' he said.

'I'm going to Stranraer,' she said, 'to see my daughter and granddaughter. That's where they live. I go down there a lot and I have to sit at the front of the bus because I get travel sick unless I can see where we're going. Do you live in Dumfries?'

Now that he was on the road home and had slept, he felt more able to reflect on what had happened that day. The overriding outcome was that Marie didn't want him, not even now he wasn't a baby and could take care of himself. Not even now that he could be of help to her. She didn't want to get to know him and be a real family. She had looked him in the eye and said so, then asked him to leave. She had shut the door on him.

Now he had to face Kathi, and he had no idea of what to expect from her. There was no way she'd still want to be his mum if she found out he'd stolen money from her purse, run away and tried to leave. She'd definitely want shot of him now that he'd been picked up by the police. He didn't know what he could do. He was only 15 years old, he couldn't even get a job.

As the wheels turned and the bus neared Dumfries, a blackness fell over him that was so heavy he struggled to sit upright under its weight. By the time he disembarked, even his eyelids felt heavy, and it took all his effort to look at Kathi. She put her arms around him, but he knew it was half-hearted and he knew for certain he'd arrived in no-man's-land.

Chapter 35

Kathi was waiting for the bus to pull into Dumfries bus station. When she saw it swing round into view, the jitters in her stomach, that she had just managed to settle, sprung back into life, like Monarch butterflies preparing to migrate. She had been in the hardware store when she got the call, looking at bathroom tiles. After she'd come off the phone with the WPC, she managed to control her panic by reminding herself that Jake was safe and sound and no harm had been done. He was just a bit shaken and feeling lost. She'd immediately called Graham. 'Jake is in Glasgow,' she'd told him.

'What's he doing there?'

'To be honest, I don't know. The police phoned me –'

'The police?'

'Yes, they told me they found him at Rutherglen train station. They're putting him on a bus to Dumfries. I'm going to meet him at the station.'

'I'm confused. Why would he be in Rutherglen? We don't know anyone there.'

'No, but I can guess, can't you?' Graham was silent. 'Marie.'

'Marie who?'

'Who do you think? His birth mother.'

'Oh Jesus, is that where she lives?'

'I don't know, but that would be my guess.'

'How did he get there?'

'I have no idea, I haven't had a chance to speak to him properly, only the police officer.'

'Christ, what was he thinking? I could kill him. What if something had happened to him? Did he find her?'

'Who?'

'Marie, did he find Marie?'

'Graham I told you, I didn't get a chance to speak to him properly, we can ask him later.' Kathi paused, she didn't have anything else to tell him, she knew nothing else, but she didn't want to hang up. She wanted Graham to tell her it was okay, no big deal, that kids run away all the time and he had done it when he was Jake's age, just like he'd done with the shoplifting. This time she'd believe him. But he didn't say that because it wasn't true.

Kathi and Graham had known each other all their lives. They'd been to nursery, primary and secondary school together. They may not have been friends all that time, but if either of them had run away from home, the other would have known. That was exactly the sort of adventure that caused an upsurge in gossip and speculation around the school and amongst parents. If someone in her year at school had run away, Kathi would have known about it. She would have gossiped about it in great detail with her friends, listened to the adults discuss it in the shops and at the post office.

She knew, too, that this was the sort of thing people still talked about. She could already feel the silence that would follow her around the Co-op before the twittering of chit-chat rose up. There would be those that had never liked her and would take a certain amount of pleasure in the fact that something like this had happened; nothing serious enough to elicit genuine sadness, but serious enough for her detractors to whisper, serves her right.

'What a daft idiot,' ranted Graham, which only added to Kathi's distress. 'What if he's met Marie, and it's all gone wrong? Maybe that's why the police were there, because something has happened.'

'They wouldn't be sending him home on a bus if that was the case.'

'How did he get Marie's details in the first place?' Graham lashed out and blamed Kathi for leaving the file somewhere accessible. 'Why didn't you hide it?' he demanded.

'I did, I hid it in the eaves.'

'What good is that? There's no lock on the door, you might as well have left it on your desk.'

'You're overreacting.'

'No, I'm not, because he did find it and he did go to find her.'

'This isn't my fault.'

'Then who's fault is it?'

Kathi didn't have an answer or a defence because she was already blaming herself. 'Fuck off,' was all she managed before hanging up. The other hardware shoppers stopped mid-conversation, staff broke from stocking shelves and turned to look at her. Mortified, Kathi abandoned her trolley and hid in the car where she cried and cried like a child who has been falsely accused of something but doesn't have the ability to defend themselves.

Eventually her tears subsided and, blotchy faced, she made her way to the bus station. She was weak and light-headed from the shock and the tears, so took her time. The bus wouldn't arrive for a couple of hours yet. The journey gave her the opportunity to think about the implications of Jake reading his adoption file and all it contained. It also allowed her to think about the repercussions if he had met Marie. She tried to remember what information the file contained. There were definitely things Jake hadn't yet been party to because it was too difficult to explain to him right now.

Jake did know that Marie had been involved with drugs and the pregnancy had been unplanned. He knew small details about Marie herself, but he didn't know about the complexity of her personal life and how she paid for her addictions. That was a conversation she knew was due, but which she'd been postponing.

Kathi and Graham didn't know what had happened to Marie in the intervening fifteen years because at the time of his birth she hadn't wanted to have any form of ongoing contact. If she'd changed her mind since then Kathi hadn't been informed. For all she knew Marie was still an addict or, even worse, dead. Her skin crawled at the thought that Marie might be alive and want Jake back. He was angry and vulnerable enough to believe that would be the best option. She pressed Graham's number on the hands-free.

'What if Marie wants him back?' she said as soon as he picked up. 'What if they've met, and she's told him she wants him back? What if he says yes and runs away to be with her?'

'He won't do that,' said Graham.

'We don't know that. He hates us right now, maybe he hates us enough to leave.'

'He can't. It's as simple as that. Even if he wants to he's not allowed to. He is a minor and we still have some control over him.' This was of little comfort to Kathi, but it was all she had to cling to as she paced the bus terminal, preparing for the speech he would give her as he stepped off the bus. She pictured his young, angry face telling her he was leaving. Varyingly, her fear turned to anger.

'What a brat,' she said to herself. 'He's been too spoiled. This is what comes of being an only child. Graham was right, we should have adopted another. He's gone too far this time. He's selfish doing this to us. We've done nothing but love him and cherish him and he keeps treating us this way.'

The anger became empathy as she remembered the little boy they met at Adoption Day. He was smaller than all the other kids and they found out later it was because of his addiction to heroin in the womb. She thought about the trauma his tiny body had been through. She pictured him as an infant in a hospital ward being fed by a nurse, not being held by his mother, not being soothed and comforted by the voices he'd come to recognise over his nine-month gestation.

She imagined his time in foster care with the other children coming and going, with the anger and trauma that follows children who are in and out of care. She saw his beautiful face and brown eyes watching the world around him buck and change; the connections in his brain being made and severed so many times he didn't know who to trust anymore.

She relived his anger and fear when he came home for the first time and how hard it it had been for them all in those early days. They'd struggled to get to know one another and become friends before finally falling in love with each other. For over ten years they had lived the dream of a happy and prosperous family who could want for nothing and had each other.

Her heart reached out to Jake. She wanted to take away all the badness and remove all memories of Marie and his adoption. She wanted to leave him with only the security and comfort of his life with her and Graham.

But she couldn't, and her empathy for all the trauma he had experienced turned to fear as she foresaw Jake packing a bag and leaving behind his toys and books and gadgets that had, until recently, made him so happy. He'd leave them behind just as he would her and Graham, his grandparents and friends. Without a heartbeat's consideration, Kathi knew he'd leave them to be with Marie and all she came with.

If Kathi was honest with herself, she wasn't sure she could blame him. Who wouldn't jump at the chance to be with their own flesh and blood? Especially if that person hadn't had the opportunity to say the wrong thing or make unwelcome decisions. A blood relative who comes with no baggage and a fresh start. A mother who has been placed upon a very high pedestal. Kathi and Graham couldn't compete with that, and the knowledge provoked an intense heat of dread to course through her. With the exception of her own parents' death, Kathi had never before felt so powerless.

It awakened in her the feelings of loss and grief and injustice she'd felt at 22 when the phone call from Marjorie came through telling her that her parents had died, severing her innocence and rendering her an orphan. 'I survived,' she said out loud. 'I'm still here and when Jake leaves me, I will survive again.'

Kathi saw Jake on the bus as it pulled in. He was sitting on the front passenger seat next to an old woman who was knitting. The woman leaned over to him and said something, but he didn't respond. His face was expressionless and his eyes never left the floor, not even to look around and check she was waiting for him. When he got off the bus he barely looked at Kathi, his movements were slow and deliberate as if they took a lot of effort. He wore a haunted expression and looked like a much younger child. As he disembarked Kathi reached out to embrace him but his fragility made her nervous he might break and she held him only lightly.

The journey home was tense. Kathi wanted simultaneously to cling to him, to tell him she loved him and beg him not to leave, and then berate him for running away and worrying her so. Her phone rang.

'Have you got him?' Graham asked.

'Yes, we're in the car. I'm on speakerphone.'

'Great, I just wanted to check you got back okay,' he said to Jake. 'I'll see you at home.' When Graham hung up, the car went back to silence. Kathi put the radio on in an attempt to lighten the atmosphere, but Jake turned it off.

'You must be hungry,' said Kathi. 'We'll get some chips on the way home.' Jake said nothing. 'Hayden's mum called this morning, they're doing a big party for his 16th birthday and wanted to check you'll be around. Hayden wants you there. It's not for months yet, not until November the third, but I think they are pulling out all the stops. They're going to hire the Telford Hall and invite family as well as friends because she's guessing you guys will all want to do your own thing the next year. I said you'd love that. I asked what he's interested in at the moment, you know, ideas for the present, but I guess you can do that, you'll know what he wants. I can give you some money towards it if you want? Get him something special. It's a special birthday, after all. What do you think? You could maybe go shopping with your dad.' Jake only grunted.

'I've been looking at tiles for the bathroom in the new property, but I can't decide on the colour. You are good at these things, maybe you can help me.' Kathi talked and talked and Jake remained silent. She forced him out of the car when they stopped at the chip shop. 'Come and see what you want. Whatever you want.'

There were a few others milling about waiting for their order and although nobody knew about Jake's trip to Glasgow, Kathi still felt self-conscious, only too aware that the tension between her and Jake was visible to outsiders. She hoped people would dismiss it as normal teenage behaviour. Kathi smiled, made chitchat, but as soon as the meal was ready they made a swift exit.

At home Graham was waiting for them, and Kathi indicated with a shake of her head that she knew nothing more than she did earlier. They waited until everybody had eaten before asking Jake about running away.

'The police officer told me they found you in Rutherglen,' Kathi began. 'Do you know anyone there? I couldn't think of anyone we knew.'

It took a long time but eventually Jake said, 'Marie. I went to see Marie. She lives there.'

'Did you go to her house?' Graham asked. Jake nodded. 'Was she there?'

'Yes.'

'Did she know you were coming?' asked Kathi.

'No. I just decided to go, I wanted to surprise her.' Jake's voice was so low that Kathi and Graham had to lean in to hear him. Before either of them could ask anything more, Jake went on. 'She didn't know who I was at first. I had to tell her. Then she seemed to recognise me, but who else would turn up claiming to be her long-lost son. She invited me in. There were lots of pictures on the wall of her and her husband. She's got two more children. Two girls, Hayley and Beth. One is blond like their dad and one is dark like her. Like me. She has lots of photographs of them. She says she has a new family now, and that she doesn't want me. I am not part of her family. She says I can't live with her. She said I had to leave.'

As soon as Jake said he wasn't going to live with Marie, Kathi could catch her breath again. Her terror slid away and she could refocus her efforts on making Jake happy here. She looked at Graham, whose relief was also self-evident as he hid his face in his hands.

'I ran back to the station,' Jake continued, 'but I didn't know what to do after that. The ticket man helped me.' Jake's lack of emotion, even of anger, frightened Kathi. He seemed unable to lift the lethargy that had hung around him since he got off the bus. When he finished his story Jake stood up and silently took his plate to the sink before going to his room. As soon as she heard his bedroom door shut Kathi burst into tears. 'That's not our son,' she said.

'No,' said Graham, 'it is not.'

Chapter 36

In the week following Jake's trip to Glasgow, Kathi had been so focused on trying to make him happy and not rocking the boat, that she'd avoided the issue of Joanne Wylie. Whenever it popped into her consciousness, she pushed it away. She didn't have the head space to think about it properly.

But as life seemed to settle down, Kathi was able to shift her to attention to Jake's relationship with her. She knew Joanne was behind Jake's trip to Glasgow but unable to work out why she was so interested in him. She asked Cherry if she could shed some light on it.

'What do you think is going on?' Kathi asked her. They'd bought a sandwich and were sitting on a bench at The Green. 'Do you think they're, –'

'No I do not,' said Cherry. 'He's only a child.'

'You do hear about things like that. I saw that movie, you know the one, with Cate Blanchett.'

'Ha!' Cherry's tone made it clear she thought Kathi was being ridiculous. 'Joanne Wylie is no Cate Blanchett. If Jake wanted to go down that route surely he'd choose someone better looking.' She was relieved Cherry thought her idiotic because the idea of Joanne taking advantage of her vulnerable son made Kathi feel sick.

'Then why are they friends? How did they even meet?'

'It's Byreburn, everybody knows everybody else one way or another. He could have met her anywhere.'

'But why would she be friends with him? I know it sounds ridiculous, but I can't help thinking Joanne is trying to get at me through Jake. I'm sure she knows more about me than she's letting on.'

'What do you mean?'

'I wonder if she is the troll who's been sending me all those messages.'

'Why would she do that?'

'I don't know, but the more I think about it, the more it makes sense. It only started happening after she moved to the town, and whoever it is definitely lives here because they've taken those photographs of me.' Cherry was silent, mulling it over.

'It could be, I suppose,' she said. 'But it still doesn't answer the question of why.'

'Why does anybody troll another person?'

'Because they're mental.'

'Is Joanne mental?'

'Not as far as I can tell, no.'

'Then there must be another reason.'

'I looked over her paperwork again, but nothing odd stood out. I've been trying to call her mother's number but haven't managed to speak to her yet.'

'Why her mum?'

'That's who her rent guarantor is. She's the only person I can think of who knows Joanne. I'll let you know as soon as I've spoken to her. I'm sorry, Kathi, but I've got to go. Listen, try not to worry too much. Things will work out, I promise.'

Cherry kissed her friend on the cheek and hurried off, leaving Kathi to mull on the relationship between her son and this much older woman. Her imagination went to some dark places. In a bid to put them to rest, Kathi pulled out Jake's old phone. He'd been bought a new one since the car crash, but Kathi hadn't cancelled the old contract. She scrolled through the dialogue between Jake and Joanne and wondered if they were still in touch. Against her better judgment, and out of desperation, Kathi typed: How are you? and sent it to Joanne.

It didn't take long for a reply to ping through.

Is that you, Kathi?

Kathi's heart leapt into her mouth, and she quickly turned the phone off. She knew she'd been caught red-handed. Should she pretend it never happened, or should she use this as an opportunity to find out what was going on? She switched the phone back on.

Yes. What do you want with Jake?

Nothing.

Why are you turning him away from me?

You don't need me to do that.

Leave him alone.

Or what?

Joanne was right. Or what? Kathi was powerless. She'd stolen her son's phone and was throwing accusations at someone she barely knew. She switched the phone off again. Kathi had hit rock bottom and run out of ideas. She needed a friendly face, so took herself to Marjorie's house.

'Only me,' she called as she went in.

'Hi love, I'm in the kitchen.'

'Hi Gran.' Kathi slumped down on a kitchen chair.

'What's up with you?'

'The usual.'

'Jake?' Kathi nodded. 'What's he up to now?'

'To be honest, nothing new. I just can't stop worrying about him.'

'Oh darling, that's understandable.'

'We seem to be swinging from one disaster to another and I don't know how to help him.' Marjorie smiled and squeezed her granddaughter's arm in sympathy.

'What is it you're worried about?'

'I found out he's friends with a much older woman. I don't think it's a physical thing, but she's so much older I can't understand why they're friends.'

'Who is it?'

'It's one of my tenants. She's new to the town and I don't know how they even became friends. She's been sending him text messages and causing trouble between us. She's the one who's egged him on to find Marie.'

'Is she a friend of yours?'

'No, I've only met her a couple of times and that was only briefly. She did seem a bit odd.'

'In what way?'

'She made reference to Graham being called out on emergencies all the time, but I don't know how she'd know that.'

'Maybe she's called him out?'

'Cherry says no. But it was more than that. She seemed determined to talk to me. I was trying to read a magazine, but she kept interrupting me. Now I think about it, it was as if she was trying to get me to react to something, get a response from me.'

'React to what?'

'To her, I think. When I was growing up, did I have any friendships that Mum and Dad didn't approve of?'

'Not that I can remember,' said Marjorie. 'You were always such a good girl.'

'What do you think Mum would do if she was me?'

'Knowing your mum,' Marjorie chuckled, 'she'd have gone right up to this Joanne and confronted her, had it out for the whole street to hear. Your mum was never afraid of getting straight to the point.'

'Maybe I should do that?'

'It's one approach, certainly.' Marjorie took a moment before saying, 'Your dad, though, he would have taken his time to find out a bit more before saying anything. You're more like him in that way. Why don't you find out a little more, or even talk to Jake about it?'

'I can't.'

'Why not?' Kathi's face coloured.

'I only know about this friendship because I looked at Jake's phone when he was in the hospital.' Marjorie looked at her reproachfully. 'I needed to know what was going on. I was desperate.' Marjorie raised her eyebrows. 'Don't be cross with me. I don't know what else to do. Everything is out of control.'

'Oh, sweetheart, I'm not cross with you. You're in a difficult position. You want to help your son but you don't know how.' Marjorie hesitated before saying, 'Have you considered that perhaps you can't help him? That perhaps he needs to go through this for himself?'

'No, I can't consider that. I can't leave him to struggle like this by himself.'

'Then you need to find out more about Joanne and why she's so keen to make trouble.'

'I also think she's the troll.'

'The one who's been sending you all those nasty messages?'

'Yes.' Kathi watched her grandmother for a moment. She remembered the last time they'd talked about the troll. It was the night Jake turned up drunk. That was the night she asked if anyone knew Lola, the girl in the mystery photo. Marjorie had behaved a little strange at the mention of the name and although she didn't say anything at the time, Kathi thought it worth revisiting. 'Did you have a chance to think about that woman I found a photograph of?'

'Which woman?'

'Lola.'

'No, darling, I didn't. To be honest, I didn't think any more about it.'

'Can you think of anyone called Lola now?'

'I'm sorry, darling.' Marjorie filled the kettle and switched it on. 'What does Graham think about it all?'

'About Lola?'

'No, about Jake and his friend.'

'We haven't really talked about it.'

'Maybe he'll be able to shed some light on it.'

'I'm sure you're right.' Resigned, Kathi gathered herself up, gave Marjorie a hug and went home.

In the living room that night, after dinner and once Jake had gone to his room, Kathi told Graham about her conversation with Cherry and her theory that Joanne is the troll.

'The time-line fits,' Graham said, turning the page of his newspaper, 'but Cherry is right. What reason does this Joanne woman have to hate you?'

Kathi went to her office and returned with the photograph she'd found of Lola. 'Look at the child,' she said to Graham. 'I think that child looks like Joanne. What do you think?'

Graham looked at her, puzzled. 'Who is it? Where do you find this?'

'It's someone called Lola. I found it in the old suitcase with my parents' papers. I had never seen it before and I don't remember them ever talking about somebody called Lola.'

'Have you asked your Gran?'

'Yes, and she looks all funny at the mention of the name.' They both looked again at the photo. 'I've been puzzling over this for ages and I think I've figured it out. I think that child is Joanne.' Graham wasn't convinced. 'Look.' Kathi pulled up Facebook and showed him a recent photograph of Joanne. 'I can't stop thinking about Joanne and why she's trying to cause so much trouble for us. I've been looking through her Facebook profile, trying to learn more about her. There was one photo in particular that reminded me of someone, I couldn't think who. Then it hit me, it was Lola.'

'There is a similarity,' he conceded. 'I would never have thought they looked alike until you said it.'

'Why would Mum and Dad have a photograph of Joanne Wylie?'

'That is something I cannot answer,' Graham reached a hand over to his wife and stroked her cheek. 'Why don't you ask her?'

'I might have burnt my bridges there.'

'What do you mean?'

'I used Jake's phone to send her a message.'

'Why did you do that?' Graham rolled his eyes in disbelief.

'I wanted to know what she wants from our son.'

'What did she say?' he asked, unable to hide his curiosity.

'Nothing, or so she says. I told her to keep away from him, but I don't think it did any good.'

'You could go back to her, ask if she has a connection to you.'

'I'm scared.'

'Of what?'

'The answer.'

Chapter 37

'Are we keeping you awake?' Jake's history teacher slammed a workbook down on his desk, forcing him to turn back to class. He'd been looking out of the window, his mind regurgitating his conversation with Marie, a conversation of which he was unable to let go. The thwump! of the book jolted him out of his daydream. As soon as he realised what was happening he resumed his sulk, glaring at his classmates and daring them to laugh in his face. He looked back up at his teacher, her expression betraying just how much of a waste of space she thought Jake was, that everybody thought he was.

'Fuck's sake,' he muttered.

'What was that?'

'Nothing, Miss.' He turned to look outside again. Anger was brewing, but he didn't want another scene. It was too draining.

'That's it,' she said. 'Get out. I've had enough of you. Go to the head teacher's office and explain your behaviour to him.' Jake stood up abruptly, his chair scraping on the floor. The sound magnified by the silence of his classmates. He grabbed his bag off the floor and left the room. He pounded down the empty corridors. I don't need this shit, he muttered to himself. They can all go to hell. He took the steps down to the ground floor two at a time and made his way out of the main entrance.

'Jake, where are you going?' the school secretary called after him, but he didn't care anymore. None of this mattered.

He went straight to Joanne's house and knocked on the door. He knocked again and shouted through the letterbox, but she wasn't home. He went down to the riverside where he'd normally find Lindsay, but she wasn't there. He pulled out his phone and thought about calling her but decided against it, texting Joanne instead. She'd know what to say.

I've had enough. Where are you?

He sat on the grass and lit a cigarette. He watched the water tumble past him. It had rained overnight and water was gushing down from the surrounding hills, swelling the River Esk until it sounded thunderous. Thunderous and inviting. He looked intently at the water, trying to follow the current, watching how it ebbed and flowed, noticing where it was deep and where it was shallow. The water looked cold, and he wondered what temperature it was. If he were to jump in now, would that fresh mountain water be cold enough to freeze a person?

He wondered if that was the sort of thing Marie would know. He didn't get enough time with her when he went to Glasgow. He still had so many questions he wanted to ask. He didn't know her any better now than he did before he had knocked on her door and told her who he was.

Her face was already beginning to blur. All he could see clearly was the look of shock on her face and how visibly the colour drained from her cheeks. He'd never seen that happen before. The smile she wore when she first opened the door immediately faded to horror. Jake wondered if she'd recognised him as soon as she saw him but hid it. Did she realise he was her long-lost son but didn't want to acknowledge him? The tears of joy he'd secretly hoped for did not materialise. There was no joy at finally being found and knowing once and for all her son was alive and well, and had forgiven her.

Prior to finding her, Jake had imagined saying, I forgive you, before she took him in her arms and brought him into the fold. He often pictured her later on, thanking Kathi and Graham for all the good work they'd done, but now she, his mother, would take over. Kathi and Graham would see how happy he was, how much he wanted to be with his birth mother, his real mum, that they could do nothing but relinquish their hold and be happy for him.

Joanne lied about that bit. This wasn't Long Lost Families, or Who Do You Think You Are? There was no happy ending for him. Jake threw his cigarette down on the ground and moved towards the water. The rush of water grew louder. It seemed to talk to him, invite him in. This wasn't a babbling brook, but a commanding torrent. It told Jake what to do; it gave him an exit. He thought about how much better things would be for Kathi and Graham without him. They were good people and didn't deserve a child as bad as him.

Come in, the water seemed to say, growing in volume and insistence. Slowly he moved towards it, still unsure he believed the river, not yet convinced it was the only way. Behind him a car door slammed and for the second time that day he was jolted out of a dream state. Jake looked at the houses behind him. He was sure they were watching him. Their windows were like eyes glowering down on him, recording his secrets and fears to share later with their inhabitants.

Nothing was secret in this town. Everybody knew he was adopted, that his mum didn't want him. It was common knowledge that Kathi and Graham had had enough of him. He would amount to nothing, was incapable of loving and undeserving of being loved. He pulled his hoodie up, lowered his head and started to walk home. He didn't want to be seen. He wanted to make himself invisible and hide from the prying eyes of Byreburn.

At home, he barricaded himself in his room. He needed to keep the world out because he couldn't deal with its demands anymore. It was too hard and there was nothing to make the hard work worthwhile. His phone pinged. It was Joanne.

I'm at work. What's up?

I have had enough. I don't know what to do anymore
Do you want to see Marie again?
She doesn't want me
Do you want to stay with Kathi and Graham?
They don't want me
Joanne didn't message back.
They don't want me, he wrote again, hoping she might be his saviour. Still she didn't reply. What do I do??
Eventually his phone beeped.
You know the answer
What does that mean? I don't understand
The answer is in your hands

'What does that mean?' Jake shouted at the phone. In frustration, he threw it across the room and it landed on the floor beside his chest of drawers. He lay back on his bed, his arms over his eyes to block out the light and to block out Joanne's cryptic messages. It was a merry-go-round of thoughts that left him dizzy. He curled into the foetal position and couldn't stop tears coming. Like an eclipsed sun and lay still for a long time, unable to move. Unexpectedly, the eclipse passed and the answer he'd been searching for revealed itself. He stopped crying, opened his eyes and sat up.

'Of course,' he thought, 'why didn't I think of it before.' He ran through the pros and cons and as far as he could see there were more pros than cons. Even the cons would be short-lived and soon forgotten. He laughed out loud at how foolish he'd been. If his brain wasn't so slow he would have worked this out months ago and saved so many people so much pain.

Jake wiped away his tears and jumped off the bed, suddenly invigorated by his newfound certainty and by the simple act of making a decision. In the bathroom he looked through the drawers and cupboards. It seemed the most likely place Kathi would keep them. The bathroom was small, and it didn't take him long to realise they weren't there. He went into Kathi and

Graham's bedroom. As always, it was uncluttered, everything was where it should be. The only clue someone slept there were the few clothes Graham laid out on a chair, ready to be changed into after work. There was nothing decorative or messy in the room. Kathi said she liked a spartan, cool bedroom, It helped her relax.

He went straight to Kathi's bedside table and opened the drawer. It was too easy. There was the little brown bottle he'd seen her popping only a few nights earlier. Jake smiled broadly as he shook the bottle, satisfied there were enough pills for his needs. Back in the bathroom, he filled a tumbler as high as it would go. In his bedroom, he carefully placed the water and the bottle of pills on his own bedside table. He wanted to leave Kathi and Graham an explanation for his actions. He didn't want them to feel bad about what he had decided to do. It wasn't their fault after all, and he wanted them to know it. But how to do it? Email? Text message? In the end, he decided a handwritten message would be best. Kathi would like that. He would tweet Lindsay and apologise for not making it to Australia with her.

He dug out an A4 lined pad and pen from his bag and settled on his bed. He swallowed all the pills in the bottle. His stomach was empty, and he hoped the pills wouldn't make him nauseous. He glanced at his bedroom door, conscious there was no lock, and wondered whether or not he should jam something under the handle. He didn't know when Kathi would be home and didn't want to be interrupted, so fitted his desk chair under the handle. Back on the bed, he thought about what he should write. What would Brenda's advice be? It took him a while to get started, but once he began he found a rhythm and all the things he had never been able to say to them face-to-face suddenly seemed easy and right. He told them he appreciated everything they had done for him, and that for the most part he had been happy. He explained that there was no place in this world for him. The anger and disappointment he felt about himself and his future was insurmountable.

He acknowledged he had caused Kathi and Graham nothing but hurt and pain and had finally understood that the best thing for everyone was to put an end to it all. Meeting Marie had only confirmed the fears he'd long held about himself. He was not worth the effort everybody had put into him.

Marie had carried him in her womb, given birth to him, was connected to him in a primal way, but even she couldn't bear to be with him. Even she didn't want to commit. As he'd grown in her belly, and on the day he was born she sensed he was not good and not the child she was destined to love and cherish. He was not what she wanted. He wasn't good enough, he knew that. It didn't matter what Brenda or anyone else said, Marie's actions told him all he needed to know.

Jake asked Kathi and Graham to tell her he was sorry. He told them he was sorry he hadn't done better by them because he knew and appreciated how much they'd tried, but it was his fault, it was in him. Badness.

By now Jake was yawning. He was lightheaded and pleasantly buzzing. The warm fuzzy feeling made him giggle, and he wished he could feel this contented all the time. How much nicer life would be. He lay down, too sleepy now to finish the letter, and reassured himself he'd written what he wanted to say, anyway.

He closed his eyes and let his mind wander. He remembered the sledge Graham had built him, made from wood and with proper runners. He remembered the Pokémon birthday cake Kathi made for his eighth birthday. He remembered the trip they took to Edinburgh Zoo and how much he'd loved the Painted Dogs with their multi-coloured coats and the strange noises they made when they called to each other.

Hayden had gone with them that day. Hayden, who now liked to remind him he was an orphan who not even his own mother wanted. The same Hayden who told Jake he didn't belong in Byreburn and should go back to wherever it was he came from. The betrayal Jake felt still hurt. In some ways it hurt more than Marie's abandonment because Hayden knew him. He'd told Hayden things about himself and Marie that were deeply personal. He knew Hayden had told others.

He didn't want his last thoughts to be bad ones so made himself think about Lindsay. He pictured her face and her long brown hair. He remembered the times they went to the river to smoke and how much they'd laughed at nothing in particular. He thought about the plans they'd made for their future and was sad to be letting her down but was certain she'd find someone else, someone better, to live out those plans with. She was amazing. She was strong and beautiful and smart. She'd be alright.

Jake started when he realised he hadn't sent her a message. He tried to get up but was too tired. His body didn't want to move. She knows, he consoled himself. She knows how I feel about her. But he wanted to tell her, he wanted to tell her how amazing she was. He tried again to rouse himself. He wanted to live a little longer, long enough to tell Lindsay how he felt. But no, it wasn't to be. The world around him faded away.

Chapter 38

As soon as Jake started to rouse, Kathi and Graham shot to either side of his hospital bed. They'd been warned he would be in some pain from having his stomach pumped and that it would affect his stomach, oesophagus, throat, nose and mouth. The very nature of extracting the pills was violent and painful.

When the doctor later explained what had happened and the severity of Jake's actions, Kathi had been too stunned to speak or cry or respond in any other way. All she'd managed to do was grasp a hold of Graham, who in turn clung to her, as they listen to the grim facts of how their son had tried to take his own life.

'We're here, Jake,' Kathi said softly. 'Dad and I are here.'

Kathi clasped Jake's hand in hers. She leaned on the bed, over the wires and cannula, in front of the beeping machines, and kissed her son's head repeatedly in a way she knew he would hate but which she couldn't stop herself doing. She needed to be close to him and be reassured he was alive and breathing. Not for the last time did Kathi blame herself for giving him space. She hadn't wanted to put pressure on him or expect too much from him as he regrouped after his meeting with Marie. Only now did she think she'd stepped back too far.

She knew Jake wasn't the same boy after his trip to Glasgow. His energy and spark had gone, even his anger had been washed away with his second rejection by Marie. She saw him head to school in a daze. She didn't put up enough of a fight when he dropped out of football and when he distanced himself from everyone, including Lindsay. At one time Kathi would have been pleased about this, but now she would give anything for Jake to show an interest in her. Kathi even missed his back chat because at least that showed he was engaged with the world. Inside Kathi kicked herself because she shouldn't have given him so much room, she should have been more insistent he engage with her.

Jake opened his eyes slowly, squinting as he gradually adjusting to the light. 'Mum,' he whispered. It was clear he found it difficult to speak, 'I'm sorry. Dad...' Jake looked at his father, his large brown eyes communicating all the embarrassment and fear he felt, the regrets of his actions.

'It's okay,' said Graham. 'You don't need to say anything. You are here, you're with us and that's the only thing that matters.'

'Dad is right,' said Kathi. 'All that matters is you are here with us, the rest will work itself out.' Suddenly the door opened and a nurse came in. She made small talk as she moved around the bed, all the while gauging his recovery and at the same time checking numbers, pressing buttons, ripping off print outs and making notes on his patient file. Kathi, Graham and Jake were silent as she moved from place to place, making inane chat to absorb the awkwardness.

Before she left she said, 'I'll let the consultant know you're awake, Jake. He'll come in and check you over.' When she left, they all gave a sigh of relief. Kathi would normally have had a lot of questions for a doctor, but right now she wanted to isolate her family from the rest of the hospital. She wanted to cocoon them within this room and shut out the world. Shut out an angry world that had hurt and damaged her son - a world that didn't deserve his beauty, his goodness, his purity. She would keep him safe in his bedroom at home, where no one could ever hurt him again.

Just as she was just about to go over and put her arms around Jake protectively, Graham beat her to it. He didn't put his arms around Jake, but managed to perch himself hesitantly on the edge of his bed. Kathi watched them hold hands, watched as something unspoken passed between them. Eventually Graham smiled at his son and all that needed to be said for the time being had been said. Kathi was envious of this apparent kinesis between them. She wished she was part of it.

They were interrupted again, this time by the consultant. He was polite but perfunctory. When he was satisfied he paused, took a breath and indicated he wanted to talk more seriously about Jake's condition. 'Jake's body has been through a lot.' He looked at Jake. 'You are going to be in a degree of pain for the next three to five days, for which we will give you something. I am pleased to say there's no lasting damage.' He turned back to Kathi and Graham. 'We're going to keep him in for observation for a few more hours, but as long as nothing emerges over the course of the day, you can take him home this evening.'

Kathi and Graham smiled at one another but dropped the smile when they saw how unenthusiastic Jake looked at the prospect of going home. The consultant also clocked it and indicated he wanted to talk to Kathi and Graham privately, and which immediately prodded awake the group of butterflies that seemed to live permanently in Kathi's stomach.

'I want to talk to you about Jake's current state of mind,' the consultant said.

'What do you mean?' Kathi couldn't help sounding defensive. Graham put his hand on her arm.

'I mean that this is the second time Jake has been admitted to hospital in recent months.'

'The car crash was an accident.'

'That is what we all assumed at the time, but in light of the past 24 hours I am not so sure.'

'What are you trying to tell us?' Graham asked, his voice calm but tight.

'I want to discharge Jake this evening because physically there is nothing wrong with him but I am only comfortable doing this on the condition that he receives regular counselling.'

'He's been seeing a counsellor, we told you that.'

'Yes you did, but I'm going to make it a condition of his discharge that for the next month he sees a counsellor twice a week. The frequency of visits can be reviewed after that time. It's a big undertaking, but given how things are, I think he needs it.'

Kathi and Graham nodded, they knew he was right and they couldn't afford to let Jake remain as he was. It was like he was in quicksand and being pulled under inch by inch. They needed to do something to help lever him out. The doctor took their silence for reluctance. 'We have psychiatrists here at the hospital if you prefer to use their services.'

'No,' said Kathi, looking at Graham for backup. 'We'll stick with Brenda, Jake knows and likes her.'

'Okay, fine,' he said, 'I will arrange for his discharge papers to be drawn up.'

When Kathi and Graham went back into Jake's room he was asleep so they each took a seat and got lost in their own thoughts. Kathi looked at her husband. His face was ashen and his expression was both stern and terrified. He looked so broken she wondered if any of them would ever recover from this. Before long Jake stirred and they were back at his bedside. Still pale, his eyes did at least have a little more light behind them.

'What did the doctor say?' he asked.

'He says he is worried about you and wants you to see Brenda at least twice a week for a month.'

'We agree,' said Graham. 'You're going to see Brenda for individual sessions and we're also going to go as a family. Your mum and I let things slip, we took our eye off the ball and didn't take as good care of you as we should have done. As you deserve.'

Kathi never been more proud of Graham. She knew he thought therapy was something for other people, not for him. Yet here he was acknowledging that something had to change and committing himself to action. Throughout their marriage she had been the one to cajole him into taking a leap into something new, including setting up his own business. It was such a welcome relief to have him take charge just when Kathi didn't know if she had the strength to do it herself. Until he said it she didn't realise how defeated she felt.

'Right,' said Graham, 'I am going to go home to get you some fresh clothes and to let everyone know how you're doing. Is there anything in particular you want?' Jake shook his head. 'Okay then, I'll see you in a bit.' When he was gone, Kathi paced the room slowly. There was so much she wanted to ask Jake, especially about his relationship with Joanne, but decided now was not the right time.

'You can go too if you want,' said Jake.

'No, I don't want to. I want to stay here with you while you rest. Go back to sleep.' Kathi stroked his hand, but he took her hand in his.

'I'm sorry Mum, I'm sorry to put you through all this.'

'Hush now, there's no need.'

'There is. You and Dad don't deserve this.' His voice croaked, and he had to swallow hard. Kathi helped him with a glass of water before moving back to the window and looking out over Dumfries, the sky low and dark but not yet raining.

'The phone call from Jamie Armstrong to tell me you'd been in a car accident took me straight back to when my parents died. I was immediately 22 again. It was as if my body remembered that day more than my brain did. My body seemed to say, you've done this before, hold it together.'

'You never really talk about your parents.'

'I think...I think it's because it still hurts so much. Our sessions with Brenda have made me wonder if I ever really processed it or accepted it, or something like that. As soon as I knew it was Jamie on the phone, I was right there again and I was angry. Angry with them, angry with you, angry with myself.'

'You've done nothing wrong.'

'Haven't I? I've hidden behind my anger and used it to stop me getting involved with what's going on in my own family. I was so scared of what I might find beneath the surface that I preferred not to look. I knew you were unhappy, and that you were feeling isolated, but rather than helping you myself, I took you to Brenda. I feel like I've palmed you off and for that I'm sorry.'

'What happened to your mum and dad?'

'They'd been to Carlisle and were driving home at Dad's usual slow pace. It used to drive all of us crazy how slowly he drove, but he was scared of crashing and couldn't be persuaded to go any faster. Not that it did him much good in the end.' Kathi fiddled with the blinds. It had been a long time since she'd talked about her parents' death and the words tripped her up. 'They were going round a bend, not a particularly blind one. You know it, the one just a few miles out of Byreburn. Anyway, they came face-to-face with an oncoming car that was going so fast even Dad's slow pace didn't give them enough time to swerve.

'It was a young boy in the car, not too much older than you are now. He'd not long passed his test and felt invincible. Both he and my parents died instantly. Trying to avoid the oncoming car, Dad's car went straight into the lorry the boy was overtaking. Even a Volvo can't compete with a lorry and they went straight under it.'

'I'm so sorry.'

'I wasn't. I was angry, so angry at that stupid boy. He destroyed so many lives that day; his own, his parents, my parents, mine. He took away my family and left me bereft and angry with the world.'

'You must be so angry with me for putting you through it all again.'

'No, I'm not. I'm angry with myself for letting things get this far. I'm not angry with you at all because I understand what it's like. I understand what it's like to be angry with the world and not know why. I understand what it's like to feel helpless and know someone has taken away what should rightfully be yours; your mum and dad, your family. I understand now that we have to work through all these things together and not leave you to do it on your own, as I was.'

Kathi moved over to the bed and sat down beside him. She stroked his face. 'I don't want you to feel that you are alone in this ever again. I hope that you've reached the bottom, survived it and now want to climb back up because your dad and I want to make that climb with you.'

They sat in silence for a while before Jake said, 'I think I have reached the bottom and I don't want to stay here. I'm just not sure how to move on.'

'So we'll find someone who can help us all.'

'Thanks Mum, thanks for not being angry.'

Chapter 39

It was agreed that Jake would take a week off school. He needed a chance to rest his body, and Kathi pushed hard to get appointments with Brenda. Some as a family, some just for Jake.

Previously, she'd left Jake sitting in his room to sink into dark thoughts. Now she insisted he get dressed and come downstairs, even if it was to watch TV or play on his console. At first Jake protested, saying she didn't need to have him under surveillance.

'It is not so I can watch you, it is so you can hear me and know I'm around. I want you to know you're not alone.' Jake thought about protesting again, but he didn't. He saw the concern and the determination in her eyes and capitulated. And actually, it was nice to feel looked after. It made him feel special and as if he could, temporarily, forget about what he'd have to face at school. He lounged on the sofa and channel hopped. Kathi brought them both a cup of tea.

'Does everyone know?' Jake asked her.

'About you?'

'Yes. About my suicide attempt.' He watched Kathi flinch at those words. 'That is what it was, Mum.'

'I know, I just hate hearing it out loud.'

'We can't hide from it.'

'You are right.' She took a sip of tea. 'Yes, I think they do. People watched when the ambulance came. They saw the lights and came outside. We would have done the same.' Kathi took a breath before saying, 'Jake, I need to talk to you.'

'What is it?' Kathi's tone immediately put him on alert.

'It's about the car crash.'

'What about it?' Jake lowered his head and seemed to sink into the sofa.

'We heard from the courts. Because Lindsay has made a full recovery, because you've never done anything like that before, and because of everything you've been going through recently, the courts have decided to be lenient with you.'

'What does that mean?'

'It means that you'll have to pay a fine and you'll be disqualified from driving for two years.'

'But I don't have a license.'

'No, I know, and you won't be allowed to get one until you're 17.' She didn't say anything for a moment. 'You've been very lucky,' she said gently. 'This could have been a lot worse.' Jake nodded his head.

'Do I need to go to court?'

'Because you were in hospital, Dad was able to go in your place. Jamie also put in a good word for you and that counted for a lot.'

'I'm sorry, Mum. I really am.'

'I know.'

'Can we go for a walk? I need to get out for a bit.' Jake had a sudden desire to escape the confines of the house. He wanted to breathe fresh summer air and feel his lungs working. 'Just to the Memorial Park. Not far.'

They put their coats on and headed out. Kathi linked her arm through his. The sky was high and wide, with only wisps of cloud in the sky. It was a warm day, but a breeze kept things cool. Trees were in full leaf, many shades and hues of green decorated the town, and the air was thick with insects making the most of the summer months. They could hear people chatting in their gardens and children's voices carried in the breeze from the nearby primary school.

'What have people been saying?' Jake asked.

'Everyone has been very nice. They've asked after you, sent their love.' Jake lowered his head, embarrassed to be the subject of such conversations. 'What's been amazing, though,' Kathi continued, 'is that more than one person has told me they've thought about it at one time or another.'

'Really? Who?'

'I don't want to say, and really it doesn't matter. The point is, they told me because they understand. They've been in a similar place to you.'

'I guess so.'

'And each of them said they were glad they didn't because life did get better. They moved on from that dark time.'

'So I will too?'

'There is a good chance, yes.' In a rare moment of sentimentality, Jake leaned over and kissed the top of his mother's head. Kathi smiled up at him, touched by his affection.

'You know what this means, don't you?' he said.

'No, what?'

'I am so much taller than you that from now on,' he joked, 'I expect to be treated with the respect my height deserves.' They laughed together, and it felt good. Jake realised this was the first time they'd done just that in a long time. It felt like the paper screen he'd put between them had been ripped and he'd stepped through to her side.

'Look,' Kathi indicated ahead of them. It was Lindsay who waved shyly.

'Hello, Mrs Beattie.'

'Hello Lindsay, how are you?'

'Fine, thanks.' They stood awkwardly for a moment before Kathi said, 'I really should get back. I have a few calls to make. Jake, don't stay out too long. You need some rest before we see Brenda later.'

'Don't worry, Mrs Beattie, I will look after him.' They watched Kathi walk away before making their own way to the park. As they walked around the perimeter neither spoke but they each wanted to. Finally Jake said, 'You can ask me.'

'Are you sure?'

'Yes.'

'Why? Why did you do it?' Jake took a moment, trying to get his thoughts in order before answering.

'It seemed the most sensible thing to do at the time. What I mean is, it seemed the best solution.'

'How can taking your life be a solution?'

'I was unhappy. I was making Mum and Dad miserable. Marie didn't want me and even Joanne left me hanging.'

'What's Joanne got to do with this?'

'All the time I was looking for Marie, she was encouraging me. In fact, it was her that found Marie's address.' Jake thought back to the day he'd tried to take his own life. 'I messaged her and told her how bad I felt. I told her I couldn't take it anymore.'

'What did she say?'

'That the answer was in my hands.'

'What on earth does that mean?' Lindsay was angry. 'She wanted you to kill yourself?'

'I don't think so. Perhaps she didn't know what to say. But I thought she'd be there for me. I thought we were friends, but it seems not.'

'She knew what you were going to do?'

Jake shrugged his shoulders. 'Maybe, maybe not. Not even I knew at that point.'

'Have you seen her since that day?'

'No, and I don't want to. She's not my friend. I don't know why I ever thought she was.' They sat down on some swings. The park was empty but for a few mums and toddlers. The older kids were in school. A few of the mums glanced over with sympathetic smiles and Jake tried not to notice.

'I'm your friend, Jake.' He looked over at Lindsay. 'You could've called me.'

'I know, I'm sorry.' He reached a hand over and she took it. 'You're actually what made me change my mind.'

'Me?'

'Yes, you. The thought of never seeing you again was horrible.' Jake looked away, embarrassed by his openness. 'It made me realise how much I love you and how much I want us to go to Australia together.'

'Me too,' said Lindsay. A moment of understanding passed between them and they smiled at one another. 'What about Marie?'

'What about her?' Jake raised his eyebrows in acceptance. 'She's made it clear she's moved on. Maybe now I can do the same.'

'Can you? You were so hurt when she turned you away.'

'It still hurts, but seeing her and talking to her has put a few ghosts to rest for the moment. I know where she is and maybe when I'm older I can try again.'

'What about now?'

'I have two parents who love me and I might even have a girlfriend.' They both blushed. 'But more than that, I have a future. A future I couldn't see before.'

'Maybe it was a good thing finding Marie.'

'What do you mean?'

'Well, if it's put everything into order for you and your path is clearer, maybe it was a good thing you found her. She's not hanging over your head anymore.'

'I'm hungry,' said Jake, exhausted by the depth of their conversation. 'Why don't you come home for lunch? Mum won't mind.' They took their time going home, hand in hand. 'What's happening with your folks?' Jake asked.

'It all kicked off after the accident. Jamie had a real go at Dad and called a social worker in to talk to Mum.'

'Wow. I had no idea all that was going on.'

'I ignored it to be honest, I didn't think it would change anything. But whatever the social worker said worked. Mum has moved out.'

'What about you?'

'I'm still at home.'

'Is it safe?'

'Weirdly, Mum moving out has given my brothers the kick up the arse they needed and they've got Dad under control.'

'Will it last?'

'We'll see, but I can always move out if I need to.'

'You can come and live with us,' said Jake hopefully. He put his arm around her, pulled her close and kissed her. When he felt her lips against his he felt the pop, pop, pop of fireworks. He felt the dizziness of a dream come true. When the kiss finished they stood, foreheads touching, and Jake enjoyed every moment.

Chapter 40

Cherry was already at the bar when Kathi arrived and was chatting to the barman with her usual ease. Cherry's ability to strike up a conversation with anyone she met, and chat as if they were old friends, was something Kathi found remarkable. It was a skill she wished she had. Perhaps it came from picking herself up and moving to another part of the country, perhaps it was simply part of her natural gregariousness. 'Hi,' she called over to Cherry as she made her way to the bar.

'Hi Kathi,' Cherry got up off her bar stool and held her friend tightly. 'How are you?'

'I'm fine.'

'How are you really?'

'Awful,' Kathi said, giving up the pretence. 'I feel awful. I didn't even want to come out tonight, but Jake made me.'

'Come on,' Cherry said, giving her a final squeeze. 'Let's get you a drink.' It was a Wednesday night, so the bar was quiet. They took a seat at the back so they could have some privacy. Kathi put her phone, face up, on the table next to her. 'Tell me all about it,' said Cherry once they were settled.

'I came home early from work. I was going to go to the hardware store to choose some paint but was too tired so headed home instead.' Kathi's eyes filled so she swallowed hard to compose herself.

'Thank God you did,' said Cherry gently.

'Exactly.' Kathi looked at her friend earnestly because she knew what might have happened otherwise. 'I had the feeling someone was at home, but Graham's van wasn't there. I called up to Jake but got no response, so I thought I was imagining things. I made a cup of tea but couldn't shake the feeling someone was at home.

'I called upstairs again but still there was no response. To reassure myself, I went up to check. Jake's door was closed, which is nothing unusual, but when I tried the handle it didn't open. That was more unusual because his door doesn't have a lock on it. It was then I heard a thump, and I knew Jake was in there.' Kathi's cheeks were wet and Cherry passed her napkin.

'Take your time,' she said.

'It was awful, Cherry, honestly. I started shouting his name and banging on the door. I tried so hard to keep it together, but I was freaking out.'

'Of course you were, who wouldn't be?'

'The door began to move and so I rammed it as hard as I could and it burst open.' Kathi put her hand over her mouth as if to stop herself calling out all over again. 'He was lying there on the bed, his arm hanging over the side, and I just knew what he done.' She took a few breaths before continuing. 'I don't know how I did it, but my mind was crystal clear. I picked up his phone, dialled 999 and at the same time put him in recovery position. I didn't even know I could do that. I found the bottle of pills and gave the operator the info and hung up. I called Graham, and he came immediately.'

'You are amazing, Kathi. I don't how you cope so well with everything.'

'I didn't when Graham got home. When he arrived, I collapsed in a heap. I was hysterical.'

'What happened when the ambulance got there?'

'I don't know what the paramedics did, but they were with Jake for what felt like ages. They wouldn't let us in the room with him. It was dreadful. Once they'd stabilised him we were all put in the ambulance. I was scared they wouldn't let us go with him, but they did. It was the longest drive of my life.'

'I bet.' They both sipped on their drinks, giving Kathi a moment to compose herself.

'I thought nothing could be worse than losing my parents, but losing Jake? If he'd succeeded, I don't know if I could have survived that.'

'It is not worth thinking about,' said Cherry, shaking her head. 'How is he now?'

'I don't know. In all honesty, I don't know anymore. I used to know that boy's every mood and thought. Now he's an enigma. He smiles and reassures me, but I don't trust my instincts anymore.' Kathi's eyes slipped back to her phone in case she'd missed a call from Graham. 'Jake told me to come out tonight. Graham is at home to keep an eye on him, but I don't know if it's the right thing to do.'

'It is,' Cherry reassured her friend. 'Jake is safe, Graham is with him, you're only two minutes from home. You need a break and a change of scene. You've been to hell and back.'

'Thank you, Cherry, thank you for always being there.'

'Of course I'm here.' Over the evening a few people had come over to ask after Jake and their genuine concern was evident, boosting Kathi's resolve.

'Enough about me,' she said to Cherry. 'How are you? Are you booked in for your operation?'

'Yes, it's happening next week. There was a cancellation. I'm both delighted and terrified. Nobody wants to go under the knife, but it'll put an end to all this worry and I can finally get on with things.'

'I'm so happy for you,' said Kathi. 'And selfishly I'm happy for me too because I didn't want to lose my best friend.'

'Don't worry, I'm not going anywhere. It'll take more than a few dodgy cells to get rid of me.' They laughed, clinked glasses and drank to that.

'You'd think this cancer business would be a negative thing,' said Cherry. 'You know, make me nervous about doing anything, but it's actually had the opposite effect. It's made me take stock of my life.'

'In what way?'

'I work every day. Don't get me wrong, I love my job, but I don't have any time off. The hospital appointments are the closest thing I've had to a holiday in a very long time.'

'You do work hard.'

'So I have decided to make some changes that mean I can have the weekends off.'

'What sort of changes?'

'Have you heard of virtual assistants?' Kathi shook her head. 'It is amazing. I can hire someone who lives in Asia or in South America, or anywhere in the world, and they can take phonecalls for me, write emails or even schedule appointments. Anything. From the other side of the world! It's amazing.'

'If that gives you more free time, it'll be worth it. But what will you do with your free time?'

'Well...' here Cherry was a little more reticent to share her plans.

'Yes?'

'This cancer scare...'

'Yes?' Kathi couldn't help but grin at her friend, guessing correctly where the conversation was headed.

'...it has made me reassess my personal life as well.'

'Uh, huh?'

'Uh huh.' Cherry fiddled with her wineglass. 'You know Brian and I have been spending time together?'

'A lot of time together.'

'Okay, yes, a lot of time and what I've realised is that after the disaster of my first marriage, I didn't want anything to do with anyone else.'

'I can understand that.'

'I am too old be running around like a teenager. Or so I thought. But, well, Brian has sort of gotten under my skin and,' she lowered her voice, 'I love him.'

'That's wonderful,' Kathi said, laughing out loud at her friend's uncharacteristic shyness. 'I am so happy for you, honestly. Brian is a great guy.'

'I know you weren't happy about us getting together.'

'That was then, this is now. Look at what we've both been through? We need good news and nothing is greater than two people falling in love.'

'Do you mean it?'

'Absolutely. One hundred percent.' Kathi was moved by the fact Cherry was seeking her blessing. 'Have you told Brian you love him?'

'Not yet.' Cherry looked sheepish. 'I haven't even told him about the cancer.'

'Cherry, you must.'

'I know, I know. I just didn't want to burden him or scare him off.'

'It would take more than that,' Kathi said. 'I've seen how he looks at you.' After a moment, Kathi asked, 'Did you manage to find out anything more about Joanne?'

'It took me forever, but I finally got a hold of her mum. She didn't sound good.'

'What do you mean?'

'She sounded like a drunk, not drunk, you understand, but a drunk. She wasn't all over the place, she knew what she was saying, but her voice was wobbly and had that mellow tone that comes with regular booze.'

'How can you be sure? Maybe she's not well.'

'Trust me, I know what an alcoholic sounds like.' Kathi wanted to ask more, but Cherry's expression told her the topic wasn't open for discussion.

'What did she say about Joanne?'

'At first she didn't know who I was talking about. I had to prompt her.'

'How can she forget she has a daughter?'

'Because she knows Joanne as Lola. Joanne is her middle name.'

Kathi's stomach flipped. And not in a good way. 'Her daughter is called Lola?'

'Yes, why?'

'I have a photograph of someone called Lola. I found it mixed in with my parents' papers.'

'You think it's the same person?'

'Positive. The girl in the photo looks so like Joanne it is uncanny. And now that we know her name is Lola, there can be no doubt. How many Lolas do you know?'

'Why would your parents have a photograph of Joanne as a little girl?'

'That is what I need to find out.'

'Whatever the reason is,' said Cherry taking a sip of wine, 'you can bet that is why she's taken such an interest in Jake.'

'It might also answer the question of who the troll is. What else did Joanne's mum say?'

'She said Joanne, Lola as she called her, had gone off the rails ever since she found out she was adopted. It turns out Joanne's mum couldn't get pregnant. She found out a cousin was having a baby she didn't want to keep, so she and her husband gave the baby a home. That baby was Joanne.

'She also told me Joanne's father died when she was eight years old. It seems they were very close, and Joanne never fully recovered from the loss. When the mum realised Joanne was in Byreburn she said she wasn't surprised because that is where her cousin is from.' Cherry paused before saying, 'She's come looking for her birth parents.'

Chapter 41

Still reeling from Cherry's news, Kathi was groggy when she awoke the next morning. Her dreams had been bombarded by Joanne. In her dreams Joanne and Lola were two different people and they followed her wherever she went, taunting her with a child's rhyme of 'we know something you don't know'. To take her mind off things, she walked up to the supermarket. She wanted to get something nice for Jake to cheer him up and make herself feel less of a failed mother. She wandered aimlessly up and down the aisles, throwing things into her basket at random.

'How is Jake?' A voice behind her asked. 'Is he out of hospital?'

Kathi turned and saw Joanne. Butter wouldn't melt, she thought. 'Yes. But I am sure you knew that.'

'You know Byreburn. Nothing stays secret for long'

'That is right, Joanne. Nothing stays secret for long.' Kathi stared hard at the woman in front of her, trying to divine from her what was going on. 'Are you happy here in Byreburn?' Joanne seemed thrown by the change of subject.

'Yes, happy enough.'

'Have your parents been to visit you yet?' Kathi asked.

'No.' Joanne's face fell. 'We had a falling out. You know how parents and children bicker.' She smiled again 'Well, I'd better be going. I hope Jake is up and about soon. It must be awful to know your son tried to take his own life and there was nothing you could do about it.' At this, Joanne cocked her head and gave a sympathetic expression which made Kathi want to punch her. Before walking away, Joanne said, 'Did he get his phone back?'

It took all Kathi's resolve to hold it together while she watched Joanne walk away, but when Joanne turned around and gave her a last smile, it was too much. 'Stay away from my son,' Kathi shouted across the store.

'I don't know what you mean,' said Joanne, looking around for a witness to Kathi's madness.

'Yes, you do. I don't know what game you've been playing, but from now on leave him out of it.' Kathi knew the other shoppers had stopped to stare but didn't care. 'I've seen the messages, I know you egged him on.'

'I think you must be in shock, Kathi.' Joanne looked at her with every appearance of being the wounded party. 'You are imagining things.'

'No, I am not.' Kathi walked up to her. 'I know it's you who's been sending me those vile emails.'

'Why would I do that?'

'I don't know yet, but I'll find out. Whatever this vendetta is you've got against my family, I'll find out what it is and haul your ass through the courts if I have to. Stay away from my son.' Kathi stood her ground until Joanne backed off and left the supermarket.

This quarrel with Joanne allowed Kathi to vent some of her fear, but it didn't answer the question of how Joanne fitted in with her own family. Through the supermarket window she watched Joanne walk away and on the spur of the moment dropped her shopping basket on the floor and followed Joanne down the street.

She was close enough to hear Joanne singing to herself but a safe enough distance away not to be able to make out what song was. Kathi didn't question why she was following Joanne, but if she had done, she wouldn't have had an answer. Kathi's gut told her she'd discover something about this strange woman she hadn't thought to look for before. There had to be a reason why Joanne had come here and befriended her son. Joanne's phone rang, and she answered it.

'What do you want?' Kathi heard her say. 'Who was it?... Didn't you ask?' There was a long pause while whoever it was spoke. 'You're useless, do you know that? Useless and a liar... I will talk to you any way I want... No, you're not. You're not my mother, you are a lying, old, useless drunk... You can't even remember who called you.'

Joanne stop talking to listen. Kathi ducked down a side street, scared in case Joanne turned around. The result was she missed the end of the conversation because when Kathi peered round the corner Joanne was already walking away from her.

Kathi resumed her shadowing. Joanne had stopped singing, but from her heavy footsteps and hunched shoulders, Kathi could tell the telephone call hadn't ended well. Joanne turned left and out of sight, so Kathi jogged towards the end of the street, keen not to lose her. When she looked around the corner she saw Joanne attempt to kick a cat, but she was too slow and the animal dodged her foot. To make up for it, Joanne stuck her tongue out at the cat. Kathi couldn't help raise her eyebrows in surprise at Joanne's childishness.

They carried on and from the direction they were walking, Kathi knew she was heading to work. The plastic bag that swung between her legs as she walked contained what looked to be her lunch. Joanne stopped abruptly and Kathi ducked into a doorway. It was just as well because Joanne did a quick sweep of the street, saw it was empty, and swiped a milk bottle from someone's doorstep.

When Joanne heard the clink of the bottle, she looked over and watched Joanne scuttle away. Kathi had seen enough: Joanne's behaviour, and the way she spoke to her mother, was enough to tell Kathi she was an angry and destructive person, and that she needed to get to the bottom of things before something else happened to either herself or Jake. It was time to confront Marjorie.

Before going to Marjorie's house, she first of all went home and pulled out the suitcase from under the eaves. She sorted through the documents and photographs again, only now she knew what she was looking for. This time she was seeking a photograph of a baby, a toddler, a young child and perhaps even a teenager that she would recognise as Joanne. She found them and she laughed when she did because it had been so easy. The photographs had been right there, just waiting for her to find them. It was also easy to see the likeness between the girl in each of the photographs and the adult she knew. Joanne had aged of course, her face was puffy and tired looking now, but the eyes and the mouth, and the shape of the chin were unmistakably the same. Something else struck Kathi and made her gasp.

She gathered up the photographs and took them downstairs to the cupboard where the photograph albums were kept. She dug out an old one, one that had belonged to her parents and flipped through to a photograph of her grandparents, Marjorie and her now dead husband, George, as a young couple. Kathi placed the photograph of Joanne as a teenager next to the one of George. The likeness was uncanny. Was Joanne a child of George's? Was this the connection?

Judging by Marjorie's odd behaviour each time Kathi mentioned the name Lola, she must know about this other family. Who could blame her for not wanting to talk about it? Her parents must also have known, Kathi reasoned, because why else would they have these photographs in their possession, hidden in plain sight? Kathi gathered everything up and took it to Marjorie's house.

'Hello darling, how are you? I wasn't expecting to see you today. How's Jake?' Marjorie hugged Kathi tightly, sensitive to everything Kathi and Graham had been through recently.

'He's resting. I think he's all right, but his body needs time to heal.'

'You must have been to hell and back.'

'Marjorie, I want to ask you again about Lola.' One by one Kathi held up the photographs. 'Why didn't anyone tell me about her before?'

'I don't know what you mean.' Kathi looked at her grandmother as if to say, the jig's up. She opened up the photograph album and once again put Joanne's photograph next to George's.

'Did Granddad have an affair? Is that why you've acted so funny every time I've mentioned Lola's name?' Kathi couldn't keep the hurt out of her voice. Why couldn't Marjorie have told her? Why was it Jake was the one to let it slip? She looked at the two photographs side-by-side, shocked at just how alike her grandfather and Joanne were. They were still in the hallway and Kathi sat down on the stairs, indicating she wasn't leaving until she had an answer.

Resigned, Marjorie went through to the kitchen. 'I'll put the kettle on.' Kathi stayed where she was. For a reason she didn't understand, she was more angry than upset about this discovery. Angry because here she was in Byreburn, in the belly of her family, and yet secret after secret was emerging. First of all Jake's secrets, then Joanne's and now Marjorie's. It was too much.

By the time the tea was brewed and poured, Kathi was ready to go into the kitchen. She placed the photographs intentionally on the table, in front of Marjorie, driving her point home. Marjorie looked at the photos and couldn't help bite on her knuckles. 'My goodness, they're alike, aren't they?' she said.

'So you do know about this?' Kathi asked.

'Yes, of course.' Marjorie's voice was gentle, and she put her hand over Kathi's.

'Was it an affair?' Marjorie's face looked drawn, and she hesitated before answering. 'What?' Kathi demanded.

'No, Kathi, it's nothing like that.' Nervous, Marjorie's voice was low, so low Kathi almost missed what she said. 'This girl is Joanne.'

'I know that. She's here in Byreburn to make my life hell.'

'She's your sister,' said Marjorie.

'What?' Kathi's blood ran cold.

'She's your older sister.'

'I don't understand.'

'Not long after your parents started courting, your mum fell pregnant.' Marjorie looked at her hands, wringing them tightly. 'They didn't think they were ready for a family.'

'I don't believe you. I'd have known.' Kathi's head reeled at the enormity of what her grandmother had said.

'They'd only been together for about six months,' said Marjorie. 'They were both so scared and decided the best thing to do was give the child up for adoption.'

'And this is her?' Kathi asked, picking up the photograph of a baby Joanne.

'Your mum went up to Glasgow for the last few months of her pregnancy,' Marjorie continued, 'and had the baby there.'

'Who adopted her? Why did mum have these photos?'

'She was adopted by a second cousin of your mum's and it was agreed that every three years the cousin would send a photo of Joanne to your parents.'

'But they stayed together. Why didn't they take her back?'

'They talked about it,' said Marjorie. 'But by then Joanne had been living with the cousin for three years or so, and as far as she knew they were her family. It would have been unkind to split them up.' Marjorie hung her head, a rare show of defeat. 'Giving her up was something your parents always regretted. They felt very guilty about it but took comfort in the knowledge she was with a good family and that reduced the pain somewhat. So did getting the photographs.'

'The dad died when Joanne was only eight. The mum is a drunk.' Marjorie's face fell. 'I have a sister. I can't believe it.'

'Are you alright, love?' Marjorie rubbed Kathi's arm and gave it another squeeze.

'I think so, but I have to admit I wasn't expecting to discover a sister today. What I don't understand is how she found out and why she's been stalking me.'

'What do you mean?' Marjorie asked.

'She's the one who's been sending me nasty messages on email and on my blog. She's been targeting Jake as well. Do you remember when he disappeared and staggered home drunk?'

'He wouldn't tell you where he'd been.'

'He'd been with Joanne. She's been encouraging him to search for his birth mother and turning him against me. I didn't understand why she was doing it, but she must know about her adoption and is taking it out on me.'

'Are you sure?' Marjorie asked, unwilling to believe it. 'Why would she involve Jake?'

'That is something I will have to ask her. I don't understand it either because she must know how difficult he is finding things right now. Why make it worse for him?' Kathi's phone rang and after checking it wasn't Graham or Jake, she ignored it. 'Do you think Mum would ever have told me I have a sister?'

'I don't know,' said Marjorie, shaking her head. 'I don't think so. It was so long ago, and it was so painful for them.' She took a gulp of tea. 'The mum's a drunk, did you say?'

'Cherry said she is, she says she was drunk when they spoke.'

'Maybe that's explains why the photographs stopped coming. After your parent's died I kept expecting you to receive a letter or photograph in the post and ask me about it, but you never did.'

They both stared at the photographs on the table, each consumed with their own thoughts. After a while, Kathi gathered the photographs together. 'I'd better go,' she said. 'I need time to digest all of this.'

'Of course, love. If you have any questions, just ask. No more secrets, I promise.'

When Kathi stepped outside she pulled out her phone. The missed call was from Cherry. 'Have you got time for a coffee?' Kathi asked, when her friend picked up.

'Yes, I need to see you, actually. I have some news for you.'

'How is Jake?' Cherry asked once they had found a table at the Silver Spoon.

'He seems fine, but that is only the half of it.'

'Oh aye?' said Cherry.

'Joanne Wylie is my sister.'

Cherry nearly spat out her coffee. 'You are kidding me? How did you find that out?' Kathi told her all about the photographs in the suitcase and the likeness to her Granddad, and about confronting Marjorie. 'It explains why she moved here and why she hates me so much. I can't believe she targeted Jake, though. That I can't forgive.' They sat in silence for a few minutes. 'She's also the one behind the trolling.'

'My God,' said Cherry, 'She's been busy. You couldn't make it up if you tried.' This made them both giggle until they became near hysterical and the more they tried to stop, the worse they got. When eventually the laughing subsided Cherry asked, 'Is Joanne aware you know about being sisters?'

'I don't think so, but she must've known I'd put it together, eventually.'

'Are you going to speak to her?'

'I don't think I have a choice. I need to put an end to this once and for all.'

Chapter 42

When Kathi walked home her head was full of all the conversations she'd had with Joanne, and about Joanne. She thought long about the fact Joanne was her sister; not a half-sister or a stepsister, but a full-blooded sister who had not lived with her or been raised by their parents. Kathi wondered how different her life might have been if she'd had a sibling growing up, or when her parents had died because they would have had a shared history and shared memories of their parents with which they could have comforted each other. Instead, she felt she'd faced that time alone and that the burden of losing both parents had been hers and hers alone.

She wondered too what Joanne might have been like if she hadn't been adopted. Would they have been close? Kathi thought about Joanne's childhood. Had it been a happy upbringing or had her relationship with her adoptive parents been strained and difficult? Kathi guessed it was the latter, otherwise why would she be here? By now it was evening and, anxious to get home to Jake, Kathi cut down towards the river and crossed over the suspension bridge and onto Eskdale Street, which took her past the Memorial Park from where she had been photographed. Kathi realised that because of recent events she'd not looked at her blog in a long time and wondered if there were any new messages. She realised she didn't care. The possibility of losing her son had snapped those messages into perspective.

Kathi looked over to the park and saw a lone figure sitting on a bench next to the war memorial. It was Joanne. Kathi's first instinct was to shout and rant at the woman for the damage she'd done since the day she had arrived in the town. But there was something about the lonely, slumped figure that stopped her. More than anything right now, Kathi wanted to understand why Joanne had behaved the way she had. Joanne bristled when she saw Kathi draw near to the bench. 'What do you want?' she sneered.

'To know why.'

'Why what?'

'Why you moved here, why you targeted Jake. Why you have been driving a wedge between me and my son and why you've been trolling me.'

'That's a lot of whys.'

'Well, you've been very busy since you got here.'

'It is not just since I got here. Ever since I found out that I was adopted, I've done nothing but think about you, our mum and dad and my family here. I pictured all of you living in this place, straight out of Monarch of the Glen, and I thought to myself, this should have been my life too. I should have been here with them,' she looked at Kathi, 'not you. But instead they tossed me aside and replaced me with you. You who was their golden child and could do no wrong. You who was so perfect they would never want their first child back.'

'That's not how it was.'

'How would you know? Living here in your ivory tower thinking life is so tough.'

'What do you mean?'

'I've read your blog. I've read your sorry tales of having nobody to speak to about your oh-so-successful business and your oh-so-perfect husband and how oh-so-hard it's been to be the mother of an adopted child.'

'It is hard, due in no small part to you.'

'Try being the adopted child.'

'I do try. I try every day to understand what Jake's going through and how hard he is finding life at the moment. I see how he's struggling and want to help him.' To her own fury, the mention of Jake made her eyes well up, but she didn't want to show any weakness.

'You understand nothing,' said Joanne.

'So tell me, help me understand.' Joanne hesitated. 'What is it? Why can't you tell me? I will tell you why. It's because your bitterness has nothing to do with your adoption. It is simply who you are. You feel the world has wronged you and that you've not been given what you deserve and so you're going to take it out on everybody else.'

'You don't know what you're talking about.'

'Yes, I do. Your mum loves you.'

'My parents are dead.'

'No, my parents are dead. Your mother is alive and well and is worried about you.' Joanne's face paled as it dawned on her somebody had been in touch with her mum.

'You've spoken to her?'

'Yes. There are no more secrets.' Joanne stood up, ready to walk away, but she turned back.

'Then you know my mum is a drunk?' Kathi looked away. 'If you've spoken to her, you know it's true. She's a lush, a soak, an alky. Your precious parents offloaded me onto an alcoholic and never looked back.'

'That's not how it was. They thought you were being well looked after.'

'How would they know? They never showed their faces again.'

'Because your mum sent them photographs. She wrote to them telling them how you were getting on.'

'How do you know?'

'Because I found them, I just didn't know who they were of.'

'I don't believe you.' Kathi dug the photos out of her bag and handed them to Joanne. Joanne was silent as she slowly looked through them. Kathi watched her face twitch and jump, trying to work out what she was thinking.

'Mum and Dad didn't just abandon you,' Kathi said. 'They did what they thought was the right thing. Marjorie told me; they had only just started dating when Mum fell pregnant. They didn't know if they would stay together and so decided to put you up for adoption. Your mum is a cousin, and it seemed to be the ideal solution.'

Joanne sneered. 'Ideal for them perhaps.'

'They thought they were doing the right thing,' said Kathi.

'I never belonged.' Joanne said after a moment, still looking through the photographs, as if she couldn't quite believe she was the little girl in the pictures, or that her birth parents had cared enough to want them. 'After Dad died, things changed. Mum used to tell me how much she loved me. She said it all the time, but I used to feel she said it to convince herself, not me. I don't know why.' Joanne stared into space for a moment, the fire and the brim gone. Kathi watched those oft repeated conversations play out on Joanne's face. She sat back down on the bench. 'I had nobody to talk to about it so I packed all that confusion and hurt away and hid it from the world.' Joanne absently patted her tummy as if confirming the pain was safely stored away inside. 'I don't think Mum ever loved me, not really. When Dad died, she got sad. I did too, and I tried to get close to her, but she closed herself off and wouldn't let anyone in.'

'What did your dad die of?'

'Stomach cancer. It was horrible. Mum nursed him right up until near the end. Eventually she couldn't cope, and he was put into a hospice for the last few weeks. She'd started drinking by then as well.'

'How old were you when he died?'

'Eight years old.'

'I'm so sorry, Joanne. That must have been awful. Was he a nice dad?'

'The best.' A smile floated over Joanne's face as she recalled happier times. 'I remember him always smiling, even when he was ill. Right up until the end, he tried to protect me from it all. But he couldn't, not really. Even at that age I could see how ill he was and that he was going to die.' They sat in silence for a long time. The evening was warm, the suns' heat still reflecting back up at them as they sat on the park bench. 'It's Common Riding soon,' Joanne said out of the blue.

'Yes.'

'Have you ever ridden a horse up the Kirk Wynd?'

'Only a couple of times when I was a child. I'm scared of horses. They're so big.'

'I'd love to have done that, but they didn't have horses on the council estate I grew up on.'

'What did you come here for, Joanne?'

'I wanted to take back what was mine.'

'What was that?'

'Loving parents, a good home, a family and security.'

'Have you found it here?'

'No.' Joanne lowered her head, her voice was imbued with sadness.

'I can understand you feeling abandoned or left behind, honestly I can. I can forgive the trolling and the worry it caused. But what I can't forgive is how you've played with Jake's mind. He tried to take his own life.'

'I'm sorry about that. Truly, I am. I didn't think it would go that far, and I didn't know how to stop it. He was determined. I just told him what he wanted to hear.'

'But didn't it occur to you that he was struggling the way you were?'

'Yes, and that's why I wanted to help him. I came here to find my birth parents. Why shouldn't he do the same?'

'Because he's a child.'

'He's not a child.'

'Yes, Joanne, he is. He's not streetwise like the city kids, you know. He's from Byreburn, for heaven's sake. Look around you, the kids here aren't as tough as city kids the same age.'

'That's what you think.'

'It's what I know. Sure, they all talk the talk, but the most 'Inner City' the kids round here get is to experience Dumfries High Street, not the Gorbals of Glasgow.'

'He'll be fine, he'll get through it.'

'I don't want him to get through it. I want him to thrive and I'm scared you've scarred him for good.'

'You can't put all this at my door. If he was so happy with his life here, he wouldn't have been so keen to find Marie.'

Kathi sighed deeply. She knew Joanne was right. Jake sought out Marie because something was missing in his life here. 'That may be so,' she said, 'but if he hadn't been egged on, he would have waited until he was older and better able to manage meeting her.'

'Well,' Joanne was defensive, 'what's done is done, no point dwelling on it.'

'You need to leave,' Kathi said abruptly. 'You've caused too much trouble. You can't stay.'

'I can if I want to.'

'Why would you want to? There's nothing for you here. Any possibility of us becoming sisters ended the day you started playing with Jake's mind. Mum and Dad are dead. There's nothing here for you. Leave.'

'There's Marjorie.'

'Do you think she wants to get involved with you now she knows what you did to Jake?'

'Yes, I'm her granddaughter.'

'No, you're not. You're not part of this family and you never will be. Go back to Glasgow, make friends with your mum, help her get off the drink. Or not. But you can't stay here.'

'I'll do whatever I want.' Joanne's face was red with rising anger. She turned to face Kathi. 'I'm not one of your lackeys, you can't boss me around.'

'I'm not bossing you around,' Kathi snapped back, 'but do you really think you can stay here now after everything you've done? The damage you've caused?' Joanne's face crumbled and for the first time Kathi could see how vulnerable she really was. 'You've told me you want a family and security,' she said. 'Do you think you'll find that here? Now, after everything you've done?' Joanne pursed her lips in response. 'Go back to Glasgow. Or anywhere. Start again where nobody knows about this.'

Joanne's body slumped, her head hung low. 'It's not fair,' she said. 'I should have had your life.'

'You still can.' Kathi was overwhelmed by momentary sympathy. She saw how different their lives would have been if her parents had taken a gamble and kept Joanne. She also saw a future she didn't want for Jake. Seeing Joanne's defeated face strengthened Kathi's resolve to do everything she could to make sure Jake always felt loved and heard. She was about to say something conciliatory but Joanne quietly stood up, looked at her sister one last time and walked away.

Soon after, Joanne packed her belongings and left Byreburn. The flat was cleaned and re-let. Kathi never found out where she went.

Chapter 43

Kathi was standing, bleary-eyed, at the open window of the upstairs dormer window watching the Town Band flute and drum its way down the street. It was 5am and she would normally have been asleep in bed, but today was Common Riding and there was a lot to celebrate.

'Here you go,' said Jake, coming in with two cups of tea in his hands. 'This'll help you wake up.' She gratefully accepted the mug and took a deep drink. Jake picked up his homemade flag and waved it out the window, whooping at the band below.

When the last of the band members had passed by, Kathi and Jake headed downstairs to the kitchen where Kathi would cook up her usual full breakfast. 'It'll keep us going,' she liked to say. Graham was still in bed, having rolled in only a few hours earlier. He'd been out with Jamie Armstrong until the wee hours, as he did every Common Riding Eve.

Later, up at the High Street, the three of them stood with Graham's parents watching the horses arrive in the market square before the speeches began. There was a big cheer once they were finished, and the horses galloped up the Kirk Wynd, keeping tradition alive. In the aftermath of the noise and the clamour of the gallop, the town quietened, and friends and neighbours continued conversations that had been interrupted by the horses and speeches.

Lindsay appeared beside Jake and they headed off to meet friends. Graham headed to a cafe to buy everyone a cup of coffee. This July wasn't as sunny as the previous year, and the clouds overhead were dark and ominous. When he came back with the tea, he handed one to Kathi and gave her a kiss on the temple. 'How's your head?' she asked him.

'Thumping.'

'Serves you right,' she teased. They stood in silence for a few moments. Kathi snuggled into Graham and enjoyed watching the world around her, feeling safe in her husband's arms. Her eye was caught by Jake, sitting on a low wall nearby, chatting and laughing with his friends, Lindsay beside him. 'Do you remember this time last year?' she asked Graham.

'I was still hungover, I think.'

'Yes,' Kathi smiled, 'you were. What I mean is, do you remember how unhappy Jake was? Look at him now.' They both watched him, and Kathi could feel Graham smiling. 'I was so jealous of you,' she said, squeezing him tightly.

'Of me? Why?'

'Of your relationship with Jake. He hated me so much, and I didn't understand why. I felt like I was making all the running and for no reward. You seemed to have this easy relationship with him and he confided in you, whereas he wouldn't even look at me.'

Graham kissed his wife again. 'I didn't know you felt like that. Believe me, he said some pretty cutting things to me too.'

'I'm ashamed to admit it, but there were moments I hated you. Only moments, and it was just my jealousy talking.'

'I'm glad we're through it. I really hope we don't have another year as difficult as this one was.' Graham and Kathi looked at each other as if to say, we should be so lucky, and laughed. 'Well, not for a while anyway,' Graham said and kissed her on the lips.

Later that day, after lunch, they went to the pub for a drink with Cherry and Brian. The pub lurched under the weight of punters. Everywhere they looked they saw friendly faces and stopped to make idle chat. The atmosphere was vibrant, and it felt like everyone was ready for a party. While Graham and Brian went to the bar, Cherry ushered Kathi to a corner where they could talk without interruption.

'Guess what?' Cherry said, a huge grin on her face.

'What?'

'This morning I told Brian about my cancer scare.'

'How did he take it?'

'He was shocked and of course happy it was benign. We had a bit of a chat about it and I thought that was that. Then,' she took a breath, 'later on, he got down on one knee-'

'-No!'

'Yes!'

'Oh my God, Cherry, what did you say?'

'What do you think? Yes, of course!'

'What happened to, I'm never making that mistake again?'

'That was before the cancer. I told you, I've been a given a new lease on life. I love Brian, he's totally different to Wayne, and I think he's worth taking a chance on.'

'Me too,' said Kathi. 'I'm so pleased for you.' She reached over and gave her friend a heartfelt hug. Timing things impeccably, Graham and Brian joined them with a bottle of champagne and four glasses.

'Have you heard the good news?' Brian asked Kathi.

'Yes, I have and I couldn't be more delighted for you.' She gave him a hug too.

'Cheers!' They all clinked glasses.

Lindsay had brought with her a can of beer from home and together she and Jake had ducked down a side street, away from the bustle of the town, to the park. They sat in the same place as they had done last year and shared the can. Their conversation this year was much more easy-going. They knew each other so intimately now, all their getting-to-know-you chat was in the past.

They talked idly and easily, discussing their plans for the summer holidays. Now that they were 16, they wanted to get jobs and start saving for Australia. 'How's your mum? Are you going to visit her?' Jake asked her.

'Yeah, I hope so. She says I can go and stay with her for a few weeks if I want.' Lindsay's mum had moved to a different town in order to escape her dad and stop drinking. 'Dad won't take me and neither of my brothers want to see her yet.'

'Do you want to go?'

'Yeah, I do. She's like a different person since she stopped drinking. I'd like to get to know her.'

'My mum will take you. Don't give it a second thought. It's important you see your mum.'

'What will you do when I'm away?' The clouds that had been getting fatter over the course of the day finally vented their fury with a loud clap of thunder and a downpour of rain. The crash of the thunder stopped them mid conversation and from the shelter of the trees under which they sat, Jake and Lindsay watched the raindrops bounce and ricochet off the foliage and earth. It quickly pooled in places, forming puddles through which they'd later have to run.

'What will you do?' Lindsay asked again when the thunder had faded into the distance.

'Get a job. I've got to repay Mum and Dad the fine money.' He reached a hand over to Lindsay and squeezed it tightly. 'Mum says she's going to book a holiday as well. She says she needs some sun.'

'I've never been abroad.'

'I wish you could come.'

Lindsay swallowed the last of the beer and they lay back on the grass, arms around each other. They lay there in silence for a long time, listening to the sound of the faraway rumble of clouds, and the heavy rain tapping the branches spread out above them.

When the cold and damp seeped into their clothes and they began to shiver, they put their coats over their heads and ran back into town.

The End

Thank You

Thank you for reading Belonging. Reviews are crucial for helping new readers discover me and decide whether or not they want to take a chance on my books.

If you could take a moment to leave a review on Amazon or Goodreads, I'd really appreciate it. Even a simple 'I enjoyed this story' is fantastic!

Recommending my work to others is also a huge help, so if you liked this book, please consider spreading the word to others!

About Emma Dhesi

My journey to publication hasn't been a straight line. It's taken me many years to return to my calling. I was once told that the job we wanted at eight years old is really the thing we want to do most in life. At eight years old I wanted to be an author, and the book that changed my life was Ballet Shoes by Noel Streatfeild. Oh, the magic of make believe!

Writing is a solitary life. As a young person, this was not for me. I lacked the maturity or confidence to sit down by myself for long stretches of time and put pen to paper (I still write longhand!). Prolonged periods of inactivity were interspersed with only short periods of intense writing.

At long last motherhood forced me to mature, and I waved goodbye to a busy social life and said hello to a life of early rises and bedtime routines. This cleared time for me to write more regularly and with increased intention.

After the birth of my second child, Post Natal Depression kicked in and took hold. As a coping mechanism, I journaled what I was going through, and often imagined what it would be like just to get up and walk away. Thankfully, I never took such drastic action myself, instead I created a fictional character who did, and followed her story.

That story became my first novel, The Day She Came Home. It has turned out to be a powerful way to share my feelings with other women struggling with PND and help them know they are not alone.

Outside of writing I love days out with my family. We're so enjoying being back in the UK. We feel like tourists, exploring Edinburgh and the rest of Scotland.

My husband and I have always loved travelling and now that the children are getting older, we hope to introduce them to the adventure that is world travel.

Here are some fun facts about me!

- I love genealogy and have spent too many hours geeking out on Census Returns, Death Registers and Ship Passenger Lists.

- I permanently borrowed a glass tumbler from Buckingham Palace – oops!

- My life hack guru is Gretchen Ruben, and she taught me I'm an Abstainer and a Rebel – it explains so much!

- The older I get, the more introvert I get.

- I am a "haggis curry". 50% Scottish, and 50% Indian.

- After travelling in South East Asia for many months, I determined to get my motor scooter license. I got it, but only just. I struggled to go any faster than 15 miles per hour, deemed slow enough to be a danger to other drivers!

Want to stay in touch? Here's how:
Website - www.emmadhesiauthor.com
Facebook – www.facebook.com/emmadhesiauthor

Also by Emma Dhesi

More Than Enough is the third contemporary family drama by Emma Dhesi.

Happily married wife, mother and entrepreneur, Kathi's world is about to be torn apart by small town secrets and a history that could destroy everyone she loves.

Kathi Beattie is married to her childhood sweetheart and is a devoted mother to their 15-year-old adopted son. But when a stranger comes into town and gets close to him, Kathi is forced to question her whole life.

On the outside, Kathi's life looks perfect. Her husband adores her and business is booming. But behind closed doors, her son is angry. It's more than the usual teenage angst and Kathi is his target.

Desperate to make her son happy, Kathi does everything in her power to bring him back from the dark side because that's all she's ever wanted – a happy family.

Kathi's situation is made worse by a stranger who seems hell bent on turning her son against her.

She must get to the bottom of who this stranger is, and why they are ripping her life apart, if she is to stop her family from imploding.

Buy your copy online today!

Printed in Great Britain
by Amazon